Claire Calman is the author of four novels: *Love Is a Four Letter Word*, *Lessons for a Sunday Father*, *I Like it Like That* and now *Cross My Heart and Hope to Die*, all published by HarperCollins.

Calman first decided to write a book when she discovered that it mainly involved making cups of tea and gazing out of the window. It was some time before a real writer friend pointed out that if she were to select an assortment of words and arrange them in some kind of order, this would speed up the process no end. Spurred on by this invaluable hint, she wrote *Love Is a Four Letter Word*, a funny yet poignant story of love and loss.

Before she got into daydreaming full time, Calman spent several years working in women's magazines, then in publishing, editing gardening books. She is also a poet and broadcaster and has performed her pithy verse at live readings and on radio many times, including for BBC Radio Four's *Woman's Hour*, *Loose Ends*, the comedy series *Five Squeezy Pieces* and for LBC. Her short stories have appeared in numerous magazines as well as in various anthologies, including *Cheatin' Heart*, the best-selling *Girls' Night In*, *Summer Magic* and *A Day in the Life*.

Claire Calman lives in L
son, and an unbelievabl

D0825465

CROSS MY HEART

and hope to die

Claire Calman

HarperCollins*Publishers*Ltd

Cross My Heart and Hope to Die
© 2004 by Claire Calman.
All rights reserved.

Published by HarperCollins
Publishers Ltd

Originally published in Great Britain
by Transworld Publishers, a division
of Random House Group Ltd: 2004
First published by HarperCollins
Publishers, Ltd: 2005
This mass market edition: 2006

The moral right of Claire Calman to be
identified as the author of this work has
been asserted.

HarperCollins Publishers Ltd
2 Bloor Street East, 20th Floor
Toronto, Ontario, Canada
M4W 1A8

www.harpercollins.ca

Library and Archives Canada Cataloguing
in Publication

Calman, Claire
Cross my heart and hope to die /
Claire Calman. — 1st mass market pbk. ed.

ISBN-13: 978-0-00-200755-9
ISBN-10: 0-00-200755-X

I. Title.

PR6053.A3915C76 2006   823'.92
C2005-905496-4

OPM 9 8 7 6 5 4 3 2 1

Printed and bound in the United States
Set in Melior

For my mother, Pat, with love

Friday

A change of plan

'Hi, it's me.' Kath reached Miranda on her mobile. 'Where are you? Can you talk?'

'Yup. I'm on my way to the station and I'm late – astonishingly – but, yes, fire away.' Miranda marched along the street at a cracking pace, parting pedestrians before her like Moses at the Red Sea.

'Now, don't go ballistic, but there's a small problem about Devon—'

'Oh, no! Kath – don't you dare tell me it's all off – you have no idea how *desperate* I am to get away – the shop's been *so* busy – half my staff have been off with flu – and my new collection's way behind schedule – and Anna's been looking forward to this for weeks and weeks – we can't let her down now – and in any case I've booked the painter to come and do our bedroom so we have no choice but to clear out – and – hang on, hang on, I have to get a ticket – where's my bloody change? God, I can't find anything in this stupid bag.' Miranda lowered her voice without pausing for breath. 'And Simon's driving me up the fucking wall at the moment, I don't know what's up with him, he's being impossible – at least in Devon I can have long walks by the sea and escape him for a couple of hours – please, please don't say we can't go – I really—'

'Miranda!'

'I promise you I will really lose it if I spend one more minute in London—' Miranda ran down the stairs to move away from a pungent drunk who was leering at her.

'Manda, will you please shut up for a second! Calm down, will you?'

'I'm completely calm—'

'Will you just let me tell you?'

'Sorry. I'll shut up.'

'Right. Devon is on. Definitely on, so you can stop panicking for a start.'

'Thank God for that – I'm so shattered – nothing could stop me going – I don't care if it's been cut off by floods or foot and mouth – I—'

'Manda!'

'OK, OK! I really am shutting up now. Hurry, hurry, there's a train coming.'

'There's just been a slight change in the line-up, that's all. It barely affects you, but it's not so hot for Anna because Sara won't be coming now. The Frasers have

4

had to pull out because Gina's dad has suddenly got a lot, lot worse and—'

'Oh, no – he hasn't? How awful! Poor her. Still – I'm not all that keen on her husband anyway. As long as *you're* not cancelling.'

'I'm *not.* So, anyway, the thing is, we asked Rob instead to – to – make up the numbers, so now he's coming, only he's bringing his girlfriend too, which wasn't part of the plan, because I thought he'd chucked her, well, he *had,* but then they got back together again, you know how hopeless he is, he can't make up his mind, well . . . anyway . . . so – oh, and my Dad's just broken his arm and can't look after himself properly . . . so . . . and this really wasn't my idea, believe me, but Rob thought . . . maybe . . . well, actually, Rob's already asked him and it's a bit awkward because we can't un-ask him now, can we? Besides, we could hardly leave him on his own with his arm in a sling, and the only alternative was for me to stay behind and play nurse and Joe wouldn't let me. You're cross, aren't you? Please say you're not cross.

'Manda? Are you still there?'

'Hang on a sec – the train's pulling in, I can't hear a thing.'

'Well?'

'My signal will go in a minute or two when we hit the tunnel. I'll have to call you later.'

'But did you hear me? It's OK, isn't it?'

5

'Doesn't sound like I have much say in the proceedings. When did all this happen?'

'I'm sorry. It was yesterday. I meant to call you, but it was very late. . .' *And if I'd told you it was because of the money, you'd have insisted on paying more and we'd have felt like impoverished students who have to be subsidized. Thanks but no thanks.*

'We could have asked the – the – what about those people at your last party – the woman with the purple suede boots and the husband with the incredibly hairy nostrils?'

'Penny and Roland? I thought you didn't like them?'

'They're OK as long as you don't look up his nose too much. Or it could have been just us lot.'

'I'm sorry. But you don't really mind, do you? I know Rob grates on people's nerves sometimes but you've always known how to handle him. I thought you *liked* him.'

'What's that supposed to mean?'

'What? Nothing. I'm just saying—'

'I do like him, of course I do. It's just that now it's turned into the Yorkes' family jamboree. . .'

'Hardly. Look, Rob and Tamsin can babysit so the four of us can go out to dinner. It'll be great.'

'Oh not Toxic Tamsin still? I'm not leaving Anna with her. Surely Rob could have dredged up something better than her by now?'

'Be fair. She's pretty harmless.'

'Excuse me? At your Christmas party, you ran down to the end of the garden – getting a pair of my gorgeous silk mules muddy in the process, I might add – just to get away from her – and you like absolutely everybody normally.'

'I overreacted because you made me drink too much mulled wine. Anyway . . . she's mellowed since then.'

'In three months?' Miranda sighed. 'This is so not what I had in mind for our holiday.'

'But you're not really cross?'

There was no response.

'Manda? Manda?'

But the signal had gone.

Kath and Joe's answerphone:
Message from Miranda

'Hi, Kath, it's me. Sorry to be a pain, but I think you may have to go without us. You know we all love Polly and Luke to bits, but it's really not fair to make Anna go a whole week without a friend her own age – especially when there are stacks and stacks of things for her to enjoy up here. Plus I'm inundated with work right now and I don't want to come and then be all stressed out – I'll only drive the rest of you crazy. You go – have a brilliant, brilliant time – and don't worry, we'll pay our full whack, of course, I'm running to the postbox right this minute with a cheque. I'm really sorry. Please don't hate me. Have fun, babe. Bye. Oh – just a thought – if you want to ring me back, get me on the mobile, I'm out and about so don't bother trying me at home, there's no point. So – on the mobile, OK? Or I'll call you.'

Miranda and Simon

'OK?' Simon wiped down the kitchen table as Miranda loaded the dishwasher after supper.

'Fine.'

'You look pale.'

'I'm *fine*.'

'I must say, I do think Kath could have phoned us to check before asking her entire family along. It is our holiday too.'

Even Simon's voicing exactly her own opinion grated on her nerves. Everything about him just now was guaranteed to irritate her; she could barely stand to be in the same room as him. And the feeling was evidently entirely mutual. She felt as if the outer layer of her skin had sloughed off without her noticing it, leaving her ultra-sensitive to the tiniest aggravation. Look – even the way Simon was holding his mug, clasped in his left hand, with its handle sticking out to the right, unused, drove her to distraction. Why couldn't he hold it properly, like a normal person?

She opened the fridge for some mineral water just so she could have the solid thickness of its door between them for a few seconds, took longer than she needed to, holding the door open as she refilled her glass, getting extra pleasure from knowing that every moment it was open must be utter torture for Simon. Inevitably, a small sigh escaped him: *Must you leave the fridge door open? It's such a waste of energy.*

'I'm closing it, for God's sake!' she snapped, although he hadn't spoken a word out loud. 'Don't blame Kath. I'm sure they manipulated her into it somehow.'

'She's not a child.'

'She was only trying to please them.'

'No wonder they're so selfish then, if she never stands up to them. Rob's like a spoilt teenager and as for her father—' Simon made a noise that combined a tut with an odd sort of squeak which emerged when he sucked his upper teeth with his lower lip, a sight Miranda currently found repellent; it was the sound of exasperation and contempt he reserved for speaking about greedy multi-nationals, oil companies, McDonald's and, apparently equally evil, people who made an extra car journey just to go to the recycling bins, thus unnecessarily burning fossil fuels while falsely claiming to be virtuous. Kath's father Giles was in a league of his own, however: not only was he wealthy, he also wore a suit and drove a gas-guzzling Jaguar; worst of all, he was a lawyer – not a lawyer who does Legal Aid cases and works on behalf of those unfortunate victims of a biased judicial system. No. Giles, a senior partner in a law practice, specialized in cases involving the petrochemicals industry. As far as Simon was concerned, Giles might as well have had 666 tattooed across his forehead.

'Now look who's being prejudiced!' Miranda drained her glass and rinsed it under a running tap for the sole purpose of getting up Simon's nose. 'You barely know them but already you've written them off without a fair trial. Rob and Giles are perfectly –' she cast around for the right words to annoy him – 'they're perfectly fine and decent human beings.' She crossed back to the dishwasher and slammed the door shut, then deliberately set it to 'Intensive' rather than pressing the green button Simon always selected: 'Eco'.

*   *   *

For a moment, Miranda imagined that Kath were sitting here in the kitchen, moaning about Rob and Giles. But she wouldn't, would she? Kath had rarely been known to utter other than the mildest criticism of her brother and father – even in circumstances which would have had anyone else spitting with rage. Like the occasion when Giles gave Rob a brand new car for his twenty-first birthday. And, three and a half years later, what did Kath get from him? A cheque. And, no, it wasn't enough for a car, it was barely enough for a half-decent bicycle. Kath's mother Constance had flushed when she'd seen the amount, then run upstairs to the bedroom, coming down breathless and bright-eyed, clutching a worn blue velvet box. Inside was her pearl necklace, Connie quickly clasping it around Kath's neck, ignoring her protests, saying she'd always planned to give it to her on her twenty-first birthday, when they all knew she'd been saving it for Kath's wedding day. Just as well, because of course by the time Kath came to marry Joe, Connie was dead.

'Si?'

Simon looked up at this rare term of affection from Miranda. He stirred the herb teabag around then tapped the spoon on the side of the mug, as if calling for attention.

'Maybe this holiday isn't such a great idea.'

He took a sip of his drink and waited for her to continue, infuriatingly patient as always.

'Aside from anything else, you know Anna spends far too much time on her own as it is – and now she won't have a friend her own age to play with – she's good with Polly and Luke, but she's bound to get bored of them pretty quickly. Don't you think it will be more stimulating for her if we stay here? There's so much more to do in London – museums, galleries, the Zoo, the puppet theatre, and she can still see her other friends.'

'I thought you said everyone was away for Easter?'

'Not everyone. I'm sure the Bradleys are around.'

'Isn't their kid the one who pushed Anna?'

'Hardly. They were messing about, that's all.'

'Anna was in tears.'

'Children are always in tears.' Miranda picked up a cloth and wiped down the already clean worktop, wishing she'd never started this conversation. 'She was fine after a minute.'

'And?'

'And what?'

'What are your other reasons for not wanting to go now? For changing your mind about a holiday that we've all been looking forward to for months?'

Miranda suppressed a strong urge to grab Simon's 'Keen to be Green' mug from his hand and smash him over the head with it.

'It's not that *I* don't want to go, Simon. *I'm* desperate for a holiday, as you very well know. *You're* the one who was just bitching about Rob and Giles – *you're* the one who'll have to put up with Rob being irritating and juvenile and bragging about his latest deal, *you're* the one who'll end up tangling with Giles about fossil fuels. Those two don't bother me a bit, I plan to read and walk, I'll barely notice they're there – *you're* the one who'll get aggravated by them.'

Simon said nothing, just stood leaning against the worktop, his expression unreadable. Miranda started vigorously wiping the still-damp kitchen table, making a show of sweeping the few remaining crumbs into her palm.

'Of course, it's true that the timing's not exactly ideal – we're absolutely up to here with special orders – everybody's wanting matching bags and shoes at this time of year.' At this, Simon gave a small but deliberate glance downwards at his own well-worn brown boots, a playful gesture that would once have made Miranda laugh. Now, she could barely even look at his boots without disgust; she was convinced he wore them almost entirely to irritate her. If so, it was a successful strategy – the boots were so brown, so scuffed, so slavishly functional; she had never seen footwear so determinedly unstylish.

She pressed on. 'Everybody gets married May, June, July, so they're all ordering their shoes now.'

'*Everybody?*'

'You *know* what I mean. It's an extremely busy time of year for us. I'm just not sure I can justify taking a whole week off.'

Simon returned his spoon to his herb tea and stirred it slowly once more. Miranda maintained an outward show of calm, while inwardly striving to anticipate his inevitable counter-argument so that she could plan her next move. He'd say she was being selfish and why should Anna miss out, she'd been looking forward to staying right by the sea for ages, so then Miranda would have to point out that they'd be able to give her lots of extra-special treats in London and that, if they didn't go, they wouldn't have to spend practically an entire day nose

13

to tail on the M3 then the A303 churning out exhaust fumes, which of course Simon hated, then he'd say—

'OK.'

'What?'

'OK. If you really feel you've got too much on, then fine, you'll be better off staying at home because you won't relax anyway and you'll spend your entire time on your mobile getting yourself in a state. Anna and I will go. I think she'll have a lot of fun there. She can mess about in rock pools and collect shells, she loves all that. She'll meet other kids on the beach, I'm sure. And we'll be out of your hair so you'll get more done. I suppose Kath will be disappointed as she's *your* friend, but as that doesn't seem to be worrying you. . .'

He shrugged.

'You wouldn't go without me?'

'Yes. Why not?' He banged down his mug. 'You mean you wanted us *all* to stay behind? *What on earth for?* Honestly, Miranda, you're unbelievable, you really are. Un-bloody-believable.' He left the room, heading for his study.

She waited a few minutes, then made some fresh, strong coffee, Simon's sole vice, and poked beneath the dark chocolate ginger thins in the biscuit tin to extract one of his home-made oatmeal and date cookies. She held it between the very tips of her fingers as if it were a mouldy apple. What was the point of a biscuit that was so obviously designed to avoid even the remotest potential for enjoyment? Wouldn't it be simpler just to avoid biscuits altogether?

'Simon?' A light, non-confrontational tap on his study door.

'Uh-huh?'

Miranda opened the door a little way, held out the coffee.

'I just wanted to say sorry. If you honestly think we should go on the holiday, then of course I'll come too. It's only that I've been so stressed lately, as you know, and it's really been—'

'Yes. Well. Haven't we all?'

'Yes, obviously. I know. But . . .'

'But it's different for you? Of course it is. That goes without saying. It's always different for Miranda, we all know that.' He leant back in his chair and stayed looking at the computer screen.

Miranda clunked his coffee down on the desk to stop herself pouring it into his lap.

'Careful!' He moved his papers to the other side of the desk. 'Christ knows I've long since given up expecting you to consider me or my needs, but you might at least spare half a thought for Anna. She's been going on about this holiday for weeks.' He shook his head slowly and spoke quietly. 'So selfish. Though God knows I should be used to it by now.'

Fuck you, you self-righteous, pompous, posturing git, she said in her mind, at once seeking solace in her own anger. Yes, she was selfish, she knew that; Miranda was not stupid, in fact she was all too aware of every single flaw she had. But no, not this time, not now. Now, she was thinking of all of them, not just herself: of Anna and, yes, definitely, of Simon. *You bastard. You self-satisfied, priggish, fucking bastardy-bastard.* She clenched her fists by her sides.

'Well, it's wonderful that you're always able to be so fair and open-minded about everything. I'm so glad you haven't felt the need to judge me at all.' She turned to go. 'Let's get an early start in the morning, shall we? Now, if I can suppress my ego for a few minutes, I'll try to make myself useful in some small, humdrum way by finishing the packing – no, no, you carry on, you have a planet to save.' She stopped at the door, looked down at the biscuit in her hand, now snapped in two. She took a step towards him and dropped it into his lap. 'Enjoy your coffee,' she said and went back downstairs to phone Kath, apologize for her earlier answerphone message, and tell her the marvellous news that they would now be coming after all.

A helping hand

'Oh, Daddy! Poor you!' Kath gently squeezed her father's uninjured arm and leaned forward to kiss his cheek.

16

'Careful! It's excruciating when people crash into it. I seem to be a magnet for every clumsy oaf staggering along the pavement at the moment.'

'I'm sorry, I didn't mean to. I thought you'd be in plaster, not just a sling. Wouldn't that give you more protection?'

'My orthopaedic chap says a sling is better in this instance as it's a relatively minor fracture and not displaced – and I don't presume to contradict the expert.'

'No, of course not. How about a nice cup of tea? Have you eaten yet? Let me make you something . . .'

'I had dinner out.' Giles rarely ate at home in any case. 'I'd prefer coffee.' Giles nodded. 'Not instant. In the—' He pointed with his left hand.

'I know.'

'Not too strong or I shan't sleep.'

'I know.' Kath spooned coffee into the filter.

'But not weak like you drink it at home. It should taste of coffee, otherwise one might as well not bother.'

'I *know.*' Kath chewed her lip and added another spoonful of coffee. 'Now, tell me what you'd like me to pack for you. Or do you want to come and *supervise* me?'

Giles got to his feet and led the way to his bedroom.

'I had to get my bag down myself.'

'So you managed then? That's good.' Kath started opening the doors of his fitted wardrobes, which ran along the length of one wall. 'Now . . .'

'When is Robert coming to pick me up?' Giles sat down on the edge of the bed, wincing as his arm moved.

'Sunday morning, I presume. They've got some swanky party tomorrow night, so they can't come down till then. You could rough it with us if you'd rather . . . but it'll be a bit of a squash with the children and all their toys and everything and I thought you might not be keen on playing I-Spy for five hours on the trot.'

'No, no, I'll wait until Sunday.' He waved his left arm towards the wardrobes. 'Not that shirt – no, no – there, that blue one, yes, and those there at the end. Not the double-cuffed ones I wear for work – I can't possibly manage cufflinks just now. What time is he coming?'

'I don't know. Perhaps you could phone him and ask him?'

'If you're speaking to him, tell him to call me.'

Kath, facing into the neat rows of shirts and suits, puffed out her cheeks and suppressed the urge to blow a loud raspberry.

'Now this is a really nice shirt. Why have I never seen you in this?'

'Short sleeves! I'd look like a second-hand car salesman! Frightful. It was a present from Mrs Thing at Christmas. Take it and give it to Oxfam. Pack a couple of sweaters, won't you? The cashmere ones. In the drawer there. No – on the right. No, below that. On the *right*.'

18

Kath carefully folded the jumpers and laid them in the case. She patted the top one, and stroked it for a moment as if it were a pet.

'These are *so* soft. Lovely. You *are* lucky.' Just one of her father's cashmere sweaters would cost at least half a dishwasher, Kath reckoned; these days, she saw everything in terms of chunks of kitchen, which she and her husband Joe had been slowly saving for over the past two years until the rising damp had been discovered, slurping up the dregs of their savings account and making the new kitchen an increasingly elusive dream. Only last week, Kath had fallen in love with a pretty aquamarine dress, and she hadn't had anything new for months, but it equalled almost half a cabinet, so she'd put it back on the rack and gone and bought herself a king-size Mars bar instead. True, she wasn't exactly in need of chocolate but at least it couldn't easily be equated to a fraction of a cupboard. 'You'll need a jacket, too. Have you got anything waterproof?' She knew her father wouldn't dream of owning any kind of anorak.

'My mac. Hall closet.'

'That's awfully smart, isn't it? It might get muddy. What happened to your old waxed jacket?'

'My Barbour? Lord knows, I haven't worn it for aeons. Oh, it might well be up in the loft if you want to fetch it down. All sorts of stuff went up there when I had the place redecorated.'

'Oh. Right.'

'There is a ladder.'

'I know.' She sighed inwardly. 'Good. That'll save me having to make a bionic leap up there then.'

'Mmm. I need to take my tablets.'

Something in the attic

'Dad, there's so much stuff up here!' Kath called down through the hatch.

'Mmm?'

She slumped onto a box then opened the one next to her. Something awkward, swaddled in newspaper. Unwrapped it. It was a teapot, part of her mother's tea service which had been handed down from her own mother. It had pretty yellow buttercups painted round it and a gold rim. When Kath was growing up, if she'd ever been ill in bed, her mother would bring her in a tray with a soft-boiled egg or a piece of home-made short-bread and what she called 'buttercup tea'; in fact, it was tea made from lemon balm and sweetened with honey, but at the bottom of the cup was a painted buttercup which Kath could see through the clear liquid.

'Drink up and let's see that buttercup,' Connie would say.

'Up – up – buttercup,' Kath would reply, a phrase that had become modified with her own children into, 'Eat up, buttercup.'

20

A shame it was all up here, going to waste. Polly would love the pretty cups, though Luke would be a bit of a liability near them.

She stood up and flipped open the lid of another box. Books. Kath picked out a couple and peered at the old leather spines: Tennyson, Keats. Her mother's, of course.

'Dad? This could take ages,' she called down. 'Do you have any idea where I should look?'

'It's quite a large box, I should think. And it should be labelled. They should all be labelled.'

'Really? I can't see any labels.' But she peered closer now and saw that there was small writing on the side. 'Tea service (old)' said the one next to her. 'C's books: poetry' said the other. She moved from box to box, reading the labels. Ah – 'Walking boots etc.' Worth a look.

'I think I may have found it.'

'Jolly good.' She heard Giles go into the bathroom, the click of the lock. Opened the box: two pairs of walking boots, the mud properly cleaned off, unlike the jumble of boots stuffed in the chest in her own hallway. Two pairs of green wellies. Ah – jacket. Yes, her mother's old navy one and her father's in sludgy dark green. She pulled them both out and closed the box again. Perching on the corner of a heavy trunk, she looked at the box beside her: 'SEWING: odds and ends,' it said in her mother's handwriting, 'Crewel

21

wool/embroidery silks/fabric scraps.' Kath thought of the hole in Polly's favourite jumper – she had been meaning to stitch a little heart over the hole to disguise it, but she might be able to match the wool instead. She dug into the box, caught herself on a stray needle and recoiled, sucking her finger. They really should have a stronger light up here. She peered in and cautiously extended her hand once more. Something light caught her eye – paper, was it? She tugged at a corner. An envelope? Several, bound together with a plait of coloured wools. Kath turned it over: Mrs C. Yorke, c/o . . . Letters for her mother sent to her at the school where she'd first taught. The envelope had a typed address. Funny to tie up business correspondence like that. She idly pulled out the top letter and opened it, unfolded it. Terrible handwriting. What people called 'artistic', i.e. almost illegible. But the top caught her eye:

My dearest

Kath peered closer, trying to read the next sentence. God, the writing was a trial. She scanned down the page, picking out odd words: 'bicycle' – rather unexpectedly, 'thinking of your . . . (indecipherable)'. She turned the sheet over: 'bea'? Looked back at the words before it: 'beary im bea'. Not likely. No. Not an 'a' at all. It must be a squashed 'd' – 'being in bed'. She felt herself flush.

22

'Kathryn!'

She jumped guiltily and quickly tucked the letter away and concealed it once more at the bottom of the box.

'Coming!'

'What *are* you doing up there? Aren't you coming down?'

'Yes, just coming now! Stand back!'

She dropped the two jackets down through the hatch, then picked up the box. It wasn't heavy at all, perhaps she could take the whole thing, so Polly and Luke could play with the scraps, make collages or something. Kath managed to balance the box against the ladder as she climbed down. Giles had picked up his own green jacket.

'You found it then?'

'And Mum's – see?'

'What did you bring hers down for?'

'Well, I thought that perhaps I could have it? I don't have a proper—'

'Oh. Right. Yes. Don't see why not.'

'Not if you mind, of course? If you'd rather hang onto it – for – for – whatever reason? It just seems a shame for it to be going to waste up there.'

'Why would I want it? Take it, take it.'

'And the other thing – ' Kath felt herself flush, even thinking of the letters. 'I found some of Mum's tapestry stuff, wool and so on – could I—'

Giles waved her away.

'Never could understand what all that was for, your mother ruining her eyesight fiddling about with her sewing.'

'She really enjoyed it.'

Giles snorted.

'That and her music. You know how much she loved—'

'Take it, I said, take whatever you want, it's no use to me.' Giles returned to the bedroom. 'Have you finished the packing?'

'Just about. Don't forget to add your toilet bag and shaving things. Oh, and your slippers.'

'I'm not an idiot, Kathryn. I have a specific injury to my elbow, that's all. It doesn't make me either a child or a cretin.'

'I'm sorry. You know I didn't mean it like that. Anyway, you're sure you can manage for now?'

'Well enough.'

'Would you like me to unbutton your shirt at least, to make it easier for you to undress?'

No response. As it wasn't an outright refusal, Kath took this as a grudging assent and moved towards him.

'How on earth did you manage to put it on this morning?'

'Slowly.' A wry smile.

Kath laughed. It was strange to be standing here, seeing her father's semi-exposed chest. She was shocked to notice how grey the hair on his body was

24

now. Of course it would be, she realized; his head hair was mostly grey, though still surprisingly thick and with a strong curl, a source of pride for Giles. It was just that she hadn't seen him other than fully dressed for years. She averted her eyes slightly, embarrassed.

'We're off at crack of dawn tomorrow, so you'll have to ring Rob if you need anything else.'

'Mrs Thing's coming tomorrow.' Giles's cleaner, who also bought his groceries, changed his bed linen and did most of the tasks that his secretary at work couldn't be expected to undertake.

'Mrs *Baines*, Daddy. That's good.'

'What time is Robert coming on Sunday with the girl?'

'I don't know.' She sighed. 'And Tamsin's not a girl, she's twenty-seven.' She leant forward to kiss him goodbye. 'I'll get Rob to phone you. See you Sunday, Dad. Take care. Don't forget your painkillers.'

Saturday

Nearly there

'I think . . . maybe . . . the turn-off might – possibly – have been back there.' Kath peered at the hopelessly small-scale photocopied map and baffling directions once more, as if the route might suddenly become crystal clear. 'Possibly.'

'*Where?*' Her husband took his eye off the road ahead and looked across at the map.

'Watch the road. Where there was that kink in the road. Just past the postbox.'

'What postbox?'

'The *red* one.' Kath gritted her teeth. 'Built into the wall. Can't you turn round?'

'Not here, no.' The narrow, rain-slicked road twisted through the Devon countryside between steep, mossy banks topped with drystone walls; it felt as if they were driving along a high-sided trench.

'Are we nearly there?' Polly piped up from the back seat.

'I need to do a wee,' said Luke.

'Very nearly there!' Kath kept her voice bright. 'We really can't stop here. Try and hang on one more minute, Luke.'

Joe backed into a gateway at the edge of a field, bumping into the metal gate with a clang, then retraced his route.

'See – *there*! That's the postbox!'

'*Good*. So how much further is the turn-off?'

'Um . . . it's immediately after.' Kath consulted the directions again.

'*Where?*' Joe slowed the car. 'How immediately? *Immediately* immediately or twenty paces past the pile of sheep dung immediately or after another fourteen miles of mud track with no signposts immediately?'

Kath shot him a look.

'*Immediately* after . . . um, going the other way.' She stared straight ahead through the windscreen, then turned to offer her husband a half-smile. 'Sorry.'

He patted her hand.

'So I need to turn round again?'

' 'Fraid so.'

'I'll reverse. It's no distance.'

Joe craned his head round to see.

'Oh, is that a good idea?'

'It's fine.'

'But you can't see.'

'No-one's coming. There hasn't been another car for ages.'

'Shall I get out and direct you?'

'No! It's *fine.*'

'Daddy?'

'Not right now, Poll. Daddy's driving.' Joe reversed cleanly round a sharp bend, then abruptly slammed on the brakes. A huge tractor filled his rear-view mirror.

'Bugger!'

'Joe . . .'

'Dad said a rude word!'

'Don't.' Joe smiled into his mirror and waved 'sorry' at the tractor-driver behind him. 'Just nobody say a word.'

He shoved the gear stick forward and shot off.

'Did you see, Luke? See the lovely big tractor?'

'Where's a tractor? I wanna see the tractor. *I* wanna see.' Luke started wriggling in his child seat.

'How the hell is anyone supposed to turn round on these roads? I mean, who designed them?'

Kath kept silent.

'Trust us to run into a tractor!' Joe gripped the wheel.

'*I* wanna see the tractor!'

'In a minute, poppet.' Kath snaked a hand round behind her to pat her small son on the leg. 'It is the country, Joe. They do have them, you know.'

'Well, *why* do they? What are they *for*? Bet you they only have them to annoy the tourists — you notice you never see one in a field, do you? You never see one actually —

31

tractoring anything – ploughing – or whatever it is – they are always, *always* on the road – no wonder British farming's in a crisis, they've all forgotten what a tractor's supposed to be for – it's some kind of anti-townie joke – bet you they all pile into the pub on Friday night and plan the whole thing: OK, Mikey, you take the narrow road between the post office and the twisty oak tree and go back and forth there for a couple of hours – Jake, do the A303 so we can get a good, long tailback going there—'

'*Daddy!*'

'*What?*' His voice softened. 'Sorry, Poll. What is it?'

She giggled.

'Luke's done a wee-wee.'

The house

Despite the fact that it had started raining yet again, the house looked as beautiful as it had in the brochure, more so even because now the daffodils were out in the front garden and all along the grass verge, their yellow heads zinging out against the muddy grass and grey stone walls. It was an old house built of mellow stone with a slate roof, from the edge of which water poured in a steady stream right by the front door. Kath comforted Luke while Joe fumbled about in the pots in the porch.

'Where did they say the key was?'

'Come on, Luke, we'll soon have you all nice and dry again. *There*—' Kath waved a hand at a platoon of pots. 'Under the primulas. Look, Luke – see the little waterfall coming off the roof? Isn't that nice?'

'The what?'

'There! Oh, hurry up, Joe – the pink ones that look like primroses. *There.*'

'Great security.' He fumbled with the key in the lock, then shoved the door open with difficulty.

Kath went in, carrying Luke, heading straight upstairs to look for the bathroom. Polly came into the hallway and looked down at the worn flagstones.

'The floor's all bumpy like the path outside. Why isn't there any carpet, Dad?'

'Because it's the country. It would get muddy.' Joe patted his daughter's head. 'It's better than carpet, Poll,' he said. 'It's very, very old.'

'Older than you?' This was one of Polly's current favourite jokes, teasing her father about his age. Joe had turned forty-three two weeks before and, ten years older than his wife, tended to be slightly defensive about it.

'Even older than me. Parts of this house have been here for nearly four hundred years and I'm only two-hundred and twenty. I'm practically a baby by comparison.'

'Shall we explore then?' Kath said, once she'd got Luke into some dry clothes.

'Explore! Explore!' Polly and Luke started jumping up and down.

On the ground floor, there was a sitting room, a separate dining room, and a large kitchen leading to a cool, stone-flagged pantry-cum-utility room, which itself contained a smaller cubicle with a lavatory. A semi-glazed door led out from the pantry to the back garden. The sitting room was large and well furnished, even overfurnished, with two long sofas, a couple of bulging armchairs, and an extraordinary number of occasional tables scattered with wipe-clean coasters depicting scenes of bygone days featuring people hunting, trapping and shooting various forms of wildlife. Off the hallway, as part of a new extension, was a twin bedroom with a small en-suite shower.

'Well, this'll give your dad a bit of peace away from the marauding hordes at least.'

'Joe?'

'Mmm. What's up, K?'

'It's just . . . I'm sorry that he's coming. This was supposed to be a real break for all of us and I know you'd rather have him administered only in small doses and I don't blame you.'

'Ach, he's not so bad. We'll get by.'

Kath smiled up at him.

'Am I being mean? He couldn't possibly have managed on his own for a week with a broken arm and it made sense for the Boy Wonder to ask him along, but I wish

Rob had spoken to us first . . . you know what Dad's like. I can't exactly see him pitching in, helping the kids make sandcastles, can you? I don't want to spend the whole week telling them to hush so as not to annoy Grandpa – it's their holiday too.' She leaned against his shoulder. 'It will be all right though, won't it? Please, just lie to me, tell me it'll all be fine.'

'It'll all be fine.' Joe pulled her close for a hug. 'Now stop beating yourself up. We know it's not ideal. But I'm here and Miranda will be here and I can't think of anyone more likely to knock Giles into shape than Miranda, can you? She'll give him a good run for his money.'

They went upstairs and Polly and Luke immediately hurled themselves onto the double bed in the main bedroom, then ran off to look at the other rooms.

'So, is this us?' Joe stuck his head round the door of the en-suite bathroom, then looked out of the window. 'Wow. This is some serious view. Come and look. You can see the sea!' He put his arm round her and pulled her close. 'This is great. The wife done well.'

'Shouldn't we offer this one to Miranda and Simon?'

'Why? We're here first. Besides, you found the place. You're the one who spent hours trawling through brochures and on the Net looking for somewhere to suit everyone.'

'Ye-e-s, I suppose so. I just thought it might help make it up to them. Sort of compensation.'

Joe raised his eyebrows.

'For what exactly?'

'Well, they're having my entire family inflicted on them as well. I feel guilty. I know I should have checked with Miranda before I called Rob, I could tell she was annoyed with me, but if I'd asked her, she'd have told me not to ask anyone else, wouldn't she? If the Frasers had already paid, it would have been different, but how could we have hassled them for their share now? "Hi, Gina, sorry your dad's at death's door – hurry up and send us your cheque, won't you?" '

'You should feel guilty: you're a terrible person. I'm having your family inflicted on me, too, so don't I deserve the nice bedroom?' He pulled her down onto the bed beside him.

'No. It's part of your job description, putting up with my family. Anyway, I'm sure the other rooms are lovely too.'

'Good. They won't mind having one of those then, will they?' He pulled his wife close for a kiss. 'We need a decent room with a big bed because I plan to be spending as much time as possible in it. Some of it even with you if you play your cards right. It's spring – aren't we due to have sex round about this time of year?' Kath smiled and fondled his ears.

'But the other thing is that Miranda said she and Simon are having a bit of a rough patch. I thought they should have the best room so they can, you know, have somewhere nice to . . . sort things out.'

'Oh no. K, you're very sweet and considerate, but if those two are going to be arguing all week, they should sleep in the garden shed. They can take potshots at each other anywhere, there's definitely no point wasting the best room on them.'

Polly and Luke came tearing back in.

'No, I'm having it!'

'No. You're a meany. Daddy, Daddy!'

'Dad, can I have the top bunk, please can I, please?'

Kath and Joe looked at each other.

'Plus there's the minor matter of where we're going to put Anna, now that we have a sixty-two-year-old man in place of an eight-year-old girl.'

'One thing at a time, petal, one thing at a time.' Joe got to his feet and rounded up his children. 'Now, let's go and sort out these bunks.'

Hemmed in

Miranda focused on the road ahead and concentrated on overtaking a huge lorry going too fast in the middle lane. Why was it so scary driving close alongside a lorry? She always felt as if it would just veer into her lane without warning, pulverizing her and her car into scrap, felt almost as if she might make it happen just by imagining it. Miranda checked her mirrors once more, then smoothly pulled back in ahead of the lorry. The rain hadn't let up from the moment they'd left home and the windscreen wipers whipped back and forth. She turned the volume of the car stereo up slightly to hear above the noise of the rain and the tyres on the wet road. They were listening to an audio tape she had given Anna for Christmas, Charles Dickens's *A Christmas Carol*. Thank God Anna was long past the Thomas the Tank Engine stage and they could at least play something that she and Simon could enjoy too. Not that she was giving it her full attention. The voice drifted in and out of her consciousness. Whole minutes would go by in which she absorbed nothing, the words no more than random sounds swirling around the car like the continuous whirr of the heater, neither noticed nor comprehended, then odd phrases, snatches of dialogue would clutch at her and she had to remind herself to keep breathing.

'Spirit!' said Scrooge in a broken voice, 'remove me from this place.'

'I told you these were shadows of the things that have been,' said the Ghost. 'That they are what they are do not blame me!'

'Remove me!' Scrooge exclaimed, 'I cannot bear it!'

Anna was looking out of the window. She wasn't allowed to read on car journeys, because it made her travel-sick, they had played the number-plate game for ages and now they were listening to a story on tape. She had heard it several times since getting it in her stocking at Christmas. Mummy and Daddy were quiet now, they were listening to the story and not being cross with each other any more about the map and the road signs and who was supposed to have written a note for the painter and who forgot to bring a bottle of water from the fridge. Anna liked the Dickens story very much, but she didn't want to hear it now this minute. It was best to listen to it snuggled up on the sofa with Mummy or Daddy and a mug of hot chocolate and you could look into the fire and see faces, Scrooge and Tiny Tim and the Ghosts of Christmas Past, Christmas Present and Christmas Yet to Come.

Now she rested her cheek against the cold of the window, looking up at the rivulets of rain travelling across the glass. If she were a drop of water, would she feel wet on the inside or only on the outside, like being in the bath? She could not picture herself as a drop, closed her eyes tight, no, only as a miniature version of herself floating in a sort of bubble, which was not the same thing. Blood was inside of you and that was wet, you could see it was when you fell over in the play-ground and scraped your knee, but you couldn't feel it being wet on the inside, it only felt wet when it came out. Granny said your blood moved round your body the whole time, even when you were asleep: the way it worked was it picked up oxygen, which was what you got in air, and it took it all over like the postman, delivering the air like little packages to your muscles and your brain and everything and then it went back to your lungs to pick up some more, but you couldn't feel it moving either. Granny used to be a doctor before she got old and she knew all about your insides and everything. Anna liked it when Granny or Mummy or Daddy told her things but it wasn't the same as when you knew something yourself, like knowing that water is wet or that sand is soft but gritty at the same time, knowing it because you could put your hand right in it, feel it on your skin, know it for sure.

'Is it this next junction, Simon, or the one after?'

'The one after.'

'OK there in the back row?' her mother said, smiling, meeting Anna's eyes in the mirror.

Anna nodded silently.

'We'll stop soon for a drink, Anna-Banana, as we don't seem to have any water in the car,' said Simon. 'Okey-doke?' Daddy called her Anna-Banana sometimes. It was a bit of a baby name, nice for night-time when he tucked her in and read her a story but not so nice when he said it in front of her friends. When she had her friend Sara for a sleepover, Sara giggled and kept saying, 'Anna's a banana! Anna's a banana!' and Anna felt all hot and red and her eyes went prickly.

Mummy looked at Daddy as if she were going to say something. Perhaps she was going to say what drink she was thinking of having when they stopped; sometimes she had a cappuccino and let Anna have the froth and the sprinkled chocolate powder from the top, but sometimes she had an espresso: it came in a small cup like for a doll but it tasted nasty, bitter, and there was no froth and no chocolate. Daddy didn't usually have coffee when they were out because he said you didn't know where it was from and it might be from a bad grower who wasn't nice to the workers and you couldn't be sure. Mummy couldn't have made up her mind, though, because she faced the front again and didn't say anything.

'Daddy?' Anna said.

'Yes?'

'D'you think it'll rain the *whole* time we're on holiday?'

The second wave

'Yoo-hoo!' Miranda called in a mock-posh-lady voice, banging the knocker and opening the front door at the same time. 'It's us! Helloooo-ooooooooooo!'

It seemed as if a herd of creatures stampeded at them from every direction: Polly and Luke came hurtling down the stairs from where they'd been playing Thunderbirds on the top bunk; Joe lumbered, rather more slowly, from the sitting room where he'd been supposedly trying to light a fire, i.e. having a nap; Kath burst from the kitchen and ran down the hallway as if Miranda were a long-lost

41

friend she hadn't seen for years, rather than for barely more than a fortnight.

Luke reached up his arms to Miranda.

'Manda! Manda!'

She dropped her handbag to the floor and picked him up.

'Hello, Lukey-Luke.'

'Me now! Me!'

Miranda put Luke down and swung Polly up high.

'How's you, Polly-Woll?' Polly gurgled with laughter.

'Gosh, you're getting as heavy as Anna now.' Miranda put her back down and gave Anna a prompting push forward. Anna was skinny but tall for her age, and two years older than Polly.

'D'you want to see my Barbie?' Polly, suddenly shy, spoke quietly.

Anna looked up at her mother, her slate blue eyes unsmiling: *Do I have to?*

Miranda gave a small nod and a smile in answer to the unstated question: *Go on – be nice, she's only little.*

'OK.'

Polly beamed with delight and grabbed Anna's hand to drag her upstairs. Anna looked back down at the adults.

'It's so good to see you!' Kath said. 'Let me come and help you with your bags.'

'No need – Simon insisted on doing it. I hate to deprive him of the chance to perfect his martyr act.'

42

'Play nicely. We're on holiday.'

'I'll give him a hand.' Joe went outside.

'At least you found it. We got lost at this last bit.'

'I'd have driven right through a drystone wall to get here if necessary by then. Anna felt car-sick when we'd barely reached the bottom of our road, it took for ever to get out of London, then she started keeping tally of the lamp-posts on the M3 until I bribed her to stop with Smarties and Simon had a go at me about using sugar as a reward. God, he's – ' she lowered her voice – 'driving me crazy just now. He's being absolutely impossible, you have no idea.'

'Oh, come on.' Kath laid a hand on her friend's arm. 'We all get like that on a long journey. Luke wet himself and Joe and I nearly came to blows.'

Miranda smiled indulgently.

'Yeah, I can imagine. That's exactly the same thing.'

'Oh, shut up. Come and have a cup of tea.'

Anna suddenly appeared beside Miranda in the kitchen.

'Oh! Please don't keep doing that, Anna! You gave me a fright.' Miranda turned to Kath. 'She's always creeping up on people, she's practising to be a cat burglar when she grows up. It's so spooky.'

'Spoo-oo-oo-ooky!' Anna snuggled close to her mother. 'Or I might be a spy actually. I haven't decided yet.'

43

'Weren't you playing with Polly's Barbie?'

'Barbie is boring actually,' Anna pronounced. 'Where am I going to sleep? Can I choose?' She turned to Kath. 'I was s'posed to share with Sara, Auntie Kath, but she can't come now because her grandad got ever so ill. They had to go to Scotland.'

'Oops, the beds!' Kath covered her mouth with her hand, as if she'd said something wrong. 'I've been meaning to sort them out. Help me, will you, Manda?'

'Sure thing.' She picked up her mug of tea. 'Anna, can you go and give Daddy a hand?' Kath led the way upstairs.

'See you bagged the best room, you big shellfish.' Miranda shook her head, stony-faced, as if saddened that it had come to this.

'I knew it! Please don't hate me. I don't care which room we have – really. We can swap.'

'God, you're so easy to wind up. You're the most unselfish person I know. Of course you should have it – you organized the whole thing. I don't give a toss where we sleep; I'm so tired I could crash out propped up in the broom cupboard.' They went into one of the other bedrooms, with twin beds. 'We can have this one – at least there's a basin.'

'Surely you want the other double? The view's better too.'

Miranda shrugged.

'Things aren't that bad, are they?'

'Pretty shitty recently.' She sighed. 'No. I don't know. Exaggerating for effect, as usual, knowing me. I haven't actually tried to kill him yet, so it could be worse, right?'

'Well, it's your choice. Rob and Tamsin aren't coming till tomorrow. I'm sure they'd *love* the double if you two don't want it.'

'No. It's OK. You're right – we'd better have the double. I can't face another row.'

'It's supposed to be a holiday. It's *supposed* to be fun.'

'Yeah, I'm sorry. I'll be fine by tomorrow, I'm just a bit shattered, that's all, we both are.'

'Same here.' Kath's voice dropped to a barely audible whisper. 'We haven't had sex for ages. We're lucky if we can manage to crawl upstairs and undress at the end of the day. Joe's fallen asleep slumped over the kitchen table the last three nights in a row. And when we do make an attempt at the weekend, Polly or Luke come waltzing into our room, saying, "Mummy, can I have toastie soldiers and Marmite?" "Daddy, what makes the fridge all cold inside?" or crying or yelling over some hideous crime that one of them has inflicted on the other. Is everyone like this or is it just us?'

'None of the couples I know has sex regularly any more, well, none of the ones with kids. Somehow it's become this kind of rare, self-indulgent luxury, like having breakfast in bed – I mean, who's got the time?

Who's got the energy? Count yourself lucky – at least you still *want* to.'

'You're just tired, that's all.'

'Hmm.'

'You'll be so relaxed after a couple of days away from it all, I bet you.'

'Mmm. I suppose you're right.'

Kath moved out to the landing again.

'Bathroom's there, by the way. There's another loo downstairs, off the utility room.' They went into the small, bunk-bedded room. 'I've put Polly and Luke's things in here for now, but we'll have to have a rethink because of Anna.'

Miranda nodded.

'I guess she could come in with us at a pinch.'

'You don't need to do that. At least she can have the twin room for tonight.'

'So, if Rob and the She-Devil have the twin from tomorrow, what about . . . ?'

'There's another twin room on the ground floor, but I thought my dad had better sleep there. It's away from the kids' noise and it's got its own shower. I just thought with his arm and everything, it might be a little easier for him.'

'Huh, all right for some.'

'Well, you have it then.' Kath led the way downstairs to show Miranda the other bedroom. 'But you can't see the sea.'

46

'This is nice. At least it's not been struck by the Curse of the Flowery Wallpaper.'

'You two have it. You can push the beds together. I just assumed you'd want the view and to be near Anna?'

'Of course we do. I'm sure you're right – besides Giles won't take kindly to being woken by the dawn chorus of the Not-So-Silent Three. He can be cocooned here in perfect peace and solitude and forget they're even here.'

Something to celebrate

Miranda set down a large box of groceries on the kitchen table.

'I know we'll need to do a proper shop, but I brought a few bits and pieces for now.'

Kath peered into the box, making exaggerated sniffs like a bloodhound.

'Mmm, what have you got? Wow! Wonderful: fresh coffee, olives, no – *two* sorts of olives, wine, anchovies, serious chocolate, posh bread, little *palmiers*, mmm yum, ooh ripe camembert and that lovely pongy cheese I like, balsamic vinegar, more wine. Golly, there's an entire delicatessen in here. I love your idea of "bits and pieces" – we brought spaghetti and tuna and cornflakes and other gastronomic folderols. Plus chicken for tomorrow.'

'Where shall I put this?' Simon came in, carrying another box.

'Is it *more* food?' Kath asked.

'Mostly champagne by the look of it.'

'Oh Simon!' Miranda turned to face him. 'Why did you bring that in? It was supposed to be a surprise, for heaven's sake!'

'What surprise?' said Kath, as Simon laid the box down in the middle of the kitchen floor and walked out.

'I *told* him to leave it in the boot for now – he *never* listens.'

'It doesn't matter, does it? Six bottles! Are we having a party?'

Miranda sighed and opened the fridge to put a couple of bottles in to chill.

'It's for your anniversary. You weren't supposed to see it, needless to say. I was planning to cook you a special dinner – unless Joe's whisking you out somewhere posh? I'm happy to babysit if you like.'

'I'm sure we'll stay in, we haven't booked anywhere – it's only our ninth after all. But *six* bottles? For seven grown-ups?'

'Take the rest home if there's any left. But, believe me, you'll want every drop of alcohol you can possibly lay your hands on once you've endured sharing a house with Simon for more than two hours.'

'Come on, you're just a bit stressed out.' Kath started putting away the groceries. 'I *like* Simon, you know I do. He's a good man. He's decent. Fair. Strongly principled. All of which seem to be increasingly rare qualities. He's an endangered species. You should treasure him.'

'*Decent*? Of course he's decent. He's Saint Simon, Saviour of our Poor, Afflicted Planet – he gets off on being principled, on making everyone else feel like some lowly, loathsome worm by comparison.'

'That's not fair!' Kath stretched up, struggling to put the biscuits on an upper shelf, out of children's sight.

'It's true.' Miranda took the biscuits from her and shoved them to the back of the shelf. 'And he doesn't give a toss about me. If I were weaving baskets and subsisting on a handful of corn in Guatemala, then maybe he'd be interested, but as it is . . .' she shrugged. 'I'm just another spoilt, white, Western woman. I'm well paid and well fed. Overfed, in fact.' She jabbed at her tummy. 'In a weird way, when I'm being calm and rational—'

'Which is all the time, of course—'

'Ha ha. You're supposed to be on my side. When I'm being rational – which is not very often, I know – then I think he's right. Of *course*, in the overall scheme of things, my problems don't matter a toss—'

'All our problems are relatively insignificant. But just because we're not starving and we have a roof over our heads, albeit a leaky one in our case, doesn't mean we don't feel pain or grief, that we don't get hurt . . . upset . . . lonely . . .'

'Yes, yes, I know that. But Simon doesn't. Or doesn't seem to at any rate.'

'I'm sure he cares about you. He loves you.'

Miranda bit her lip and said nothing. A barely perceptible shake of the head.

'Well, he's hiding it extremely well at the moment, I assure you.'

'It's probably just tiredness. You know he's crazy about you. Here, come and sit down. Let me make you some tea.'

A lady of letters

They sat at the kitchen table, drinking their tea.

'Do you think we should perhaps test one of those biscuits?' Kath said.

'Check they're not stale before we inflict them on anyone else? Good idea.' Miranda got them down.

'You used to be so proud of him,' Kath pointed out. 'You said it was extraordinary to be with someone who was actually making a difference in the world, you said he made you feel more hopeful about life – don't you remember? You used to get this little glow when you talked about him.'

'Did I? Bleugh. Well, I grew out of it. That was then and this is now. I'm sick of being made to feel guilty all the time. It's so tiring being around Simon, you've no idea. Every tiny decision has to be gone over and over, every little purchase – every light bulb, every apple –

50

where did it come from, is it low energy, are the pickers well treated, how many miles has it travelled, where did I buy it – it's so bloody boring. For once, I'd love just to walk into a supermarket and hurl things into the trolley without spending two hours reading the labels.'

Kath said nothing.

'I know. I know I'm sounding like a spoilt brat. OK, maybe I am a spoilt brat, but I haven't got the *energy* to be like him – it makes life such hard work. I'm happy to recycle our bottles – God knows the amount I've been drinking recently, I really *am* making a difference single-handed – and I buy organic veg, free-range eggs, fair-trade coffee. I get out my credit card when I see programmes about Ethiopia or Rwanda or the street children of Brazil, but that's about it. I don't know how to be a better person.'

'Don't be so hard on yourself—'

'Why not? It saves Simon the bother. And it's not just that, for weeks and weeks now, he's been really prickly, I know you think I'm just being daft but I swear I'm not imagining it. He picks on everything I say, so now I find I'm being defensive the second I open my mouth.'

'Come on. We all go through bad patches.' Kath leant forward and squeezed Miranda's arm.

Miranda pushed the packet of biscuits away.

'Please, hide these from me. I've got no self-control.'

'And I have?'

Kath took them and disappeared into the pantry off the kitchen.

'Anyway, what's happening with you? Any exciting news? I'm sorry – I've been blethering on about myself. That's because I'm a narcissist, according to Simon. It must be true because – as we know – Simon is never, ever wrong.'

'Oh, you're not, don't be silly.' Kath emerged from the pantry looking slightly flushed. 'Actually, there is something exciting. I came across some old letters. I think they could be love letters.'

'Oo-ooh, love letters! Who to? Who from?'

'To my *mum*.' Kath dropped her voice to a whisper. 'They were hidden beneath her tapestry wools. Hang on a tick, let me go and fetch them.'

Miranda put their mugs in the dishwasher, then transferred the rest of the champagne to the pantry. It was much cooler in here than in the kitchen, due to the stone-flagged floor and the air vents. Dim and cool, like the shade beneath a tree. Perhaps she could spend the entire holiday in this strange stone cell, emerge from time to time for a cup of tea with Kath or to see Anna, then return to her resting place, sitting unnoticed on one of the long wooden shelves or propped in a corner.

'Here they are.' Kath reappeared clutching a slim bundle of letters, tied round with a plait of tapestry wool in shades of green, moss and apple and pine.

'So, what do they say? Are they rude? Tell, tell.'

Kath shook her head. 'I haven't read them yet. I took a quick peek at one, thought I saw the word "bed" and stuffed it back in the envelope. And the handwriting's a bit of a challenge.'

'God, you're a saint. How can you be so un-nosy?'

'I'm *not*. I only found them yesterday when I went to help Dad pack and I haven't had a single minute to myself since then. And – and – to be honest, though of course I want to read them, at the same time I feel a bit weird about it—'

'That's only natural – God, I mean, who the hell wants to read about their parents having – *juices* etcetera—'

'Manda!' Kath hit her with the bundle of letters. 'You are totally disgusting! Now I need another biscuit to drive away that thought.'

Miranda refilled the kettle.

'Can you imagine letters between *my* parents?' Miranda said. 'You know what my mum's like – bet you they'd be totally devoid of romance and utterly matter-of-fact: "Dearest Charles, I often think of you putting your penis into my vagina . . ."'

'Will you *stop*? It is odd though. Can you think of anyone less likely to have an *affair* than my mother?'

'No.' Miranda shook her head. 'Though I guess we all act out of character sometimes, don't we? I have days when I'm just so tired of being Miranda and I'd give anything to escape from me and be someone else – even for one day. Don't you?'

'Not really. I'd like to have more money and I'd like to be less tired, but I don't want anyone else's life. Why would I?'

Miranda smiled.

'You have no idea how lucky you are.'

'Ha, come round to my crumbling kitchen and say that.'

'No, you are. Not everyone has the capacity to be contented. You should give lessons: Happiness for Beginners, a step-by-step course for the complete novice. I'd sign up for sure.'

'I'll try to remember that next time I'm standing at the sink gazing at the exposed plaster and cracked tiles.' She fiddled with the woven braid around the letters.

Miranda laid her hand on top of Kath's.

'Hang on a minute. Maybe you're right to be cautious? I mean, you don't really need to read them, do you? Perhaps you should destroy them? Or lock them away safely and forget about them? Surely Connie wouldn't have meant you to read them?'

'I don't know. But it seems wrong to get rid of them. Once they're gone, they're gone.' She suddenly pushed the bundle across the table towards Miranda. 'Here, why don't you take a look instead?'

'What?'

Kath nodded.

'Yes. Then if there's anything, you know . . . too . . . physical or whatever, you can warn me.'

'Really?'

'Mmm. It makes perfect sense. You can check them then read me out the slushy bits: "Darling, I dream of you night and day . . ." and then I can hide them away again. The kids might find them fascinating when they're older.'

'But Kath . . .'

'Go on. Please. For me.' Kath took the top letter out of its envelope and handed it to Miranda.

'Well, if you're sure you're sure . . . ? Do you know who they're from at least?'

'No. They were sent to her care of the school. The writing's awful, but it's not Dad's anyway, I know that much.'

'Well, I hardly thought they were from Giles!'

'Why do you say it like that?' Kath frowned.

'Oh, nothing. I just meant, well, he doesn't seem the type, does he? To write love letters. And – and – he'd hardly write to her at work, would he? Besides – you said yourself "an *affair*", so of course I assumed—'

'He did *love* my mum.'

'Of course he did. I'm sorry. I was just, you know . . .'

Joe appeared in the doorway.

'All right, girls?'

'Fine!' they said in unison.

'Love letters?' Joe nodded at the bundle in Miranda's hand. Miranda flicked a glance at Kath, saw her lips clamped together.

'I *wish*. Nothing so thrilling, I'm afraid – just some old family stuff we're sorting out.'

'What are we doing about food tonight? Do you need me to go and get some groceries in?'

'And check out the local pub on the way back?' Kath teased him.

'Well, if you really want me to . . . I suppose I could.'

Kath consulted with Miranda and quickly scribbled down a short list of supplies.

'There probably won't be anywhere open tomorrow as it's Easter, so can you get those things for now? I can give the kids pasta with tuna for their supper tonight, and we brought those two chickens for tomorrow.'

'Where are they, by the way?' Miranda asked.

'Upstairs playing, they're fine.'

'Where's Simon?'

'Last time I saw him, he was sitting in the car, reading.'

'Oh, for God's sake, how childish!'

'Deep breaths. Help me do the pasta, will you?'

'Sure. Joe – do me a favour, will you? Take Simon with you. You'll earn big Brownie points.'

Joe looked at Kath.

'You're doing a Polly face: Mum, do I *have* to?'

'I wasn't. I'll ask him but I can't make him come.'

'Say you want his advice about something, he can't resist that. You know how he loves to be the expert.'

He went into the hall.

'Feel free to leave him there . . .' Miranda called after him. She turned to Kath. 'Why don't you want Joe to know about the letters? I thought you two never had secrets from each other?'

'We *don't*. Normally. But Joe's hopeless at keeping a secret. He's bound to mention them in front of everyone without thinking. It's easier if he doesn't know for now.'

There was a thundering as the children hurtled downstairs.

'Mum! Luke keeps spoiling our game.'

'I *never*.' Luke was on the verge of tears. 'Mummy, Polly pushed me and—' Kath drew them to one side and prepared to arbitrate.

Anna was silent.

'You having fun up there, hmm?' Miranda tucked one of Anna's wild curls back behind her ear.

Anna nodded but said nothing, then looked down at the letters in her mother's hand.

'What are they?'

'Letters.'

'Can I read them?'

'No, sweetheart. They're not mine.'

'Whose are they?'

'They're just boring, grown-up letters.'

Anna ran a finger along the woven wool plait.

'Sorcha in my class has got a bracelet like that.'

'I can't give you this one, sweetie. We can make you another if you'd like.'

Anna nodded.

'Why can't I read them?'

'Because – ' No point using the word 'private' or that would make her even more curious. Miranda glanced down at the top letter and smiled. She held it out for Anna to see. 'Because the handwriting's too hard to read, see?'

'I bet *I* could read it.'

'Well, I'm sure you could if we had all day.'

'Can we go to the beach then?'

'You know we would if we could. But look out of the window, darling. It's tipping down.' Miranda stood up. 'Now, who'd like a nice biscuit and then why don't we do some drawing?'

Miranda doled out a biscuit to each child then spoke quietly to Kath about the letters.

'I'd better take these upstairs, away from roving little hands and eyes, OK?'

'Good idea. Oh – and Manda?' Kath dropped her voice to just above a whisper. 'For God's sake, whatever you do, don't leave them lying around anywhere where Dad might see them, OK?'

Miranda made a dopey face.

'Uh-duh. Really? I thought we might all sit round the fire and take it in turns to read bits out.'

'I'm just *saying*.'

'Yes, miss. Don't worry – they're safe with me. I'll put them in my knicker drawer, OK?'

Bedtime

'Mummy?' Anna started to sit up in bed.

'Yes?' Miranda smoothed her daughter's hair back from her brow. 'Snuggle down now. You've had your story.'

'You know how you said we could go to the beach every single day when we were on holiday?'

'Ye-e-e-e-s?'

'Well, we didn't go today, did we?'

'No – but we don't really count today because we didn't get here until this afternoon. Also, it hasn't stopped raining, has it? We'd have got ever so soggy.'

'You *like* the beach in the rain. And so does Daddy. You like it when it's all wet and windy and no-one else is there except for us.'

'Yes, I do.' Miranda smiled. 'But now it's wet and windy and *dark.* There wouldn't be any point going now – we wouldn't be able to see anything.'

'We could take a torch maybe. Or a candle.'

'Or we could go to sleep maybe.'

'I'm not a bit sleepy.' Anna started to pull the quilt aside. 'Please, *please* can we go now?'

'We'll go to the beach tomorrow, I promise.' Miranda tucked it firmly back again.

'But what if it's rainy and dark all day? Then you'll say we can't go again.'

'I won't. We'll go even if it's horrible, OK? We can

even go twice to make up for today. We'll put on our wellies and our macs and we'll go and watch the waves crashing against the rocks. And we'll get soaked to the skin and then we'll rush back here and have big mugs of hot chocolate.'

'You promise?'

'Yes.'

'You absolutely and truly promise, cross your heart and hope to die?'

Miranda duly crossed her heart with her index finger and absolutely and truly promised. Then she bent to kiss Anna goodnight.

'Warm enough or shall I find you an extra blanket?'

'Snug as a bug in a rug.'

Miranda smiled.

'Mummy?' Miranda detected a note of anxiety in Anna's voice.

'Don't worry – I'll leave on the landing light, OK? See?'

Anna nodded.

'Is Daddy coming up soon?'

'Of course he will. Nighty-night, sleep tight.'

'Ni'-night.'

Anna is swimming . . . her waist-length hair fanning out behind her like an undulating dorsal fin. She arcs her back and wheels up and round in slow loops, looking at the glinting surface of the water above her, then the rippled sand beneath. Each time she returns to the sea, she notices that her skin is gradually losing its pasty pinkness. She shimmers through a shaft of sunlight, her tiny scales an iridescent mosaic: silver and aquamarine and lapis lazuli, their curved edges shiny as newly minted coins. Already her legs kick and bend together as one, and her feet are changing, too; she can see the light through them as she points them away from her, fusing at the heels to make a curving V. She swims with greater grace, more strength each time; to prove it to herself, she kicks hard and watches her fluid form shoot forward, carving through a shoal of fishes. They part before her like courtiers in the presence of a queen, swishing away as one, a curtain of silver. She smiles at them and stretches up her arms to swim towards the surface.

Anna opened her eyes and pulled Nessa, her blue velvet doll, in beside her, kissed her goodnight. Nessa's smile was a little lopsided, made in a hurry by Miranda one time when Anna lost her favourite doll and was inconsolable. It gave her a rather wry expression, not at all doll-like, as if she were assessing the world with a coolly amused eye.

It was not a dream, being a mermaid, because Anna was not yet asleep. It was what she called a 'thinking', like being in a cinema seeing a film, the colours clear and true, while everything else around her was dark and forgotten. Only with a thinking, Anna was inside the film, watching yet making it happen at the same time. She knew that she was not actually a mermaid, of course, but it seemed so real that when she opened her eyes again and the picture disappeared, still she felt for a few moments that her legs *were* joined, that her eyelashes were tipped with silver, that her hair was long and billowing and beautiful. For almost a whole minute she lay absolutely still, keeping the feeling alive, but she could not resist. She poked one hand up above the covers to touch her hair . . . and found the same shoulder-length tangle of curls snaking across her pillow as always.

She turned onto her side, facing the other twin bed. It felt funny sleeping in a room with another bed in it, especially an empty one. When she had a friend to stay for a sleepover, Sara or Emma or Lily, Mum set up the fold-out bed next to Anna's bed and she had to give her friend her own bed and sleep on the fold-out one. But when she went to stay at their houses, they slept in their own beds and she had the camp bed or the pull-out bed or the mattress on the floor. Mum said you must always let the guest have the best bed or the best chair and first pick of the chocolates and the nicest bit of the roast chicken, the breast with the crispy skin, even if that was your absolute most favouritest bit.

She wished she were downstairs with the grown-ups. She could hear them talking and laughing and clinking their glasses and having fun. It wasn't fair. When you were a grown-up, you could do whatever you like, you didn't have to go to bed when you were told and you could go to the beach in the middle of the night if you wanted to. You could go in your nightie even, you could skip along the beach eating chocolate fudge and yelling your name out over the sea, shouting it to the Moon. But most of the time grown-ups didn't go to the beach or eat chocolate fudge after midnight; they ate yucky olives and drank bitter coffee and wine and beer and they were tired the whole time, all they wanted to do was lie down and put their feet up and they were always just going to close their eyes for a few minutes but when you went into their room ten whole minutes later they'd say, 'Daddy's just having a little nap now, why don't you go and read a nice book and Daddy'll come down in a little while?'

Mummy said it was hard being a grown-up because you had to pay lots of bills, taxes and phone and water and electricity and everything. Her mum had two lots of bills because she had a shop as well. And she had to pay the people who worked in the shop and the people who made the shoes she designed. Daddy didn't have a shop, he had a desk at home and he sat there and telephoned people and wrote articles or he went into the newspaper office and also he wrote two whole books about how you can help save the planet. Mummy said that the books were really wonderful and they had very good reviews. Daddy said that the books didn't sell many copies, but then it wasn't exactly a big surprise, was it, if people cared enough to buy the books, then they'd care enough not to be destroying the planet in the first place, wouldn't they?

When Mummy was not being cross with Daddy, she said he was brilliant and she stood behind him to squeeze his shoulders and he sat back and closed his eyes and made mm-mmm noises. But there had been no squeezing of shoulders or mm-mmm noises for a while, not since her mum's last trip, Anna thought. Sometimes there was shouting and sometimes there was silence, but mostly they talked to each other in a funny way now, as if they didn't know each other. They were really polite, like how you were supposed to be when you're at someone else's house, and you say, 'Could you pass the salt, please?' and 'It's very cold today, isn't it?' You were supposed to be on your best behaviour then but parents don't have to be like that with each other because they are already in the same house and they are not guests or anything.

Domestic bliss

Miranda pulled her chair back from the table and started clearing the plates from supper. Kath sprang up to help.

'So what day's your anniversary?' Simon asked.

'Thursday,' said Kath.

'Wednesday,' said Joe at the same time.

'He always gets it wrong.' Kath shook her head and went through to the kitchen.

'I do not.' He called out. 'Is it really Thursday?'

'Yup.' She came back in. 'Definitely.'

Joe laid his head on the table and Kath patted him.

'Don't worry, I won't hold it against you. I'm used to it after nine years.'

'Well, here's to you both anyway.' Simon raised his glass. 'Nine years of marriage and still speaking to each other, that's something to be proud of.'

'Plus over two years before that,' Kath added. 'But you two have been together almost as long.'

'Over ten years.' Simon nodded.

'Gosh, it seems barely more than a century, doesn't it, darling?' Miranda smiled brightly.

'Every day is an eternity when I'm with you, dearest.'

'At least we're not married. I'm not holding you against your will, am I?'

Simon stood up.

'I'm sure Kath and Joe aren't interested in our petty domestic squabbles, especially in the run-up to their anniversary. Now, who wants coffee? Or tea? Herb tea?' He took their orders and went through to the kitchen.

'Have you still got that gorgeous outfit you wore to

our wedding, Manda? It was stunning. You remember it, Joe?'

He looked up at his wife in disbelief.

'K, I can't remember what *I* was wearing yesterday, never mind anyone else. You know I never notice that kind of thing.'

'You remember my wedding dress at least, don't you? Answer carefully, husband.'

'Course I do. White. With crunchy bits at the front that kept getting caught up in my jacket buttons.' He made a scrabbling motion at his chest. 'And you had a sort of thing on your head, like you get under the cakes in a posh tearoom. A doily?'

'Yes, the headdress was possibly a bit of a mistake,' said Kath, laughing. 'The dress was ivory. With beads. I'd never fit into it now.' She patted her hips.

'You looked beautiful, doily or no doily. I can't believe it's really nine years, I remember it as if it were only last week.' Miranda tilted her head to one side. 'Actually, better than last week. My short-term memory's gone out the window. I run upstairs to get something from the bedroom but by the time I've got there I haven't a clue what I wanted, I have to go out and go in again, it's pathetic. How can I be senile already? I'm not even forty yet. Does everyone else keep forgetting things?'

'Who are you again?' said Kath. 'Is this the bus stop?'

A perfect day for a wedding

It is a bright, fresh day, with only a few marshmallowy clouds puffing across the sky, a perfect day for a wedding. It has been raining almost without a pause for most of the week, but this morning a thin wash of early April sunshine made a tentative appearance and now it is almost warm enough to kid yourself that you're quite comfortable without a jacket. Miranda slips off her sandals and wiggles her toes into the close-cropped lawn in front of the hotel to remind herself how wonderful today is and how happy she should be. Mentally, she ticks off reasons to feel good about today: 1) She loves Kath and today is Kath's Big Day and nothing must be allowed to spoil it, especially not Miranda's looking depressed. 2) It is not raining, an unexpected bonus and, Miranda decides, definitely a positive omen though she is usually fiercely dismissive of such superstitious notions. 3) Joe is wonderful and so right for Kath – unlike many people who mistake Kath's reticence for aloofness and restraint for dullness, Joe 'gets' Kath. He and Miranda have developed an unspoken pact to bring her forward more so that the rest of the world can see what they see. 4) Four, she thinks, four. Well, OK, three big reasons then. This is a wedding, she tells herself – shape up and start smiling, you miserable bitch.

On the journey there, Miranda drives clenching the steering wheel like a lifebelt. She chews gum and turns the radio up loud to make herself concentrate. Normally, she is a confident driver, fast and assertive, nipping neatly from lane to lane, but now she forces herself to drive as if she has swallowed the Highway Code, speaking her movements aloud: 'Mirror – arsehole zooming up too fast in the outside lane – wing mirrors – watch the red estate behind – signal – pull out smoothly –' She drives like this for the whole two-hour trip, fearing that if she lets her concentration lapse for a moment, she will be overtaken by the urge to steer straight into the central reservation or swerve into the path of a massive lorry. She realizes that she should not have driven, but she had no choice: the car was already packed with clothes and presents and the train journey involved two connections and by the time she'd had the huge row with Simon it would have been too late for her to catch them. She should not have driven because, at the moment, it is all she can do to keep hold of the most basic information. Yesterday, she found her car keys in the fridge. Last night, she had painted her toenails, then noticed this morning as she stood in the shower that she'd only done her left foot.

There is a reason for all this, of course. Actually, there are two reasons. Less than a month ago, Miranda's father had died of a massive stroke. When her mother returned home from work, she found him sitting in the big leather armchair in his study, the newspaper fallen to the floor beside him. Pamela, peeping in briefly, had thought him asleep and gone and made them both some coffee. It was only when she came back carrying the two mugs that she looked at him properly and realized that he was dead. Pamela, a doctor who worked at a family planning clinic, didn't panic. She calmly set down the mugs, then reached to see if he had a pulse. But the temperature of his skin told her everything: he had been dead for hours. She'd sat with him for some time, perched on the arm of the chair, cradling his head against her, then eventually she rang another doctor and finally her two daughters. To Miranda, she'd said, 'I'm afraid I have some rather bad news. Your father has had a stroke.' No 'Perhaps you should sit down,' no telltale catch in her voice that might have warned Miranda that her life was about to fall apart. Miranda had stammered out, desperate for a last few seconds of hope, 'Is he in hospital? He's going to be OK, isn't he?'

'No, dear, I'm sorry if I wasn't clear. He's dead.'

Her father was dead and in a fortnight's time Miranda would turn thirty. For the last month, she'd felt as if her body no longer belonged to her; simply going down the street seemed as if she were walking through water, her limbs heavy and slow. And then this morning she'd had that massive argument with Simon. Not just an I unloaded-the-dishwasher-last-time-it's-your-turn kind of a row, but a serious why-are-we-together-what's-the-point row. She couldn't quite remember how a minor altercation about her daring to throw away window envelopes rather than tearing out the plastic bit then putting the rest in the paper and magazines recycling crate could have got so out of hand, but it had indeed, with the result that she had shouted, 'Fuck you and your fucking recycled envelopes, you self-righteous, preaching goody-goody. No-one – no-one *sane* – tears the windows out of window envelopes for God's sake.' Simon, inevitably, came back with a veritable treatise on figures of paper tonnage and kilowatts of energy saved, until she simply walked out to prevent herself from giving him a good kick in the shin. She had a cigarette at the far end of the garden, spinning it out for ten minutes, hoping he'd give way first and join her. Then she came back in and said, 'Well, the car's packed, I'm packed and ready to go.'

'Fine,' he said, not moving.

She raised her brows.

'You're not coming then?'

'Well, you clearly don't want me to, or you wouldn't have started such a ridiculous row.'

'I didn't start it. I don't give a toss about window envelopes.'

'It's not about window envelopes, is it, Miranda? You don't give a toss about envelopes, about my work, about our planet, or about our relationship, do you? You regard everything as expendable, including me—'

'That's ridiculous – just because I—'

'No, it isn't. It's true.' He paused, as if only realizing it as he said it out loud. 'And you don't really care that much if I come to the wedding with you. You just don't want to go on your own in case anyone thinks you're heading for the Big Three-oh and are still single.'

Now she really did want to hit him.

'God, you really are being such a charmer this morning, aren't you? That's a horrible thing to say.' *Even if there's a tiny grain of truth in it*, she thought. 'Thanks, Simon – thanks for being so supportive – I can really handle this kind of crap now.'

'You always dismiss any criticism of you as being somehow invalid, don't you?'

'And Kath and Joe invited you – they'll have done you a little name card in twiddly lettering – how can you not go?' She laughed, hoping to lighten the mood between them.

'Give them my congratulations. Tell them I've had to go away for work if you don't want to tell them we've had a row.'

'I could tell them you refused to come because you think I'm cavalier about window envelopes.' She was smiling now.

'Tell them whatever you like.'

She tried to swallow, suddenly feeling she might cry. Bollocks to him, standing there with his virtuous face, trying to make her into the bad one again. She would not cry, she would not. If she did, he would fold her in his arms and whisper sorry, sorry into her hair, cup her face in his hands the way he did, relishing these brief moments when she allowed herself to be weak, when he could be the strong one.

'Right. I'm off then. I'll be back tomorrow. Late afternoon, I should think.'

He nodded, unsmiling. 'Drive safely,' he said.

In her hotel room, Miranda hangs up her outfit and bounces gently on the edge of the four-poster bed, as if considering whether to buy it. Then she goes through to the bathroom to check out the freebies, picks up a miniature bottle of shampoo. Her eyes prick with tears – her father used to bring back all the hotel shampoos and guest soaps from conferences and work trips for Miranda and her sister when they were children. Marianne, the Neat One, put hers out in a row next to her dolls. This annoyed Miranda, who thought that any fool should be able to see that the scale wasn't right – it would be like having a bottle of shampoo that came up to your knees. She wasn't neat, but she was particular – fussy about things that didn't bother anyone else; she drove her mother crazy with her refusal to wear clashing colours – she had once thrown a tantrum at the relatively grown-up age of eight when her mother had demanded she wear bottle-green trousers with an orange T-shirt, saying they were late and she must put them on RIGHT NOW, there was nothing else clean and dry. Miranda had screamed back, the two of them head to head, equally stubborn, determined.

She faces herself in the mirror and addresses her reflection:

'You will not – repeat NOT – cry. There's not enough time, for a start.' She quickly unpacks and hangs up her outfit, briskly scoops up the mini shampoos and shower gels and drops them into her case.

Miranda is habitually late, but the church is less than ten minutes' walk from the hotel and even she cannot fail to be there in plenty of time. Feeling awkward and conspicuously alone, she lingers outside and looks at the gravestones for a while. For the first time in her life, she suddenly thinks how odd it is that couples choose to get married in a building that is surrounded by dead people. But perhaps it makes perfect sense, a reminder that life is all too short so you'd better crack on, find a mate and start having babies because any second now you'll have had your stint and you'll be out here pushing up the daisies.

More guests start arriving and there is a flurry of talk and laughter and cheek-kissing, the women picking their way awkwardly up the uneven path, one hand clamped to their heads to stop their hats sailing off in a sudden gust of wind. She spots a few familiar faces, smiles and waves. Miranda enters the church at last and then Rob is suddenly right there in front of her, handsome and assured in his usher's grey morning suit. He smiles warmly and kisses her.

'Hey, beautiful, how's it going? Are you, um, OK?'

It is the first nice word anyone has said to her today, and it is all she can do not to start crying.

'Yeah, I'm doing OK, thanks. Are you going to ush me?'

He winks.

'Anytime.' Rob fiddles with the cream rose in his button hole, which is slipping forward as if it is about to fall out.

'Shall I fix that?'

He nods and looks down at her as she repins the rose firmly into place, pats his lapel.

'OK?' he asks.

She smiles and nods, feeling tearful.

'Where's Himself?'

'Don't ask.' She looks away, into the church. 'So – where do you want me?' He takes her arm and leads her down the aisle right to the front.

'No, surely this is for family only?'

'You're as good as family. Actually, better than family – don't tell them I said that. Kathy said she wants you at the front. No arguments.'

The church fills, then at last the organ strikes up and all stand and turn as one. Kath seems impossibly tiny next to her father and she is almost having to run to keep up with his long strides. When Miranda sees

Kath clinging to Giles's arm, a bolt of pain strikes her, a sudden shock of grief for a moment that she herself can never have, a moment that before now she never knew she even wanted. The irony is not lost on her. Miranda, who from her teens had detested the symbolism of being given away like a chattel, had always warned her father that she wouldn't be going in for all that if she ever got married. But now, here, she pictures herself walking down the aisle with him, his voice as he says something funny to settle her nerves, his arm strong and steady beneath hers. Tears fill her eyes. Everybody cries at weddings, she tells herself. But these are not wedding-guest tears that can be neatly dabbed away with the corner of a hankie. A huge bubble of grief rises inside her and she slips out the end of the pew and quickly down the side aisle. Stumbles past the photographer stationed by the door. Barely able to see, she bursts outside into the sunlight as the sobs take her. Her body spasms and she gulps for breath. Clutches at a grave-stone for support.

After a minute, she manages to stem the tide, pulls herself upright once more. She scrabbles in her bag for a tissue and her hand-mirror to set her face to rights. The gravestone in front of her, like many of the older stones in the churchyard, is tilting at a precipitous angle. Perhaps it's because too many people like her keep leaning on it, she thinks, overwhelmed by emotion at weddings, christenings, funerals. The inscription is hard to read, weathered by time, the letters blurred by lichens, grey and yellow and green, but she can just make it out:

Here lies
Mary Swithin
Died 14 August, 1857
Aged 29 years
Beloved Wife and Mother
A Virtuous Woman
Gone to a Better Place

Twenty-nine, the same age as Miranda. She pats the stone tenderly. And what would be her epitaph if she were to die tomorrow?

Miranda Miller
Dumped by her Boyfriend
Childless and not very Beloved
Not at all Virtuous
Didn't believe in a Better Place
Good Worm Food

Now is not the time for self-pity, you snivelling snot-nose, she tells herself. Rubs roughly beneath her eyes, rakes her fingers through her hair, then sneaks back into the service.

And so to bed . . .

Miranda hung up her clothes in the wardrobe while Simon used the bathroom. She hummed quietly to herself, trying to focus only on the task in hand. Set out her toiletries neatly on the chest of drawers in front of the mirror. Laid her make-up purse on the pink cut-glass tray and caught sight of her reflection, her tired eyes and dry skin. She pulled at her cheeks. God, you look about 102, you wizened old bag, what's wrong with you? Miranda looked herself firmly in the eye: *you* can *do this*, she instructed her reflection, *just hang on in there and keep your cool and it'll all be OK. Remain calm. It's only one week. Seven days. It'll zip by in no time.*

Simon came back in.

'Bathroom's free.'

'Thanks.' She picked up her towel and toilet bag. 'I've left you some hangers if you want them.'

He didn't respond and she left the room.

When she returned, Simon was in bed, sitting up reading the newspaper, a notepad and pen by his side.

'Anything interesting in the paper?' Her voice bright.

'Not really.'

Miranda undressed quickly with her back to him, slipped on a pair of pyjamas. When she turned round, he raised his eyebrows but said nothing.

'In case I get up in the night,' she explained. 'If Anna has a nightmare or something. I don't want to frighten our housemates.'

A corner of his mouth twitched and his gaze dropped to the paper once more. Miranda carefully slid beneath the bedclothes and removed one of her pillows.

'It's a lovely house, isn't it?' she said, lying on her back, looking up at the ceiling.

'Mmm. Kath made a good choice.'

'And brilliant to be practically on the beach.' *I am trying here. Feel free to join in, why don't you?*

'Yes indeed.'

'Well, we'll get to see it tomorrow anyway.'

'Hmm-mm.'

'Well. Goodnight then.' She leant towards him to plant a quick kiss on his cheek. 'Sleep well.'

'Night.'

Miranda turned onto her side away from him and nestled her cheek into her pillow. After a few minutes, there was a rustle as Simon folded the paper and dropped it onto the floor by the bed. He sighed and the light was switched off. The bed creaked as he vigorously plumped up both his pillows, patting and rearranging them, then he lay down, tugging the quilt towards him. After a minute, she felt him move a little nearer and the slightest warm breeze of his breath on the back of her neck.

'Miranda?' His voice was quiet, barely more than a whisper.

She slowed her breathing and kept her eyes closed. After another minute, the bed creaked once more as he turned away again, and then there was only silence.

Sunday

A promise

Miranda woke suddenly to find Anna's face just a few inches from her own.

'Oh, you scared me! What is it? Are you all right?'

'Happy Easter, Mummy! Can we go to the beach now? I'm ready – see!'

Miranda laughed and shut her eyes.

'You, madam, are unbelievable. Happy Easter to you too! What time is it? It feels like the middle of the night.' She reached for her watch by the side of the bed, wrinkled her nose at it.

'It's practically seven o'clock!' Anna pulled at her mother's arm. 'Come on! I've been up for ages and ages.'

'Noooooo, it's way, way too early. You're not human. Go and pick on someone else.' Miranda leaned up on one elbow and glanced over her shoulder at Simon. His face was buried in the pillow and he was snoring quietly. Perhaps she could accidentally lean on his head as she turned over – oops, sorry, darling! – then he could take Anna to the beach? Tempting, but – in the interests of furthering peace negotiations – not perhaps the best way to kick off the day.

'You said we could go. You *promised*.'

'We will go, but not right this minute. The beach won't run away. We can go after breakfast.'

'I'm bored.'

'Go and play with Polly then.'

'She's playing with her Barbie. You come and play with me.'

'I'm barely awake. Don't be a pest. Go and read quietly. Or why don't you get Polly to play Spies with you? Go on, she'd love that. Be nice. Or Explorers? Or you could be ballerinas, but not too much leaping, OK? Mummy needs some coffee, then I'll come and get you some breakfast. Have a banana for now if you're hungry. Or some cornflakes. I left them out on the kitchen table. Or cornflakes *and* banana – see, no end of exciting possibilities?'

'OK,' Anna said reluctantly, then trailed off. Ten seconds later, she returned. 'Mum?' She leaned against the bed and smiled. 'You know how it's Easter and everything? Do you think that maybe somebody might have got some chocolate Easter eggs hidden somewhere?'

'Which somebody would that be? Let's see – in the bed?' Miranda pulled up the covers and pretended to look. 'Uh-uh, can't see any. Did *you* bring some?'

'Mu-um! Stop it! Have you got me an Easter egg? It doesn't have to be a big one or anything. If you gave me even just a little tiny one, then you wouldn't have to get up and make breakfast and you could stay in bed for ages and ages.'

Miranda shook her head with a laugh.

'In your dreams, beanlet. We will be having a special Easter egg hunt later in the garden which I suspect may well involve chocolate. But not until *after* lunch. Go and tell the others.'

Anna left once more, this time with an energetic skip.

Miranda heaved herself upright and pulled on her dressing gown, then padded downstairs to make the coffee.

*   *   *

Well, today's the day, she thought. The invasion. With any luck, the infiltrators would break down on the motorway or the traffic would be so dreadful that they'd simply give up and go back home. Or they might have an accident – nothing too horrible, maybe just a small crunch. She started to picture it in her head, but immediately a vision of wrecked and charred metal sprang to mind. Miranda screwed her eyes up tight, trying to shut it out. Will you stop this, she told herself. This is horrible. You're horrible. Stop it right now. Just don't think about it. Focus on the practicalities, concentrate on something specific, something you can organize.

Right: beds. The beds were definitely a problem with this new line-up. OK, what are the possibilities? It made sense for Anna and Polly to share the bunks room, but then what about Luke? There'd be a spare bed downstairs in the room Giles would have, but even though Luke was Giles's grandson, she could hardly see them sharing a room. What if Luke woke up with a nightmare? Would Giles fill the breach, providing the required cuddle and lullaby? Er, probably not. Not exactly the paternal type. Patriarchal, certainly, but not paternal or grandpaternal. Anna could come in with her, and Simon could share with Giles! Fantastic plan. They could stay up all night, throwing statistics at each other. She could lock them in, then brick up the doorway and leave them both there. Or Rob could share Giles's room, Kath could bunk in with Tamsin and Luke could sleep with his dad. At least that would put paid to the week-long shagfest that was bound to go on in Rob and Tamsin's room. Bloody hell, what on earth had Kath been thinking of, asking Rob along? He must have talked her into it. It was like one of those infuriating puzzles where you kept moving the little squares around to try to get them in the right position. At a pinch, they could put the spare mattress on the floor of her and Simon's room for Anna, but it didn't seem fair. It wasn't Anna's fault that all the arrangements had gone doolally. Anyway, a mattress would only fit between the side of the bed and the door, so they'd have to have the door open all night. So everyone else would see them arguing and not having sex. Terrific.

Time to practise being pleasant. Miranda poured out a mug of coffee for Simon, then decided to take him up some toast as well. She needed him to be nice to her today, or civil at the very least, and if that meant bribing him with toast and honey, then bribe she would.

The Mermaid

Kath and Miranda were enjoying a brief respite, reading the Sunday papers, while Simon and Joe played Snap and Happy Families with the children on the sitting-room floor, when there was a knock at the front door. Miranda checked her watch. It was only just after ten a.m. Far too early for it to be Rob and the others, unless they'd left at the crack of dawn. Dear God, please not yet. She got up and went to answer it.

It was Mrs O'Neill, the owner of the house, who'd just popped by to check that everything was all right.

'It's beautiful, thank you. And the views are fantastic.'

'Been down to the beach yet? Or is it too wet for you?'

'We were all set to go first thing, but then it started tipping it down. But we will definitely get to the beach today come hell or high water.'

Anna sneaked up behind Miranda.

'Oh, hello! What's your name, my love?'

'Anna.'

'And how old are you?'

'Eight and nearly a quarter.'

'Well, that's ever so grown-up! Now, you're a pretty little thing, in't you?' Mrs O'Neill turned to Miranda. 'Beautiful eyes, in't she? Just like the sea. You off down to the beach then, my love?'

Anna nodded.

'Mummy promised. As soon as it stops raining, she said.'

'Well, it's no distance, is it? A flea'd get there in three jumps. Bottom of the garden, down the steps and there you are, you could do it in your sleep. You take care on them steps now, they're steep, and slippery when the rain's been at 'em.'

Joe came out to the hall and was introduced. He explained that he'd had a lot of trouble lighting the fire and the landlady went in to demonstrate the magic routine required to overcome its idiosyncrasies.

'There's plenty more wood out the back and an axe in the shed if you're up to chopping it yourselves. But I'll bring you up some more kindling, seein' as you been having so much trouble with it,' she promised, coming back into the hallway afterwards. 'Go down when the tide's out,' she told Miranda, 'and you'll see the Mermaid.'

Anna's eyes widened.

'Oh, it's not a real one, bless you! It's just a big old rock out in the bay there. You can walk right out to it at low tide. They say you touch her and you can make a wish. Come high tide, there's only just the top of her above water though.' She gently lifted one of Anna's curls. 'Look at these curls! I can tell you eat up your greens!' She turned back to Miranda. 'The wishing's just silly superstition, but no harm for the kiddies, eh? It's not much to look at, to tell you the truth, just a daft old rock.'

Miranda smiled and nodded, then asked if there were any good places to eat nearby.

By the time Mrs O'Neill had left, Anna had put on her jacket and blue wellington boots.

'You're off out then, are you?' Miranda teased. 'Are you taking the car? Pick up some extra milk while you're out, will you?'

'Mu-um!'

'Wha-a-a-t? Why have you got your jacket on?'

'To go to the beach. The rain's stopped. You promised.'

'You're right, I did, I did. Put your fleece on underneath – it might be quite windy right by the sea. Let me get my coat, you go and see if the others want to come, too.'

'At least it's stopped raining.' Joe dug his hands deeper into his pockets as he and Miranda walked to the gate at the bottom of the back garden. Kath and Simon had decided to stay behind. 'But it's not exactly a balmy spring day, is it?'

Miranda snuggled her chin down into the coil of her scarf and reached her hand out to take Anna's.

The wooden steps were steep and creaked ominously. Joe picked up Luke and watched out for Polly.

'No coming down here without a grown-up, OK, kids?' Miranda said.

Once at the bottom, the children broke away and charged across the sand, whooping and shouting. The turquoise hood of Anna's fleece flapped up and down behind her as she ran, like the wing of some exotic bird against the washed-out colours of sea and sand and sky.

'I know the weather's not been brilliant so far, but this was a really great choice, wasn't it? The beach right on our doorstep.' Miranda inhaled deeply. 'Kids don't get enough of this, do they?'

'When I was a kid, we practically lived outdoors no matter what the weather. We didn't *want* to be stuck indoors. Not that we had DVDs and computers and—' Joe began, then broke off. 'God, I sound like my Dad. I'm becoming such an old fart.'

'You're not. Well, we all are. Anyway, it's true. It's not *that* long ago when we were kids, but we disappeared for hours at a time and no-one thought anything of it. My sister and I used to cycle round our village or make camps in the woods. I don't think our parents fretted about us the way we all do about our lot.'

'My dad used to chuck us out and tell us not to come back till it was dark. And my mum would say, "Get out from under my feet! I've to wash the kitchen floor." We got up to no end of mischief.' He smiled. 'They've no idea what they're missing, this generation, have they? They'll get to eighteen and they won't even know how to take a bus on their own.'

'True. Part of me – the sensible part – knows that we've got to let go and encourage them to be independent and think for themselves. Despite the fevered rants of the tabloids about demonic paedophiles lurking in every bush, I know way, way more kids are killed in traffic accidents than are abducted. If we spent more time teaching them how to cross the road and less time putting the fear of God into them about evil strangers, we'd be doing them all a favour. I do *know* that – it's just –' She shook her head. 'It's so hard to be laid-back, isn't it?'

Further along the sand, the children were seeing how near they could stand to the waves, daring each other to go closer.

'Kids! Stay out of the water!' Miranda called across. 'They'll get soaked.'

'They're OK.' He kept watching the children. 'Um, Kath said you brought some champagne for our anniversary? That was really kind of you, you didn't have to do that.'

'My motives were entirely selfish, as always. Just happy to have an excuse to get drunk.'

Joe smiled but said nothing.

'Do I detect a problem?'

'Well, I'd kind of booked this posh hotel for dinner . . . as a surprise. Only, being me, I booked it for the wrong night in any case, it's for Wednesday. I tried to change it, but they're full up on Thursday. Maybe we could have a drink here first?'

'It's no problem. I did ask Kath, of course, but – obviously – she didn't know. Look – why not have two dinners? Have your romantic tête-à-tête one evening, then we can all celebrate together the next and I can cook for you?'

'Good plan. Thank you. Can't see why anyone else would want to celebrate it other than us, but I appreciate the thought.'

'I imagine we like to mark other couples' anniversaries because it makes us feel hopeful – at least we know it's actually *possible* to stay together for years and still love each other. Still *like* each other, more to the point. It's nice to know it can be done. Even if . . . well.'

Joe glanced at her and opened his mouth, as if about to say something, then shut it again.

'Yeah,' he said. 'I'm a very lucky man.'

'Well, you're not so bad yourself.'

'Mummy, Mummy!' Anna ran up and tugged at Miranda's coat. 'Is that the Mermaid over there? Is that it?'

Miranda and Joe followed her to the edge of the waves. Jutting up from the water at one side of the bay was the top part of a craggy column of rock.

'I think it must be, I can't see anything else, can you?' Anna shook her head.

'But why is it called a mermaid? Where's the tail?'

Miranda ducked down to Anna's level and faced out to sea with her, pointing to the rock.

'Hmmm, good question. Well, it's hard to see properly now because the tide's too far in so she's partly covered up, isn't she? But, look there, scrunch your eyes up a little – see, that bulge could be her head and the sticky-out bit's her arm, then where it goes in, that's her waist, see? Shame we can't see the rest of her now. Perhaps she does have a tail, but it's covered by the sea?'

'Can we make a wish on her?'

'Why don't you just blow her a wish for now?'

Anna looked disappointed.

'Go on. Then we can come back at low tide – perhaps we can phone Mrs O'Neill to ask her, you know, the nice lady who came earlier? – or we can probably pick up a tides table at the local shop, I should think.'

'Or we can walk to the end of the garden and have a look,' Joe suggested.

'Good point. Trust me to overlook the obvious.'

Anna skipped off again to join the others; the children ran along the beach, chasing each other and shrieking, and trying to do cartwheels.

'It's such a shame the Frasers couldn't come, isn't it?'
Miranda said.

'Yeah. Well. Yes and no. I wouldn't mind if it was just
us lot, would you?'

'Absolutely – God, I didn't mean I didn't want to
be here just with you and Kath, it's just . . . y'know,
this new line-up's not exactly what I had in mind for
our holiday. It's not that *I* care really, but Simon's
being very prickly right now – and Giles is so provocative and you know what Rob's like, he so loves to
wind people up. I don't want to spend the entire week
playing referee.'

'Right.'

'Please don't tell Kath I said that, I wouldn't want to
hurt her, but she has got a bit of a blind spot about her
family sometimes.'

Joe nodded.

'Don't blame Kath. To tell you the truth, she's not
exactly overjoyed about it either. She asked Rob partly
because he's been a bit down lately and she thought he
could do with a break. She really didn't know he'd got
back with Tamsin – and then of course Rob invited Giles
without checking if it was OK with us.'

'Typical Rob. Is he really depressed?'

'Who knows?' Joe shrugged. 'He's not exactly let's all
sit in a circle and share our feelings, is he? Kath thinks
he's going through some sort of crisis, had enough of
being an estate agent, can't see it going anywhere with

Tamsin, she thinks he might suddenly throw it all in and scoot off to a desert island, build himself a hut and go native.'

Miranda smiled at the thought.

'I can't imagine Rob lasting more than a week if he even had to go without his Calvin Klein aftershave, can you? Anyway, I thought he'd got the whole back-packing bit out of his system? God, he should have at his age.' Her brow furrowed, as if she were struggling to remember something. 'He swanned off round the globe not long after your wedding, as far as I remember. He was away for ages, wasn't he?'

'That's right. Over a year. Originally, I think the plan was to go only for a couple of months, but I suppose once he got started, he got hooked and there wasn't anything worth coming back for.'

'No, I guess not.' Miranda adjusted her scarf and did up another button on her coat. 'It's pretty chilly – we should go in soon. So much for the joys of spring.'

Waiting

'Come on, Kath. The kids need to eat and I can't hang on for ever either,' Miranda said through a mouthful of bread and butter.

'Is this you hanging on?'

'I was getting all low-blood-sugary.' Miranda opened

the oven and took out the roast potatoes to turn them yet again. 'Why are they taking so long?'

'They look pretty brown to me.'

'*Not* the potatoes – *your* family.'

'It'll look so rude if we start without them. Maybe we could cut off some chicken for the children?'

'Oh, for God's sake!' Miranda shoved the roasting tin back in and slammed the oven door shut with a bang. 'If you were running a restaurant, you'd have given away their table half an hour ago. Well, I'm feeding Anna.' She opened the oven once more and pulled out the tin containing the two chickens. Extracted a piece of cara-melized onion and ate it. 'Mmm.'

Kath carved off the legs and wings while Miranda cooked a few vegetables for the children.

'And some breast,' Miranda dictated, hurling sliced carrots into boiling water.

'Dad prefers the breast.'

'There are two big chickens, Kath – he's not having all of it. Besides, Anna won't eat leg either – she says it makes her think of the chicken trying to run away and not having any legs.'

Kath smiled.

'So why isn't she veggie?'

'She tried to be for about a fortnight, but she kept wanting to make exceptions – fish fingers, roast chicken, spaghetti Bolognese . . . She says she's going to try again when she's a bit older because it'll be easier then.'

Miranda poked her head into the hallway and bellowed, 'Kids! Lunch! Now, this minute! Wash your hands!'

'She said that?'

'Yup. Then she said, "Grown-ups can be good if they want to, but it's harder for children because they have to be naughty sometimes, they can't help it."'

'I'll try and remember that.'

'Surely Rob has a mobile? Can't you ring him and find out where they are?'

'I don't want to seem as if I'm hassling them.'

'Why ever not? They're very late.' Miranda set out plates and cutlery for the children. 'Use my phone if you like, but you'll have to go outside – the signal's hopeless in here. The patio seems to be best.'

'It's OK, I'll take Joe's.'

Kath came back in and put the phone on the worktop.

'Well, perhaps we'd better eat too then.'

Miranda raised one eyebrow.

'I trust they're having a delicious lunch wherever they are?'

Kath nodded.

'I'm sorry. They stopped off. You were right. You're always right. It's most annoying of you.'

The children came running in and scrambled onto the kitchen chairs.

Kath tucked napkins round them and started to cut up Luke's chicken. Joe came in.

'I'm starving. Aren't we having ours now, too?'

'We were sort of waiting for Dad and Rob, but – '

' – We've decided not to on the grounds that they've stopped for lunch on the way and didn't bother to phone us.'

'They were just about to.'

'I don't doubt it for a moment. Anyway, we can have ours in a few minutes – let me just make the gravy and put on some more veg. Joe, would you mind setting the table? In the dining room – it's too squashed for all of us in here.'

'Sure. Where's the cutlery?'

Miranda yanked out a drawer then returned to her gravy-making.

'And perhaps you could round up Simon, too?'

'No need, I'm here.' Simon came in and hovered over Anna. 'Ooh, yummy roast chicken. Aren't you having any carrots, Anna?'

'She's perfectly capable of helping herself if she wants some, Simon, they're right there. Can you give Joe a hand setting the other table please?'

'I *know* she's perfectly capable.' Simon came closer and dropped his voice. 'I hardly think I'm stunting her progress if I offer her carrots. They're full of vitamin A and beta-carotene.' He looked around at the worktop. 'Where do they keep the cutlery in this place?'

Miranda pointed at the open drawer.

'Is there some reason why Kath and I are expected to

know the exact whereabouts of every knife, fork and tea strainer in this kitchen while you act as if you've never even been in any kitchen in your life *ever* – it's not as if we've lived here for years and you haven't – we all arrived twenty-four hours ago. Why are *we* supposed to be the experts when it comes to locating cutlery, loo rolls, clean mugs, teabags while the males, surprise, surprise, have newly landed on this planet and so are, naturally enough, unable to find a fork or make a cup of tea.'

'Gosh, we've never heard this speech before,' Simon said quietly.

'We're all just a bit hungry,' Kath said. 'I get really ratty when I haven't eaten, ask Joe.'

'I'm *not* being ratty. I'm merely pointing out—'

'That everyone else is dreadful and selfish and unfair and hopeless.' Simon dug out a fistful of cutlery. 'It's a wonder you manage to get through the day. How do you stand it, being the lone oasis of perfection surrounded by a desert of idiots?' Although his voice was quiet, it was blistering with rage. He brushed past her and went through to the dining room.

Miranda was about to call after him, but stopped herself, literally biting her lip to make herself shut up. She poured a generous splash of wine into the gravy and kept whisking. Felt Kath's hand squeezing her arm.

'Are you OK?' Kath whispered.

Miranda nodded, then turned round to look at Anna.

'All right there, kids? Enjoying your lunch?'

Polly and Luke nodded vigorously, mouths full of roast potato and chicken. Anna looked back into her mother's eyes, unsmiling.

'Yes, thank you,' she said.

Miranda turned off the burner and tipped the gravy into a jug, spilling some down the side as her hands were shaking.

'Here, let me.'

'Thanks. Kath, can you take the plates through? Sorry – must just nip up to the loo. Be down in a tick.' She dropped the tea towel, then turned and headed for the stairs. Running up them now. The bolt sliding home.

The hunt

They were all outside, watching the children hunt for miniature chocolate Easter eggs and chicks which Miranda and Kath had hidden all over the garden, when they heard the toot-toot of the car horn. Kath tried to drag Polly and Luke away, but they refused to be deflected from the quest for chocolate. She ran to greet the new arrivals, followed by Joe moving rather more slowly.

'Shouldn't we go, too?' Simon asked Miranda.

'What for? So we can hang out the welcoming bunting?'

100

'It'll look rude.'

Miranda shrugged.

'Since when did you care? Besides, I think it's pretty rude not to bother to phone us when we were slaving away all morning cooking lunch for them. You go if you like – I'll stay here and keep an eye on the kids.'

Luke came up and tugged at the fringe of her crimson pashmina.

'Manda! There aren' any eggs. Polly's takin' them all.'

Anna was competing with Polly, clambering over the rock garden at the far end, which had been dotted with foil-wrapped eggs.

Miranda bent down and took his hand.

'There are plenty left, I promise. What say you and I hunt together, eh? Girls! Please leave some for Luke, OK?' She steered him towards a pot on the patio. 'Hmm, can you see anything shiny in there, Luke?'

The sound of car doors slamming, voices raised in greeting.

'What about up here, Luke?' Miranda directed Luke towards the drystone wall further up the garden, from which small ferns poked tongues of shiny green. 'It looks as if there are lots of little hiding places in here.'

Now they would go into the house to drop off their things, have a look round. But no, she could hear Kath bringing them straight down the path at the side of the house, telling them that the egg hunt was under way.

Crunch of gravel underfoot as someone stood on the edge of the herb bed. Miranda stayed crouched by Luke, put her arm round him to pull him close for a cuddle.

'Well done! You've found another one!' Holding him longer than he wanted, feeling him start to pull away, eager to carry on.

Miranda looked round, slowly stood up, glanced to where she'd last seen Anna, but she was no longer there.

Tamsin stayed on the patio, watching the hunt in full swing. She put her arm through Rob's.

'Aaaaaah . . . Aren't they sooooooo sweet?'

'Don't be fooled by appearances. Polly and Luke are little devils in disguise. Trust me.'

'How can you say that! Your own niece and nephew!'

Rob patted her arm.

'*You're* very sweet – defending the demon trolls without even knowing them. I wasn't a hundred per cent serious, baby.'

Anna turned to watch the new arrivals. She crouched behind a low bush, pretending to be a spy. When visitors come, you are supposed to go and say hello, how do you do? And you have to smile and be nice and remember not to pick your nose or ask too many questions like how old are you or haven't you got big bosoms or why is your hair so red? When visitors come, grown-ups stop talking to you and go and do that funny kissing thing that is not

102

proper kissing, only sometimes they do hugs instead, like Mummy and Auntie Kath. Anna peeped out from behind her hiding place, watching her mother, waiting for her to go and say hello, to see if she would do kisses or hugs, but Mummy couldn't have seen them because she was still with Luke, helping him to find the eggs. Polly was getting upset now, pulling at the tall man, saying it wasn't fair, Manda was helping Luke but no-one was helping her, it wasn't fair, but Anna knew that you only got help when you were really little, like Luke. She didn't want anyone to help her, she wanted to find the eggs herself. She looked down at her clutch of eggs, glinting in the nest of her palm, pink and silver, blue and gold. Thinking, calculating, how many to have now and how many to save, keeping the silver and blue ones for last, the best ones, silver and blue, sparkling like a mermaid's tail.

'Hey, Manda.' Rob strode across the lawn to Miranda, put one arm around her waist. 'Don't say hello, then.'

'Hey, Rob.' Miranda stretched up on her toes, turning her face so that they kissed cheek to cheek. 'Sorry, I have a one-track mind when it comes to chocolate.'

'You're looking well. Really well.' He squeezed her arm, then let her go. Simon quickly joined them on the lawn. 'Simon.' They shook hands. 'Good to see you again. How's life, work, etcetera?'

'Excellent, thank you.' He nodded. 'How was your journey down?'

Rob rolled his shoulders.

'Bit short on legroom. We came in Tamsin's car – mine's at the garage again and Dad won't let anyone else drive his precious Jag, pretends the company insurance forbids it.'

Miranda and Tamsin exchanged air kisses, said yes, of course they remembered meeting before at Kath and Joe's Christmas party, of course. Luke came up to Rob, demanding a piggyback; Rob lifted him up high onto his shoulders and cantered off down the garden.

'Will you give *me* a piggyback?' Polly asked Tamsin.

Tamsin eyed Polly's muddy shoes and pulled her pale cashmere coat closer around her.

'I'm sure your Uncle Rob will give you one in a minute.'

'And Giles, too, of course! How lovely – the whole tribe at once!' Miranda stood still as he leant forward to kiss her, his hand tight around her elbow. 'Goodness! Poor you! Does it hurt much? Now, tell me . . .' She gave him a mischievous smile. 'Did you fall – or were you pushed?' She felt Anna come up close behind her, half-hiding behind her legs.

'Amusing as always, fair Miranda. And who is this charming young lady?'

'This is Anna. She's a bit shy.'

'No, I'm not!' Anna said, still clinging to her mother's side.

'Well, you can be sometimes. You remember Polly's grandad, don't you, darling? You met him once at Auntie Kath's house. Or were you too little?'

Anna looked up at Giles without speaking.

'And how old are you, Anna?'

'Why don't you run off and play with Polly – go on, hurry up, before all the eggs are gone!' Anna skipped away. 'So. How are you, Giles? I mean, aside from your arm. Obviously.'

'Fit as a fiddle. Aside from my arm. Obviously.' He smiled.

'How did it happen?'

'A secretary of ours, a complete and utter cretin I might add, left a baby's car seat on the floor right outside my office door and I tripped over it, not surprisingly. Anyone would have done. Thank God it wasn't a client at least. If she hadn't been an employee, I would have been more than happy to sue, I can tell you. She'd brought in her baby to show people in the office. I mean – a *baby* – to the *office*. Quite inappropriate.'

'Oh Giles – you *are* funny. I'm sure you play up your old fogey act purely to be provocative at times. I bet you're just as soppy about babies as anyone else.'

'I doubt it very much.' He fumbled with his left hand in his jacket pocket.

'Can you manage?'

'It's just my cigars. Could you . . . ?'

Miranda reached into his pocket and pulled out a packet of slim cigars, took one out and unpeeled it from its plastic, lifted it to her nose.

'God, I used to love these.'

'Please, have one.'

'No – no thanks. I mean just the smell. My dad was a cigar man.' She handed it to him. 'Matches?'

'Same pocket.'

Miranda lit the cigar for him, cupping her hand around the flame as he puffed. Giles nodded his thanks.

'We'd better bring our stuff in – do you know which is our room?' Rob addressed Miranda.

'You'd better ask Kath, she's Chief Organizer.'

'And where's your little girl? Isn't she with the others?' Tamsin asked.

From the corner of her eye, Miranda spotted Anna's blue-shoed feet sticking out at one side of a bush.

'Oh, she's somewhere around . . . you know how kids are . . .' She waved her hand airily. Turned towards the path. 'Let me give you a hand in with your stuff.'

Settling in

Rob dumped his holdall on the floor, then flopped back onto one of the twin beds.

'How come we don't get a double bed?' Tamsin looked around for a surface large enough to accommodate her outsize suitcase, then, seeing that there wasn't one, hefted it onto the other bed and unzipped it.

'We didn't even know we were coming until a couple of days ago, baby.'

'I'm just saying . . . don't you think it's, like, really, really selfish? Bet you Simon and Amanda don't even . . . *use* it.' She took out a number of garments and opened the wardrobe. 'There aren't enough hangers.'

'Miranda, not Amanda. Come on, Tam – we'd have snaffled the other double if we'd got here first. We can hardly blame them for doing the same. It's no big deal. We'll shove the beds together.' He prodded her thigh with his extended foot. 'Come and test it out.'

'I have to unpack first. I bet they've got more hangers than we have.'

He sighed and stood up.

'I'll go and see.'

Rob banged a complicated series of knocks on Kath and Joe's bedroom door, still using the elaborate code he and Kath had devised as children: *It's me, Rob – what are you up to?*

'Halt! Who goes there?' Joe called out.

'It's me. Just looking for spare hangers,' Rob called back.

Joe opened the door.

'Sorry, thought it must be Polly. I was having a bit of a lie-down.'

'Don't blame you. I'm pretty shattered myself.'

'Hah. Wait till you have kids, mate, then you'll look back with longing on the days of being merely shattered. Hangers, was it?' Joe opened the wardrobe. 'Here, there's loads, help yourself. I couldn't be arsed to hang anything up myself.'

'Cheers.' Rob grabbed a jangle of wire coat hangers. 'So . . .' He turned round. 'How's tricks?'

'You know how it is.' Joe shrugged. 'Come round and marvel at our kitchen. I'm thinking of entering it in *The Guinness Book of Records*: the Most Slowly Built Kitchen of All Time. Still, we splashed out on the cupboard handles last week, so that brought a bit of excitement into our lives.'

'Your cupboards are in then? I thought Kath said—'

'No, no. *Handles.* The cupboards are way off. We take it in turns to stand there, holding them up around the room to sort of get the general effect.'

Rob laughed.

'And you?' Joe asked. 'How are your cupboards? So to speak.'

'Actually, my cupboards are crap – top-of-the-range, overpriced, genuine veneered chipboard by the look of them. One day, maybe I'll get round to building myself a new kitchen. Wouldn't mind having a crack at being creative again.' Rob had – briefly – tried his hand at designing and making his own furniture several years before, but, in the absence of instant success, had abandoned it in favour of something more immediately lucrative: becoming an estate agent; now, he had his own thriving agency. 'Yeah. And while I'm at it, think I'll make a rocket ship and head off to Jupiter for the weekend.' He sighed theatrically.

'Oh, I'm doing *OK*. The market's a bit sluggish right now, so business manages to be both boring and stressful at the same time – still, what else is new?'

'And, um – ?' Joe nodded towards the door. 'We had the impression you'd gone your separate ways?'

Rob leaned back against the door, until it clicked shut. Shrugged again.

'We're always splitting up, it's become a habit. It's Monday – what shall I do? I know – split up with Tamsin. It's Friday – shit, better get round there and grovel.' Rob dug his hands down into his pockets, leaned one foot back against the door. 'Yeah, I know, I'm a bastard and don't know when I'm well off. She's gorgeous, isn't she?'

'She's very attractive.'

'Yeah. And we mostly get on OK when we're not splitting up – I mean, it's not just the sex. Well . . . it's mainly that, but . . .'

'So what if it is? Enjoy it while you can, mate.'

'Why do married couples always say that? Do you all just go off each other after a year or two, is that it?'

Joe smiled.

'Not in the least. Or not for me at any rate. It's just exhaustion. If you've got any kind of job that involves more than paper-shuffling or pissing about on the Internet all day, then you're knackered by the time you get home. You come in, try not to look at the baked beans ground into the carpet, give the kids their bath, read them a story which means three stories, pick your way through the devastation in the kitchen in search of sustenance, usually whatever's lying about because you can't summon the energy to hack your way through the elaborate obstacle course of packaging on a frozen pizza, so you microwave two leftover fish fingers or half a plate of mangled, spurned spaghetti, knock back whatever wine or beer you can lay your hands on, then, if you're lucky, you manage to make it upstairs to the bedroom without passing out at the kitchen table with your face in a plate of cold pasta. It's all you can do to take your clothes off and brush your teeth. So you give each other a kiss and say, "Let's have sex at the weekend, when we're more relaxed, when we're not so tired." "Good idea," you reply, "let's do it at the weekend, maybe Saturday morning." Then Saturday comes and at 6.32 a.m. two manic elephants come in and start using you as a trampoline, but you're so tired you can't even be bothered to tell them to stop. And you realize this isn't a day off, it doesn't even remotely resemble a day off, because today you've got them solidly for many, many hours and you spend the entire day dragging them from place to place, from park to café to museum to park – heaven forbid they should ever be bored for more than two seconds. Then one of them gets asked to a party so you think, "Hurrah! A couple of hours off." But no, because of course you have to go too to show that you're a nice, involved, caring parent who likes nothing more than watching the same creepy clown make toy balloon animals that you've seen at the last forty-three parties. So then it's Saturday night but you can't go out to dinner with your wife because by the time you add on the cost of a babysitter and a bottle of wine and a taxi home you've shelled out enough for half a kitchen cabinet, the same kitchen cabinets you've been saving for for the past three years and, besides, what's the point of going out to dinner when you're too tired even to read the menu, never mind appreciate what a fine Bordeaux you're having or to attempt to make proper conversation. So you end up having an Indian takeaway or you say, "I'll cook for a change, darling," and you make pasta scrots and salad because that's basically all you can cook that isn't fish fingers and baked beans. And you have two bottles of wine because God knows the one thing you're never too tired to do is to have a drink, then you both fall into bed. And then it's Sunday and the whole thing starts all over again but, if you haven't actually *died* by the time it's three o'clock in the afternoon, you put *Thomas the Tank Engine* or *The Little Mermaid* in the video for possibly the fiftieth time in a fortnight and you know that if you run upstairs right this second and cut straight to the sex and don't bother with too much foreplay, you should just about manage it before one of them comes tumbling into your room crying or yelling about whose turn it is to press the funny-forward button.'

Joe finally wound to a halt.

'Ach, don't mind me. Just needed to get it out of my system.'

'No sweat, seemed like you were on a roll. What the hell are pasta *scrots* when they're at home?'

'Oh, sorry. That's just our name for them. The knobbly ones with stuff in the middle. Tortellini? Tortelloni? They look like little scrotums.'

'Ah – all is clear to me now. How appetizing. But some of it's good, right? I mean, marriage and all that?'

Joe blinked.

'Marrying Kath's the best thing I ever did in my whole life and I'm not just saying that because she's your sister. And the kids? They're brilliant.'

'But you said they tread baked beans into the carpet and come and bounce on you when you're asleep.'

'So?' Joe waved him away. 'What's a few baked-bean stains? You just wait till you have your own. You'll see.'

'Well, I may just relish the calm before the storm for now. Kath's always badgering me to settle down – but you're not much of a salesman, you know.'

'OK, take it from me, Honest Joe says, "Get Married, Have Kids – You Know it Makes Sense." Now are you convinced?'

'A hundred per cent. You're wasted in the probation service.' Rob turned to go.

'But Rob?'

'Yeah?'

'If you're thinking about it, don't bother picturing yourself walking up the aisle with your beautiful bride or shagging on the beach at sunset. Think how she'll be with her head over the toilet bowl or whether she's going to help you scrape up those baked beans from the carpet.'

'Cheers, Joe. Enjoy your rest.'

'Cheers, mate.'

Deciphering the past

After the new interlopers had arrived and unpacked, Tamsin had claimed that she'd left behind something vital and dragged Rob with her to try to find a chemist that would be open on Easter Day. Giles had withdrawn to his room to attempt the crossword. The children had tea towels tied round their heads and were playing Crossing the Desert, which mostly seemed to involve their spilling the contents of their shared bottle of water and staggering theatrically around the house.

Miranda was stripping the meat off the lunchtime chickens so she could make stock from the bones for soup when Kath came in.

'Need a hand?'

'Nah, seize your chance to take it easy for once. Go on, you've been buzzing round like a bee ever since we got here.'

Kath picked up the kettle and filled it with water.

'So have you,' she pointed out. 'I think I've forgotten how to take it easy. I keep thinking I should be doing something. I don't know how to *do* holidays any more. Do you want coffee? Tea?'

'Mmm. Tea, please, if you're doing. Thanks.' Miranda started pulling apart the chicken carcasses with her hands. 'I'm making some soup, OK? And there's enough chicken here to do a fricassée or something for tonight.'

'Wonderful.'

'Can you have a look in the fridge for the herbs I brought?' Miranda held her hands up like a surgeon who's just scrubbed up. 'I don't want to get everything greasy.'

Kath rummaged in the fridge and brought out a plastic bag.

'Manda?' Her voice dropped to a stage whisper. 'Um, you haven't had a chance to look at those letters yet, have you?'

'No, I'm sorry. It's been hard to get a moment to myself.' Miranda looked at Kath's face, saw the anxiety there. 'Tell you what, let me get this stock on the go, then I'll make a start on them, OK? I'll nip down to the beach for a bit of peace and quiet.'

Miranda tucked the packet of letters inside the front of her coat and carefully descended the steps. Although there was quite a strong breeze, with each step away from the house she felt herself start to relax. They shouldn't have come. Stupid, stupid, stupid Miranda for thinking it might be possible. She should have feigned illness, put sugar in her own petrol tank, thought of something, anything – at least to give herself more time to think. And now it was too late. She clutched the rail tightly, reluctant to relinquish its support, then finally stepped away down onto the rocks and picked her way across them to the flat sands.

It started raining again so Miranda flipped her stole over her head and tucked her hair in. She inhaled deeply. At least it was good to be here on her own, without having to keep an eye on anyone else for a few minutes. It was a nice beach, a cosy little beach, not large enough to draw big crowds or merit so much as an ice-cream kiosk, but not so small that there weren't nooks and crags and pockets that couldn't be seen all at once. Hanks of seaweed were slumped on the sand. When Miranda was a child, she'd loved popping the greeny-brown seaweed with bumps along its strands like beads; her aunt had called it mermaids' necklaces and Miranda had said the same to Anna.

Strange how certain things were handed down through the generations, not necessarily jewellery or valuable paintings, but funny things, silly things, tricks and quirks, phrases and sayings, recipes and stories. Even her own mother, who was as far from fanciful as it was humanly possible to be, had shared their family treasure chest of oddities with Miranda from an early age. Always smash the bottom of your boiled egg after you've eaten it – so that the witches can't use it as a boat to sail away in. Never give someone a present of a knife or anything sharp without asking for a small coin in return, or the friendship will soon be severed. Great-grandma's recipe for shortbread. Making fresh lemonade on the first day of June to herald the beginning of summer, rain or shine, pouring it from the green glass jug, ice cubes clinking. Closing a letter with 'love frok me', a now deliberate mimicking of her granny's haphazard typing.

She found a large, steady rock out of the wind and sat down. Turned up the collar of her leather coat. When she pulled off the woollen plait that secured the letters, the wind flapped at them ominously. That would go down well: 'Sorry, Kath, your mum's letters were blown out to sea so you'll never know what they said.' She gripped them more tightly, stroking her thumb across the top envelope. It wasn't such a bonkers idea, though: surely it would be better for Kath not to know, wouldn't it? Of course, Kath seemed excited about the *idea* of the letters – she thought they were romantic, intriguing, showing a side of her mother she'd never suspected. But if the letters revealed what Miranda presumed they would, Kath would be devastated. Miranda checked the postmarks, sighing softly to herself, then quickly flicked through, re-sorting the envelopes into date order so that the first letter was now at the top of the pile. Well, there was no ducking the issue – perhaps they would be simply romantic, they wouldn't necessarily spell everything out in unambiguous detail. She pulled out the first letter and held it securely, spread it open on her knee, trying to keep it flat in the wind. In this first one, the writing was relatively legible – perhaps before he got carried away by the depths of his surging passion?

Dear Connie,
Please accept my apologies.

That wasn't very romantic. Maybe they weren't love letters after all?

Well, it's finally been made official: I am an idiot. Just in case you were in any doubt. I'm so sorry, Connie; believe me, I'm not usually in the habit of enfolding my pupils in an embrace, even if they do happen to have beautiful hazel eyes. But seeing you cry like that ... I take it it wasn't just the Bach, was it? There I go again. I know it's none of my business. I do understand if you want to discontinue your lessons and I'm sorry if I made you suffer even a moment's embarrassment or awkwardness (or nausea?

Please say not). But if you ever need a sympathetic ear and an absorbent shoulder (or, failing that, just a piano lesson), well, you know where I am. Perhaps you could let me know about next week's lesson?

Warm regards
Frank

Not exactly a Don Juan, by the sound of it, but it was a nice letter. Not pushy. Miranda opened the next one, screwing her eyes up with the effort of decoding the handwriting. This one began:

Dear ♩

I don't think you have the slightest idea just how amazing you are, do you? And I'm not just talking about your eyes, your lips, your freckles . . . all of which are wonderful, but everything about you – your voice, your mind, your thoughtfulness, the way you crinkle your nose like a child when you're concentrating . . .
. . . God, it felt good to hold you . . . I hate it that you're so unhappy. I don't want to make things worse, or to complicate your life – tell me what I can do to bring the smile back to your lovely face. Call me anytime, day or night if you want to. But no pressure.

Until next week then. I'll bring you some Chopin. Something tricky. I'm too soft on you.

Miranda shut her eyes and leant back against the rock.

If only Kath hadn't come across the letters. Unless Miranda claimed that they were graphically sexual, Kath would inevitably end up reading them. She was bound to, it was human nature. If Miranda had found letters in her parents' attic, she'd no doubt have read them at once, gorging herself on secrets, unable to stop until she'd savoured every last word, even if she felt horrified or repelled at the same time. Kath was much less nosy, of course, and more restrained, but even she wouldn't be able to resist the temptation for ever. And then at the very least she would know that her mother had been unhappy, unhappy enough to have been unfaithful to Giles, and Kath would feel sad and powerless. If only people could let things alone, let the past stay in the past without digging it up and dusting it off and examining it all the time like zealous archaeologists, resurrecting what would have been better left buried.

She wished that she herself owned a stash of exquisitely written letters that Anna might come across in decades' time, clearing out the loft after Miranda was dead. Letters that showed that Miranda had once been beautiful, exciting, loved. She had received love letters, but precious few that had really been worth saving; there were a handful of rather rude, sexy ones from one boyfriend when she'd been in her early twenties. They'd lived nearly a hundred miles apart and only seen each other at weekends, but they'd both penned letters detailing what they'd like to do to each other at their next meeting. But they weren't exactly romantic and the prose was pretty basic – rough and to the point rather than lyrical. There were a couple of soppy ones from that very wet guy she'd seen for a few months; she'd tried to convince herself that he was desperately romantic because he used to kiss her hand and he once floated rose petals in her bath, but really he was just a bundle of clichés, trying to adhere to some magazine-fantasy romantic ideal that he imagined that women wanted, and after a while she realized that she didn't even like him all that much, it was just the idea of him that seemed attractive.

And there were Simon's letters, of course. She laughed out loud suddenly at the thought of them. When Simon went away for work for more than a few days, he always wrote – usually a letter for her and a postcard for Anna. His letters were interesting, but not remotely romantic, almost anti-romantic even. He'd tell her about what he'd seen and done, quirky details about people he'd met and peculiar, cheap hotel rooms he'd stayed in. He was funnier on the page than in person, she realized – in letters, his attention to detail and powers of observation became a source of pleasure rather than irritation, and his remarks about the dodgy wallpaper or the way some interviewee's strange beard resembled an old bird's nest could have her giggling away. But they weren't like proper love letters – there was no 'Darling, how I dream of you,' or 'At night, I bury my face in the pillow and wish that you were beside me,' 'I miss your scent, the way your hair tickles my cheek when we're in bed,' – none of that. He'd tell her about the recycling plant he'd been to see or the hydroelectric scheme or the new housing development with houses that were 30 per cent more energy-efficient. Then, at the end, without elaboration or any extra sentiment, he'd put:

'I miss you.'

If he were to go away now, he probably wouldn't even bother with that, not unless it had become automatic and he didn't notice that he'd written it – or only noticed afterwards and didn't want to draw attention to it by crossing it out, which would be too rude and aggressive even by Simon's current standards. He seemed to be so angry all the time at the moment, not just in the way he usually was – with politicians, corporations, industry – but with her, specifically with her. But then she was no picnic to live with, she knew that. Maybe he'd just had enough and was deliberately being impossible so that she'd finally say, 'OK, that's it – it's all over.' Maybe he simply didn't have the courage to say it himself and so wanted to poke at the lion through the bars until it went berserk? Well, OK then, another couple of weeks like this, and she'd be all too ready to tear him into bite-sized chunks.

But *Anna*, she thought. What about Anna?

A shadow fell across the letters in her lap and she looked up. It was Simon. She let her hands drop loosely on top of the pile.

'Catching up with your mail?'

'They're not mine,' she said quickly, clutching them more tightly.

Simon raised his eyebrows.

'They're Kath's. Or, rather, Connie's. Look – it's a bit awkward, she asked me to read them, but I need to be discreet about it, that's why I came down here.' She looked into his eyes. 'I'm sorry, but she asked me not to show anyone else.'

'Fine. I'm not interested in prying into other people's private business, Miranda. If you claim that they're not yours, then what possible reason could I have not to believe you? No-one's asking you to compromise your moral integrity.' He laughed briefly. 'I'm going for a walk. A long one. Along the cliff path.'

'Oh – shall I—?'

'I only came down to tell you because it's getting on. Are you OK doing Anna's supper and bath if I'm not back in time?'

'Of course! Why wouldn't I be? No need to make it sound as if you do everything.'

'A little paranoid, don't you think? I was simply checking that you would be available.'

'*Available?* Why ever not? Where else would I possibly be? Down at the local disco? Of course I'm available.'

Simon put his hands into his pockets and nodded.

'Well. There are a few more distractions now though, aren't there?'

She looked him right in the eye.

'Not for me there aren't.'

He sniffed and said nothing.

'Have a good walk,' she said. As he strode away, she lowered her voice. 'Do try not to fall off any cliffs, won't you?'

Sleeping arrangements

'OK, now we really better sort out these sleeping arrangements.' Kath stood in the doorway to the children's room. 'Any bright ideas?'

'How about I share with you, then we can talk all night?' Miranda leaned against the bunks. 'Bagsy top bunk. Actually – I'd better not, I'd break them.'

'I'd love to share with you, but I'm not sure Joe . . .'

'Hello? Not entirely serious, babe.'

'Sorry. So? Ideas? *Sensible* ideas.'

Miranda folded her arms.

'I *have* been mulling it over – I think the least crappy solution is to bring up the spare mattress from Giles's room and try to squash it in here.'

Kath frowned at the diminutive space.

'Will it fit? Maybe we could have Luke in with us instead?'

'I thought you were desperate for sleep? And sex.'

'It would be nice . . .'

'Well then. That's that sorted.'

'Let's get the chaps to bring up the mattress.'

'Why? We can manage.'

Kath made a face, but led the way downstairs. She knocked tentatively on the door of Giles's bedroom.

'Dad?'

'Come!'

Giles was poring over the crossword, the newspaper folded open on his lap.

'Can we borrow the spare mattress from here? For the kids' room.'

'Certainly.' He looked up at Miranda.

'Why are you skulking in here?' she teased him. 'Are you avoiding the rest of us?'

'Now, why on earth would I want to do that?' He smiled.

'I can't imagine.'

Kath tugged at the bedspread and started stripping the bed.

'I'm afraid I can't be of much use right now.' Giles indicated his injured arm. 'Get Robert to do that for you.'

'We've got it,' Miranda said firmly. She and Kath pulled the mattress onto one edge and started dragging it out into the hall. 'Can't you lift it?' Miranda said. Kath peered at her over the top of the mattress.

'Said the giraffe to the garden gnome. No, I can't.'

Joe came out of the kitchen, eating a biscuit.

'Here, what are you doing? Let me do that!'

'We're fine.'

'Actually, it *is* a bit awkward.' Kath relinquished her end. 'Thanks. Hang on, Manda, let me get Rob for your end.'

'Right!' Miranda grasped hold of the mattress, walking backwards. 'Ready for the stairs? Up we go.' She glanced behind her and moved onto the first step.

'You OK there?' Joe asked.

'Yup. No prob.'

She backed up another two steps.

Rob sauntered into the hall.

'Kathy said you needed a hand.'

'No, thanks!'

He started trying to squeeze past the mattress on the stairs to take Miranda's end.

'Come on, give it here!'

'I can manage. It's only a mattress.'

'Yes, yes – we all know you can manage anything. Don't be silly – why not let someone help you for once?'

'Because I don't *need* help. Though I daresay it would be considerably easier if there weren't a large and irritating obstacle cluttering up the stairway.'

'Why are you always so stubborn about everything?'

'Did I ask for a personality assessment?'

'Excuse me?' Joe said. 'Can you save the chit-chat for later? I'm not standing scrunched here all day, it's doing my back in.'

'For God's sake – will you just let me do it!' Rob wrenched the mattress from Miranda's grasp. 'I've got it now, Joe – you can let go.' He easily hefted the mattress single-handed up the stairs to the landing. 'Where shall I put it?'

'One or two orifices spring readily to mind.' Miranda opened the door to the children's room. 'In there.'

'It won't fit.'

'It has to fit. There isn't anywhere else.'

They manoeuvred it into the room and, by laying it at an angle, managed to set it down, with one end wedged into the open doorway and the other end under the bottom bunk.

'This is how you want it? Really?'

'Well, you come up with something, Sparky.'

'What's the actual problem? That the kids all want to share? What?'

Miranda sighed.

'No. The *actual* problem, if you take two seconds to think about it, is that originally Anna was going to

126

share with her friend, only then they had to drop out and Kath took it into her head to invite you for some bizarre reason and you – dear genius – roped in your dad. So after all Kath's efforts to track down the perfect house with the perfect number of rooms and beds, now it doesn't work after all. If you have any suggestions for a better plan, then do please tell rather than just lobbing criticisms at everyone else.'

She leaned against the bunk beds and folded her arms. He came closer and echoed her posture.

'Arm-wrestle you for top bunk?' He smiled. 'Or do you prefer to go on the bottom?'

She shook her head with a smile.

'Any other ideas?'

'Mmm, I can think of any number of suggestions.' He laid his arm along the length of the top bunk, his hand resting near her upper arm.

'No doubt. Any that might be of some *practical* use?'

'I guess you could always put Simon on a fast train to London, then there'd be a nice, vacant space in—'

'Still wouldn't solve the problem. The children, remember?' She stood upright.

'Can't one of the kids sleep on a sofa downstairs?'

'Uh-uh. That means no-one can use the sitting room after about half eight in the evening. Besides, Anna sometimes has bad dreams – she likes to be near us.'

'She's going to be a bit of a heartbreaker, isn't she?'

'You think?'

'Yeah. Beautiful kid. Definitely takes after your side of the family, I'd say.'

Miranda snorted.

'*I* was never a heartbreaker. I didn't exactly have them queuing round the block when I was a teenager – I was always so tall, so awkward and witchy-looking – and I was so desperate to be all small and pretty with nice, straight blonde hair and cute little freckles. So I made it worse by being loud and sarcastic and abrasive, showing them I didn't give a toss whether they fancied me or not. Great strategy. They were probably terrified and who can blame them?'

His eyes met hers.

'Manda . . .'

'Ah, great, you managed to get it up here then?' Kath stood in the doorway, arms full of bedding. 'Oops, it's a bit of a snug fit, isn't it? We can't close the door.'

'No raucous parties for the grown-ups then.'

'Luke sleeps through anything. We can always put Polly to sleep in our bed, then move her through here.'

Miranda took the bedding from Kath and they started making up the mattress.

'Well, I'll get out of your hair.' Rob leapt over the end of the mattress. 'I'm off to get some fags. Anyone want anything? Miranda? Fags? Marlboro Lights, still?'

'I don't smoke any more, Rob. I haven't smoked for over six months.'

'God, how did you manage that? I thought you were the one person I could rely on to be as depraved as me. Don't tell me I'm the only smoker here?'

'Yes, and don't go trying to tempt her, Robbie. You're a bad influence.'

'What? Me? How can you say that?' He smiled broadly and thundered down the stairs.

Miranda knelt down to tuck in the bottom sheet.

'Funny how all the men disappear as soon as there's anything like bed-making to do. Perhaps they're worried they might have an allergic reaction?'

Kath laughed.

'They don't see it. They see a bare mattress and think "there you go, a place to sleep." Joe has selective blindness. He can walk across a floor absolutely covered in Lego and toy cars without thinking to pick any of it up. Simon's pretty house-trained though, isn't he?'

'He's an odd mixture: he can rustle up a meal, though he's having an unfortunate phase of doing couscous with everything just now. I'm hoping he'll grow out of it. And of course he has the world's most elaborate recycling system under his iron rule. He does load the dishwasher but I can't bear to watch because it's such an unbelievably long-drawn-out, painstaking process – he has this one-man mission to work out the exact, ideal position for each mug and teaspoon that will maximize washing efficiency and minimize consumption of water and detergent and any time I shove so much as a saucer in there, he repositions it according to Simon's Law, which no sane person could possibly hope to grasp in a million years. But he has a slobby side, too – if it were left up to him, we'd never change our bed linen –' She tilted her head on one side and adopted Simon's manner: ' "There's no need for this *obsessive* laundering all the time – when you think just how much energy is used by a single washing-machine load . . ." Aaaaarrggh, I just want to hit him.'

Kath plumped up a pillow and threw it to the other end of the mattress.

'Um, so did you get a chance to read the letters, by the way?'

'God – yes – I'm sorry – I knew there was something I meant to tell you. I only had a brief look – inevitably, Simon sprang up from behind a rock the second I started to read them, so I only had a minute—'

'And? And? Who are they from?'

'Her piano teacher it looks like. They seemed pretty innocuous, the bits I saw.'

'Well, perhaps I can read them myself then?'

'Actually, there was a slightly . . . you know . . . juicy . . . bit – maybe I'd better hang onto them a little longer, if you don't mind – just to make sure—'

'Of course.' Kath's voice sounded flat. 'Oh – did you notice when they were written? I didn't even see a date—'

'Oh, bugger! I meant to ask Rob to get me something from the shop – ' Miranda turned towards the door. 'I might just catch him.'

'He'll be halfway there by now. Didn't you hear the door slam?'

'Yes, yes, of course, I wasn't thinking.' She shook out the duvet and spread it on the mattress. 'God, and the other thing that drives me mad about Simon is that he doesn't clean the loo properly.'

'Neither does Joe. Maybe it's an atavistic trait? Primitive territory marking?'

'Ha! Don't make excuses. Maybe it's because we cave in and clean up after them? No wonder they all believe in the Cleaning Fairy. If your dirty socks always magically reappear all clean and fragrant in your sock drawer, why should you believe any different?'

'At least you really have got a Cleaning Fairy.'

'True. Iris is the most important person in my life. Well, aside from Anna, of course.' She stepped carefully over the end of the mattress. 'And you.'

'I'm honoured. Am I really *above* your cleaner? What about Simon?'

Miranda shrugged.

'Nope, I'd have a nervous breakdown if I had to last a week without Iris. Simon toddled off for a few days recently to write a feature on that tidal-power project up in Shetland and I revelled in every second of it. Is it time for tea yet? I'm in need of a biscuit.'

Kath led the way downstairs.

'It's always time for tea. God, you sound like Luke – "Mummy, I *need* a biscuit." '

'Well, I do. I do *need* a biscuit. I may even *need* three or four.' She glanced at her watch. 'Hey, bugger the tea. I do believe that it's late enough to start on the wine.'

The big bulge club

'Even my bulges have bulges.' Kath slumped into a kitchen chair and lifted up her top. 'See? I'm growing a whole colony of bulges.'

Miranda lifted up her jumper to compare. She clutched at a fold of flesh and moved her navel like a mouth. 'Hey, Leetel Bulge, you wanna join my club? I am the Beeeeg Bulge, but I let you join.'

'Can I breeng my fambily? I have many, many Bulges to support,' Kath's navel mouthed back.

'Sure – the more Bulges, the better.'

'Oh! Hi!' Tamsin came in. The bulges went back into hiding. Tamsin crossed to the fridge and took out a bottle of mineral water. 'God, I know how you feel, I really, really pigged out last week and I'm such a fatso now. Look at this!'

She attempted to squeeze some flesh from her perfectly flat tummy through her top.

'We were just . . .' Kath began.

Miranda glared at her.

'. . . having some wine,' Miranda finished. 'Grab yourself a glass.'

Tamsin reached up to a cupboard to get a glass, revealing a tanned and toned midriff sporting a tiny, tasteful red jewel piercing the navel.

'I can't, thanks, I'm on a detox today.'

'Gosh, that sounds fun,' Miranda said, drawing up her legs to avoid the anticipated kick from Kath.

'What does that do then?' Kath said.

'It really, really helps to cleanse your whole system—'

'Like an enema, only from the other end? Myself, I prefer a good dose of Ajax and a thorough scrubbing.'

Kath scrunched her nose reprovingly at Miranda.

Tamsin drained her glass of water and poured herself another one.

'So, you just drink water? Is that it?' Kath asked.

'It depends. Like if you do the detox-fast, that's like twenty-four hours and you just have water. Or there's the detox-plus, which is where you have water plus seedless grapes.'

'Oh. Right. Grapes. That's good. How many are you allowed?' Kath avoided meeting Miranda's eyes.

'Me – I can hardly so much as look at a seedless grape without piling on the pounds.' Miranda knocked back the rest of her wine as if taking a slug of whisky. She frowned at her empty glass. 'How about wine instead of the grapes? I could probably survive on nothing but wine for a month without too much difficulty.'

'Ooh, no, you're not allowed alcohol. But you can have as many grapes as you like – so you can really,

133

really pig out. Grapes are, like, *sooooo* the best thing for a detox – they actually contain actual micrograms which purify the blood.'

'Micrograms of what?' Miranda said, then caught Kath glaring at her. She made a face at her, then turned to Tamsin. 'I'm very impressed. I don't have an ounce of self-discipline, do I, Kath? My idea of restraint is only having one bottle of wine in an evening. Well, good for you.' She avoided Kath's eye. 'It's *really, really* admirable.'

The Mermaid's Tale

They had decided in the end that the girls would take turn and turn about on the top and bottom bunks, with Luke – bribed with the promise of a new yellow toy tractor – on the mattress on the floor as he was too little to go in the top bunk.

'Mummy – tell me about the mermaid,' Anna said.

Miranda bent down to sit on the bottom bunk.

'Ssh-shh, whisper or you'll wake Polly and Luke. Which mermaid? The one in the bay?'

Anna nodded and curled her hands over the top of the quilt.

'Shall we make up a story about her?' Miranda's voice was soft and quiet. 'Hmm, let's see . . .'

'You tell it.'

'Mmm. Well, how shall we begin?'

'Silly. Once upon a time . . .'

'Ssh. Once upon a time, there was a beautiful girl with eyes the colour of the depths of the ocean and hair that lapped around her shoulders like the waves against the stones on the shore . . .'

'Did she live on the beach?'

'She lived . . . um . . . yes, she lived in a tiny cottage right by the sea. It was made of driftwood and she had stuck shells all around the windows and the door – cockles and mussels and periwinkles. There was a proper log fire inside and smoke curling out of the chimney . . .'

'And she cooked on the fire – she toasted marshmallows and crumpets and sometimes she made her own bread with organic flour and she never had to eat broccoli.'

'OK.' Miranda suppressed a smile. 'She never ate broccoli.'

'Or yucky green peppers.'

'Or yucky green peppers – she could eat whatever she liked because it was her cottage and her fire. Maybe she had boiled seaweed?'

Anna made a face.

'Anyway, one day, she was collecting shells on the seashore when she saw a small boat drop its anchor in the bay. Two figures got into a rowing boat and were soon pulling up on the sands where she stood.'

'Were they princes from a foreign land?'

'Uh-uh, better than princes. They were sailors and one of them was very, very handsome.'

'Did he fall in love with the girl?'

Miranda nodded.

'He certainly did. For not only was she very beautiful . . .' She stroked her daughter's hair rhythmically back from her brow. 'She was also extremely clever and sweet and funny and lovely.'

'And then what happened?'

'Well, if I tell you, you must promise to go straight to sleep after the end of the story.'

Anna nodded, her eyelids drooping.

'Well, the sailor told the girl he loved her and promised he would come back to marry her . . .'

'But he didn't, did he, Mummy? I know he didn't.'

'Um, that's right. He meant to but he had to go away to sea and his boat was caught in a huge storm.'

'Did he get drowned?' Anna was struggling to keep her eyes open.

'No-o-o-o-o, he didn't drown. He was shipwrecked, though, on a desert island far, far away in another ocean on the other side of the world. He was washed up on the beach and when he woke up, he had lost his memory.'

'– he forget all about her?' Anna murmured.

'Hmm-mm, he couldn't remember anything . . .' Miranda bent to kiss Anna's forehead. 'He made himself a shelter and lived on fish and coconut milk and wove himself a bed of palm leaves and every day he sat on the beach, watching the waves and trying to remember . . .'

'Then wha'—?'

'You're falling asleep, little bean.'

''m not. Tell. Please tell.' Her eyes fluttered open once more.

'The beautiful girl waited and waited her whole life for him to come back. Every day, she sat outside her cottage looking out to sea, watching and waiting, waiting and watching, but of course he never came. Then, when she was very old and—'

'Did she die?'

'Just as she was dying, and this is only when she was really, really old, remember, a local good witch took pity on her and transformed her magically into a mermaid hewn from the rock of the seashore so that she could watch for her sailor for ever and ever. And there she sits to this day, looking out to sea, waiting.'

Hmm, that hadn't quite come out as she'd intended. Not exactly a happy tale. Oh dear. Miranda looked down at her daughter, feeling as always a deep well of love for her when she was like this, asleep and unaware. And silent, she reminded herself, don't get too sentimental. Easy to love a sleeping child, when it wasn't crying or shouting or being stroppy. So much harder to be an endlessly loving and patient parent when you'd put up with a whole day of squabbling and stubbornness and whiny demands for Coke and sweets and nasty plastic toys. One good thing about Simon was that he had endless reserves of patience, he could stand any amount of persistent questions and he rarely got cross. Well, he rarely got cross with Anna at least – but perhaps that was because at the moment he was expending so much energy being angry with Miranda that he simply used up all his reserves and there was no anger left for anyone else?

She bent down to kiss Anna's brow.

'Nighty-night, little bean. Sleep tight.'

Monday

A convivial breakfast

'What are *you* doing up so early?' Kath was surprised to see her brother padding into the kitchen in his boxer shorts shortly after 7.30 a.m. 'Oh, did the beasts wake you? I'm sorry.'

'Uh-uh, force of habit – I'm normally up at seven to go to the gym before work – though I did also hear a horde of rhinoceroses charging down the stairs at some ungodly hour. Did you round them up?'

'Herded them into the sitting room to watch cartoons.'

'Is that what's known as *quality time*?' he teased her.

'Absolutely. Quality time for *me*. Don't try and guilt-trip me, I'm having a week off.'

'Hey, I was a cartoon junkie, remember? And look at me!'

'Dear God! I better go and rescue them now.'

'Hush up, you.' He went over to the worktop. 'Is there any coffee on the go?'

'I'm just about to make some.'

Rob pulled out a kitchen chair and sat down, propping up his feet on another chair.

'Why's it so cold in here?'

'It isn't. You've just been spoiled by your swish underfloor heating. Course, you could try wearing a dressing gown and slippers like normal people. I'm sure not everyone wants to see you lolling about in your underpants first thing in the morning.'

His face crinkled into an expression of disgust.

'I'm too young to wear slippers.'

'*I* wear them.'

Rob looked down at her feet, which were clad in large sheepskin moccasins.

'So this week in Devon's just a prelude to your epic trek across the snowy wastes of Antarctica, is it?'

'They're very warm and very comfortable.'

'I bet Joe finds them irresistible, too – especially teamed with that outsize T-shirt, the sweat pants and the bathrobe. What is this – the barrier method? It must take him an hour just to unpeel you.'

Kath turned away from him and spooned instant coffee into two mugs.

'Not everyone's as shallow as you, you know. Once you're married, all sorts of other things become more important, not just what you look like.'

'Isn't there any *real* coffee?'

Kath silently tipped the instant back into the jar.

'Well, I just hope whoever I eventually marry won't let herself go, that's all.'

'Thanks, Robbie. You really know how to cheer a person up.'

'I didn't mean *you* necessarily—'

'Yes, you did.'

'So? Doesn't matter what I think, does it? If Joe finds terry towelling a turn-on for some reason, then good for you.' He sighed and fiddled with a stray teaspoon on the table.

Kath poured water into the cafetière and stirred it vigorously.

'Toast?'

'Cheers. Is there any marmalade?'

'Not sure. Feel free to get up and have a look, why don't you?'

'The floor's too cold. I'm marooned here!'

'Oh, for goodness sake! That's why people have slippers!' Kath rooted around in one of the cupboards. 'Here you go.' She tilted the jar so that he could see the label. 'Is this to Sir's liking? It should be good, Miranda must have brought it. Now, are you sure you can manage to spread it all by yourself?'

'Yeah, yeah, sod off.'

'Robbie?' Kath closed the door to the hallway and lowered her voice.

'Mmm?'

'Does that mean you're definitely not planning to settle down with Tamsin?'

He shrugged.

'What?'

'It's just you said "whoever" and "eventually" . . .'

'Yeah, well, you weren't planning on dashing out this morning to look for a fancy hat, were you?'

'No-o-o, but still . . . ?'

'What am I waiting for and why am I messing about if she's not The One? Can't we change the record? It's boring now.'

'You're not twenty-two any more, you don't have time to faff about. And also, it's not fair on her, is it? You can't string her along if you're not really serious.'

'Tam's OK with it, so why should you give a toss? Look – it's sweet of you to worry about me, but there's no need. I'm *fine*. I'm not saying I'm deliriously happy every minute of the day, but who is? I get along. Anyway – why the hell should I be miserable and celibate just because I can't have the woman of my dreams?'

Kath frowned. She slowly plunged the cafetière, then poured the coffee into their mugs.

'I didn't realize you'd already met her.'

'Didn't say I had.' He looked at her sharply. The toast sprang up from the toaster and Rob quickly stood up and went to fetch it.

'You said "can't have", not "haven't met".'

144

'So sue me, Miss Pedantic. I'm barely awake yet.'

He plonked a plate with toast on it in front of her.

'Thanks. What about Amy? Was it her? You liked her a lot, didn't you?'

'No idea. Which one was she?'

'You're impossible!' She shoved him playfully. 'Or Natalie? I was really fond of her. She was sweet.'

'Aah, I'm happy for you both. Will you tell Joe or shall I?'

'But there is someone, isn't there? You had someone in mind when you said that.'

'God, you're getting as bad as Dad. Why aren't *you* a lawyer? Then you'd be fantastically overpaid and you could have a swish kitchen – all at once instead of handle by handle.'

'Please, don't. There's an embargo on mentioning the kitchen while we're on holiday. I'm trying not to think about it. Anyway, don't change the subject.' Kath sat back in her chair and smiled. 'I'm right, aren't I?'

'Don't be smug.' He rubbed his face with his hands, then took a gulp of coffee. 'Look, there is – was – this person – who I kind of had a bit of a thing for – we had a brief – fling – nothing really – a one-night stand – no biggie – and it was ages ago – but I – anyway, it didn't work out, OK? End of story.' He dug down into the jar of marmalade with his knife. 'Ah, really chunky, just the job – did you bring this?'

'No, Manda did, I told you. So, come on, what

happened? Who is she?' Kath leaned forward. 'Do you still see her? Are you madly in love with her?'

'Whoa – hold on. Don't get your hopes up. It's not going to happen, OK?' He put his feet up on the corner of her chair once more. 'I can't *believe* how cold this floor is. Anyway, what are we up to today? Any plans? Loafing in nice old country pub somewhere?'

Kath ignored his attempt to steer the conversation elsewhere.

'Stop avoiding the issue. Why won't anything happen? How can you be so sure? Oh, God, she's married, isn't she? Oh, Rob, that's really not—'

'No, she isn't. Don't go leaping to conclusions. She—'

The door suddenly swung open and they both jumped.

'Hey.' Miranda stood in the doorway, wearing ivory satin pyjamas beneath a plum silk robe, a pair of beaded plum velvet mules on her feet.

'Hey,' said Rob. 'So it *is* possible to find nightwear that isn't specially designed to be male-repellent.'

'Good morning,' said Kath. 'Do you have to look so gorgeous first thing?'

'Hardly.' Miranda yawned. 'Why's the door closed? Are you having a private bitching session? I can't believe you started without me.' She reached for the coffee pot. 'You know it's practically the only thing I'm any good at.'

'You're good at millions of things.'

Miranda waved her away. 'Anna's watching cartoons with the others.'

'I know, I peeked in on them. Thank you. Has she eaten anything, do you know? She gets a bit low-blood-sugary sometimes.'

'I gave them each a banana and some bread and jam.'

'Thank you, angel.' Miranda kissed the top of Kath's head, then went to the worktop to cut some more bread and put it in the toaster. She leaned back against the counter. 'Aren't you cold, Rob? Much though I like to eat my toast with something to look at, I normally make do with the newspaper.'

'Why – it doesn't bother you, does it? I can go and put on a suit and tie if my naked chest offends you for some reason?'

Kath frowned at Rob and nudged him disapprovingly with her knee. He didn't meet her eye.

'Nope. Doesn't offend me in the slightest.' Miranda stared fixedly at his chest. 'Has no effect on me of any kind. Though it might be marginally more appetizing if you didn't have toast crumbs trapped in your chest hair – mind you, that's just a personal preference – perhaps Tamsin likes it that way? Who knows?'

Now Kath frowned at Miranda as Rob vigorously brushed at his chest to remove the crumbs.

'Does anyone want cereal as well as toast? Rice Krispies? Cornflakes? Coco Pops?'

'No, thanks.'

'Uh-huh.'

The toast popped up and Miranda buttered it.

'Kath, do you want another piece? Rob?' She came over and started to pull out a chair, then stopped. 'Sorry, were you seriously talking about something private when I came in? Shall I bugger off? I don't mind.'

'Don't be daft.' Kath patted the chair beside her.

There was silence for several seconds.

'Um, we were just talking about relationships,' Kath said, ignoring Rob's glare.

'Oh.' Miranda laid her head on the table. 'Wake me when you move on to something interesting, won't you?'

'Jeez, I hate the way you couples are all so smug! Once you're settled, you're unbelievably judgemental about anyone single.'

Miranda slowly sat up again, looking back at Rob.

'Sorry – did I miss a scene somewhere?'

He thunked down his coffee mug.

'You know what I mean.' Rob tilted his head to one side and affected a drawl. 'Oh, how terribly, terribly dull and boring, talking about the problems of single people, oh what a drag – cheers, Miranda, no-one's forcing you to join in, I was talking to my sister, OK? Feel free to beetle off if it's not fascinating enough for you.'

Kath laid a hand on his arm.

'Robbie, she didn't mean that—'

Miranda looked straight at him.

'*Rob.*' She waited for him to meet her eyes. 'I hate to jolt you out of your paranoid fantasy, but if you bothered to think about anyone other than *yourself* for two minutes, you'd have realized that you are *so* way off the mark that you will now be *cringing* inside with embarrassment. I know I can be a pain in the arse, I know I get on people's tits sometimes, but I am never, *ever* smug about relationships and for *you* to say that – even to think it – ' She shook her head and dropped her gaze. 'I *meant* – ah, forget it.' She stopped abruptly and stood up. 'Besides, you're not single, are you? Isn't there a woman upstairs in your bed? Or is she merely a travel accessory you thought might come in handy for the holiday?'

Kath pulled at Miranda's sleeve.

'Come on, can't we all get on? It's just a silly misunderstanding.' She glared at Rob. 'Be nice.'

'Yeah – hey, Miranda – I'm sorry, OK? I thought you – it seemed – I got the wrong end of the stick. Here, sit down – have some more coffee.' He topped up her cup. 'Look – I'll let you punch me if you like.' Miranda laughed. He stood up facing her. 'Go on – punch me right here.'

'Ooh, can't I have a go?' Kath said. 'How come you never let me punch you? It's so unfair.'

'Have you been working on your abs, then?' Miranda smiled and laid her hand flat against his taut stomach. 'God, you *have.*' He looked back at her, his face serious.

'Go on,' he said again. 'I'm not kidding.'

She shook her head.

'Uh-uh. Don't tempt me.' Miranda patted his flesh lightly then withdrew her hand. 'I might get carried away.' She picked up her toast and coffee and opened the door. 'Guess I'll seize my chance to grab a shower before all the others are up.'

'Oh, Manda? Can you stand to fit in a quick supermarket trip with me this morning? Apparently, the huge one outside town is open. I can't believe how much food we're getting through.'

'Sure thing.'

'Shall I babysit? Anna seems a pretty sweet kid – not such a handful as the demon spawn, is she?' Rob ducked out of the way as Kath aimed a swipe at him.

'Thanks, but Anna will probably come with us. She loves supermarkets.' Miranda turned and left the room.

Kath started clearing away the rest of the breakfast things.

'Rob? You know what you were saying before?'

He bent down to kiss her cheek.

'Later, eh? Must go and get some clothes on – I'm freezing. And I'd better go and give the old man a hand getting dressed, too. See you in a bit.'

In search of politically correct sausages

Anna wanted to push the trolley; Miranda and Kath walked immediately behind, keeping an eye on her so that she didn't veer into the other shoppers.

'Can I read the list?' Anna asked. 'Can I?'

'OK – why don't you read out what we need then and I'll push?' Miranda said.

'It says Pots!'

'Potatoes. Right. Lots of pots, yes?'

Kath nodded.

'What shall we do for supper tonight?'

Miranda made a face.

'Dunno, guv. I'm already out of ideas and it's only Monday. Anna – what do you fancy? Pasta?'

'We *always* have pasta *all* the time.' Her face suddenly lit up. 'Can we have sausages? Please can we, please?'

Miranda squidged her cheeks.

'Oh you poor, wee, deprived thing! Never being given sausages by nasty, cruel Mummy! Don't do that little hard-done-by face, missy. You're not Oliver Twist.'

'But can we?'

Miranda looked at Kath.

'Fine by me. Easy. Cheap. Polly and Luke love them. Luke would happily eat nothing but sausages breakfast, lunch and supper if he could.'

'Can you say it's your idea?' Miranda said quietly.

'So you-know-who doesn't give me a hard time about buying junk food?'

'Sausages aren't really junk food, are they? That's a bit tough. He won't have a go at me, will he?'

'No, course not. He thinks you're wonderful. It's one of the very few things on which we agree at the moment.'

They made their way to the right aisle. Kath picked up a packet of sausages. 'These OK?'

Miranda shook her head and sighed.

'We're looking for ones from outdoor-reared pigs, with minimal additives and no added colouring. Come on, Anna – help us look.'

Anna picked out some immediately.

'*These* are the ones Daddy always gets.'

Miranda looked surprised.

'When did you have sausages with Daddy?' She turned to Kath. 'So much for me trying to second-guess him and be a good mother.'

'When you go away we always have them, and sometimes we have them on Saturdays if you have to go to the shop.'

'Do you now? Well, why don't we all have them then? Kath? Sausages and mash with onion gravy?' Miranda grabbed some more packets. 'Will everyone eat that?'

'I don't want gravy. These are free range.' Anna turned to Kath, showing her the packet. 'My dad says

152

it's cruel to keep pigs all squashed up inside. They're really intelligent.'

'Well, I'm sure he's right.' They walked on, with Anna skipping along ahead of them.

'Can you fetch some orange juice, Anna? See – it's just over there.'

'Organic?'

'OK, if they have it. Better get two cartons.'

'We'd better get extra milk, too.' Kath reached for some more. 'Luke still gets through gallons.' Anna came racing back clutching the cartons close to her chest. 'Anna, do you think you could find a bottle of tomato ketchup as well – for the sausages? Ask a lady to get it down for you if you can't reach.' Kath took the juice from her. 'Manda?'

'Mmm? We may be forced to get ice cream, don't you think?'

'Definitely. Um . . . have you . . . you haven't forgotten about the letters, have you?' Kath looked down at the contents of their trolley. 'Not to hassle you or anything.'

'Course not. Don't worry. I'm sorry I've made so little headway – reading the handwriting's like trying to unravel tangled knitting.'

'So what was in the bits you did read? Why didn't you tell me this morning?'

'Well . . . Rob was there for a start, being Mr Universe, strutting round the kitchen practically naked: I was trying to be discreet for once. I didn't know if you'd even told him about the letters?'

Kath shook her head.

'Well, then. So I was right not to mention it?'

'I s'pose so. Do you think I should tell him?'

'There's no law, it's up to you. Look – let me carry on and read some more – there's no point dragging anyone else into it until we know what the letters say, is there?'

'I guess not.' Kath started twiddling with a strand of her hair. 'But, if my mum . . . if she *did* have an affair with someone else while she was married, then I suppose I ought to . . .'

'Tell your dad? Why? There's no need for that.' Miranda moved up the aisle towards the cheese. 'Come and help me – what cheese shall we get?'

'How come you always know what to do? I do envy you.' Kath stared blankly at the shelves of different types of cheese in front of her. 'I dither over even the tiniest decision, I always worry that I'll do the wrong thing. If I buy Canadian Cheddar, will everyone be cross with me because I should have chosen Irish? Or Scottish? What's the difference anyway? It must be wonderful just to decide and not fret about it. So . . . you really think I shouldn't—'

Miranda looked at her friend sideways.

'You think I'm confident about my decisions?' Miranda shook her head. 'You think I don't fuck up?

154

Jesus. Oh, Kath – there are things I've done – awful, terrible things you wouldn't believe . . .'

'You're always so hard on yourself. Anyway, you *seem* so confident and that's more than half the battle, isn't it? You have this natural sort of authority. Presence. When you come into a room, people stop what they're doing and wait for you to speak.'

'Yeah, right.' Miranda grabbed some Cheddar, Stilton and goat's cheese and held out the packets for Kath to approve. Kath shrugged and Miranda dropped them all into the trolley.

'They *do*! And you do make the right decisions, don't you? Your business is going from strength to strength, your house is like something out of a magazine, you found a wonderful school for Anna . . . '

'Business is mostly non-stop stress and I live with a man who seems to hate me.'

'He doesn't hate you. You know how you love to exaggerate.'

'Kath. We haven't had sex for over two months. Actually – it's nearly three. Not since my last trip to Milan.'

'Well, we're all so tired. You said yourself—'

'No, it's not that. He doesn't—' Her eyes suddenly filled with tears. 'He doesn't – want – to – touch me. He looks at me like – like I'm a – a bit of shit on his shoe. No.' She laughed, rubbing at her eyes with the heel of her hand. 'No – he has some respect for shit. At

155

least manure's organic and recyclable. You can spread it round your plants and it'll do some good. Sometimes he comes into a room and he looks surprised, as if he can't imagine what on earth I'm doing there in the same space as him.'

'Oh, Manda . . .' Kath pushed aside the trolley to hug her. 'It'll be all right, I'm sure it will. You'll see.' A woman coughed pointedly near them and penned them in with her trolley, then made a show of leaning over to reach the cheese.

'I'm so sorry,' said Kath, quickly moving their trolley aside, then she and Miranda caught the woman's expression and both laughed as she sniffed and moved away.

'God, did you see? That'll make the local paper – Lesbians in Supermarket Shock!' Miranda looked round, the laugh suddenly stopped in its tracks. 'Where's Anna?'

'Gone to get the ketchup.' Kath frowned. 'She'll be back in a tick.'

'But she's been ages.'

'It's only a couple of minutes. You stay here in case she comes back and I'll whizz round and look for her.'

'No. You stay, I'll look.'

Miranda walked briskly up the aisle to the end and looked along the supermarket. No sign. Turned into the next one, trying to peer through the shoppers and their trolleys, speeding up now, calling Anna's name. Pushed past people, banging into them, blurting excuse-mes and sorrys. The next aisle now, starting to run, telling herself not to panic. Images flooded her mind: the toddler who was abducted from a shopping centre by older children then murdered, the girl who was raped in a supermarket toilet. She started to pray, the atheist's last resort: *Please, God, please – let her be fine – let her be just in the next aisle and I'll do whatever you want – I'll be good – I promise to be good – I'll give more money to charity – I won't snap at my mother on the phone – I'll try harder with Simon, I promise – please God, please.*

The next aisle included chocolate and confectionery. Anna was staring at the Pick 'n' Mix selection, carefully placed at child height, completely transfixed as if under hypnosis. She was holding a bottle of tomato ketchup.

'Anna!'

Anna looked up, startled to see her mother bearing down on her at some speed. Miranda scooped her into her arms, then crouched down next to her.

'Here you are! I thought you were lost.'

'I'm not lost.'

'No, but I thought you were. You must stay in sight of me and Auntie Kath all the time.'

'But she asked me to get the ketchup!' Anna protested. 'Look, I got it!'

'I know, darling, well done. But just stick with us now. Like glue, OK?'

'OK.' Anna touched Miranda's cheek. 'Are you sad, Mummy?'

'No, course not – just got a bit of a runny nose.'

'Oh. Mummy? You know how it's a holiday and everything?' Anna eyed the sweets.

Miranda wiped her nose and kissed her daughter's cheek.

'Go on, then. Just a few. Let's fetch Auntie Kath and pick out some for Polly and Luke, too. But no toffees – they're too bad for your teeth.'

Splitting up

'Well, I don't know what the rest of you are up to, but Anna and I are going for a walk along the coastal path,' Simon announced as it was coming up to lunchtime.

'Shall I come too?' Miranda ignored the fact that Simon hadn't issued any kind of invitation. 'We could take a picnic.'

'Sure, come if you want. It's a free country.' He zipped up his fleece. 'Can you be ready to go in ten minutes? By which I mean ten minutes, not half an hour. There's no need to faff about doing your make-up. No-one cares what you look like, you know.'

'Charming. I don't want the seagulls vomiting at the sight of me, though, if it's all right with you. Plus it'll take me a little while to get a picnic together.'

'I can do that.'

'Will you? Are you sure?'

'Yes, I'm not completely incapable.'

'No-one's saying you are. OK – so . . . great – can you do some sandwiches and fruit? There are biscuits in the pantry. And maybe raw carrot sticks? There's plenty of cheese. Bottled water's in the fridge. Oh, and if you want coffee, I brought a Thermos – it's in the—'

'We're not taking a ten-course banquet and a butler, Miranda. Why do you have to turn everything into such a palaver the whole time? It's only a bloody walk!' He stomped out.

Miranda made a face at Kath and mouthed, 'See?'

'What's up with Saint Simon?' Rob laughed. 'His halo's slipped a bit this morning, hasn't it? Jeez.'

'We all have our off days.' Kath started clearing away the coffee mugs.

'Right. Some of us more than others. Some might call it an off day and some might call it being fucking rude for no reason.' Rob stood up. 'Well, Tam, given that His Holiness clearly doesn't want us tagging along, shall we shoot off for a drive round? Find ourselves a decent pub for lunch? Anyone else want to come? Manda – sure you don't want some time out?'

Miranda shook her head.

'Well, who could compete with the many temptations of a fun outing with Mr Jolly?'

'Not helpful, Rob, thank you. I'd better get ready.' She ran upstairs.

'What about you two? Up for a pint?'

Joe met Kath's eye.

'No, you go off and have fun,' he said. 'I could do with a lazy day, to be honest.'

'OK. Dad?'

'No, thank you. I believe I'll stay here, too. I have some reports to read.'

'Oh, Dad, you're not really going to work, are you?' Kath moved up the sofa towards him. 'You're on holiday. You should be relaxing. Why don't you go?'

'I am *not* on holiday, Kathryn. I am on *compulsory* sick leave. I have plenty of work to do. Just because I can't use my right hand, I can still read.'

'Yes, of course, but why don't you take the chance to get out and about, enjoy the sea air and . . .' She fizzled out, seeing Giles's expression. 'Well, whatever you think's best.'

'Quite.' He looked down at the newspaper folded on his lap. 'Unless you're saying you'd rather have me out of the way?'

'No. No, of course not. I was just . . . please stay. We want you to stay.'

Giles nodded once and looked away again.

Staying behind

Joe was kicking a ball around the garden with Polly and Luke, while Kath heated up some of Miranda's

160

chicken soup for their lunch. She went into the sitting room to find Giles. He was poring over a thick stack of papers.

'Dad? How are you doing? Fancy some soup for lunch?'

'I'd love some, thank you.'

'It's really quite warm outside. We thought we might eat out on the patio.'

'Righto. I'll join you shortly.'

They ate at the garden table. Luke and Polly were messing around, slurping their soup noisily. Kath caught Giles's expression.

'Do try to eat nicely, children,' she said, sitting up a little straighter in her chair.

'Grandpa, does your arm really hurt a lot-a lot-a lot?' Polly clanged her spoon into her bowl loudly.

'Sometimes,' he nodded, carefully raising a spoonful of soup left-handed. 'But the doctor gave me some tablets to make it less painful.'

'Did you cry when it got broke?'

'*Broken.* No.'

Polly tore up her bread into little pieces and dropped them into her soup and mashed them around.

'You must be ever so brave then.'

He smiled.

'Not especially. But grown-up men don't cry.'

'I saw Daddy cry. And he's a grown-up.'

Joe shifted in his seat, frowning.

'When did you see me cry, Poll?'

'When Uncle Jim died and I came into the kitchen and you and Mummy were there and you—'

'Oh, yeah. Right. People do cry when someone dies, Poll.'

She nodded.

'Yes. But why do they? Does it hurt, like when I fell over in the playground?' She turned to Giles and held out her leg towards him. 'I had a really big scab here on my knee. And then I picked it off and it started bleeding again.'

'Don't talk about scabs while we're eating, Polly,' Kath said. 'Anyway, yes, it is a bit like that, only it's on the inside rather than the outside and when you have pain on the inside it makes you feel very sad. And sometimes it hurts for a long, long time.'

'*Why* does it?'

'I think this one might make rather a good lawyer, Kathryn. She's certainly persistent in her enquiries,' Giles said.

'She must take after you.' Kath turned back to Polly. 'Well, I think it goes on hurting because you miss the person and you know you won't be able to see them any more. Remember how sad you were when your hamster died?'

'Yes, but then we got Geronimo instead.' She turned to Giles. 'He's our budgie.' Polly tilted her head on one side and prodded one of her sodden bits of bread with

162

her spoon. 'But if you didn't like somebody all that much and then they died, you wouldn't miss them and it wouldn't hurt, would it?'

Giles laughed.

'Quite. You're a sharp young lady.'

'No, I don't think that's true.' Kath frowned, speaking quietly and apparently directing her remarks to her soup bowl. 'I think even if you had a bad relationship with someone, especially if it were someone you'd tried to be close to, and then they died, it would be extremely painful. Maybe even worse, in a way, because you'd have lost any hope of making the relationship better.' She fiddled with the crust of her bread. 'At least while they're still alive, there's some sort of chance . . . Anyway, that's what I think. Does anyone want seconds of soup? Bread? Polly, don't keep messing about with it. Eat up, Buttercup, OK? There's a good girl.'

Polly switched her spoon to her left hand and tried to eat her soup, spilling most of it down her front.

'Grandpa, it's really hard having to eat back to front, isn't it? I bet you spill things the whole time!'

Up to the cliff

Miranda, Simon and Anna went through the gate at the bottom of the garden; to the right lay the steps down to the beach, but they now turned left, following the narrow rocky path that climbed steeply to the cliffs. At the top the coastal path snaked around the headland then followed the course of the shore, jinking in with each small cove or curving like a broad grin above a wide bay.

Up on the cliff, it was breezy but the sky was clear and the sun was shining. Beside the path the grass was close-cropped and dry, so there was room for them to walk alongside each other if they chose. Simon set off at a brisk pace until Anna begged him to slow down, tugging at the edge of his fleece and making him laugh. Above, the gulls hung in the air, almost motionless, or wheeled round and down to the waves in leisurely arcs, taking their time.

'Isn't it a beautiful day?' Miranda said.

'It's the most beautiful day ever!' Anna walked in a zigzag, stopping frequently, now to look up at the gulls, now down at the path, the grass, the tiny plants crouching low against the wind.

'Mum?'

'Hmm-mm?'

'You know Tamsin?'

'Ye-e-e-s? What about her?'

'Did you see she's got a ruby in her belly button?'

'Yes, I did.'

'Did you see it, Dad?' Anna traced circles in the grass with her foot. 'It's really pretty . . . '

'No, I didn't.'

'Do you think that maybe I could—'

'No!' Miranda and Simon spoke together. They turned to each other, suddenly laughing. Miranda smiled, then looked away, as if she'd shared a moment of unexpected intimacy with a complete stranger.

'Stop laughing at me!' Anna flailed at them both, then broke into a run. Miranda and Simon quickly gave chase and Simon caught up with her after just a few paces. He held her arms.

'Quick! Tickle her! Show no mercy!'

Miranda put on an evil-sounding cackle, curving her fingers like talons. Together, they collapsed into a laughing heap, all tickling and teasing each other, then falling back, breathless, looking up at the bright sky.

'Is it time for lunch yet?' Miranda asked. 'I'm hungry.'

'We've only been going five minutes. You're *always* hungry. You must have a tapeworm.'

'Mummy's got wo-o-o-r-or-ms! Mummy's got wo-o-o-o-o-r-m-s!'

'I probably have. So you'd better hurry up and feed me or they'll come crawling out and they'll slither all over you looking for lunch!'

Anna shrieked and rolled away.

'Now, come on.' Simon stood up and checked his watch. 'Let's keep going for another fifteen, twenty minutes at least, then we can stop.'

'Oh, go on, can't we eat now?' Miranda looked up at him.

'I'm sta-a-a-a-a-a-a-r-ving, Dad!'

'No, you're not.'

'I am!' Anna clutched her tummy and lay back on the grass. 'I'll starve to death if I don't have a picnic right now, I can tell.'

'Me too! I'm staaaaaaarving, too.' Miranda hammed it up dramatically, sprawling out on the grass next to Anna. 'Oh, please can we eat, dear, lovely Simon, please can we? And then there won't be so much to carry.'

Simon took off his small rucksack and set it on the ground.

'How on earth would you two cope if you ever actually had to go without for more than ten minutes?'

'We wouldn't.' Miranda rolled onto her side, then plucked a piece of grass to tickle Anna under her chin.

A small favour

Back at the house, Joe and Kath cleared away the lunch dishes while the children played in the garden.

Joe nuzzled up to his wife's neck.

'Don't suppose I can lure you upstairs for a bit of R and R?'

She turned to kiss him lightly on the lips.

'What about the kids?'

'Your dad can watch them.'

'When he has vital reports to read? The crossword to complete? You *are* kidding?'

He sighed.

'Go on, *ask* him. He never babysits. It won't kill him for once. Just for an hour. Or three.'

'What would I say? "Dad, can you mind the kids while I have sex with my husband?"'

'Yeah. Why not?' Joe put both his arms around her, pulling her close. 'We're allowed.'

'I couldn't possibly!' She covered her face with her hands.

'Right. I'll ask him.' He broke free.

'No, no! You can't!'

'I certainly can.'

'OK, OK. Let me do it. I'll say we want a nap.'

He looked down at her.

'Coward. No backing out now?'

She shook her head and went out to the garden. Giles was still sitting outside, head tilted back, eyes closed.

'Um. Dad?'

'Mmm-mm?'

'I was just wondering . . . if . . . well, not if you're tired, obviously . . . it's just I was thinking . . . well, we both were really . . . if you might . . . it was only a thought . . . but you know . . . Joe's very tired, he's been working really hard . . . and the thing is . . .'

Giles opened his eyes.

'Could you possibly come to the point?'

'Yes. I am.' She cleared her throat. 'Yes. Right. Well, you see, what it is . . .'

Joe came out and stood by her side.

'We'd really appreciate it if you could keep an eye on the kids for an hour, Giles.'

'Are you going out?'

'No. We'd just like a little bit of time together, that's all. Alone. You know.'

'For a nap,' Kath added.

'Oh, I see. In the middle of the day? Well, why not? Why not indeed?'

'Thank you,' said Joe.

'Yes, thank you, Daddy!' Kath quickly bent to kiss his cheek.

'Ah – now what am I supposed to do with them?' Giles asked as Kath and Joe turned to go back inside. 'I mean, are you expecting me to – to *play* with them or something? My arm is rather—'

'You don't need to do anything.' Joe gave his wife a small push to stop her returning to become embroiled in elaborate instructions. 'Just don't let them go out the back gate down to the beach on their own. If they get very bored or start whining, whack in a video for them. There's a stack next to the telly. OK?'

Giles nodded.

'Don't be too long, will you?'

Choosing favourites

'Can we come here next year?' Anna asked, lying back with her head against Simon.

'Are you having a good time then?'

Anna nodded vigorously as she tried to say 'yes' through a mouthful of sandwich.

'Wouldn't you rather we came on holiday just the three of us?' Simon opened the bottle of water and passed it to Anna.

She wrinkled her nose, then struggled to lift the bottle to her lips without spilling it. Miranda steadied it for her.

'It's nice for you to have Polly and Luke here, isn't it? Even though they're not as grown-up as you.'

'I don't mind playing with Polly, actually, even though she's only six, but Luke's still practically a baby, isn't he?'

'Well, he is only three, Anna. You weren't so different at that age.'

Anna looked highly sceptical and Miranda laughed. 'You're right – you were never a baby.'

'I like being with the different grown-ups.'

Miranda looked at Simon, who delved once more into the rucksack. He passed a piece of kitchen roll to each of them.

'Really? Who do you like best then?'

'Oh, Simon – that's just silly.'

'Why is it? I'm interested. Anna?'

Anna sat cross-legged and her brow furrowed, deep in thought.

'Well, actually, I like Auntie Kath and Uncle Joe best . . . '

'Of course you do. You've known them the longest.'

'Then Uncle Rob—'

'He's not your uncle!' Miranda and Simon said together.

'You said he was Auntie Kath's brother, so why isn't he?'

'Well, Auntie Kath's not really your auntie, Anna, you know that.' Miranda took a swig of water. 'It's a sort of honorary title, like—'

'What's honorary?'

'In this case, it's to show Kath that you think of her as being like a real, blood auntie,' Simon joined in. 'It's like a privilege. You know what that is?' Anna nodded.

'So, why do you like Rob so much then?' Simon continued, casting a glance at Miranda.

Anna thought for a moment.

'He's not like most grown-ups. Even though he's really tall and everything, he likes playing. This morning, he gave me a horseback ride all up and down the hall for ages and ages and then he did Polly and then Luke. He didn't stop after one minute and say he was tired and he didn't mind even though he got all dusty.'

'You're a bit old to be playing horsey now, aren't

you?' Simon doled out an apple each.

'I can! I'm on holiday!' She bit into her apple. 'And another thing, I told him all my best knock-knock jokes and he really laughed. Properly, not just for pretend.'

Simon snorted.

'Well, that figures.'

'And what about Tamsin?' Miranda asked. 'Do you like her?'

'She's very pretty. I like her hair – it's really straight and shiny and blonde. And she's very skinny, isn't she, Mum?'

'Mmm.'

'But she doesn't like children.'

'Of course she does. What makes you say that?' Miranda sat up more.

'Because she won't give us piggybacks or play with us.' Anna crunched on through her apple. 'And she doesn't know how to talk to us. She puts on a silly voice as if we're babies.'

'And what about Polly and Luke's grandpa?' Simon asked. 'Do you like Giles?'

Anna nibbled carefully all around the edge of her apple core, then shrugged.

'Don't know.'

Miranda and Simon both frowned.

'What do you mean, you don't know?' Miranda leaned in closer.

'I mean I don't know *yet*,' Anna pronounced firmly.

'I think he's a little bit sad actually. And he doesn't talk very much and he doesn't know how to play. I'll have to tell you later once I know him a bit better.' She stood up and looked out to sea. 'Can we go and see the Mermaid again later? When the tide's out? I need to see if she has a proper tail and I have to make a special wish.'

'Maybe. We'll see how the day goes. And it depends on the tide,' Simon said. 'What's your wish, Anna-Banana?'

She half-turned towards them.

'I'm not telling, it's a secret. And don't call me Anna-Banana, it's a stupid baby name.'

Simon rolled his eyes at Miranda and she smiled back.

'All right, Miss Lloyd-Miller, have it your way!' He started gathering up the debris from the picnic. 'Come on, let's walk to the end of the next headland.'

Seize the day

Kath and Joe ran up to their room and quickly got undressed. Joe leapt under the covers and held back the other side of the quilt for Kath.

'Quick, quick! Get in!'

She slipped under the quilt and snuggled up close to him.

'I can't believe we're doing this. Bed in the middle of the day, it's such a treat.'

'See, it wasn't such a crummy idea of Rob's to ask your dad along, was it?'

Kath wrinkled her nose.

'Do you think he knows we're doing it or do you think he thinks we're just having a quiet cuddle?'

'K, I don't know and I don't care. I'm sure he understands that even married couples have to have sex occasionally.' Joe started caressing his way down Kath's body.

'Joe?'

'Hmm-mm.' He kissed her neck, her breasts. 'I'm concentrating.'

'You don't think it's a bit weird, do you? I don't really like the idea of being rude while my dad's downstairs knowing what we're up to.'

'Don't think about it then.'

'But I am thinking about it.'

'We're not "up to" anything weird. We're not fifteen, are we?'

Kath stared straight up at the ceiling.

'Maybe we should wait until later?'

'Oh, no. Not later.' He took her hand and guided it down below the covers. 'I can't wait until later, see?'

She smiled and turned towards him, returned his kisses.

Joe pulled Kath on top of him and they both sighed softly.

'It's been too long, wife.'

Suddenly there was a long-drawn-out wail from

downstairs, followed by loud sobbing. Kath froze.

'Oh, Joe – I should—'

'No, you shouldn't. It'll be fine. Let your dad sort it out. He's perfectly capable. That's the whole point of getting someone else to babysit.'

'But what if something awful's happened?'

The crying continued.

'Then your dad'll come up and get us. You know what Luke's like. By the time you get downstairs, he'll be grinning away with his jaws wrapped round a choc-olate biscuit. Come on, K. Just relax.' He started to move once more.

There was another wail, a terrible, plaintive sound, like the moan of an air-raid siren.

Kath struggled to move.

'I'm sorry but I'm going down.'

'He's *fine*.'

'He's *not*.'

'*Muuuuuuu-uuuu-mm-eeeeeeeeeeeeeee*!' The sound of small, chubby legs gamely clambering up the stairs.

'Quick!' Kath pulled away from him.

Joe groaned and turned onto his side.

'For God's sake! Just five minutes' peace, that's all I ask.'

There was a bang on their door, then Luke charged in and climbed onto the bed.

'Muuu-mm-eeee!' He started crying again.

'What is it, Lukey, hmm?' Kath folded him close for

a cuddle, kissing his tear-stained cheeks.

He gulped between sobs, unable to tell them.

Then Polly came running up the stairs and hurtled into the room.

'It wasn't me, Dad!'

'All right, Poll. Tell me what happened.'

'We were playing "it" and Luke fell over the back step and hurt himself. It wasn't me.' Polly climbed onto the bed as well. 'Why are you in bed? Are you sleepy? I'm not. I'm never sleepy.'

'We're just having a cuddle. And maybe a small nap. Go on, you two. Go off and play.'

Luke pouted and laid his head against Kath. Polly leaned against her father.

'We're bored. Can't you come downstairs now?'

'No,' said Joe firmly. 'You've got Grandpa down there. Let Mum and Dad have a bit of a rest, eh?'

'Grandpa doesn't like us.'

'Oh, that's not true!' Kath looked at her daughter.

Polly spread out on the bed.

'It *is* true. He never plays with us.'

'Oof, Poll. Budge up a bit.' Joe shoved her over.

'Your grandpa's hurt his arm very badly.' Kath tucked Polly's hair back behind her ears. 'You can't expect him to play with you just now. You must try to be extra-specially nice to him.'

'He never plays with us in any case. Even when his arm isn't hurting.' Polly lay on her back and started cycling her legs in the air. Luke pulled away from Kath to try to copy her.

'Well, not all grown-ups have the energy to play with children,' Joe said. 'It doesn't mean he doesn't like you. I'm sure he likes you a lot.'

'Yes.' Kath pulled the covers around herself and tried to sit up. 'Of course he does. And he loves you both very much, OK?'

Polly made a non-committal face, then clambered off the bed again.

'Are there any little chocolate eggs left?'

'What happened to all the ones you collected yesterday?'

Polly shrugged.

'Don't know. They got lost.'

'You mean you *ate* them all, Piglet.'

'It's not fair. I hardly had *any*. Oh please can I have one, please can I?'

Joe and Kath turned to each other and sighed.

'Try again later?' she said.

He nodded.

'Children.' He shook his head. 'The greatest form of contraception ever devised. How on earth do people get round to having six or seven kids?'

'Do you want seven kids, Dad?' Polly asked. 'I don't want them if they're all going to be like Luke, silly crybabies.'

'That's enough, Polly,' Kath said. 'Don't be mean.'

176

'No, thanks. No more children – you two are as much joy as I can handle. Right, shove off, everybody. Kids – downstairs. No arguing. We'll be down in two minutes. Now! Go, go, go!'

Wishes

'Tide's out, folks!' Joe came in from the garden. 'Who wants to go down to the beach?'

'Me! Me!' Anna and Polly started jumping up and down.

'Me! Me!' Rob followed suit.

Anna ran into the kitchen and started tugging at Miranda.

'Mum, you have to come and wish on the Mermaid – the tide's out. You have to come right now! Quickly!'

Joe went round the house, calling the others.

The tide was almost completely out, the sand still wet from the withdrawing waves. Joe pointed it out to Polly.

'See that, Poll? That means you can tell that the tide's still on its way out, not on its way in, right? So it's safe to walk out to the rock.'

The children were wearing wellies, but they all wanted to take them off so they could splash barefoot through the water, where it still lapped against the base of the rock. Simon had brought his camera with him and he took pictures of the children as they tugged off their boots and left them lying on the sand. Kath and Joe gathered them up and set them at the bottom of the steps to pick up on their return, three little pairs in a row, blue and pink and red.

'I'll stay here and watch.' Giles seated himself on a large flat rock, looking out to sea.

'Oh, come on, Giles, we promise not to splash you!' Miranda teased. 'Don't you want to come and make a wish on the magic Mermaid?'

'Does she fix multimillion-pound lawsuits?'

'I suspect you may have to ask extra nicely.'

He stood up again and joined the others.

Luke, trying to run through the shallows to keep up with Anna and Polly, suddenly fell headlong, face first into the water. It was barely more than an inch deep, but he was taken by surprise. Joe reached him almost at once and picked him up, brushing the wet sand off his face.

Kath ran up to her husband and son, wanting to take Luke back to the house to dry him off, but Joe insisted on going back with him himself.

'You go on with the others. Go on, you're always missing out.'

As they drew closer to the rock, Miranda bent down to speak to Anna.

'See – she has got a tail after all.' She pointed out the

way the rock thickened at one side. 'Well, sort of.'

Around the base of the Mermaid, the water was slightly deeper.

'Should have taken our shoes off, too, eh?' Miranda leaned against Kath for a minute as she balanced to pull off her loafers, then Kath did the same. Miranda placed hers carefully on a small ledge of rock.

Polly ran forward and touched the base.

'I'm making a wish!'

'That doesn't count. That's not the Mermaid,' Anna said. 'It's just the rock she's sitting on.'

'It does count!'

'No, it doesn't, does it, Mummy? That's not the special magic part.'

'I think it's all equally magic, Anna.' Miranda caught sight of Polly's trembling lower lip.

Anna shook her head firmly.

'No, it isn't. You have to touch her — her *hair* while you wish.' She pointed upwards. 'That bit up there. Or else it's not real magic and your wish won't come true.'

Rob came over, laughing. He picked up Polly, twirled her round, then lifted her up high.

'There you go, Polly-Wolly Doodle.' He stood closer to the rock. 'Can you reach?'

Polly stretched out and touched the rock with her fingertips.

'I did it! I wished!'

'Anyone else for a leg-up?' Looking at Anna now, turning towards her.

'Anna!' Miranda called out. 'Come round this way. I think you might be able to climb up.'

Simon lowered his camera and quickly joined them.

'I'll give you a lift up.'

'No, Dad. I want to climb up all by myself.' Anna scrambled up the lower part of the rock.

'It's still too wet and slippy.'

'Let me *do* it.'

'Well, you be careful now, OK?'

Miranda stood immediately beneath her.

'It's OK, Simon. I'm right here.'

A sudden peal of giggles as Tamsin was lifted up by Rob.

'Have you made a wish, baby?'

'Can you go closer? I can't reach.' Her fingers touched the rock. 'Done it!' She smiled down at him. 'Do you think it'll come true?'

Anna found herself a foothold and awkwardly pulled herself up, then she edged onto a narrow shelf of rock next to the Mermaid's tail. Carefully, she wedged her foot into a tiny toehold further up.

'Ooh – careful, Anna!' Miranda stood even closer, practically hugging the rock beneath.

Anna stretched up, fingertips reaching above her head for the Mermaid's magic hair. She scrunched her eyes tight shut for two, three seconds, laying her cheek flat against the cold face of the rock.

I wish I could be a real mermaid . . .

'Are you done?' Miranda called up.

'Yes!' Anna half-turned to try to get down again, but now the ledge seemed much further away beneath her feet. 'Mu-um?'

Rob strode to their side.

'Hey – just jump off and I'll catch you!' He spread his arms out.

'Promise?'

'I promise. I won't let you fall, honestly.'

'Really and truly promise? Cross your heart and hope to die?'

'C'mon, darling.' Miranda sighed. 'Jump if you're jumping.'

'Cross my heart and hope to die!' Rob shouted.

Anna pushed off, leaping out clear across a slice of sky and sea-slicked sand. Rob caught her easily and swung her round, then lifted her high up, up and onto his shoulders, holding her on by her legs.

'Can I go again? That was brilliant!'

'We should be heading back now.' Simon hovered close by Rob's elbow. 'It's getting cold.'

'Yes, and I have to get your supper on, Anna.'

'I'm not hungry.'

'Not now, maybe, but you will be by the time it takes to do the sausages and potatoes.'

'I won't. I won't be hungry for ages and ages and ages!' Anna gurgled with laughter as Rob turned in circle after circle in the wet sand.

'Look,' he pointed out. 'The tide's completely out now. We should have waited a few minutes.'

'Get down now, Anna.' Simon pulled at one of her legs. 'You're too old for piggyback rides.'

'Yes. And you'll do poor Rob a mischief,' Miranda added. 'He's not as strong as he looks, you know.'

'Aren't I? Bet you I could pick you up at the same time. Anna's light as a feather.' Rob galloped away from them across the sands, with Anna bouncing wildly on his shoulders, shrieking with fear and delight.

'I really need to make a start on supper,' Miranda told Simon, turning away from Rob.

'You go back then. I'll stay with Anna.'

Rob came charging back towards them.

'Mum!' Anna called down from her perch. 'Did you make a wish yet? Everyone has to make a wish.'

A wish? Jesus, I don't need a wish, I need a bloody miracle. Miranda stepped close to the rock once more and pulled herself up onto the narrow ledge. Now that she saw it up close, she thought for a moment she could discern the rough features of a face in the planes and fissures of the rock just a few inches from her own face. A wistful face. She cupped her hand gently behind the Mermaid's head, laid her hand on the hair as if she were stroking it.

Please, just let everything be all right.

'You go now, Dad!'

'All right, bossyboots.' Simon moved forward and laid his hand firmly against the rock. For a moment his brow furrowed as if he were concentrating on a puzzling dilemma.

I wish . . .

Then he withdrew his hand and turned away.

'And you!' Anna beat a light tattoo on the top of Rob's head. He looked up at her and saluted. 'Everyone has to have a go!'

'Yes, ma'am! Born to command – can't think where you got that from . . .' He cast a sidelong glance at Miranda. 'OK, what shall I wish then?'

'I don't know. It's got to be your wish. And it's got to be a secret. But you can tell me if you like – you'll have to whisper.'

'Hmm.' Rob's eyes briefly met Miranda's. 'Now, let me see . . .'

'Hurry up!' Anna pulled his ears.

'Ow! Didn't anyone ever tell you to be kind to your horse? Be gentle with me or I'll chuck you into the sea.'

He stretched up with one hand, towards the Mermaid's head, the other still holding Anna's leg to keep her steady. He patted the rock, then laid his hand flat for a moment.

I wish . . .

He turned then and looked up at Anna.

'Do you think my wish will come true?'

She nodded.

'It will but only if you wished really, really hard. And you have to believe that the Mermaid's really magic or it won't work.'

Miranda folded her arms.

'I'm going back.' She spoke to Simon. 'Don't be too long, hmm? It's getting cold.' She called across the sand. 'Kath? Coming?'

'Yes. Polly! We're going now.'

'Why are we? Can't I stay? Oh please can I?'

'We'll bring her back,' Simon said. 'Don't worry. You go ahead.'

'Mummy, you didn't wish!' Polly shouted.

Kath ran back and touched the rock briefly, closed her eyes.

I wish . . .

'And Grandpa!' Polly skipped along the sand towards Giles.

'Yes, Giles. What about you?' Miranda turned to speak to him. 'Or is there nothing on Earth you wish for? I suppose you have everything already?'

Giles laid his left hand against the rock.

'There are all too many things I wish for,' he said, looking back at her. 'But perhaps I'll confine myself to just one for now.'

I wish . . .

Kath and Miranda walked back across the damp sands.

'Glad you came?'

'Mmm, of course.' Miranda looked back over her shoulder and paused to wave. 'Why wouldn't I be? Anna's having a wonderful time.'

'She is, isn't she? She seems really, I don't know, relaxed today. I mean, she's always so grown-up, most of the time I forget she's only eight, but now – capering about with Rob and Polly and being silly, she was just like a happy, excited kid.'

Miranda nodded.

'Yes, I guess you can trust Rob to bring out the inner infant in anyone.'

'Well, that's not such a bad thing, is it? Who wants to be a grown-up the whole time?'

'Too true. Certainly not me. You're right – Anna is a little too serious. She spends too much time around us and not enough with other kids.'

'Have you thought of having another baby?'

Miranda snorted.

'What? Now? After all this time? Wouldn't be much of a playmate, would it?'

'Noooo, maybe not at first, but still . . .'

'Besides, we're getting on too badly even to consider it right now. I don't imagine a baby's the magic answer to all our problems, do you?'

Kath smiled.

'Maybe you should have wished for one on the Mermaid? It does work, you know, if you really and truly wish hard.'

'Ha ha. What did you wish for? Snazzy new kitchen? Posh granite worktops? Dishwasher that also mops the kitchen floor and brings you tea and toast in the morning?'

'Oh, bum! I didn't even think of that. I'll have to have another go tomorrow.'

'Are we allowed another go?' Miranda wondered out loud.

'Why not?'

'I'll have to check with the Oracle – Anna seems to be the expert on this wishing lark.' They reached the bottom of the rickety steps. 'So, what did you wish for then? Come on. Untold riches? Health and happiness for all time? World peace?'

Kath started to climb the steps.

'Uh-uh.' Her shoulders drooped. 'I just wished that my dad would like me more, that's all. Was that silly?' Kath kept facing ahead, but she slowed her steps.

'Oh, Kath . . .' Miranda reached forward to squeeze her friend's arm. 'He does like you. And he loves you, of course he does.'

At the top, Kath turned round, then slowly shook her head.

'Well, one would hope so. And yet . . . you know, I really don't think he does. I'm not being victimy about it. Or paranoid. At least I don't think I am. It's just most of the time it feels as if there's this gaping great chasm between us and I'm desperately trying to find some way across from my side to his and he . . . he . . .'

'What?'

'He's just sort of absorbed in his work and his view of the world but he hasn't even noticed this huge chasm is there . . . maybe because he doesn't care?' She shrugged. 'I don't know what to do about it. Perhaps there isn't anything I can do, I just have to be a grown-up and accept it?'

'But, Kath, don't you think it's partly just his generation? And his background? Upper middle class, public school, father not around for most of his childhood, chilly distant mother with no time for him – it's no wonder he's not given to hugging everyone and expressing how he feels, is it? But it doesn't mean—'

'Did you guess all that or did you know?' Kath frowned. 'I'd no idea you knew so much about Dad?'

'Oh, we had a conversation once about our respective backgrounds – ages ago, can't remember when. Anyway, the point is—'

'Wow. Dad never talks about that stuff.'

'Well, you know me – Miss Nosy; I winkled it out of him.'

Feet first

'Ooh, you're wearing Miranda's shoes!' Kath pointed down at Tamsin's feet. Tamsin had showered and changed after their walk on the beach.

'No, they're not. They're mine.' Tamsin backed away a step, as if Kath might suddenly make a grab for them. 'Perhaps she has some that are, like, a little bit similar?' Tamsin smiled. 'Actually, it was really, really naughty of me to have bought them, I, like, *sooooooooo* overspent on my credit cards last month. And I got some in red, too. Don't tell Rob, he thinks I'm hopelessly extravagant. They are bliss though, aren't they?' She turned her foot this way and that for Kath to admire them.

'Yes, they're lovely. And they definitely are Miranda's. Have a look at the inside.'

Tamsin removed one strappy aqua mule and lifted it up.

'See?' Kath said. 'Miranda Miller. I told you.'

Tamsin frowned, still not getting it.

'No, that's the designer's name, you see.' Smiling now, explaining as if Kath were not very bright. 'You know, like Jimmy Choo or Salvatore Ferragamo or . . . or . . .' She looked down at Kath's feet, currently clad in a pair of battered trainers. 'Or Dolcis or whoever.'

'Exactly. Miranda. Miranda Miller.'

Slowly, the light dawned. Kath waited, as realization finally crossed Tamsin's face.

'Miranda is Miranda *Miller*?'

Kath nodded, suddenly feeling ridiculously proud, as if Miranda were her daughter.

'Oh, but I really, really *love* her stuff! I'm, like, sooooooooo embarrassed! And she has that heavenly little shop in Marylebone!'

Kath nodded again.

Miranda swept in, carrying four dirty mugs.

'Do you think the Y chromosome makes men genetically unable to clear away their own coffee cups?' She strode across to the dishwasher, then saw that it was full of dirty things already. Sighed, put in detergent, and set the machine going. Dumped the mugs in the sink and started to wash them.

'What time shall we have supper tonight for the grown-ups? Tamsin, we're doing sausages and mash like the kids had – is that OK with you?'

'You're really Miranda Miller?' Tamsin was wide-eyed.

'What?'

'I just told Tamsin who you are.'

'So?' Miranda looked down at Tamsin's feet at once, and smiled, nodding her approval. 'Oh, right. You must have got those very recently – they're only just in.' She dried her hands and came closer. 'Nice feet, by the way. And good varnish. Goes well with the mules. Really sets them off.'

Tamsin giggled.

'How are you finding them?'

'Oh, they're complete bliss. I absolutely love them!'

'Can you walk in them OK? Are they comfortable?'

'This is the first time I've worn them. I don't care anyway. I take taxis like the *whole* time if I'm not driving, I'm really, really naughty.'

'Kath's just the opposite: comfort is all – now I only give her the loafers and pumps.'

'Miranda tried to get me to wear those really high-heeled ones, the satin ones with the little feathers on the straps, have you seen them? By the time we got home, Joe had to carry me from the car to the house.'

'And I can't wear them or I'd be even more of a giraffe than I am already.'

'Oh, but I'd just die for those! They're such bliss! I was planning to go back and get them next week.'

'Come to my Marylebone shop rather than to one of the concessions. Give me a call first, make sure I'm there.'

Rob came in.

'Any coffee on the go, girls?'

Kath bobbed up at once and crossed to the kettle.

'I'll give you a special discount,' Miranda told Tamsin, then cast a sideways glance at Rob. 'I guess you're practically family now really, aren't you?'

Tamsin smiled and giggled. Rob raised one eyebrow.

Reaching out

Through the wall, Miranda could hear the rhythmic creaking of bedsprings from Rob and Tamsin's room. Well, wasn't this fun? La-la-la, if only she'd thought to bring earplugs. Maybe Kath had some spares, because of Joe's legendary snoring. She pressed her head firmly into the pillow. Simon suddenly snuggled up to her, spooning her from behind as naturally as if he did this every night.

'It's been a good day today, hasn't it?'

'Yes. It really has.' *What's brought this on?*

'So you're glad you came then after all? Do you know, I don't think you've mentioned work once today?'

'No, I haven't even given it a thought.' *Though now that you've brought it up, it's reminded me that I have to do about a thousand e-mails ready to send tomorrow. Cheers.* 'Anna's loving it here. It's great to see the kids running around in the fresh air so much. And thank God the rain seems to have taken a day off at least.'

'Yeah, it was a really beautiful day.' His arm snaked around her waist. 'Tired?'

'Mmm. A bit.' She patted his arm. 'You?'

'I'm fine.' He kissed the back of her shoulder. 'I'm sorry I was a bit . . . y'know . . . this morning. Hmm?'

'That's OK. I don't think I'd have won any prizes for charm either. We're just tired.'

'But not too tired?'

Miranda turned to face him. Tilted her mouth towards his. They kissed softly, then more deeply as she pressed closer to him.

'Take these off, hmm?' Simon stroked the front of her slippery satin pyjamas, then started to undo the buttons.

'I'm a bit cold.'

'Live dangerously. I'll warm you up.'

She awkwardly shucked off the trouser bottoms, kicking them to the end of the bed. Simon slid his hand down her back.

'Your bum's freezing.'

'Wait till you feel my feet.'

'Oh no, not the feet! Not the feet! *No*!'

'Please! Oh, *please*!'

'OK, but not on my legs.' He reached down to clasp one chilly foot between his hands and rubbed it briskly. 'How do you get them so cold? You can't be human.'

'I'm not. I am of the warrior race Vrek. For two point seven hours a day, I must place my extremities in your primitive domestic refrigeration units in order to survive.'

'I knew I should have been more suspicious about your green tongue.'

'Too late, Earthman.' Miranda darted her tongue back and forth, then slid it softly between his lips.

His hand moved down to the curve of her tummy, slipped between her legs, not wasting time in teasing her but touching her at once in the way he knew aroused her. She pushed harder against him and kissed the hollow of his neck.

'We haven't done this for ages,' he said.

'Ages and ages.'

'Shall I . . . ?'

'Hang on, where are the condoms? Did you bring any—?'

He carried on caressing her.

'Come on . . .' Easing himself gently on top of her now.

'Simon?'

'Mmm.' His hand slipping down to fondle her.

'Wait a sec.'

'Can't we just go with the flow? Hmm?'

'*Simon*! No. We agreed.'

'You won't get pregnant anyway, you only just had your period,' he pointed out.

'True. OK, just this once, but we're not making a habit of it.' She parted her legs and guided him in.

He inhaled sharply, eyes closed, then he looked down at her and smiled.

After so many years together, sex was no longer a source of great surprises for either of them, but it was generally highly satisfactory for both. Like a gin and tonic with just the right amount of gin, it hit the spot. They knew what worked and what didn't. There was no need for extensive foreplay or seduction games: a brief bit of mutual fondling and they could crack on with the main event and, with very little effort, they could manage it so that Miranda came first and Simon shortly afterwards. Minimum expenditure of energy, but with a reliable and desirable result.

Afterwards

Simon came with a shudder and a brief groan that was somewhat louder than usual. He dipped to kiss her.

'Uh,' he sighed. 'God, that was good.'

'Certainly was.' Miranda exhaled with a satisfied sigh and swept her hair back from her face. *And about bloody time, too.* 'We don't have to leave quite so long a gap next time, do we?' She smiled, softening the implied criticism, and reached for some tissues.

'Hmm.' He rolled off and onto his back. 'We use up too much energy in arguing, that's our problem.'

And whose fault is that? Miranda managed not to say it out loud. *You're the one who usually starts it.* She clenched and unclenched her toes beneath the covers, telling herself to shut up.

'Mmm,' she said vaguely. 'Maybe we should hook ourselves up to the National Grid?' Keeping her voice light, teasing. 'Every time we have a row, we could provide power for half the kettles in north London.'

Simon nodded, pretending to consider it seriously.

'And it's renewable,' he pointed out.

'And safe,' she added.

Simon moved so she could settle into the crook of his arm and Miranda nestled her head against his shoulder, tilted her face towards his.

'This is nice,' she said. 'Being like this.'

He smiled and kissed her nose.

'You know,' she continued. 'When we're getting on like this, it feels so right and so – so normal, doesn't it? You'd think we'd be like this all the time. And then I can't remember how we manage to get ourselves into so many arguments – can you?' Miranda mused out loud, but as she turned to meet his gaze, she realized she would have done better to keep her thoughts to herself.

Simon's face clouded over and his eyes seemed cold and blank.

'Did you have to spoil the moment, Miranda? Why couldn't you just enjoy it?' He sighed loudly.

'*I was* enjoying it – I just couldn't help thinking—'

'You couldn't help thinking that a few moments of simple contentment had to be dissected then trampled on?' He pulled roughly away from her. 'Honestly!'

'That's not fair.' She sat bolt upright, tugging the duvet up around her breasts. 'It's only that we've been getting on so – so – not so well recently – and I—'

'*You* have been particularly self-absorbed of late and self-indulgently *wallowing* in stress as part of your I'm-so-important-I'm-so-busy persona you seem to be so fond of. It's not *we* anything, is it?'

'Thanks. Funny how you didn't feel the need to point out my appalling self-absorption before you decided you were in the mood for a fuck, isn't it? Cheers, Simon.'

He sniffed and said nothing, then rearranged his pillows into their final configuration before settling down to sleep.

'I'm going downstairs to make some tea.' Miranda got up and quickly pulled on her robe. Opened the wardrobe and took out her laptop in its case. 'And I'd better do my e-mails now, too. Gosh, it's just me, me, me, isn't it? Oh, yes, and if I don't do them and keep my business vaguely ticking over, we won't be able to pay the mortgage and the house will be repossessed, but – hey – that won't matter a duck's arse, will it, because at least Simon will get to revel in his absolute favourite pastime of witnessing me fuck up.'

She left and closed the door crisply but quietly behind her. Fought the urge to stomp loudly downstairs, and settled instead for a more dignified glide.

In the kitchen, Miranda put just enough water for one mug in the kettle, then noticed what she was doing – *see, he's controlling your movements even when he's not in the same room, you sad, brainwashed ninny.* She filled the kettle up to the MAX point and clicked it on. Stood leaning against the worktop, wishing she'd worn her slippers. Ten seconds later, she sighed and tipped out most of the water. Just because Simon was being a complete and utter arse didn't mean she had to act like a spoilt and wasteful slob, did it? Bloody hell. His ways had insinuated themselves into her life and now so many of them had become habits. She'd been Simonized.

Miranda looked around for a power point and phone jack for her laptop. Plenty of sockets by the worktop, but nothing for the modem. Then she noticed a crack of light under the door to the dining room. Cautiously opened the door.

Rob was sitting at the dining table, frowning at the screen of his open laptop. He was wearing faded jeans. Nothing else.

'Hey.' He smiled. 'I'm glad it's you. I heard you clanking about, but I thought it might be – someone else.'

'Hey. Did you find a phone point by any wild chance?'

He clucked his tongue and winked, gestured to the skirting board behind him.

'You go first if you like.'

'No, it's OK.' She turned back towards the kitchen. 'Do you want some tea?'

'Mmm, please.' He nodded. 'Actually – no – fancy some wine instead?'

'God, I could murder a glass.' She smacked her lips. 'Or three. After all, we haven't had a drop of alcohol for – ooh – at least two hours . . .'

Rob got up and went through to the pantry, his bare feet slapping lightly on the hard floor.

They sat opposite each other, drinking wine, nibbling cheese and crackers, composing e-mails, and sporadically exclaiming over their work.

'God, this guy's such an arsehole.' Rob took a mouthful of his wine. 'Get this – he's now saying he could sue us under the Trades Descriptions Act because his survey claims the roof needs work. The man's barking – I mean, what estate agent ever guaranteed a roof, for fuck's sake?'

'Why not rename your company Honest Rob's? "The Estate Agent Who Tells It Like It Is."'

He nodded.

'Mmm – great way to run a business: Ideal opportunity for gullible first-time buyer: botched two-bed conversion with poky kitchen and possible subsidence.'

'Overpriced, tarted-up Seventies semi with poncy pillars and tacky fake panelling in hallway.'

'Experience the sophistication of "Soho loft-living" in exclusive new development in . . . Peckham.' Rob lowered his head slowly, resting his chin on his arms on the table. 'Remind me why I'm doing this again.'

'To pay for your fabulous state-of-the-art penthouse with solid maple flooring and Philippe Starck taps?'

He scrunched up his face and pouted at her.

'That's attractive, dear.'

'I'm getting too old for this game.'

Miranda reached forward and patted him lightly on the hand.

'We're all too old for this game. Being a grown-up is a ridiculous occupation.' She stretched out her feet. 'I spend half my life engaged in activities that are almost entirely pointless. Then Anna comes back from school and I see what she's managed to achieve in a single day. She's learning *all* the time. Every day she comes back buzzing with new stuff – it's just amazing. When did you last feel *you'd* learned anything?'

'Jeez. Don't make it any worse.'

He sat up then leaned back in his chair. Drank some more of his wine. He slowly shook his head, then looked at her. Miranda returned his gaze, neither smiling nor looking away for several seconds. Then she dropped her eyes to the screen in front of her once more. Rob reached for the packet of cigarettes on the table and was about to light up.

'You're not smoking in here?'

He shrugged.

'Why not? You don't mind, do you? Don't tell me you've turned into one of those anti-smoking zealots? Why are ex-smokers always the worst?'

'Not me. Think of the children. We agreed no smoking in the house.'

'They're upstairs. It'll have cleared by the morning.'

'No. Please don't, Rob. It hangs around for ages. Go on – have it outside. Please.'

He tutted and stood up.

'All right. But you've got to come with me. If I've got to be out there freezing my nuts off, you can jolly well suffer, too.'

They huddled in the back doorway.

'It's too cold for this.' Rob inhaled deeply. 'You're a tough woman, Ms Miller.'

'Well, why aren't you wearing more clothes?' She shivered. 'No-one said you weren't allowed to put a shirt on, did they? You seem determined to show off your chest on this holiday.'

'I wasn't expecting the Board of Censors to come marching downstairs to inspect me, strangely enough.' He laughed. 'Besides – look who's talking! Don't tell me that wafer-thin wisp of silk is keeping you warm.' He stared pointedly at Miranda's nipples, erect under the thin material in the cold night air.

She folded her arms across her chest.

'I'm fine! I'm perfectly warm.' She shivered again. 'Look – when I put it on, I wasn't planning on waltzing about outside. God, please can we go in now?'

'OK, OK. In a minute.' He offered her a cigarette. 'Sure you don't want one? I hate smoking on my own.'

'Oh, go on then – but not a whole one. Give me a drag of yours. Just one puff – don't let me have any more, not even if I beg.'

He handed her his cigarette and she inhaled deeply, closing her eyes.

'Good as you remember?'

She shook her head.

'Uh-uh. Better.' She handed it back. 'And don't you dare tell anyone.'

After the ceremony

During the dancing, Miranda goes outside and starts rummaging in her handbag for her cigarettes. Where is her fucking lighter, for fuck's sake? Matches? From that awful restaurant the other day, the one with plates the size of tea trays and a menu where the chef clearly thought no dish was complete without a *coulis* or a *jus* of something or other sitting there like a stagnant pond. Somewhere in here – she squats down on the grass and tips out the contents of her bag – tissues, purse, four lipsticks (too many, even for her), two mascaras, an eyeliner pencil missing its lid, several loose swatches of fabric including one she'd spent over an hour looking for just last week, more tissues, at least one of which had spontaneously self-destructed into a thousand fragments, creating puffs of tissue dust in the bright air, a small roll of Sellotape, handbag mirror, three pens and two pencils, one with no point, a pair of scissors and a measuring tape, a travel sewing kit from some hotel, two notebooks (full), some unopened post, a dry-cleaning ticket which she had been carrying around for two weeks, her Filofax and – aha! – a book of matches. She tugs sharply at the flap, then hears a click; a small flame appears a foot in front of her face.

Rob stands beside her, cupping his hand around the flame.

Miranda leans close to light her cigarette, inhales deeply, nods a curt thank you.

'Very droll, Rob. Nice timing.'

'What is it with women's handbags?' He smiles at her, looking around at the scattered contents, then crouches down to help her gather them up.

'I don't know, Rob – what *is* it with women's hand-bags?'

'You know what I mean – so much stuff. Sellotape? Scissors? Is that in case you're suddenly overcome by a wild urge to wrap things?'

'Endlessly useful. What about the glove boot of your car?'

'Ah. Point taken.'

They stand side by side, looking out at the fields beyond, smoking in silence for a few moments. She can feel him wanting to say the right thing.

'Um . . .' he begins. 'I'm sorry about your dad – Kath told me.'

'Yeah. Well. It's crap, isn't it?'

He nods. 'I guess so. I still miss my mum, but it's not as if we were ever that close to start with. It was much worse for Kath.' He exhales loudly. 'I was going to call you, but . . .'

'You couldn't be bothered?'

'No.' He looks wounded. He shrugs, and drops his cigarette butt on the ground. 'I thought you might not want to talk to people and . . . I didn't know what to say.'

She lays a hand on his arm.

'Sorry. I didn't mean to give you a hard time. I don't know what you're supposed to say either.'

'So – are you OK?'

Miranda wrinkles her nose.

'This probably sounds stupid, but I'm not really sure.' She scans his face, wondering whether to carry on. 'I mean, my moods have gone a bit haywire but aside from that I'm sort of all right because it hasn't sunk in yet, see? Well, I lost it a bit in church today, but –'

He nods.

'It's not that I just haven't taken it in properly – I mean that I don't quite believe that it's really true.' She reads his face, that tiny lift of the eyebrow. 'It seems ridiculously *unlikely*. Like some sort of huge administrative cock-up – and any second now, he'll phone me and explain and we'll laugh about it. He was far too full of life to just let go so easily. I mean, he had this really loud laugh – actually, it used to drive me crazy, when I was a kid I hated going to the cinema with him because when anything funny happened half the audience would turn round to stare at my dad. But people always listened to him. He made the decisions, he got things done, he cut through the crap. You wouldn't have thought he'd have *allowed* himself to die. If God had said, "Well, that's that, Charles – sorry, your number's up," I can't imagine Dad going quietly – he'd have said, "No can do, I'm far too *busy* to die now." ' She puffs out her cheeks and blows a restrained raspberry.

'Meaning?'

'That's for God.'

'Oh. Right. Fair enough.' A quiet smile. 'How's your mother doing?'

'Mother is coping absolutely *marvellously*,' Miranda booms in an accurate impression of her mother's mannish tones. 'As always. She *is* sad, of course she is, but, God, how she loves to get her teeth into a crisis. Something she can really organize the hell out of. It's List City at their house. Her house. 1) Clear out Charles's side of the wardrobe. 2) Select wording for headstone. 3) Cancel journal subscriptions. 4) Cry.'

Rob laughs.

'Oh, come on. Didn't they have a good marriage? I mean, she loved him and everything?'

'Yes. In her way. But they weren't – I think the marriage suited them both extremely well, intellectually, they certainly still talked a lot – but . . .'

'What?'

'I'm not sure there was much passion between them.

204

Ever.' She shrugs. 'Maybe I'm wrong. A marriage is a bit like a Tardis, isn't it – you can't tell what it's like on the inside just from looking at the outside.'

He smiles warmly, his blue-grey eyes locked on hers.

'I've never looked at it *quite* like that before. Still, we have different expectations now, don't we? We expect passion as some sort of right rather than as a bonus.' He shoves his hands deep into his pockets. 'But, with or without the passion, she must miss him enormously?'

'Ye-e-e-s. Not that you'd guess it from the way she's acting at the moment. Ma believes that all you need to do with anything is to document it, file it or organize a committee to discuss it, then that's it sorted. I was up there last weekend and she said, "Now Miranda, are you managing to grieve? It's not healthy to still be in the denial stage at this point, dear." I wanted to hit her.'

'She meant well, I'm sure.'

Miranda snorts.

'I'm not grieving to a fucking timetable.'

'Maybe it's her way of coping.'

'Thank you, Professor Freud. Yes, I *think* I'd gathered that about my mother after nearly thirty years.'

'Talking of which, I've got you an early birthday present.' He raises his eyebrows. 'I may have to lure you up to my room later. I can't believe you're going to be thirty.'

'Don't say it like that. It's bad enough without your making it sound like a hundred and thirty.' She looks at him directly. 'I thought we were the same age?'

'I'm only twenty-eight.'

'Why are you grinning as if you've just won the Olympic pentathlon? Twenty-eight, twenty-nine – who cares? We're both going to end up in the same place.' She jerks her thumb downwards.

'Hey!' Rob frowns. Then his voice softens. 'Hey . . .' he says again. 'Come on . . .' She can feel him looking at her but she stares straight ahead, out at the grass, the trees, the sky beyond.

'It's been a wonderful wedding, hasn't it?' Miranda's tone sounds oddly formal to her own ears, as if she is speaking to some distant, elderly relative. 'Kath is absolutely radiant and Joe's speech was wonderful – so warm and funny. I know they're going to be so happy.' She continues to stare straight ahead, not wanting to meet his eyes.

'Yeah – I've never seen her looking so good – she looks really pretty, doesn't she?'

'No need to sound so surprised. Kath *is* pretty – it's only that most of the time she likes to hide herself in those awful baggy jumpers and is too scared of her lousy hairdresser to switch to someone new. She'd be really lovely if she made half an effort, don't you think?'

He shrugs.

'Well, she's just Kathy to me – you don't think about how your own sister looks, do you?'

'You do if you're me. My sister is stunning.'

'Is she here? Is she single?' He makes a show of looking behind and beyond Miranda.

'Sod off. No, she isn't. She's very married and also very in Australia, thank God.'

'Does she look like you?'

'A bit, only prettier, more delicate, more petite – but then who isn't, let's face it? Shorter, slimmer, smaller nose – not so galumphing.' Miranda drops her cigarette butt to the ground, crushes it firmly underfoot.

'Don't do yourself down – I like tall women.'

She watches him sideways, trying to tell if he's taking the piss out of her. Standing next to him, she notices she does feel less galumphing – he is a good four inches taller than she is, and broad-shouldered without being meaty. He carries his height well – he doesn't look especially big, just . . . she tries to think of the word . . . in charge.

'What?' He's looking at her.

'What?'

'You're staring. Have I got lettuce stuck between my teeth?'

'Sorry.' She smiles. 'I thought you had a smidgen of mayonnaise on your chin.' Puts out one finger and draws it across his lower lip.

They look into each other's eyes, unabashed. He covers her hand with his own, quickly pulls her close, looking down at her.

She hadn't realized until this moment how much

she has wanted this. From the first time she met him –
no, before that even, when Kath was showing her some
photos and Miranda had said, 'God, who's *that*?' having
no idea he was Kath's brother – Miranda has been
attracted to Rob. At first, she told herself it was simply
a silly crush, fancying your best friend's big brother,
the sort of thing you do when you're thirteen – how
pathetic. Every time she's been to a party at Kath's, she
finds herself taking considerably longer to get ready
than usual – she does her make-up with greater care,
blots her lipstick properly the way you're supposed to,
even tries on different pairs of earrings, seeing which
catch the light best so that he'll be aware of her, even
from the other side of the room, telling herself she's
being ridiculous. Rob always flirts shamelessly with
her, sometimes right in front of whichever woman he
happens to have in tow. She has never seen him bring
the same woman to more than one party. Somehow,
the flirting has always stayed at flirting and Miranda is
not quite sure why – is it because he usually favours
women several years younger than him? Is it that she's
so tall and . . . statuesque? Galumphing. Or just that he
sees her as his kid sister's mate? It can't be because, for
the last year or so, she's been with Simon – Rob hardly
seems like the kind of man who would let a little thing
like that stand in his way and Simon usually avoids
parties if he can. So he's just not interested then – the
flirting must simply be a bit of playful jesting, not to be

taken seriously. Fine. A little harmless sport. She has always taken it in this vein, while striving to ignore the stirring in her stomach she feels when she first hears his voice, the slight flush she senses coming to her face – Miranda, blushing! Miranda, who makes most men quake in their shoes.

Rob is holding her by her arms, as if she might try to get away. His mouth is hot and firm on hers, kissing her so hard she can barely breathe. He lets go of her arms only to encircle her, pull her even closer. Miranda presses against him, feeling him harden against her. She pulls back slightly, just for a moment, for air. They both laugh suddenly and he tugs her close again, his eyes locked on hers.

'I can't tell you how long I've wanted to do that.'

'What stopped you?'

He shrugs.

'Wasn't sure if you were really interested . . .'

'Oh, come on! When have I ever not seemed interested? Short of wearing a big sign saying "I fancy you, Rob", I think I've made it clear enough.'

'Hmm – but when we flirt, I always think you're just teasing me – toying with me.'

She laughs, nodding.

'*I* always think *you're* toying with *me*. Besides, this is practically the first time I've seen you without a girl glued to your arm.'

'Hey – if there's a free banquet on offer, you can't expect me to sit at home eating a stale sandwich, can you?'

Miranda scrunches up her face in distaste.

'I'm not sure if that says you're an arrogant git or you just can't come up with a decent metaphor.'

He laughs.

'How come you're always so tough on me?'

'Someone has to be. Kath looks up to you so much – God knows why.'

'Yeah, right.' He tries to read her expression. 'Does she really?' He pulls Miranda close and kisses in a line along the length of her eyebrows. 'You know, I always figured she'd warned you off me, told you to steer clear of me.'

'Now why would she do that, do you suppose?' She smiles up at him. *Up!*

'Maybe she figures I'm not a good long-term bet.'

'What's your longest ever relationship?'

'Um – I think it was Helen. Or maybe Jill.'

'No, I meant how long, not who with.'

'Oh.' He shrugs.

'You must know.'

'A year or so, I guess.'

Miranda smiles.

'Or so? Say, six months?'

'Oi! More like nearly eight.'

She shakes her head and tut-tuts flirtatiously at him.

He smiles and bends his head to kiss her again.

'If I go and get us some more champagne, will you still be here when I get back?'

'*I'm* not the one who has a problem staying around,' she reminds him.

Tuesday

Giles unlaced

'Oh – do you need a hand, Giles?' Miranda walked into the kitchen, where Giles was awkwardly attempting to fill the kettle. Then she spotted that his shoelaces were undone. 'And your laces are undone – you can't go around like that, you could trip—'

'And break my arm? Perish the thought.' He smiled. 'True – these aren't exactly the most practical shoes right now.'

'Here, let me help you.' She quickly knelt down to tie his laces. 'Don't you have any loafers? Or slippers even?'

'Unfortunately, Kathryn neglected to put them in my bag when she packed.'

'Yes, of course it's all *her* fault. Honestly, Giles. Be fair.'

'I shall consider myself chastised. I wonder why you feel the need to be so hard on me, Miranda?'

'Don't imagine you're special – I'm equally nasty to everyone. Ask Simon.' Miranda turned away to fill the kettle. 'Maybe you could borrow some more suitable shoes for now? Simon doesn't have any loafers, but—'

'Do you think I'd want to *borrow* . . . *anything* that *belonged* to . . . another man?' His voice was controlled, but he looked furious.

Miranda spun back to face him.

'For God's sake, Giles – it's only for a few days. I'm trying to be helpful here.' She sighed. 'Surely you won't mind having some of Rob's then at least – aren't you about the same size?' His cool blue gaze met hers steadily and she flushed deeply and looked down, as if assessing his shoe size. 'I mean, you're . . . what . . . a size ten?'

'An educated guess?'

'Well – it's one thing I ought to be at least vaguely good at by now. Anyway – ' She set out the teapot and grabbed the box of tea bags. 'So – tea, tea, tea – OK for you? Or coffee?'

'Tea's fine. Thank you.'

'We could go and get you some more loafers if you like? I mean, I could come with you – I spotted two or three little shoe shops in town. Not that you exactly need my expertise to choose a pair of loafers, obviously. It's probably not worth it. You won't be in a sling for much longer, will you?'

There was a pause. Miranda poured the boiling water into the teapot and mashed the tea bags energetically with a spoon. Busied herself with cups and saucers and teaspoons, milk and sugar.

'Anyway, it was just a thought . . .' She leaned her head out into the hallway and called, 'Tea, everyone! In the kitchen!'

'Thank you.' Giles lowered himself carefully into the chair at the head of the table. 'That would be nice.' He nodded. 'It's good of you to offer. I'd appreciate your guidance. Never refuse expert help when it's available . . . or amenable company, of course.'

Miranda took her tea and went back up to the bedroom to put on some make-up. Simon was standing at the wardrobe mirror, flossing his teeth.

'I'll have to go into town later today. It's amazing how much food we're getting through, you'd think we were doing nothing but sitting with our noses in the trough all day long, wouldn't you?' Miranda ducked awkwardly to use the other mirror, on top of the chest of drawers. She swept cleansing lotion lightly over her face, then reached for a ball of cotton wool. 'And I've offered to take Giles shoe-shopping at the same time. He can't manage laces just now. Obviously.'

'How very philanthropic of you,' Simon said into the mirror, rewinding the floss around his fingers.

'God, Simon, do you have to turn *everything* into some kind of dig?' She flung the cotton wool in the bin and reached for another ball. 'What's the big deal? He's a sixty-two-year-old man with a broken arm who can't tie his own shoelaces. Have a bit of feeling, for God's sake. I just offered casually – someone has to go into town in any case, so what difference does it make?'

'Why doesn't Kath take him then? Or Rob for that matter? How has it magically become your job all of a sudden? You're not his . . . relative.'

Miranda ignored his deliberate pause.

'I was *trying* to be nice.' She half-turned from the dressing table.

'Really? What brought that on? It's not Christmas already, is it?'

She sighed with impatience.

'Oh, *stop*, will you? Think about it: Giles is used to being in charge and powerful – and suddenly he can't even dress himself properly. I think he's feeling a bit – I don't know – *lost*, I guess. And at least if I go with him, it gives Kath a break.'

Simon flicked the dental floss between his two front teeth, making a small clicking noise.

'He's certainly very critical of her.'

'Giles is critical of everybody. He gives Rob a hard time, too, don't you think?'

Simon frowned and scrunched up his used floss. Turned to face her.

'Hmm, not in the same way though. He's more . . . competitive, wouldn't you say? More as if they were brothers? Rivals even.'

'A little perhaps. Though I suppose that's not unusual for fathers and sons, is it?' Miranda shrugged, peered at her reflection, looking for lines at the corners of her eyes. 'I hadn't really given it much thought.'

In the mirror, she saw Simon raise his eyebrows. She dropped her gaze and reached for her bottle of toner.

Mummies and Daddies

Late morning. Outside, on the patio, Miranda and Rob were watching the children play Mummies and Daddies.

'I'm Mummy and I'm picking up all the toys off the floor.' Polly mimed tidying up, sighing loudly. 'And now I'm going into the kitchen to eat all the biscuits when no-one else is looking.'

'I'm the Daddy,' said Anna, tapping away at an imaginary keyboard. 'I'm writing articles for the newspapers about why there should be windmills everywhere and also I'm looking after the planet and telling off all the bad people at the nasty oil companies.'

'No! *I'm* Daddy!' Luke pushed Anna, then immediately lay down. 'I'm watching a video and making pig noises.'

'*I* want to be the Daddy. I'm sick of being the Mummy. Being the Mummy's boring.' Polly lay down next to Luke and began to snore loudly.

'Out of the mouths of babes . . .' said Miranda.

Rob laughed and lit up a cigarette. He offered Miranda one, but she refused.

'Go on.' He looked at her out of the corner of his eye. 'You know you want to.'

'You're a bad influence. My mother always told me to stay away from boys like you. I'd love one, but I can't.' She nodded towards Anna. 'The secret police have me under surveillance. Let me just stand next to you and torment myself by sniffing the air.'

'It's funny – I can't say I ever figured you for the maternal type.'

Miranda swung sharply round to face him.

'I'm extremely maternal actually. Just because I don't spend my days baking cookies with a beatific smile on my face doesn't make me a bad mother. Real mothers get exhausted and tetchy and sometimes get stroppy with their kids, I'm not the only one on the planet, you know.'

'Hey, chill out, will you?'

'And don't tell me to chill out.'

'I didn't mean it that way – I just meant that you're so . . . so . . .'

'Aggressive? Self-centred? A hard-nosed bitch? Incapable of being caring or affectionate?'

'Jeez, what's with you today? You must be coming down with Simon's Syndrome.' He laid a hand on her shoulder. 'That's so not how I see you, Manda. You know it isn't.'

He rarely used Kath's pet name for her. Miranda softened and was silent. She suddenly felt her eyes welling with tears, looked down at the patio, eyes locked on the paving as if she were making a detailed appraisal of it.

'Manda?'

She focused on her shoes now, the way she always did when she wanted to feel strong.

'Hey?' His voice was soft and low, barely audible to anyone more than a few inches away.

A quick glance.

'So . . . how *do* you see me then?'

She was fishing, she knew, but she couldn't stop herself. She allowed herself another covert glance up at those extraordinary blue eyes, then hastily looked away again, felt guilty as if she'd been caught stealing.

'How do I see you? Ah, there's a question and a half.' His gaze met hers for a long, long moment, then he looked away, back towards the children. 'Well . . . there are a number of ways to answer that, but I'd better behave myself – let's see – as highly successful, of course. You're dynamic, you've got loads of drive. You've really made it happen for yourself. You didn't just – ' He shrugged. 'Give up as soon as it got tricky. You stuck with it – and now look at you! On every chic foot in the country!'

'Hardly!' she laughed, covering her disappointment. 'Sometimes I wish I had given up though. I'm permanently exhausted – it's one headache after another – always fretting about my overheads, my margins, I've had hitch after hitch with my suppliers, the workshop, staff crises, flood damage, delivery fiascos, you name it, I've had it. It's certainly not the glamour-fest people seem to imagine it is. Sometimes I think "Why on earth am I doing this? Why don't I go and get a normal job like everyone else?" Then I could just sod off home at six o'clock and forget about it, instead of waking up at two in the morning worrying about sub-standard buckles.'

'And how long do you think you could stand a normal job?'

Miranda looked him in the eye and smiled.

'OK, OK. About a week. Tops.'

'Exactly. Trust me, you don't want to sell out and end up doing some boring shit that does your head in.' He dropped his fag end on the ground and stubbed it out with his foot, grinding it into the patio.

'Come on – it can't be that bad. You've got your own business. You're your own boss at least. You're hardly a downtrodden wage slave, are you?'

'It's not the same thing and you know it. I mean, it's not exactly the realization of a lifelong dream, is it?' His voice shifted, playing the patronizing grown-up. 'And what do you want to be when you grow up, little boy? An astronaut? A footballer? A doctor? Oh, you'd like to be an estate agent! Gosh!'

'It's not too late. You're not even forty yet. Don't give up on yourself so easily. Be brave, change direction if you want to. It's not impossible . . . unless you'd really set your heart on being an astronaut?'

He shook his head and was silent.

'Do you still make things?'

'Uh-huh. What's the point?'

'Um – because you're bloody good at it? Because if you walked into someone's house and saw one of your tables standing there, you'd get one hell of a kick out of it, I know you would. I *know* you, Rob – you need fulfilment and you need recognition, too.' She clocked the expression on his face. 'It's not a bad thing, there's no shame in it – you just need to know it about yourself. Did you know – Tamsin was wearing a pair of my shoes yesterday? The moment I saw them, it gave me such a buzz. I love the designing and – when it's not driving me fucking crazy – I even love trying to solve all the problems, but what really gives me a high is that moment when I see some woman at a party or walking down the street and she's wearing a pair of my shoes and you can tell that they make her feel like a million dollars.'

He lit up another cigarette.

'Rob?'

'Mmm.'

'I still have that box you made me, you know.'

He frowned.

'The one you did for me years ago. With the inlaid lid and the teeny-tiny secret compartment. For my thirtieth birthday. You gave it to me beforehand because you'd finished it and you couldn't wait to see my reaction, remember? At Kath's wedding,' she added. 'And, of course, you went off on your grand trip shortly after that, so you missed my big party anyway. Remember?'

'Oh. Yeah. Right.' He nodded. 'It was just a box.'

'It's beautiful.'

'Took me about two weeks solid. I spent forever just on sanding and polishing it, trying to make it smooth as skin. That's not commercially viable, is it? If I charged for my time properly, it'd cost about two grand – who's going to pay two grand for a piddly little box? I only did it because I used to love working with wood. That plus I was desperate to get into your knickers, of course.'

Miranda looked away again.

'Well, you got that out of your system pretty quickly at least.'

'Other way round, more like.'

She frowned, puzzled.

'Look, Rob, let's not forget, you were the one – Oh, shit.' She sent Rob a warning glance, then turned to face Simon with a smile.

'Hi!'

'You're not smoking again, are you?' Simon ignored Rob.

'Not guilty.' She held up her hands, palms facing towards him. 'Just watching the kids play Bitches and Martyrs.' Waited for him to look baffled so she could pause then add 'Mummies and Daddies', but he didn't react.

'I came out to tell the children that their lunch is ready. I'm doing them some pasta.'

'Oh, good.'

'Kids! Lunchtime! Spaghetti! Come and get it!'

The children ran past in a stream.

'You might want to come and lend a hand.' Simon moved towards the house. 'If it won't interrupt anything important.'

Miranda made a face at Rob and followed Simon in.

In search of shoes

After lunch, Miranda finished making her shopping list.

'Right. Anything else for anyone? Chocolate? Toothpaste? Tampax? Last call!'

'I'm all right for Tampax, but I wouldn't mind coming for a recce if you're going into town'. Rob looked up from his sprawled position on the sofa, where he was apparently absorbed in one of Polly's Dr Seuss storybooks.

'Silly!' Tamsin giggled and gave him a playful slap on his arm. 'Can I come, too?' She shook back her long, straight hair like a horse swishing off flies from its mane, then pulled it into a perfectly neat ponytail, which she secured with the velvet scrunchie she wore on her wrist like a bracelet.

This wasn't supposed to be an elaborate expedition, Miranda thought, just a quick foray to grab some groceries and a pair of shoes.

'Of course. Why not? You two can do the shopping, if you like, while Giles and I suss out what funky footwear is available.'

'Shopping's not really my bag,' Rob said, yawning widely. 'Unless it's wine.'

'Thank you, Rob. Helpful as always.'

He made a face at her.

Miranda waited for Tamsin to volunteer at least.

'I'm, like, really, really hopeless, too. Mummy says I have to write it down even if I only want a pint of milk or I'd come back with a bag of potatoes or something.' She giggled. 'I actually have to get a pen and paper and everything and put, like, one pint of milk. Like a list, you know?'

Miranda caught Rob's eye briefly, then looked away.

'Fine. I'll do it. Rob – can you pick up some wine at least? Say two of each?'

'Just enough for tonight then?'

'Quite. I'm not mad keen on Chardonnay, by the way. Or not if it's oaky.'

'Ah, it's *so* last year, isn't it?' Rob teased.

'Yuh, it's Viognier now,' Tamsin said seriously. 'That's like *the* white wine, you know?'

They spoke little on the way there, with occasional squeals from Tamsin as Miranda sharply took a corner or brazened it out with an oncoming car, making the other driver reverse on the single-track road. She drove faster than usual, though whether to keep the journey as brief as possible or to make some kind of point she wasn't sure.

'You don't drive like a woman,' Giles observed.

'Yeah – more like Ayrton Senna!' Rob called from the back seat. Miranda looked at him in her rear-view mirror and stuck her tongue out at him.

'Um, isn't he the one who – who crashed?' Tamsin asked.

'Certainly did.' Rob frowned at Miranda. 'Jesus – get us there in one piece, won't you?'

'It's rather refreshing.' Giles shifted awkwardly in his seat, holding his right arm steady with his left. 'Kathryn drives like an old woman. Twenty-eight miles an hour—'

'And that's on the motorway hogging the middle lane,' Rob joined in.

Miranda veered round a blind bend, then slammed on the brakes. The silver Saab screeched to a halt a foot short of a battered and muddy Land Rover. The driver hooted and remained where he was.

'Stupid bugger.' Giles sat more upright. 'Stay where you are.'

'*Dad*, don't be daft. Better back up,' Rob said.

'I don't see why. Let him reverse.'

Another long hoot of the horn.

'Because his car's got more dents in it.' Rob sighed. 'Miranda's the one with the snazzy motor. I'm sure he'd be more than happy to ram us and crush us into the hedge. Besides, we're the tourists, he's local – it's standard protocol.'

'I'd have thought you were the *last* person to suggest giving way.' Miranda met his eyes briefly in the mirror. 'I don't think I know anyone more stubborn than you.'

'There's a time to be stubborn and a time just to be gracious and get on with it, don't you think?' He smiled in what she felt was a condescending way. 'In the interests of our not spending the rest of our days stuck in your car on this bobsleigh run. Fun though it undoubtedly is.'

A double hoot. The driver's door of the Land Rover opened. Miranda waved her hand in a conciliatory gesture and yanked the gear into reverse.

In the town, Miranda ignored the signs pointing to the car park and drove on right into the high street. Spotted someone pulling out of a space ahead and flicked on her indicator. Pulled ahead then reversed neatly at some speed, earning approving nods from both Rob and Giles.

'Golly – you even park like a man!' Rob teased.

'Yes, that was extremely well done.'

'Thank you, the Patronizing Partners. Unbelievable.'

They agreed on a time to meet back at the car. Rob and Tamsin wandered off together to look for an off-licence.

'Right, let's have a dekko at these shoe shops, shall we?' Miranda stood so that Giles could lean on her as he got out of the car. He moved awkwardly but avoided taking her arm. 'Any preferences? What are your other loafers like?'

'Maroon leather.'

'Maroon! God, that's a word I haven't heard for a while. Funny how no-one uses the word maroon any more, isn't it?' Miranda prattled away. 'It's burgundy now.'

'No-one except the ancient doddering Giles, is that it?'

'Oh, Giles – don't take offence. I didn't mean anything by it – I was just, you know, babbling away the way I do. You should know by now that you have to ignore ninety per cent of what I say – most of it's utter nonsense. I've got no edit button.'

'Miranda, that is patently a preposterous lie. I would say that much of the time you choose your words very carefully indeed.' He paused a moment to adjust his sling slightly. 'As do I.'

She gently took his left arm and steered him towards a shoe shop.

'Anything you fancy?'

Felt his eyes on her, willing her to look at him. She indicated a slightly pointed pair in black leather. 'Those aren't too bad, are they? Or too pointy for you?'

'Pimp shoes.' Giles curled his lip and they walked on. Miranda gestured towards another shop further up the hill.

Inside, she persuaded him to try on a pair of loafers in dark brown suede. He stayed seated, gently flexing his feet.

'Stand up. Have a good walk round. Make sure they're comfortable.'

He looked at her and she thought perhaps she was being too bossy as usual, but he smiled and stood up.

'Not too tight at the toe?' She suddenly knelt before him and felt the end of the shoe, the way she would when buying shoes for Anna. Glanced up at him. His eyes met hers, and a warm smile lit up his face. Miranda felt herself flush deeply. She stood up and stepped back a pace, avoiding his gaze.

Giles nodded.

'They're fine.'

'Good.' She turned away from him. 'Excellent. So nice to shop with someone who isn't a ditherer, I must say.' Miranda waved at the assistant. 'Yes, can we take these, please?'

They stood by the till while the assistant boxed them up.

'Aww, you poor love,' she said to Giles, indicating his sling. 'Took a nasty tumble, did you? It's ever so slippy what with all the rain we been having, you want to watch your step. Still, nice weather for ducks, eh?' She laughed uproariously.

Giles nodded and murmured a vague 'mmm'.

'Still, good you've got your daughter brung you out to the shops and that, eh? Always a treat to have a bit of a family outing, that's what I say.'

'Oh, no, I'm not – he's – we're not related actually.' Miranda dared not look at him.

'Oh, sorry!' The woman flushed pink. 'Me and my big mouth!'

Giles signed the credit card slip in silence and they left.

'Giles . . .' She laid a hand on his left arm. 'She was just a silly woman. It doesn't—'

'It doesn't matter? Don't patronize me, Miranda, it's not worthy of you.'

'I wasn't going to say that. I –'

He waited without interrupting her.

'I was going to say that it doesn't *mean* anything, what some daft shop assistant thinks. I don't think she was exactly the sharpest knife in the drawer, do you?'

'Not a candidate for *University Challenge*, certainly. But I'm a man of sixty-two and you're a woman still in your prime. Very much in your prime.' He flared his nostrils, but more at himself than anyone else, it seemed to Miranda. 'What else would she think? That I'm your husband? Your . . . lover? Your sugar daddy possibly . . .'

'Don't say that!' In her anger, she brushed against him and he winced in a sudden spasm of pain. 'Oh – I'm so sorry. Giles – are you all right?'

He nodded, but his face was pallid and drawn.

'Here, let's go and sit down and have a coffee somewhere.'

'I'm perfectly all right. I don't need a nursemaid.'

'Well, *I* need a coffee even if you don't. I'm tired. Please – come on.'

A cosy gathering

A couple of minutes later they were seated in the Anchor Tea Rooms, and had ordered tea and toasted teacakes. Giles fumbled in his pocket for his tablets while Miranda asked for a glass of water for him.

'Is the idea so repellent then?' He appeared to be addressing the jar of painkillers.

'Of your being a sugar daddy? Of course. Well, ridiculous rather than repellent. I'm too old and too independent to hook one for a start.'

'I wasn't referring to that.'

At that moment the waitress arrived and started clattering down cups and saucers. Miranda busied herself fiddling with the tea strainer and repositioning everything on the tiny lace-covered table.

'Gosh, it's like doll's house furniture in here. I can barely get my ginormous thighs wedged under this table.'

'Miranda—' He laid his hand gently on her bare forearm.

The bell rang as the tea room door opened.

'Well, well. Fancy seeing you here. How very cosy.' Rob's voice was loud and clear just a few feet from their table. Miranda quickly withdrew her arm and picked up her teacup. 'Any luck with your impossible quest for the Holy Grail of Footwear – a casual shoe that Dad doesn't dismiss as something for either a pensioner or a pimp?'

Heads turned towards them, hands clutching cake forks froze in mid-air.

'Sssh!' Miranda glared at him.

The waitress came over.

'Shall I move you to a bigger table so you can all sit together?'

'That'd be super!' Tamsin beamed. 'Thank you.'

'Yes. Super,' Miranda echoed flatly, standing up to move their tea things.

'This is really, really scrummy.' Tamsin took a tiny bite out of her teacake. 'I can't believe I'm being *such* a pig.'

Oh please, thought Miranda, give me a break, that's practically the first thing you've eaten this week.

'Is that why you're so fat?' she said, deadpan.

'God, I *am*, aren't I?' Tamsin took Miranda at her word, but seemed entirely unoffended. 'A total hippopotamus. I can't believe Rob can even bear to touch me, but he's such a total, total sweetheart, isn't he?' She smiled at him.

'I was joking, Tamsin – I wouldn't dream of telling someone they looked fat, especially when they can't possibly be more than a size 10. You must know you're absolutely stunning, so why not enjoy it? Women are always running themselves down, it's ridiculous. You don't hear men whingeing to each other, do you? "Ooh, my hair should be declared a disaster zone – look at my bald patch." "Oh no, my pot belly makes me look pregnant – I'd better not eat for three months." They just ignore it and get on with their lives. That's probably why they're the ones running the corporations, the media and the country – they're not wasting half their time peering into a mirror looking for flaws to moan about or beating themselves up because they still haven't signed up for sodding Pilates sessions.'

Miranda reached across Rob for the milk.

'Ha! And you don't run yourself down, I suppose?' Rob laughed and shook his head.

'Not especially.'

'You *do*. Whenever I tell you you're looking great or say something nice about what you're wearing or your

234

hair or whatever, you always either ignore it completely or throw it back in my face.'

'Rob, that's such bollocks. How the hell would you know? I can't recall an instance of your complimenting me – no, I'm not fishing, just stating a fact. Name a time, name one single time.' She lifted the lid of the teapot and poked at the contents with a spoon. '*Recently*,' she added.

He looked thoughtful for a few moments.

'OK. I will. OK – yeah, I know. When we arrived on Sunday and you were in the garden and I came up and I said, "Hello, you're looking gorgeous," and you pretended not to hear me.'

'You didn't say that.'

'I did. I remember it clearly.'

Miranda put down her cup with a crash.

'No, you *didn't*, Rob. You said, "You're looking *well*." *I* remember exactly. Not gorgeous. *Well*.'

'Well, *I meant* gorgeous, you know I did. You're just being annoying and Miranda-ish.' He took a deep drink of his tea, apparently satisfied that he had won this round at least.

Miranda suddenly became acutely aware of Giles and Tamsin, their eyes flicking from Rob to her, watching and silent. She fought the urge to tip the contents of the teapot over Rob's lap in an attempt to wipe the smirk off his face. To her right, she could sense Giles watching her profile, looking for her reaction. Tried to keep her face impassive.

'I can't help being Miranda-ish. It kind of goes with the job of being me, unfortunately.'

Rob laughed and leaned his chair back so that it was balanced on its back legs for a moment, then he rocked forward again.

'Aren't you finishing your teacake, Tam?'

Tamsin shook her head.

'I've had enough.'

'Can I have it then?'

'Well . . .' Miranda signalled to the waitress for the bill. 'I'd better crack on – there's still loads to get.'

'Shall I come?' Giles asked.

'Um, actually, if you don't mind . . . I can zip round really fast on my own. Why don't you stay here a bit longer and finish your tea?' She handed over her car keys and slapped some money down on the table, which Giles waved away. 'See you all back at the car in half an hour.'

For God's sake, she thought, striding across the road to the bakery, deftly nipping between the cars, I'd have been better off bringing bloody Simon than this merry troupe.

Pulling out of the town after their shopping trip, Miranda switched on the car CD player.

'Mind if we have a bit of music?' She turned up the volume before anyone could have a chance to reply. 'If you want to make any amusing comments about my driving, you'll have to shout, I'm afraid!'

Rob made a show of bracing himself in the back.

'Buckle up tight, Tam!' He flattened his mouth. 'Prepare for the G-force.'

Someone else's life

After Miranda had put away the shopping, she quickly ran up to her room. Picked up her novel, let her gaze roam over the page for a minute, then put it down again, remembering she ought to carry on reading Kath's letters. She took out the bundle from her underwear drawer and lay down on the bed. Ah, a few minutes' peace. A few minutes' thinking about someone else's life rather than her own.

My dearest ♩

Well, the weather is grey and drizzly and it is raining yet AGAIN. Don't you wonder why the sky doesn't simply run out of rain eventually? Is your sky full of clouds? If it were up to me, you would have your very own oasis of sunshine that would follow you about, a patch of perfect blue sky shimmering above you. You are less than three miles away from me, but it might as well be 3,000. Ten times a day I have to stop myself from leaping onto my less-than-trusty bicycle (another puncture yesterday! Now my tyres have more repairs than tyre . . .) and zipping round there to take you in my arms right on your doorstep (Heavens! What would the neighbours say? Especially that woman opposite. Does she actually do anything else all day other than hover by her front window keeping an eye out for rogue piano teachers?) Dear God, I just reread the beginning of this letter and I'm talking about the weather! What's wrong with me? Perhaps it's just to stop myself from saying what I want to say? Romantic things. Loving things. Lustful things, too. This morning I tormented myself by playing 'our' Bach sonata and thinking of your neat little fingers dancing across the keys. I look down at my own hands and they seem ridiculously large and ungainly by comparison – how can you tolerate being in the same room as a man who has such ugly hands?

You know – I'm all done with the weather and my hands now – I suspect I fell in love with you long before you let me kiss you. And I have a confession to make. Months and months ago, I moved the pupil who had a lesson straight after yours so that I'd never have to rush off again. I liked staying and talking with you, lingering over coffee, talking about music, books – and you showing me around your beautiful garden, trying your best to teach me the names of all your plants, teasing me as I muddled them up yet again. I make a poor student. And a slow learner – it took me a long time to admit to myself how I felt about you. I've probably broken some ancient and venerable code of ethics, the equivalent of the Hippocratic oath but for piano teachers – the Vivaldian Vow or something. Promise not to shop me? In turn, I promise to spend less time thinking about being in bed with you.

Right – I must go now. Twelve-year-old Adrian will be poised on his piano stool. His mother believes he is destined for greatness, but she may have a long wait. He never practises. If he were as assiduous with his lessons as he is with his excuses, we might start getting somewhere.

See you on Wednesday then, as always. I'll be racing up your path like an overkeen schoolboy.

Are you ready for some Beethoven, my ♩ ? I'm thinking of something devilishly difficult for you. Be prepared!

Your

Nothing too graphic so far at least: no nipple talk, no musing on the softness of Constance's inner thighs. Still, the later ones might be more revealing – in every sense; maybe she should have read those first? Miranda leafed through the stack. But that would be like skipping ahead to read the last page of a detective story. Strewth, his writing was hard work. She propped herself up against the pillows and peered at the next letter.

My ♩

What do I have to offer you? So little. And so much. I wish I could paint myself in a rosy light, wish I could come to you with at least a house of my own to welcome you both to. I know you don't want a mansion, but I can picture you in a cottage by the sea. Three bedrooms – one for us, one for little Robbie (not so little, he grows so fast that boy! What are you feeding him?) and one for . . . I am getting ahead of myself as usual. How dare I ask you to come away with me, to leave him, your house and garden, lifelong security, the chance of a top school for R? All I have to offer is myself and I can see that's not much of an offer. I'm no handsome Casanova (in case you hadn't noticed . . .) I'm not tall, I'm not rich. Hang on, I'd better start thinking of my good points. I know I had some once, perhaps I mislaid them? I'd make a hopeless salesman. I have a good heart, a modicum of talent, a means of earning an adequate living. I have an ocean's worth of love for you – but that you know already. This, I think – I hope – would be enough for you. But there is Robbie to consider, and I know you think it would be wrong to tear him from the life he knows – his home, his father – at such a tender age. I would like to think that maybe one day I could be something like a father to him. But that is in your hands.

Oh, dearest C – I think about you constantly. I imagine the deep, quiet pleasure of waking up beside you each morning, seeing your precious face so close to mine, feeling your warm breath on my cheek. We have to let our love happen, my C, we have to.

Your

Hmm, surely that one alone would be enough to upset Kath? But how could she stop her reading it? Miranda rolled her shoulders back and yawned. Tucked the letter back into its envelope. Time for her twenty-fourth coffee of the day perhaps? She ran downstairs, trying to keep her tread as light as possible. That was the trouble with this kind of group holiday – you could never just make yourself a drink without catering for an entire platoon of people; you weren't allowed to be selfish.

Miranda knew it was silly, but she had to admit that she felt decidedly envious of Connie. What must it be like when your fingers closed around that crisp, promising envelope, knowing it contained a chain of magical words, words that would make you feel beautiful, desirable, beloved? And Frank sounded like a real person, too. His letters weren't puffed up with grandly romantic statements, proclaiming his love to the stars; he wasn't given to over-the-top compliments or ridiculous flattery. He sounded like a man genuinely in love.

Her eyes filled with tears and she briskly rubbed them away. Is that what you want, you daft cow? To have some dashing knight ride up and sweep you off your feet? How pathetic. What was the point of having wrinkles ('laughter lines'? Ha-ha, ha-ha, ah, yes, how she loved to chortle merrily as she looked in the mirror . . .) and creaky knees and a big mortgage and a pension plan, if she were in actuality no more mature than she'd been at thirteen, mooning about hoping that the desirable and impossibly grown-up seven-teen-year-old boy from down the road would notice her as she shuffled awkwardly past him, earnestly studying the paving at her feet?

She was just about to go back into the bedroom when she heard footsteps thundering up the stairs behind her.

'Mum!' Anna ran up to Miranda and grabbed her from behind.

'Oops! Careful! Hot coffee!'

Anna walked jerkily on her heels across the landing.

'Come downstairs and play with us.'

'I'm reading right now.'

'Come and read downstairs then. You're *always* telling me to join in.' Anna pulled at her mother's belt loop. 'Come *on*.'

Fun and games

It had started raining again. The children were playing Ludo with Kath and Joe; Tamsin was upstairs washing her hair; Giles was poring over a thick stack of papers. Miranda was making her fourteenth attempt to get past the first ten pages of the novel she had brought with her. She had reread the same page at least three times.

The game of Ludo came to an end.

'Let's be gymnasts!' Polly said, balancing precariously on one leg. 'I'm on the beam. Mum, you've got to give us marks out of ten.'

Anna and Polly started doing somersaults and would-be cartwheels across the carpet, squealing, while Luke tried to join in, crashing into Giles's crossed legs. Giles cleared his throat pointedly.

'Don't disturb Grandpa, Luke. He's trying to read.' Kath crossed her eyes and made a silly face at Joe.

Luke got up and tried again, rolling lopsidedly into Polly. She cried out and pushed him and he started crying. Giles looked up from his papers and peered at Kath.

'Pops – you're doing your Victorian patriarch look again.' Rob shook his head, laughing to himself. 'Kids make noise, they fight and they cry. A lot. It's completely normal. It doesn't mean there's been a terminal lapse of discipline – heaven forbid.'

'I'd no idea you were such an expert on children, Robert? Have you been hatching a secret brood somewhere?'

'At least I spend some time with them occasionally. When did you last babysit?'

'Yesterday afternoon, since you ask.' Giles looked back down at his work. 'I seem to recall I was also a parent of young children once myself.'

'Ah, yes, how we remember the many, many happy hours spent somersaulting across the drawing room with you.'

'Don't be mean, Robbie. Dads didn't do things like that so much then. It's different now.'

'Robert seems to have acquired a talent for rewriting history,' Giles pronounced, not looking up from his papers. 'I frequently took him fishing. Riding. Archery. If he'd bothered to stick at it, he might have become rather good.' He made a small mark on the top sheet of paper. 'If only I'd known that somersaulting was his activity of choice, I might have saved myself considerable money and effort.'

'Mmm, lucky me.' Rob turned to Miranda. 'It was a whirlwind of fun, fun, fun, I can tell you. I'm not sure why Kath got let off the merry-go-round.'

'Girls have different interests,' Giles said, not looking-up. 'Or at least they did back then in those pre-politically correct days before the dawn of the Feminist Age.' He cast an anxious glance in Miranda's direction. 'I suppose one's not even allowed to say that any more?'

Kath and Miranda looked at each other and started to laugh.

'Oh, Daddy! I was born right at the peak of it.' Kath

smiled affectionately. 'Even Mum had a secret copy of Germaine Greer hidden away, you know.'

'Giles, you're hilarious, you really are.' Miranda put down her book, still giggling softly to herself. 'Well, I think I need some air before my Inner Goddess snaps and gets out her shotgun.' She stood up. 'Anna? Coming for a quick walk?'

Anna nodded.

'Can we go to the beach?'

'Yes. Get your jacket and boots on. Anyone else? Members of the Sisterhood only.'

Faces turned towards the window, with the rain streaming down outside.

'You one crazy lady, Miranda.' Rob smiled. 'I'm glad I'm excused.'

'It's only rain, you big softie. You could be our token male.'

'What an honour, but I think I'll pass. Bet you come running back in after ten minutes, moaning that your hair's gone frizzy. I could stay out there for days if I had to.'

'Do you have to turn everything into a competition? Fine – you'd survive out in the wilds for days, eating nothing but seaweed and the odd raw hermit crab, I believe you.' She turned to go. 'By the time we come back, my bet is that you'll have snuck off to the pub. Hope you can manage to battle successfully against the elements snuggled up to a blazing fire armed only with a pint of beer and a packet of cheese-and-onion crisps.'

'What an excellent plan.'

Only a shower

Miranda stood by the back door, tucking her hair into her scarf.

'Wait, Mum! Dad's coming with us!'

'Is he?'

'Yes, he was reading upstairs. You forgot to ask him if he wanted to come.'

'So I did. Silly me.'

Anna tried to walk on her toes. 'It's really hard to go on tiptoes in wellies.'

'That's probably why you don't see many ballerinas in them. Is he ready then? Do you want to tell him to hurry up?'

'He's putting his boots on. Can we take some hot chocolate? Say yes, say yes! Oh, *please*.'

'You're getting to be *such* an old ham.' Miranda looked out of the window. 'I don't think we'll be outside long enough to want it, Anna. It's pretty wet.'

'It's only a shower.' Anna repeated one of Simon's favourite expressions and her mother laughed.

Miranda was just pouring the hot chocolate into the flask when Simon came into the kitchen.

'I can't believe I left my binoculars behind, I'm such an idiot.'

'Well, there won't be many birds around in this, will there?'

Simon hunched over the sink, peering out.

'It'll clear up any second now. It's only a shower.'

'Maybe one of the others has a pair?' She shrugged. 'Worth asking anyway.'

He nodded and clumped off to the sitting room in his boots.

'Joe, you wouldn't have any binoculars with you, by any wild chance?' Simon poked his head round the door of the sitting room.

'Sorry, mate.'

'You're welcome to borrow mine,' Giles said, without looking up. 'This is a great part of the world for bird life.' He frowned towards the window. 'Though perhaps not right at this minute.'

'It's easing off now.' Simon hovered awkwardly, half in and half out of the room. 'Well, if you really don't mind . . .'

'Not at all.' Giles stood up. 'They're in my room.'

Simon began to follow him, then stayed in the hallway well away from the door to Giles's bedroom.

Giles tugged at the handle on one side of a drawer, but it stuck almost at once. He jiggled it, trying to free it one-handed, turned towards the door.

'Ah, it's a little awkward, you see—'

Simon came in and pushed the drawer back in, then smoothly pulled it out with both hands. Stood back while Giles took out the binoculars and handed them over. Simon nodded approvingly.

'Good make.'

'The best,' Giles confirmed.

'I wouldn't have figured you for a bird-watcher.'

'Well, even the most diehard exploitative capitalist has to have the occasional hour off.'

Simon laughed half-heartedly.

'Thanks for these.' He looked round at the room, the badly made bed, the clothes slung across the chair. 'Um, are you managing all right? With your arm, I mean? It must be tricky. Have you got any help at home?'

'Such as . . . ?'

'A – well, a – a – someone to help.'

'Kathryn packed for me – which explains the necessity of my buying a pair of shoes earlier today – and my cleaning lady attends to certain practicalities in any case . . . shopping and so forth . . .'

Simon shifted from foot to foot.

' . . . but it's at times like this that one does feel in want of a wife, it's true.' Giles closed the drawer and adjusted his arm.

'Not just to tidy up though presumably?' Simon said pointedly, then his tone softened. 'Well, perhaps you'll marry again?' He turned to leave.

'Perhaps. I rather doubt it.' He followed Simon out of the room. 'I'm afraid I am occasionally pursued by ageing widows or women half my age keen to become better acquainted with the contents of my bank account – but – alas – the kind of woman one would really *desire* . . . tends to be already spoken for.'

248

'Yeah, well. It's always the way, I guess.'

'But who knows – perhaps I'll be lucky enough to find myself a wonderful woman fleeing some ingrate who doesn't appreciate her true worth?'

'Um. Well. Yes, perhaps you will.' Simon zipped up his jacket and headed for the kitchen. 'Thanks again. I'll bring them right back.'

Giles waved in an expansive gesture.

'No rush.'

Skipping stones

Simon helped Anna negotiate the slippery steps down to the beach. At the bottom, she jumped the last three, then ran towards the waves, the soles of her boots scrunching against the stones before she reached the sand. It was raining steadily now and they were the only people on the beach.

Simon bent to pick up a small, flat stone. He turned side on to the sea, scooped his arm back and low, then flicked it forward, sending the stone skipping out over the water.

'Be better when the sea's a bit calmer.' He stood up straight.

Anna lobbed a pebble underhand into the sea and it plonked down at once below the waves with a small splash.

'Show me how to do it, Dad! Why can't I do it?'

'It's just practice, sweetheart. And having the right stone: look for a nice big, flat one.'

All three turned their attention downwards, scanning the shoreline for the best stones. Then Simon squatted down behind Anna, guiding her arm, showing her how to throw. The stone jumped once, twice, then disappeared beneath the waves.

'I did it!'

'Well done!' Miranda and Simon said together.

'You have a go, Mum.'

'I'm no good at it. I haven't got the knack.'

'Dad can show you how, can't you, Daddy?' Anna came and took her mother's hand and pulled her closer to the water's edge.

'I know *how* to do it, Anna, I'm just lousy at it.'

'You always say I shouldn't give up just because I'm not good at something. And Miss Strauss says you have to try, try again.'

Simon smiled at her.

'The trick is to get your arm down low,' he told Miranda. 'And try to flick it, give it a bit of a spin.' He turned her sideways. 'Stand like this.'

'There's no point. I'm absolutely useless, you know I am.'

'What kind of attitude is that? Whatever would Miss Strauss say?' He looked intently into her eyes. 'Don't you ever want to improve . . . yourself?'

'Of course I do.' Miranda snatched the stone from his hand and swung her arm back, flung it forward, fast and low. It skittered across the waves in a string of bounces.

Miranda stood upright, feeling ridiculously pleased with herself.

'That was so brilliant, Mummy!' Anna jumped up and clapped her hands.

'There you go,' said Simon. 'Not so hopeless when you choose not to be.'

'Cheers.'

Now, the rain started to ease off and became no more than a thin drizzle. Anna tugged her hood down, back from her face. Miranda tried to pull it up again.

'It's wetter than you think, beanlet.'

Anna pulled away.

'I don't like it up. It feels funny.'

Miranda turned to Simon to share a weary-parent look.

'Do we think it's time for hot chocolate?' she ventured.

They stood huddled against the rock face, looking out across the water. Simon tried out the binoculars.

'These are miles better than mine.' He passed them down to Anna. 'Fantastic. Look how far you can see.'

'I can't see anything. I want to see the Mermaid. Where's she gone?'

Simon bent down to her eye level and helped her refocus the binoculars.

'There, see? She's not far out at all. Right there!' He pointed out to the left of the bay. 'You're aiming too far to the right. Let me line them up for you.'

'I see! I see her now!'

The flask had only two cups. Miranda passed Anna a half-full cup of hot chocolate. She gave the second cup to Simon.

'What about you?'

'I'm OK.'

He took a sip and passed the cup back to her.

'We can share.'

Miranda tipped the cup to her lips, breathing in the warm chocolatey smell, feeling the steam on her cheeks. She glanced across at Simon, who was watching her. He smiled tentatively and she lowered the cup and smiled back. Why couldn't it always be like this? She opened her mouth to say something, then thought better of it. Every time she spoke, she seemed to say the wrong thing. Better to shut up. Dipped her head to drink once more. She handed him the cup again and risked another small smile. He drank and sighed happily, sniffing from the hot liquid.

'Good hot chocolate.' He nodded. 'Just the job.'

Anna leaned back against him, and looked up at them both, her smiling mouth topped by a hot-chocolate moustache.

'What are you grinning at, little bean?' Miranda bent over her and kissed her. 'You're all chocolatey.'

Anna licked her lips, then puffed out her cheeks.

'I just like it here, that's all.'

Just us

Rob and Tamsin had decided to drive into town to try a restaurant there for supper and, with a minor amount of arm-twisting, Joe had persuaded Rob to take Giles' with them.

The children were bathed and asleep in bed, the adults' glasses were filled with wine, supper was steaming on the table.

'Ah . . .' Miranda spooned out the rice onto plates, ladled on generous portions of chilli con carne. 'God, it's so nice to be just us, isn't it?'

Joe cast a glance at his wife.

Miranda passed Kath a plate.

'Sorry, Kath – you know I don't mean to be horrible.' She looked briefly at Simon. 'I guess it comes naturally to me, doesn't it, darling? It's just a bit easier without . . . everyone all at once.'

'Still, Tamsin's on quite good form, isn't she?' Kath said. 'She's being rather sweet really.'

'*Really, really* sweet. Like, totally sweet. *Mummy* would be proud of her.' Miranda dolloped chilli onto

Simon's plate and handed it over. 'Sorry, sorry – I'll shut up.'

'Actually, I agree with you, I much prefer it like this. Dad's being even more grumpy than usual. I feel like I have to watch the children every single second of the day to make sure they're not stepping a toe out of line, it's exhausting.' Kath gestured to Simon. 'Chuck us the salad over, will you, Simon?'

He passed her the bowl.

'Well, when people are in pain, they tend to lash out. Like an animal does. It's hardly surprising really.'

'My God – Simon defending Giles, now I think I've seen everything.'

'Miranda, whatever else you may think of me, I hope you at least accept that I'm a fair man.'

'Yes, yes.' She waved the ladle around impatiently. 'Of course I do. In fact, I think you're extremely fair. *Irritating* much of the time,' she couldn't resist adding with a smile. 'But certainly fair.'

'Good, I'm glad you concede that at least. Whatever differences Giles and I may have in the way we see the world . . . considerable differences, obviously . . . we do share a common humanity and—'

'Ha! What's brought about this sudden change of heart? *You're* the one who's always acted as if Giles were practically the devil incarnate – what about the time he said we should all be as wasteful as possible because it would create more jobs and be good for the economy? You looked like you were ready to punch him.'

'Oh, Manda, I'm sure Dad didn't really mean that!' Kath said through a mouthful of chilli. 'You know how he loves to be provocative.'

Simon nodded in agreement.

'I'd say all of us enjoy the stimulus of a good argument, don't we?'

'Mmm, some of us more than others.' Miranda took a gulp of her wine. 'Me, I think I've had more than enough stimulation of that kind on this holiday so far.'

'Anyway, my *point* was simply that of course I am capable of having compassion for a fellow human being who's in any kind of pain. And not just physical pain. Perhaps Giles is starting to feel his age, too? He can't be all that far off retirement, not easy for someone used to a certain degree of power and status. I imagine it must be quite difficult for him, anticipating his old age . . . without the focus of work . . . without . . . well, alone.'

Kath smiled at him.

'We all know you're full of heart, Simon. You have oodles of compassion.'

'Yes, oodles and oodles,' said Miranda, suddenly getting the giggles. 'Your oodles are beyond reproach. Personally speaking, I'm extremely fond of your oodles.'

Kath started laughing too.

'Shall we have oodles on toast tomorrow?'

'In sauce? Or do you prefer your oodles *au naturel*?'

'What's up with you two?' Joe shook his head. 'Oodles of wine, I think.'

*   *   *

After supper, they retired to the sitting room with their coffee and slumped onto the sofas in companionable silence for a while.

'I'd love a bath in peace for a change, without people impatiently pacing up and down the landing,' Miranda said, slowly levering herself to her feet. 'Will anyone think me antisocial if I trot off?'

Lazy shaking of heads.

'Leave it in, will you?' Simon looked up at her. 'I'll have it after you.'

'Of course. I wouldn't dream of *wasting* any water.' She smiled down at him, then leaned over to kiss him lightly on the top of his head. 'I was planning to make Kath and Joe have it after me as well. Then we can invite the neighbours in for a turn if you like.'

Lying back in a glorious deep, scented bath, islands of bubbles drifting around her, Miranda heard the others returning from their supper, the thoughtless banging of doors, Rob's loud voice. Oh joy, oh joy, let the revels begin once more. She sank lower into the bath, letting her ears go below the surface to blot out the intrusive new sounds, so that only the oval of her face was above the water.

When it became merely warm rather than her preferred boiling-oil temperature, Miranda got out and dried herself. She changed into her pyjamas and robe, then went downstairs to tell Simon that the bath was now free. Simon only ever had second-hand baths, otherwise he showered and even that at some speed, but whether that was just to save water and energy or because he was impatient with any kind of hedonism she was never entirely sure.

She poked her head round the sitting-room door.

'Anyone seen Simon?'

'I think he's outside,' Joe said.

Miranda headed for the back door, flicking on the kettle as she passed. Simon was on the patio, looking up at the night sky.

'Your bath awaits,' she said, following his gaze. 'It's nearly a full moon. Beautiful.'

'Mmm. Couple of nights till it's full.'

'The stars are so much clearer here. You don't realize how many there are when you're in London.'

'No. Too much light pollution.'

'Yes. Well, at least that makes us appreciate the stars when we can see them.'

He nodded and turned to go.

'Have a nice bath.' She felt suddenly quite soft and mellow, wanting to be pleasant towards everyone. 'Do you want a drink of anything brought up? Wine? Hippy tea?'

'No, I'm fine, thanks. See you upstairs in a bit.'

Beneath a starlit sky

After less than a minute, Miranda went back in to make herself a herbal tea. She wanted to watch the stars a little longer, so she grabbed her coat from the hall and put it on over her dressing gown. Returned to the patio.

A step behind her. No need to turn round to see who it was. The click of a cigarette lighter.

'Call me a hopeless old romantic.' Rob inhaled deeply by her side. 'But doesn't a night like this make you want to lie on the grass next to someone you love looking up at all those stars?'

'Yup. Pretty much.'

'I miss this, living in London. Don't you?'

She nodded in the darkness.

'Mmm. I always forget just how different it is once you're out in the country. When I was a kid, my sister and I used to lie on the lawn like starfish, trying to work out the constellations.'

'That's the Great Bear up there.' He pointed. 'Bet you thought a city boy like me wouldn't know that.'

'Everyone knows the Great Bear, Rob. Though I still think it should be called the Saucepan. Besides, you have no idea what I think. About anything.'

'Don't I?' He proffered the packet of cigarettes. 'I think you would love a cigarette. Am I right?'

Miranda looked nervously over her shoulder, then quickly took one.

'You're right about that, but not necessarily about anything else.'

He leaned slightly closer so that the sides of their arms were almost touching. She felt what seemed like a buzz of static fizzing between their flesh.

'I think Miranda would like to lie back on the grass to look at the stars. And I think Rob would like to lie next to her.'

Seconds of silence. A sky full of stars.

Miranda stepped to the edge of the patio.

'The grass is probably too damp.'

Rob bent down to lay the flat of his hand against it.

'Bone dry. Well, almost.'

She looked back towards the house.

'Just for a minute then.'

He led the way to the far end of the lawn, beyond the apple tree. There they lay side by side, looking up, their eyes shining in the light of the moon and the stars. Her hand rested open palm up, the fingers loosely curled like petals. Then she felt his hand by hers, one finger gently dabbed the centre of her palm. She breathed in, feeling overwhelmed, small and fragile and tender under the vastness of the sky above.

'Manda,' he said. 'Do you remember?'

'*Sssh.*' She shut her eyes for a second to give herself a moment's respite from the hugeness of it all. 'What do you think?' she said. 'How could I forget?'

Remembering

There is bad sex, average sex and good sex. If you have bad sex, you can only hope for it to be so lousy that it at least makes it worth recounting to your friends at a later date: the boyfriend who thought it was deeply erotic and sensual to insert fruit into your personal regions but was somewhat less adept at removing it, so you had to shove half your arm up there, like a vet up to your elbow in innards, trying to root about for three grapes (seedless at least) and the top half of an overripe banana, and you've never been able to so much as look at a mashed-banana sandwich since; the one whose penis was so minute you had no idea whether he was inside you or was still fiddling about with his thumb; the one who tried to trim your pubic hair with nail clippers while he thought you were asleep; the one who attempted to lift you up and take you manfully against the wall but hadn't realized how heavy you were and you had to stop and shoehorn him into your car to drive him to an osteopath for emergency treatment; the one who jiggled bits of you at high speed, saying, 'There, yes!? Is that good for you? You're getting wet now, right?' while somehow managing never to touch your clitoris, not even accidentally; the one who wanted you to put bulldog clips on his nipples . . .

Average sex is like a bath that's already not quite as hot as you wanted it to be the moment you get in – and you know the longer you stay in, the more you're going to want to get out, and yet you can't quite be bothered to bring it to an end so you lie there until you're completely cold. It's mildly pleasant, at least to start with, but you'd probably have enjoyed yourself more with a decent book, a nice drop of Chenin Blanc, and set menu no. 2 from the Peking Garden. And you'd have had a free pair of disposable chopsticks thrown in.

Good sex makes you smile suddenly when you're waiting for your train the next day, so that you have to bury your face in your book and pretend that *How to Become More Organized and Get Things Done* is unexpectedly amusing.

And, of course, there is *sex. Sex* so amazing that it has to be thought of in italics, *sex* that makes your skin tingle not just the next day or the next week but two, three years later when you happen to pass someone who has the same sort of smell, *sex* so good you lose the power to think or to speak, so good you don't know whose body is whose and don't care, so good you forget where you are and who you are. The kind of sex you dream about, then wake up feeling flushed and embarrassed, knowing that your face has that freshly shagged glow, the kind of sex you imagine that other people have all the time, the kind of sex you want to have again. That kind of sex.

The air seems hot and close in Miranda's hotel room. Eventually, Rob unsticks himself from her and they lie side by side, breathing heavily.

'Jeez,' Rob says. He tilts her face towards him and kisses her almost numb lips. 'Now I really can't believe we haven't done this before.'

'We have a major backlog to catch up on, I hope you realize.' She smiles, then starts to get up.

'Noooooo – where are you going?'

'Loo. I'm leaking.' Miranda clamps her legs together and kangaroo-hops across to the bathroom. She leaves the door slightly ajar. 'Good grief, had you been stock-piling it? I should have a shower.'

'Later. Come back to bed.'

'Bossy. I'm glad I don't have a big brother.'

'And I hope he wouldn't be telling you to come back to bed if you did have one.'

Miranda crawls back in alongside him, nestles into his shoulder.

'This is a bit like incest though, isn't it?'

'How so?' His breath is hot in her hair.

'Kath's sort of like a sister. Admittedly, a lot nicer and less infuriating than my actual sister, but . . . And your mum was always so lovely to me. She always used to give me a big hug and wanted to hear what I'd been up to.'

'Well, personally, I'm damn glad I'm not your brother under the circs.' He drops a kiss on her forehead.

'Aren't you getting on with your mum? Kath thinks she's fantastic.'

Miranda nods.

'She *is* fantastic. Absolutely fantastic. No doubt about it. As well as working at the clinic, she visits schools, gives talks, she goes all over the place, educating people about contraception: advising, listening, helping – she's a marvel. I really admire her.'

'But?'

'But.' Miranda sits upright and plumps up her pillow. 'I don't interest her. She can't understand why I don't want to be a doctor, like her, or an aid worker, or a prison reformer or something. She thinks I'm shallow and selfish and trivial, that I just want to have my own shop with my name in big letters above the window and have my shoes appear in *Vogue*.'

'You're not like that.'

'Oh, but I am!' She turns to look at him. 'I am absolutely shallow and I'd kill to have my own shop. I *am* selfish. I don't want to save the world, I wouldn't know where to start – I just want to walk down the street spotting glamorous women wearing gorgeous shoes designed by me.'

'That's not so bad, is it? What's wrong with wanting to be successful and make your mark on the world? Isn't that what we all want, in one way or another? I mean, you're not wanting to take over the country and execute anyone who refuses to wear your shoes, are you? Or are

263

you?' His hand slides down the soft curve of her tummy, lingers at the crease of her thigh for a moment. Her eyes flutter closed and she pushes against him.

'Now that – ' she says, her breath growing thick, 'is a first-rate plan.'

'Rob?'

The silence was cut by a voice. Kath's voice, not loud, but clear in the night. Kath, hovering on the back doorstep in her towelling dressing gown. Rob sat up quickly.

'Yup. Just having a quick fag.'

'I think Tamsin's wondering where you are. I wasn't sure . . . '

Miranda swept at herself, attempting to brush off any loose bits of grass.

'We were trying to spot constellations, but we were just coming in anyway.'

'Good.'

Rob and Miranda went back inside, not looking at each other. With Kath, they turned off the lights and locked up, then they slowly made their way upstairs and parted to go to their separate rooms.

Wednesday

A helping hand

'Dad?' Kath tapped quietly on Giles's bedroom door. There was no answer. She tried again. 'Um, Dad? I've brought you a cup of tea.' Still no response.

She opened the door a little way and squeezed her head round the gap.

The lavatory flushed, water running in the basin. Giles emerged from the en suite shower room, struggling to zip up his trousers left-handed. He was bare-chested.

'Oh, sorry. I didn't mean to disturb you. I thought you might like some tea.' She held out the cup at arm's length, as if proffering a live mouse to a peckish python. 'Hasn't Rob been in to – to help you with . . . things . . . ?'

'Apparently not.' Giles checked his watch on the bedside table and made no comment.

'Maybe he's having a lie-in. Shall I . . . ?' She took one small pace towards him. 'Or would you rather wait for him?'

'I can't skulk in my room until noon, drifting about half-dressed like some depressed idler.'

Kath crossed to the wardrobe and Giles pointed out his choice of shirt.

'Now, how do we do this exactly?' She held it out tentatively.

'Not at speed preferably,' Giles said, deadpan. 'Robert insisted on wrestling me into it yesterday as if up against the clock.' He showed her how to hold the shirt open so that he could ease his injured arm in first.

Kath laid a gentle hand on his left arm.

'This is tough for you, I know. You don't like being a patient, do you?'

Giles wrinkled his nose in distaste.

'What sane person does?'

'*Lots* of people. Joe's almost never ill, but when he is . . . he takes to his bed like a *grande dame* of opera, coughing pathetically and calling out in a pitiful voice for hot drinks and to have his pillows plumped up.' She carefully pulled the shirt round so that Giles could slide in his good arm. He smiled and nodded his approval, then Kath did up the buttons.

'Now. Your sling.' She frowned in concentration as she helped him on with it, then he sat down while she reknotted it. 'Not too tight?'

'No. That's good.' He stood up. 'You might have made a half-decent nurse, Kathryn.'

'Er . . . thanks. I think they get paid even less than teachers do. Rob says I should have become a lawyer like you, but I haven't got the right sort of mindset for it. I'm too gullible. And too soft. Your laser brain and – and – shrewdness and everything must have all gone straight to Rob, so I didn't get a look-in.'

'You're hardly a stupid woman, Kathryn.' Giles reached for his tea, which was well beyond his grasp. Kath quickly passed it to him. 'Constance was extremely bright, as you know. And I'd say you're looking more like her every day.'

'Thank you. Am I really?' She flushed and turned away, picked up one of his jumpers from the back of a chair. 'Would you like this round your shoulders?' Kath stretched up and carefully placed it across his broad back, came round the front to knot the sleeves loosely, looking up at him. 'I wish I'd inherited some of your height at least.'

'Hmm. I've lost a good inch or two, you know. I'm being eroded slowly and surely like a cliff face.' He smiled and shook his head. 'Growing old is a terrible business, Kathryn, you have no idea.'

'You're not old, you're distinguished.' She smiled and stepped back to look at him. 'There. Very hand-some. You look quite the country gent.'

'Flatterer.' He picked up his watch and passed it to her without further comment for her to strap on his wrist. 'Remind me – is your anniversary today? I suppose I should have got you some sort of present?'

'No, it's tomorrow. We don't need a present. It's only nine years, not a special one. Well, they're all special to us, of course . . . but—'

'Your mother and I were married for twenty-nine.'

'I know, Dad. I do remember.'

'Quite an achievement.'

Kath frowned.

'That's one way of looking at it.'

He glanced down at her, then looked round for his shoes.

'Can you see my new loafers?'

She scurried across to pick them up from beneath the chair.

'These are smart. It was kind of Miranda to come with you, wasn't it? Not everyone gets to have such an expert style adviser.'

'Do you think she came out of pity then?'

'No, of course not. What a funny thing to say. I just meant it was *kind,* that's all, you don't need to read anything into it. But not everyone would take their best friend's father shopping, would they? Miranda is a kind person. She always paints herself as some sort of harpy from hell, but it's not at all true. People often read her wrong, just because she can be a little bit . . . brusque at times . . .'

Giles laughed.

'What? Don't be mean. You like her, don't you?'

'Do I *like* Miranda?' He smiled down at her, then shook his head as if humouring her. 'I think *like* is too – too *anaemic* a word for such a woman, don't you? She's not a slice of Madeira cake. Miranda is not a person anyone could have such a mild opinion about, I'd have thought.

Not at all.' He laughed again, but to himself it seemed. 'Thank you for your help.' He nodded, dismissing her. 'I'll be through shortly.'

An unexpected suggestion

Miranda opened her eyes to find Simon lying on his side, apparently watching her as if she were some exotic or interesting object that had washed up on the shore.

'Simon? What is it? What's the matter?'

'Nothing.'

'Oh. Are you . . . all right?'

'Yes, thanks. I'm fine. You?'

'Mmm.' She twisted her head round to see the clock. 'Is Anna up?'

He nodded, smiling.

'She's downstairs, deep in a book and a bowl of Coco Pops.'

Miranda looked sidelong at Simon. He still hadn't moved. What on earth was he up to? Being pleasant first thing in the morning.

'Shall I go and make some coffee?' she offered, feeling slightly unnerved.

'Don't move just yet.' He moved down the bed a little, and inched closer to her, his hand resting lightly on the duvet near her breast.

She turned her head towards him.

'You know, you have such an amazing face.' He reached out and stroked his fingertip down the centre of her face from hairline to chin.

'Yeah. Right.' OK, this was starting to freak her out now. She dug her nails into the side of her thighs, stopping herself from saying, *What's brought this on? What do you want? Can you stop now?*

'I forget how beautiful you are . . .' He teased out one of her curls, holding it as gently as if it were a butterfly.

'Don't worry – I won't hold it against you. Every time I look in the mirror and am confronted by this haggard old bag, I forget how beautiful I am.' She gave him a puzzled smile. 'You are taking the piss, aren't you?'

He shook his head in silence.

'Really? Ah . . . well . . . thanks.' She glanced at him sideways. His eyes were dark and shining, as if he were near tears. 'It's OK, you know – I don't expect a non-stop chorus of appreciation after all these years.' She found herself starting to babble, desperate to break the intensity of his gaze. 'Of course, we all stop noticing each other, don't we? It's normal. When you live with someone day in, day out – well, you're bound to – I mean – sometimes I wonder what I'm – I know I – I take many of your good qualities for granted – your – your – decency – and – and – sincerity and things . . . your sharp mind. Your patience. Kindness.'

'But it's not *good* to stop noticing,' Simon said quietly. 'And it's not just the noticing. After a while, you don't

272

really see the other person any more. They just become part of the landscape, like . . . I don't know . . . '

'Like that pile of clutter that always accrues at one end of the kitchen worktop? It's irritating, but it would feel peculiar if anybody ever got round to tidying it away? There'd be an odd gap.'

He laughed.

'A bit like that maybe.'

'It's good to hear you laugh.' She smiled sadly. 'We don't laugh as much as we used to, do we?'

'Mmm.'

With his fingertip, he traced a meandering path over her face, making her skin tingle. She shivered slightly and felt her nipples stiffen against the crisp cotton of the covers. *I don't understand*, she thought, *I can't cope with this. Why are you suddenly being nice?* She tried to keep her body rigid, resisting the urge to curve towards him, striving not to soften, to yield. Her eyes fluttered closed for a moment.

'When you're asleep, you look like a painting.' Simon tenderly touched the corner of her eye.

'Who by? Don't say Hieronymus Bosch.'

'No . . . that's when you're awake.'

'Git.' She thumped him playfully.

'There's definitely a touch of Rubens in there.' His hand cupped the smooth roundness of her shoulder.

'Ha! Everyone's favourite euphemism for a fatso! So, Rubens for my thighs and undulating folds. Lovely.'

'Curls courtesy of Botticelli.'

273

'OK, now I know you want something. What is it? You want me to sign over my pension fund to Friends of the Earth? You want us to take in a whole family of refugees?'

'Don't be so suspicious.' He kissed the dip behind her collarbone. 'It's not *so* extraordinary for me to be nice . . . is it?'

'Mmm,' she said quietly. 'Perhaps niceness has been a little thin on the ground lately?'

He said nothing, but his hand crept slowly beneath the covers as he sidled closer towards her. He stroked-the dip of her waist, his thumb enjoying the give of her flesh. Miranda pressed her thighs together tightly. *Was this his new strategy? Keep her sex-starved most of the time, so she'd be raring to go any time he condescended to feel in the mood. Still, twice in one week? But maybe she should get the good now. Feast while you can; famine could be just around the corner.*

'Miranda?' Simon kissed her lightly on the lips.

'Mmm?' Still wary.

'You know, I've been thinking.' His hand sliding over her hip towards her thigh. 'Maybe we *should* try for another baby.'

Dear God. The man must be ill.

'What about overpopulating the planet?' she said lightly. 'Why the sudden change of heart?' *What about the fact that we've barely had a civil conversation for nearly three months?*

'We-e-e-ll, yes, there is that, of course. But, strictly speaking, we wouldn't be creating a net increase, would we? Because we'd only have produced replacements of ourselves – numerically speaking. Of course, there'd be a temporary increase, during the overlap, but as soon as we died . . .'

'That's certainly a joyful way of looking at it.'

'You *know* that's not how I feel about it; I'm simply putting it in a logical context so that we can see it clearly. So that we know we're taking the decision responsibly rather than because of some irrational urge. There's no point getting emotional about everything.'

'We're talking about a *baby,* Simon. A new life. Not a numerical replacement. It's not about how many kilowatts of energy a wind turbine can produce, it's about-making a new, little person – why shouldn't I be emotional about it – what could possibly be more emotional than that?' Miranda sat up and plumped up the pillows behind her. 'Besides, don't you think we've left too big a gap? A baby won't be much company for Anna, will it?'

'I was reading a study the other day which showed that, in fact, sibling relationships with an age difference of six years or more can be extremely healthy and mutually supportive. Apparently, there are far fewer problems with rivalry and jealousy when there's a larger gap. The older child tends to feel protective rather than threatened.'

'Plus there is the additional minor problem that I'm completely knackered most of the time as it is. I'm not sure I want to put us through all that again – sleepless nights, nappies, teething, tantrums.'

'But *you* wouldn't have to be put through it. That's the fantastic thing: I've been giving a lot of thought to this. I'm based almost entirely at home these days in any case. It'll be very different from last time. And, now that you're doing so well, I could work fewer hours if you liked, perhaps even take two or three years out completely. All you'd need to do would be to express enough milk for the night-time feeds, and for the days, too, obviously, if you needed to be at the shop or at meetings. And I'd do everything else. You would hardly have to be bothered at all.'

Miranda got out of bed and pulled on her dressing gown. Looked into his eyes. Yes, he was definitely serious.

'Well, it sounds as though you have it all worked out.'

Simon nodded.

'I've tried to consider all the factors. And, financially, it certainly seems to make sense this way. Remember how much we spent on childcare when Anna was small. Crazy, really, when you think of it. And a hired person is no substitute for a – a real parent in any case.'

'So, let's get this straight: you'd impregnate me, so I guess I'd have to be around at that point – and presumably my involvement would extend to my putting up with morning sickness and piles and stretch marks and being poked and prodded and cut about, but otherwise I could pretty much keep out of it – then I'd hand the baby over to you – I'd get hooked up to the milking machine twice a day – and you'd have a nice, cosy set-up with a paid-for house and a new baby and as long as I kept bringing in the money I wouldn't have to be *bothered* with feeding the baby or changing it or cuddling it or – or – *loving* it, is that correct?'

Simon got up and quickly grabbed yesterday's cords and T-shirt, which had been lying on the floor.

'How very like you to choose to misconstrue me completely, Miranda. You've managed to turn an entirely considerate, unselfish offer on my part into something that makes me sound like a selfish sponger.' He yanked on the T-shirt and reached for his fleece. 'A paid-for house? You think I'm asking to be a kept man? Yes, we all know the house is in your name and that you pay the mortgage, as you like to tell people at every opportunity, but I've always paid my way. Naturally enough, in this skewed world we live in, work like mine may not be financially rewarded very highly, though feeling that one is making some small contribution is reward enough, of course. Not everyone is *obsessed* with being successful, not that everyone would define success as making huge sums of money by selling silly, spoilt, rich women shoes they can't even walk in when they already have forty-five other pairs at home even though presumably they only have the one pair of feet. You pander to the worst tendencies of rampant consumerism in our society, Miranda, yet – bizarrely – for some reason you seem determined to make out that *I'm* the bad guy.'

'I see.' She pulled on her robe and stood by the door, ready to make a quick exit. 'And you wanted to have a baby with this particular overpaid, evil, exploitative capitalist for what reason exactly? Perhaps you were hoping your Saviour of the Universe genes would be dominant enough to cancel mine out altogether? But what if your cunning plan went awry? What if we bred ourselves a fledgling banker? A lawyer? A demon child – maybe his sole ambition in life would be to rebel against you and to go and hack down the rest of the rainforest to make the world's largest prairie of genetically modified wheat. Then what would you do?'

Simon slumped onto the bed. Miranda paused for a moment, wondering whether she had gone too far. Ach, bollocks to him – he'd started it. Did he really imagine that having a baby would shore up their crumbling relationship? Surely he couldn't be that naïve? She slung her towel casually over her shoulder, as if she were off for a swim.

'Well, I guess I'd better have a shower. See if I can have a clean body at least, even if my soul is beyond help according to you.'

She longed to slam the door, but she gritted her teeth and pulled it closed carefully behind her, to avoid arousing even more curiosity. The others must be sick of it already – living all cramped together like this, they could hardly be unaware of the raised voices and tension. *My soul is beyond help*? For God's sake, Miranda, that was truly ridiculous – if you're so desperate to have the last word, at least say something with some sort of point, that was pathetic. It was the kind of thing Simon might say.

Wet, wet, wet

Bugger – the bathroom light was on and she could hear the shower. There was a chance it might be Kath, bumped to this bathroom because Joe was in the other one. Miranda could hear Simon banging about in the bedroom – if he came out and she were still loitering on the landing having made her prima donna exit, she'd look ridiculous.

She tapped tentatively at the bathroom door.

'Sorry – um, are you going to be much longer? Kath?'

'Is that you?' Rob's voice.

'Yes.'

The door opened a crack. He was dripping wet, a white towel tucked round his waist.

'God, I'm sorry – you meant Tamsin, of course! I wasn't thinking.'

He shook his head.

'No, I didn't. Quick – come in!' He grabbed her arm and pulled her inside. They heard her bedroom door open, and he shoved the door shut. Miranda slid the bolt across and they both stood leaning against the door, their heads close, listening. Simon's footsteps crossing the landing, pausing outside the door. Miranda looked up into Rob's eyes, held one hand up, motioning for him to be silent.

The footsteps moved on, then she heard Simon thudding downstairs.

Slowly, Rob raised one hand and brought it to her face. He wound his finger gently into one of her curls, then softly touched her cheek, traced a line over its contours, then paused at the corner of her mouth. His fingertip pressed the pad of her lower lip and she silently kissed it. And now he pulled her tight to him, effortlessly enfolding her with one arm, bent towards her.

'Manda . . . my Miranda.' Cupping her cheek again. 'So, *so* lovely.'

She tilted her face up to his, feeling her hips automatically pressing close to him. His mouth on hers now, lips brushing lips lightly for a moment, then opening, his tongue sliding into her mouth, entering her. His wet hair dripped onto her upturned face like rain, and she closed her eyes the better to feel it. He crushed her even closer, almost too hard, his arm strong around her, as his other hand reached down – slip-sliding down the front of her silk robe, seeking the opening – tugging at the tie-belt, laughing at himself, clumsy in his eagerness – she pulled the bow loose and the robe fell open – his breath caught in his throat as he saw her, a low, raw sound like an animal – he pushed aside the soft silk from softer skin – dipped his head to one breast, nipping at the nipple with his lips, then taking it into his mouth, his tongue wet and warm on her – she fumbled at his towel – his hand sought her – strong and certain – brushing against the tops of her thighs for a moment to tease her – his fingers finding home, rubbing her, then sliding into her, still holding her up with one arm as she gasped and crumpled against him. He dropped his towel to the floor and pulled off her robe, clutched her tight to him. In silence, they looked around at the tiny floor space, the too-small bath, the squashed shower cubicle. Wordlessly, they spread out their towels in the narrow gap between bath and wall. Rob dropped to his knees and ran his thumb along the top of her dark pubic hair, leaned forward to kiss those damp curls, entwine his fingers. He took her hand, pulling her down, down to lie with him. His dark head close to hers now, then journeying down, his mouth moving over her skin, hot, hungry, tasting every—

'Miranda?' Kath's voice. Right outside the bathroom door. A tentative knock.

Miranda put one finger to her lips, clutched his shoulder.

'Miranda! Is it you in there? Are you all right?'

Miranda struggled to sit up and looked at Rob, panic in her eyes. He nodded.

'Yes! I'm fine! Don't worry! Won't be long!'

'Are you sure you're OK? I thought I heard a noise.'

She bit her lip.

'Yes. I – I've just got a bit of a dodgy tummy, that's all.'

Rob shooed his hand at the door, as if it might make Kath go away. His fingers crept back between Miranda's legs and she shuddered and tried to push him away.

'Oh, sorry. I saw Simon striding off down to the beach. You haven't had a row, have you?'

'So what else is new? It's nothing major! Don't worry about it!'

'Have you seen Rob at all?'

Rob lowered himself closer to Miranda and planted a silent kiss on her lips. Then he gently sucked her bottom lip between his teeth.

'No!' She cleared her throat. 'Why would I have seen Rob?' She mouthed at him: *Stop!*

'It's just Tamsin seemed to think that he was still in the shower . . .'

'No, he isn't.'

Rob made a face and Miranda pinched him. 'Oh, actually I think I spotted him from the window – he must have gone off for a walk.'

A pause.

'Manda?'

Miranda bit her lip.

'Is everything OK? I mean, you're not *doing* anything in there, are you?'

Miranda mouthed 'fuck' as Rob nodded. He picked up her ankles and pulled her closer so her legs were around him.

'You think I'm slashing my wrists because of bloody Simon?' Miranda called out. 'Look, Kath, I honestly have a bit of tummy ache – just give me a few minutes' peace. I'll be down in a tick. Honestly. OK?'

'OK. Sorry. Hope you feel better soon.'

'Thanks.'

Miranda flopped back onto the towels.

'Bit of a passion-killer.'

He rested on his elbows on top of her, wincing as he caught his shoulder on the towel rail, then slowly started kissing her neck, the soft swell of her breasts.

'Mummy?'

They froze.

'Yes, darling? Mummy's on the loo just now.' Miranda tried to scrabble away from Rob.

He laughed silently and brushed her hair out of her eyes.

'Auntie Kath said you've got a tummy ache.'

'Yes, but I'm all right. Go and play in the garden and I'll come out in a minute.'

'Mummy?'

'Yes?'

'You know those little cakes you got at the shop yesterday . . .'

'Yes, *yes*. Have one. Have two if you like – ask Auntie Kath to get them down for you. Leave Mummy in peace. Off you go now!'

Footsteps running downstairs. A sudden thud as Anna jumped the bottom three. Miranda patted Rob's arm and motioned for him to shift off.

'Ayyy!' He banged himself on the towel rail again. 'Jesus!'

They lay on their sides, squashed close, facing each other.

'Rob . . . '

'Yeah. I know. Budge up.'

'I guess the timing could be better.'

'Timing's never been my strong point.'

'Same here.'

'Manda?' His face close to hers, eyes dark and serious.

'Mmm. We'd better get out of here.'

'What do you want to do?'

'What – now, you mean?' Knowing he didn't.

'Uh-uh.'

'Well, what do *you* want to do?'

He smiled and kissed her elbow, bent awkwardly between them.

'I asked you first.'

'I want you to fuck me so hard that I have to walk like a jockey for three days.' She saw him smile again, then a

284

slight frown furrowed his brow. 'And then I want you to take me away somewhere and make love to me slowly . . . ,' she stretched up to kiss him, '. . . for days and days.'

'And then?'

She shook her head.

'I can't think that far ahead.'

They both started as there was a sudden bang on the door.

'Mummy! Can I have some Coke as well?'

Miranda closed her eyes and shook her head.

'Half a glass. And only if you brush your teeth straight away afterwards. Promise?'

'I promise! Cross my heart and hope to die!' Thundering footsteps down the stairs again.

'Dear God,' said Miranda, 'who'd be a parent?'

She pulled herself up by the side of the bath.

'Come on, we can't stay in here all day. Up, up!'

'*I* could.'

'Another two minutes and we'll have the whole pack of them pounding on the door.'

He stood up and looked down into her eyes.

'What say you get dressed and run away with me?' His eyes shining, intent. 'Right now this minute.'

'Sure, that'll work. We could leave a brief note on the kitchen table: Sorry, got bored with this life – gone to get a new one.'

'I can be packed and ready to go in two minutes.'

She peered at him, frowning. Could he possibly be serious?

'Fine, I'll just fold my daughter into my suitcase, will I? Wake up, Rob – we're not in a movie.'

'She could come with us!' He grabbed her arms, but she gently pulled back from him.

'Rob, don't joke about this. It's not funny.'

'I'm not.' He tried to hold her again.

She shook her head.

'I'm not eighteen, I can't just chuck a pair of knickers and a toothbrush in a case and walk out on my life.'

'You could. You can do anything you want. If you really want to.'

She sighed.

'Come on, we have to get out of here.'

'Exactly what I'm saying!'

'Out of the *bathroom*.'

Rob clutched her close to him briefly, kissed her hard on the lips.

'I'm not mucking around, I swear it.' He picked up his towel and tucked it around his waist once more. 'Even if you don't want to do a runner right this minute. Just think about it, Manda, OK? I mean it.'

Missing

Miranda quickly got dressed and attempted to apply some mascara, but her hands were shaking so badly she succeeded only in blotching herself with smudges as if she'd tried to do her make-up during a fairground ride. She opened her underwear drawer again, then snorted at herself and shook her head and shoved it closed. Grow up! As if she could really go sailing off into the sunset at a moment's notice. Of course, it was tempting . . . fine if she *were* in a film, the camera could pan across the pink-tinged sky, take in the trio silhouetted against the rosy sands, two carefree lovers, the young girl skipping happily between them, three lines of footsteps, then the credits would roll. La-la-la, and they all lived happily ever after . . .

But life wasn't like that, was it? It wasn't a game of Barbie dolls where you could just enact a different scenario every time you got bored; it was complicated and messy and it brought demands and responsibilities and consequences. Romance belonged to the world of love letters and fiction and—

She yanked open the drawer once more. They should be right here, where she'd left them. Miranda rifled through a tangle of tights, socks and pants.

The letters had gone.

Calm. Keep calm. They hadn't gone, she'd obviously just put them down somewhere else, she must have done. She was always leaving things in stupid places. Silly, silly Miranda. She must try and be more organized. Closed her eyes and tried to visualize what she'd done with them. Reading them yesterday, yes, then what? She hadn't even looked at them today, hadn't had a moment to, what with – with everything. So . . . yesterday then. But she'd been reading them right here, in the bedroom, hadn't she? Yes. Then . . . ? Oh, she'd gone downstairs to make a cup of coffee and maybe she had them in her hand, clutching them automatically? Miranda quickly ran downstairs. Into the kitchen, eyes sweeping the room, pointlessly peering behind the kettle, opening the bread bin, the fridge. Through to the hall, wading through the heap of children's jackets and fleeces on the chair by the front door as if they could somehow have become buried beneath those. Think, think. Pantry? No. Downstairs loo? No. Oh, God, what would Kath say? Went into the sitting room. Enquiring faces looked up.

'OK?' said Rob, giving her a meaningful smile.

'Hmm. Just mislaid something, that's all.'

'Anything important?' Giles asked.

'No, no. Nothing really. It doesn't matter.' She started to leave, then turned back. 'Has anyone seen Simon?'

'I believe he said something about popping out to save the planet . . .' Rob stood up and stretched, then extended his arms in a Superman pose. 'Make way for SuperSimon, Eco-Warrior! Saving the Globe from Evil Oil Barons and Estate Agents!'

'That's helpful, Rob. Really – have you seen him?'

Shaking of heads.

Miranda ran back upstairs into the bedroom. Checked her drawer again – maybe she'd just somehow not seen them? Heard the front door, then footsteps on the stairs. Simon came in.

'Oh, *there* you are! I couldn't find you.'

Simon raised his eyebrows.

'Why the sudden need for my company?'

'Don't be like that. Look – you know those letters you saw me reading?'

'Letters?'

'Kath's letters – remember?'

'Are those the incredibly private, incredibly secret letters that you had to skulk down to the beach to read? Those letters?'

'Yes.' Miranda sighed. '*Those* letters. The ones belonging to Kath. Not mine. *Kath's.*'

'Hmm, yes I think we've gathered that by now, Miranda. And this concerns me how exactly? Given that they're so top secret that you didn't want me even to see them? Yet now you want me to show an interest?'

'Um – well – it's just – they seem to have disappeared and – well – I was wondering if – possibly – if you'd . . . ' She dropped her gaze.

'You think I took your stupid letters?'

'No-o-o-o-o, not necessarily. I mean, of course not. I just thought you might have seen them? Maybe. Or – or – moved them? Accidentally. Or whatever.'

'You really think I'm interested in nosing into your

private affairs? How pathetic! Is that how you see me? As some sad little snoop? Do you think I have no self-respect whatsoever?'

'No. Of course not, Simon – don't be so melo-dramatic—'

'Says the drama queen—'

'Oh, *please*! For God's sake. They're not *my* private affairs. They're not *my* bloody letters, for the ninety-eighth time. They're Kath's – I promise you – but she entrusted them to me – and I—'

'And you lost them?' He folded his arms and smirked. 'You *do* surprise me. You were given something precious to safeguard and yet you treated it as expendable rubbish? How extraordinary.' He shook his head. 'Well, perhaps it will teach you to be a little less casual about things that are vitally important to other people . . . '

Miranda frowned.

'Simon?'

'I'm off for a walk up on the coastal path. With Anna.' He stopped at the door. 'Oh, and, for the record, I haven't the slightest interest in the ins and outs of whatever sordid little affairs you have going on, so I won't be poking through your things hunting for evidence, OK? Do whatever you like, I really couldn't care less.' He left the room and she heard him running down the stairs, calling for Anna to hurry up and get ready for their walk.

Dazed, Miranda slowly went downstairs. She couldn't

seem to feel her feet. She looked down, watching them beneath her, moving down each step. Was she making them move or were they acting independently? So Simon must have guessed at once that something was going on between her and Rob. Was it really so obvious? Shit, what a godawful mess. Her legs were shaking, she noticed, again thinking they seemed remote from her – strange, alien things over which she had no control. She slumped down and sat at the bottom of the stairs, clutching the banister, laid her hands flat on her knees, trying to steady them.

'Are you all right there?' Joe came into the hall. Miranda stared up at him blankly. 'Miranda? Are you all right?'

'Mmm? Oh. Yes, I'm fine. Sorry. I was just . . .'

'Can I get you anything? Coffee?'

'Yes. Please. Thank you. I mean no. No. I'm fine.' She stood up. 'Sorry – just having a bit of a dozy moment – I felt a bit – so what else is new?' She made a face at her own supposed dizziness. 'Ah, is Kath around?'

'She went down to the beach. Needed a bit of time out.'

'Ah. Don't we all?'

'Sure you don't want a coffee? Let me get you something.'

Miranda shook her head.

'No, thanks. Think I'll just step out for a bit myself. Get some fresh air, clear away the cobwebs.'

'Shall I keep an eye on Anna for you?'

'Uh-uh, no need. She's with Simon.'

Joe nodded.

'Good. Miranda?'

'Mmm.'

'I know it's none of my business, but . . . well, you just take care of yourself, will you?'

Down on the beach

Now, if I were in a bad sitcom, I would rehearse what I have to say in front of the mirror, Miranda thought as she descended the steps to the beach. Um, Kath, I'm really sorry, but I seem to have lost your precious, secret letters and I have absolutely no idea where they are. Simon says I'm cavalier about things and he's right. I'm hopeless. I was sure I had them safe, but I've obviously left them lying around and someone else has picked them up. I don't know what to say. I am so, so sorry.

Kath was sitting on the big, flat rock that squatted squarely almost in the centre of the bay, a natural resting point. The collar of her jacket was turned up against the breeze and she was looking out to sea.

Miranda walked over to the rock.

'Hey. Mind if I join you?'

Kath shook her head, without turning to face Miranda;

it was so very unlike her that Miranda was immediately alarmed.

'Kath? Are you all right?' Miranda stepped in front of her.

Kath was crying silently, tears pouring down her face. Clutched in her right hand was the packet of letters.

'Oh, Kath, Kath . . .' Miranda sat next to her and put her arms around her friend. 'I'm so sorry. Poor you. It's awful, I know.'

Kath let herself be held for a minute, then pulled away slightly.

'It's just the letters, you see.' She looked down at them in her hand.

'I know . . . I guess it must be a real shock . . . I can't imagine how you feel. I really am sorry.'

Kath frowned, head tilted on one side.

'A shock? Not really.' She turned towards Miranda, looking confused.

'Well – perhaps that's the wrong word. I – I meant I'm sorry you're upset, that's all.'

Kath sniffed and dug about in her pockets for a tissue.

'I'm not upset either. Well, not really.' She smiled and blew her nose loudly.

'You're doing a good impression of it.'

'No. I'm OK. It's not what you think . . .'

Miranda sat silently, waiting for Kath to continue.

'And not what I thought. Funny how we all assume so many things, isn't it? I caught sight of the word "Dearest" and immediately assumed that Mum must have had a secret lover—'

'Well, who wouldn't assume that?'

Kath shrugged.

'I don't know. Maybe not Joe? He's very fair.' She scrubbed at her nose with the tissue. 'After you said how nice the letters were and not too rude or anything . . . and, well, I'd been getting more and more impatient to read them, as you know, and . . .'

'And I was taking too long—'

'And you were taking *ages*,' Kath teased. 'So I decided to read them and I looked for you but I couldn't find you, so I popped into your room, you said you'd put them in your knicker drawer and I knew you wouldn't mind . . .'

'You might have told me. I thought I'd lost them.'

'Sorry. I meant to tell you but then I got caught up in the latest it's-not-fair battle and it slipped my mind.'

'But you can't have read them all yet?'

'I didn't try to read every word. And – remember I'm a lot more used to crummy handwriting than you are. Some of my pupils . . . even the eleven-year-olds. Terrible. It's because they never write properly any more unless they have to. They e-mail or text each other.'

'Anyway. So why were you crying?'

'I don't know. Partly because I'm happy that Mum had someone who loved her like this. I mean, *really* loved her.' She looked down at the letters in her hand, stroked the top one tenderly with her thumb. 'And I'm sure she loved him. She must have done. But she didn't sleep with him, I know she didn't.'

'How can you be sure? I mean, well . . .' Miranda looked down.

'Here. You think I'm kidding myself?' Kath passed her one of the letters and pointed to a passage. 'Read this bit.'

. . . I imagine making love to you and it's all so vivid, it's driving me crazy (but I don't want to stop). Part of me – the noble yet foolish part – admires you for being so strong, for refusing to embark on 'a seedy affair' as you put it the other day. The other part of me wishes you weren't such a good woman! Couldn't you try being immoral just for an hour or two? You might like it.

I'm sorry – how low can I sink? You know I can't imagine anything between us being seedy. I do love you.

To me, taking you in my arms and my bed could never be anything other than wonderful and right and true. We will make love, one day – one day very soon, I know it.

'But Kath . . .' Miranda's voice softened, as if she were speaking to a child, 'she could have slept with him after this. Even if it's not in the letters . . . some might be missing.'

Kath shook her head.

'That's just what I thought, of course, but it doesn't look like it. And that doesn't fit when you read the last letter.' She passed Miranda another letter. 'See, that bit there – why would he say that?'

Miranda nodded.

'I think you're right.' She started to re-read the final letter Kath had shown her over again, making sure. 'But this is *incredible.* Really incredible.'

Kath shivered and stood up.

'Can we walk a bit? I'm cold.' They moved off along the sand. 'Why is it incredible? Lots of people must fall in love yet not actually end up having sex together. Especially back then.'

'Kath, it was right at the end of the Sixties – it was exactly when people were bonking away like billy-o.'

'Well, you'd hardly call my mother a swinger, would you?' They both smiled at the absurdity of the idea.

'You're right. It's only because I'm such a cynical old hussy—'

'Excuse me, may I point out that you're the one who gets annoyed that women run themselves down all the time? You're always saying we should be more proud of ourselves.'

'I'm *not* running myself down. It's a simple statement of fact. I think I've lost all sense of romance – that's if I even had any in the first place. If someone invited me over for a candlelit dinner, I'd go steaming in and say, "What's wrong with the bloody lights?" How depressingly sad is that? I can't imagine an affair of the heart, really of the heart, unless it also involved sneaking off for a shag.'

'Oh, shush. It's only what most people would assume, isn't it? You're no worse than anyone else. We're all so cynical these days. I bet the average person would jump to the same conclusion, of course they would.'

'Mmm.' Miranda nodded. 'They would.'

Smoke rising

Rob was perched on the low front wall of the house, smoking and waiting for Tamsin, who wanted to go back into town to have another look at a really, really sweet little hat she'd seen in one of the small boutiques. While he was leaning there, a battered and muddy old Volvo pulled up.

'Hi.' Rob stood up. 'Are you lost? Can I help?'

It was the landlady, Mrs O'Neill. She introduced herself and handed him an open egg tray with a dozen eggs in it.

'Don't know what's got into the hens this week, anyone'd think we pay 'em overtime, so I thought I'd pop by with these for you.'

Rob thanked her and told her how much they were enjoying the house and the surrounding landscape. He had left the front door slightly ajar and just then Anna came skipping out.

'Oh, hello again, my love. Did you see the Mermaid then?'

Anna nodded.

'And did you make a special wish on her, like I told you?'

'Yes, I did and everybody else did too. And we made up a story about her.' Anna looked away at Rob, suddenly shy. 'Um . . . is it . . . can you . . . are you allowed to make more than one wish or do you only get one?'

'Well now . . .' Mrs O'Neill winked at Rob surreptitiously. 'I'd say you can probably have three wishes on her. That's the magic number usually, they say. No more now, mind. It doesn't do to be greedy.' She smiled broadly.

Anna turned to Rob.

'Mummy says, um, do you want a cup of coffee out here?' She looked at his cigarette. 'Smoking's ever so bad for you, you know. It makes your lungs go all black and horrible and then you die.'

'I know.' He smiled. 'I promise I'll give up very, very soon. Tell Mummy yes, please, coffee would be very nice.'

Anna skipped off again. Rob asked the landlady if she could recommend any pubs that served decent food.

'Well now, I said to your wife when I was here the other day. Didn't she tell you? The Crow's Nest does good, big portions – that's popular with the men. Or there's the Compasses. They do local seafood. You go along this way . . .' She started to direct him.

'We're not married actually.'

'Oh well. These days, who is, eh? It's only stuffy old folks who mind about that any more.' She laughed.

298

'Your daughter's all set to be a beauty, the little love.' Nodding towards the house.

'Hmm?'

'Your little one there. With the curls and the blue eyes. Quite the spit of her daddy, in't she?'

Rob sat back down on the wall.

'Oops, mind the eggs!' She leaned forward to steady the tray. 'There we go.'

He clutched the tray tight, as if it were a rail on a wildly pitching boat. Looked up at her as though trying to peer through a veil of mist.

'Thank you,' he said, looking back down at the eggs. 'Thank you very much. Really.'

'It's no trouble.' She nodded at the eggs. 'It's the hens what do the work, after all. Enjoy the rest of your holiday now.'

Tamsin came bounding out of the front door.

'Ready!' She put her arm through his and dangled her car keys in front of his face. 'There. I know you can't stand my driving, you meanie!'

He shook his head, letting himself be led to her car.

'No. It's OK. You drive.'

A la carte

Joe tugged at his tie again and perched at the edge of the pale green velvet banquette in the hotel's lounge.

'Sorry, K. I didn't realize it would be such a starchy place. Maybe we should have gone to the pub?'

'No, this is a real treat. And it's nice to have a reason to dress up.'

'You look lovely.'

'Thank you. So do you.' She leaned forward to tweak his tie and smiled at him.

'Have you noticed how everyone always whispers in these places?'

'Mmm. Including us. It's like a library in here.'

A waiter glided over to them.

'Would you care for an aperitif before dinner?'

Joe looked at Kath.

'Not for me.' She turned to the waiter. 'We just had some champagne at home. With our friends.'

'Perhaps Sir would care to peruse the wine list then?'

'Yes please.'

The waiter withdrew.

'Why are you telling him we had champagne?' Joe hissed at his wife.

'I didn't want him to think we were just being mean. Not having an aperitif. But I couldn't manage that on top of the champagne and wine.'

'He doesn't *care*. Why would he?'

She shrugged.

'I don't know. I just said it.'

The waiter returned with the wine list and two menus,

each of which was the size of a large atlas.

Kath peered over the top of her menu at Joe, resting her nose lightly on the edge.

'Just checking you were still there. Why do they make the menus so *huge*?'

'To match the prices.'

'Oh my God, it's *so* expensive.' She inhaled sharply. 'We can't eat here. Let's sneak out and go to the pub. Quick, quick – before he comes back.'

'No, you deserve a proper treat.' He pulled at his tie again. 'It's not so bad.'

'But, Joe, what about the kitchen?'

'Look, can we just have one week off from fretting about the sodding kitchen? We can afford a decent dinner out on our anniversary. Don't worry about it. Have whatever you like. Have the – the lobster. Go on.'

Kath studied the menu.

'I don't really fancy a starter, do you?'

'You're having a starter.'

'I don't need one, I'm not all that hungry.'

'It's not about *needing* one. It's our anniversary. Have one.'

'I don't—'

'Will you just have a bloody starter, for Pete's sake!'

'Don't be like that!' Kath raised her menu in front of her face.

Joe leaned forward and peered down at her over the top of it.

'K?'

'Yes? What?'

'I'm sorry, petal. I just wanted it to be all nice for you.'

'I know you did. I'm sorry too.'

He planted a quick kiss on her lips.

'K?'

'Mmm?'

'Can you do a bit of translating for me? What's the thing second from top? Fillet of something, is it?'

'The *feuilleté de girolles*? Sort of puff pastry with mushrooms. Bit like an overgrown vol-au-vent.'

'Oh.'

'What about the warm salad of chicken livers? You like that.'

'Where's that? I didn't see that.'

'*Salade tiède de foie de volailles.*'

'Oh, yeah. Why don't they have the menu in English? We're in Devon, for God's sake.'

'You know why. Because they think it makes it posh and they can charge more. Shall I ask what the *Soupe du Jour* is?'

They called over the waiter.

He clicked his pen at the ready.

'What's the soup today please?'

'It is a *velouté* of Jerusalem artichokes drizzled with truffle oil. Very good.'

Joe looked at his wife and she shook her head discreetly.

'Jerusalem artichokes? Isn't that what we had that time when . . . ?'

'Yes, it is, so no, you can't have it,' Kath whispered back. 'Especially as we're sharing a house. Unless you particularly want to drive everyone away tomorrow.'

'I've heard of worse ideas.'

'Behave.' She turned to the waiter. 'I'll have the salmon pâté please, followed by the lamb.'

'And I'll have the chicken liver thing – the salad, then the duck. Thanks.'

'Chef prefers to serve the duck cooked medium rare, Sir . . .'

'And Sir prefers to eat it well done. Thank you.'

'Any vegetables with your main course?'

'Doesn't it come with some?'

The waiter shrugged as if he'd never heard such a bizarre suggestion before. Joe curled his lip and Kath kicked him under the table then ordered a *bouquetière* of vegetables to share.

'And the wine? You have chosen?'

'Not yet. Here, K, you have a look. You're better at all that.'

Kath quickly scanned the list.

'Happy with red?'

'Sure.'

'A bottle of the Cabernet Sauvignon then. This one please.'

The waiter nodded.

'And some water for the table? Still or sparkling?'

Kath ignored Joe's wrinkling his nose.

'Um, sparkling, please.'

'Your table is ready for you any time you want to go through.'

'Why do they always say that?' Joe hissed loudly as soon as the waiter had turned away. 'Some water for the table? What does the table want it for? Why don't they just say, "And can we rip you off still further, sir?" Bloody overpriced bottled bollocks!'

'Sssh! Well, why didn't you just ask for tap then?' she hissed back.

'It's our anniversary – this is one evening in the year when I reserve the right to be overcharged for things I don't want!'

'Oh, Joe!' Kath darted forward and kissed him, laughing. 'I do love you!'

Table d'hôte

'Need a hand?' Rob ventured into the kitchen.

'You could set the table if you like?'

'Simon not around?'

'Upstairs. Reading Anna a story.'

'Ah.'

'Cutlery's in the drawer there.'

Rob slowly opened the drawer and stood gazing into it.

'It's not a crystal ball, Rob. You won't find the answer to the mysteries of the Universe in there. At least, I don't think you will.'

'All right, I'm just looking. Now, let's see, there's you, me, Tam—'

'Five of us. We're having beef casserole with jacket potatoes and salad. We need knives, forks and maybe extra knives in case people want cheese and fruit after.'

'Pudding spoons?'

'Why – did you whip up a quick crumble this afternoon, Rob?'

'Not exactly my forte. And I was rather *occupied* this morning. Did you?'

'Nope. What with the rolling in the wet sand and the squabbling, there just wasn't enough time left somehow.' She turned back to the worktop and carried on slicing cucumber for salad. 'There's some ice cream if you want it.'

'Miranda?'

'What?'

'Can you just stop chopping for a sec and look at me?'

'There's an awful lot to do.'

'I need to ask you something. You've been avoiding me all day.'

Miranda speeded up her slicing, the knife thunk-thunking through the cucumber onto the wooden board.

'I haven't. Can't it wait? Supper's in a couple of minutes.'

'It's pretty important.'

Miranda ducked down to rummage in a cupboard for a large bowl.

'Miranda?'

'Yup.' She scooped up the washed salad leaves from the colander and tipped them into the bowl.

'You know what this is about, don't you? And I don't just mean this morning.'

'I'm not playing guessing games, Rob.' She met his eyes briefly, then looked back down at the salad, pulled out leaves to tear them into smaller pieces. 'I thought you were setting the table?'

'You're making this very hard.'

'I'm not doing anything. I'm just trying to make supper.'

Simon came in.

'Everything under control?'

'Fine.' Miranda glanced briefly at him. 'Perhaps you could give Rob a hand setting the table? He seems to be finding the task a bit daunting.'

Simon looked at Rob, who shrugged and rolled his eyes.

'Hiya, everyone!' Tamsin entered the kitchen. 'What can I do? You must, must let me help. Just tell me what to do.'

'Well, it's mostly done now actually. Thanks anyway. The boys are warming up for the new team event of

306

Setting the Table, but – who knows? – they may need an extra pair of hands to help them master the challenge of putting out five knives and forks. Or you could open the wine. Grab some napkins.' Miranda quickly washed the tomatoes, then started chopping them.

'Sorry, where are the napkins?'

'In the pantry. Top of the washing machine.' She spooned Dijon mustard into a jug then laid a clove of garlic on the board and crushed it with the flat of her knife for the salad dressing. 'And can someone please give Giles a shout to tell him supper's almost ready!'

'Not necessary.' Giles appeared suddenly, speaking almost right into her ear.

'You startled me!' Miranda frowned, indicating the large knife. 'I could've cut myself.'

'Apologies. It was unintentional, I assure you.'

Hors d'oeuvres

'God, it's good to get away from that lot, isn't it?' Joe raised his glass to Kath. 'Just for a couple of hours anyway.'

'Meanie. I thought you were having a good time?'

'I am. I *am*, K. It's just that every time I go into a room, I feel I should be wearing body armour. There's either Miranda and Simon taking swipes at each other or Miranda and Rob polishing their repartee. I keep

307

wanting to send them out into the garden and tell them not to come back in until they've made it up and can behave themselves.'

'Mmm, Miranda's incredibly tense and on edge. Even you must've noticed how touchy Simon's being with her? I know she can be difficult, too, but I really don't think she's being paranoid this time.'

He shrugged.

'She gives as good as she gets. But you're right, she does look wiped out.'

Kath nodded her agreement.

'I'm worried about her.' She frowned, then quickly smiled as the waiter arrived with their starters. 'Thank you.'

'Mmm. This looks good.'

They sampled each other's dishes.

'Joe?'

He said, 'Yes?' through a mouthful of chicken liver.

'You know what you said about Rob and Manda?'

Joe nodded.

'Is it – is there something going on, d'you think?'

'How should I know?' He forked some more salad into his mouth, speaking through a frill of fancy lettuce. 'I thought she told you everything?'

'So did I.' Kath took a swallow of her wine. 'But . . .'

'But she wouldn't necessarily if she was being knobbed by Rob? Yeah. That makes sense.'

'Joe! Don't put it like that! I know she and Rob have

always been a bit flirty, but it's just the way they both are, it doesn't mean anything.' She shook her head decisively. 'Miranda wouldn't . . . I'm sure she wouldn't be unfaithful to Simon.'

'You said yourself they're getting on really badly.'

'Yes, but sleeping with — with someone else isn't going to help, is it?'

'Too true. Kath, can we talk about something else now? It's a bit depressing on our anniversary dinner.'

'Of course, yes. Sorry.' She scooped up a piece of salmon pâté on a corner of toast and leaned across the table to feed it to him. 'But one last thing?'

'Go on.'

'I know you're going to say I'm being ridiculous, but this morning Miranda was in the bathroom for ages and ages—'

'So?'

'I think Rob was in there, too. Tamsin thought he was — but I told her he'd gone for a walk and I dragged her out to the garden to keep an eye on the kids.'

'Why? If Rob and Miranda want to act like silly teenagers, it's not your job to protect them, is it?'

'No-o-o, I know that. I was thinking of Tamsin, I feel really sorry for her. Rob's not serious about her and she's desperate to get married and start a family—'

The waiter came to remove their hors d'oeuvres plates and Kath sipped at her water, waiting for him to go.

Joe leaned towards his wife.

'Well, better she knows what he's really like then. Welcome to reality. She's not exactly the brightest bulb in the box, is she?'

'True – but that makes it worse in a way, it's like playing a mean trick on Luke or something. It's not right. Rob should be honest with her, then she could forget about him and move on.'

'Hang on – I thought you were worried about *him* and his happiness? You're always fretting about him.'

'Am I?'

'Of course. You're like a mother hen clucking over a stray chick.' He reached across to stroke her hand. 'Hey, I'm not knocking you, it's nice that you care about people.'

'Hmm, you *say* that, but I know what you think.'

'What do I think?' Joe laughed.

'You think that he's thirty-seven and old enough to look after himself and in any case he's my brother not my chick so it's not my worry. See? I know you so well.'

'Wife?' He took her hand and squeezed it. 'It's not that I *think* Rob's thirty-seven etcetera – he *is* thirty-seven and if he isn't old enough to look after himself by now then he never will be. What I do think though is that you worrying about him won't make a blind bit of difference. Face it, Rob is not one of life's contented souls. It's nothing to do with Tamsin. You could comb the entire globe and present him with the perfect woman, he'd still find something wrong with her. He needs to sort himself out and have more realistic expectations.'

'I see. Is that what you did with me? Am I the sad compromise you ended up with once you gave up your quest for the perfect woman?' She pretended to sulk.

'Yup, I scraped the bottom of the barrel and there you were. Still – you're not so bad for a last resort.'

The waiter returned with their main courses.

'Duck. *Well-done,* sir?'

When the waiter had finished fussing round them, Joe took his wife's hand once more.

'K? The only reason I gave up my quest for the perfect woman was . . . because I *found* her.'

Kath stood up and came round the table to kiss him.

'That is such a lovely thing to say.'

Joe flushed and motioned her back to her seat.

'Even if it's a ridiculous exaggeration,' she added.

After supper . . .

Back at the house, Miranda picked up her coffee and marched through into the sitting room.

'Anyone else fancy a little undemanding television? There might be a bad movie on if we're lucky.' She scanned the TV listings, ignoring Rob's trying to catch her eye, then she clattered through the stack of videos on the floor.

'Not much on telly. Anyone for *The Little Mermaid*? *Toy Story*? *Bob the Builder*? *Mary Poppins*? I've sat

311

through this lot a thousand times. I can't believe we didn't bring anything for the over-eights.'

Simon stood up.

'I think I'll have a bath.'

Miranda looked at him, but said nothing. A fresh bath of his very own. Oh God, he must be desperate to escape. Pity he'd thought of it first, now she couldn't try that one.

'Have you really got *Mary Poppins*?' Tamsin asked.

'Hmm? Oh. Yes. Yes, of course. Please – carry on. It's great, isn't it? Anna never gets tired of it.'

'I really, really love it. "A Spoonful of Sugar" is, like, one of my absolute all-time most favourite songs.'

'Good.' Miranda inserted the tape and passed the remote control to Tamsin. 'There you go. Think I'll just nip upstairs and find my book.'

*   *   *

Miranda finished clearing the supper dishes then set out crockery and boxes of cereal on the kitchen table for breakfast. Her mother often used to lay the breakfast table the night before and now Miranda found it strangely comforting to echo the habit. No matter what might happen – illness, an unexpected turn of events, a hurricane even – breakfast would be served. If only everything else could be anticipated with such easy certainty. She straightened the cutlery, then opened the back door and stood there, breathing in the cool night air.

'Miranda.'

She didn't turn round.

'I was just coming in.'

'Come outside.' Rob took out a cigarette and laid a hand on the small of her back.

'It's a bit chilly.'

'Then get your coat.'

'OK. Don't boss.'

She grabbed her stole from the back of a kitchen chair and followed him out onto the patio. He offered her a cigarette and she took one. His hands were trembling as he held out his lighter. For almost a minute, they stood smoking in silence, looking out at the moonlit garden, smelling the salt air.

'She's mine, isn't she?' Rob looked up at the stars.

'What? Who?'

'Don't fuck about. She is, isn't she?'

'No. Of course not. She—'

'Miranda!' Clutching her arm tight. 'This is too big for silly games. You got pregnant that weekend, didn't you? At Kath's wedding. Anna's eight and a quarter, she said it herself.'

'It was *after* that weekend. I went home, patched things up with Simon and we . . .' She shrugged.

'And that's why she's the spitting image of Simon? Just look at her for Christ's sake!'

'She takes after my side of the family. My father's eyes were—'

313

'Oh, please.' He took her other arm, holding her tight. 'Miranda. I need to know. You can't keep this from me. Am I her father, yes or no?'

She tried to pull away from him.

'How come it's taken you all these years to ask this question, Rob? Kath must have told you I was pregnant back then – and where were you? I don't remember you rushing over to hold my hair back while I was vomiting every bloody morning or – or – even calling me to see how I was. And it's not as if you haven't set eyes on Anna since then—'

'Have I? *Barely*. I did my belated bumming round the world bit for a year, remember? And when I came back, you and Simon had moved to Bristol and you were there for, what, three years? Four? Exactly how many times have I had so much as a *glimpse* of Anna since she was born? Come to think of it, on a couple of occasions when I've dropped by at Kath's, you've suddenly upped and hurried Anna out the door like you were smuggling her past Customs.'

'That's ridiculous! A complete fantasy. You know where we live, you've got my number – if you had really thought for even one second that Anna might be yours, why didn't you come round – why didn't you—'

'So she *is* mine then?'

'No.'

'Then why are you saying all this? Why do you care that I didn't come round if she isn't mine?'

'Because.' Miranda buried her face in her hands for a moment, then looked up at him. *'Because* I'm just saying that, whether or not she is actually yours, you didn't care enough, weren't concerned enough even to *ask* me before now. It simply never occurred to you . . . did it?'

He let her go.

'I didn't think.' He ran his hands through his hair. 'I don't know, I feel so stupid – but every time I saw you at Kath's – at parties or whatever – you were on your own. I almost never saw you with Anna – or with him – I – I always think of you just as you.'

Miranda laid a hand on his arm. Rob looked at her, frowning.

'But is she? You said "whether or not" – but you must know?'

She shook her head.

'I'm sorry. I really don't. I admit that that there is a small possibility, but I'm not a hundred per cent sure. Simon and I did . . . she could just as easily be his. In fact, that's much more likely.'

He grabbed her arms again.

'But there are tests now! I'll have a DNA test and that'll prove she's mine for certain and then—'

'And then *what* exactly?' She yanked away from him. 'What if you're right? Then we tell Anna: "Sorry, the man you thought was your daddy isn't. Here's a new one. Sorry about that." Terrific idea.'

'But if she's *mine*? If I'm her *father*? Doesn't she have the right to know? Don't *I*?'

Miranda looked down then back up into his eyes.

'I'm not sure that rights have much to do with it. She's too young to deal with all this now. Even if you are her biological father – and God knows it's one hell of a big *if*. She loves her daddy so much . . . she loves *Simon*.'

'But she would grow to love *me*, wouldn't she? It's just she doesn't know me – she hasn't had the chance.'

'Of course she would love you if she knew you.' Miranda smiled tenderly. 'Who wouldn't? But – Rob – I can't just explode her life from under her. And what about Simon? I really think it would kill him. He loves Anna – she means everything to him.'

'Huh – well you didn't seem to be too concerned about him when you were spreading your legs on the bathroom floor.'

She drew back as if he had struck her.

'Cheers, Rob. That's charming. I notice you weren't exactly thinking about anyone else either—'

'I'm not virtually married and with a kid—'

'Just as well. I can't see you being faithful to anyone for more than a week.'

'That's not true.'

'Isn't it? Be honest – you're saying you've never cheated on Tamsin?'

'That's different!'

'Why is it different?'

'Because I'm not in *love* with Tamsin!' His voice was suddenly loud in the still night. Rob took her hand. 'But if I *were* with someone I was in love with, then I wouldn't be unfaithful. I wouldn't want to be. I wouldn't want anyone else.' He ran his thumb round and round her palm. 'And I think if you were really in love with Simon, you wouldn't even be standing here with me now.'

'We've been together a long time. No-one's still in love after ten years.'

'No? Look at Kath and Joe.'

Miranda smiled.

'They must be aliens.'

Rob took her other hand, drawing her round to face him.

'We could have that.'

She shook her head.

'No, we couldn't. Kath and Joe are a different species. Easy-going. Considerate. Unselfish. They've mastered the art of living together without driving each other crazy. I don't know how to be like that . . . and I'm not sure you do either. It's just not the way we are, is it?'

'Don't you even want to try?'

Miranda pulled her hands away and let them fall to her sides.

'Why did you go away?'

'What?'

'After Kath's wedding – after our – our – well, what turned out to be a fling – I thought – well – and then

317

you revealed that you were trotting off round the world for a year as if you were eighteen.'

'But I only went because you rejected me!'

'*I* rejected *you*! Yeah, good one. Don't lie about it, Rob. I was there, *remember*? You can't just rewrite history.'

'Excuse me – I made it pretty bloody clear that I wanted us to carry on and you brushed me off like you couldn't be bothered with me any more – you'd had your no-strings fuck, then you wanted to hurry on back to your real relationship. You made me feel like some irritating insect buzzing round you.'

'Only because I was so angry. And hurt. And can you blame me?

That night

'God, I'm starving.' Rob turns on his side facing Miranda. 'Aren't you?'

'Pig. How can you be after all that food?'

'Hey, I didn't have that much.'

'Too busy drinking.'

'Too busy trying to seduce you.'

'That didn't take long.'

'True.'

Miranda elbows him in the ribs.

'You'll have to wait till breakfast – they don't have twenty-four-hour room service here.'

Rob gets up and pulls on his boxer shorts, then his trousers.

'I'm going to raid the kitchens. Want to come?'

She shakes her head.

'Too sleepy. Don't be long.'

'I won't. Have you seen my fags?'

'Uh-uh. You had them when we were outside, didn't you?'

He puts on his shirt without buttoning it, grabs his jacket, and tiptoes with exaggerated care to the door. Blows her a kiss and creeps out.

Miranda plumps up the pillows and sits up in bed. She wiggles her toes into the crisp hotel sheets and sinks into thinking about Rob, feeling a thrill of self-indulgence as if she were about to dig a spoon into a cream-slathered dessert. Would he want to move into her place? His flat was way too small for both of them and hers wasn't much bigger. Probably best if they got somewhere new together. Maybe even make the ultimate commitment and have a joint mortgage. A clean slate anyway, that was the thing. Part of the trouble with Simon was that they'd slid into living together. She hated his flat, which was in a dodgy area and had bars on the windows, so bit by bit he'd spent more and more time at her place until she'd said he might as well give up his own. Recently, she'd found herself feeling slightly invaded, as if he were a house guest who'd outstayed his welcome. Especially as he'd somehow managed to colonize the spare bedroom as his study, claiming he had to have space to accommodate the endless files and cuttings needed for his book, so Miranda ended up working at the kitchen table and shoving all her stuff into plastic crates which were then stacked in a teetering tower on top of the washing machine.

Presumably, Simon will be gone by the time she gets home, even if he hasn't taken all his belongings. Well. It would be easier this way. If he'd already walked out on her, there'd be no need to drag Rob into it. Less heartache all round. She could just skip nimbly from one to the other as if between well-placed stepping stones. Knowing Simon, he would insist on some dreadful post-mortem though, analysing every single thing that's wrong with their relationship and with her. She is selfish, egocentric, hard to please; if she weren't cluttering up his life, he could get on with the rather more important matter of saving the world. Fine and good luck to him. That last row, when he'd suddenly refused to come to the wedding with her, well, it said it all. OK, he hadn't actually said the words 'it's all over' but then why state the bloody obvious?

Miranda gets up and crosses to the dressing-table mirror. Peers at the mascara smudges beneath her eyes. Tugs out a tissue. Moonlight shines through the window and she turns towards it. It is a beautiful night, cold but clear, the waxing moon only a night or two away from being full. She opens the window to breathe fresh air. Footsteps on the path beneath. Stretches out a little way to see. It is Rob, heading for the bench to find his cigarettes. She is about to call out to him, then stops herself, relishing the pleasure of just watching him, his rangy walk seen from above, his broad shoulders. Rob reaches the bench, picks up the cigarettes, takes one out and lights up. Plonks himself down and takes out his mobile phone.

'Hey, babe. It's me. Sorry – did I wake you?'

A laugh.

'Yeah, it was great. Loads of champagne.'

'No. Course not . . . One dance with some woman, some friend of Kath's . . . no . . . no . . . And she trod on my feet. Not my type.'

'You got the tickets already? Oh. But I thought we said we'd get them next – Right . . . No . . . Yeah . . . No, no probs. Course I do . . . Don't be daft.'

'Oh, did they? But it's – shit, that's only a fortnight away. It's a bit soon . . . yeah but . . . OK, OK . . . '

'Yeah. You too, baby. I'll call you tomorrow. Bye. Yeah. Bye.'

Miranda silently closes the window. Perches on the corner of the bed for a minute, then goes into the bathroom and shuts the door.

A gentle tap-tap at the bedroom door. Miranda pulls on a bathrobe and lets Rob in, manages a bright smile.

'Any luck?'

'Only fruit and some biscuits. I couldn't even find the kitchen – this place is a maze. Found my fags though.' He bends to kiss her. 'You're all wet.'

'I needed a shower.'

'You should have waited for me.'

'I felt grubby.'

'I could have licked you clean.'

She laughs a little too loudly.

'Anyway.' Rob puts down the fruit. 'Come back to bed.'

'Shouldn't you be getting back to your room?'

'Why? Are you worried about your reputation?'

'Desperately. No. I just thought . . . you know . . . it might be a little awkward.'

'Oh. Really? For who?'

'And, of course, Simon's bound to call.'

'I thought you said you'd had a huge row?' Looking at her intently now. 'I kind of got the impression that he was history . . .'

'Hardly. Just a lovers' tiff really. He always phones me late if we're apart.'

'Oh. Right.'

Rob picks up an apple.

'Well, I'd better skulk off before anyone sees me then.'

'Probably best.' She reaches up to receive his kiss, lips sealed shut.

He holds her close for a moment.

'Well. That was . . . amazing.'

'Mmm.'

He pulls back from her and looks down into her eyes, as if hoping to find something.

'So . . . I guess I'll see you . . . ?'

'Back in London. At Kath and Joe's next jolly gathering no doubt.' She squeezes his arm and kisses him on the cheek. 'It's really been great fun.'

'Fun. Yes.'

He turns to go.

'Miranda – I – is there – this just seems—'

'Hmm?' Distracted now, looking at the fruit. 'Think I'll have a banana.'

'Yeah. Good plan. Well.' He kisses the top of her forehead, as if she were a child. 'See you around. Take care of yourself, you hear?' Then he closes the door and is gone.

Miranda holds herself together as long as she can, physically clutching herself as if she might otherwise disintegrate. She starts to count out loud, telling herself that if she can just reach a hundred, then that means that she'll be all right. Everything will be all right.

She gets to fourteen before she gives way, mouth gaping; staggers to the bed and crawls on top of it, arms shielding her head as if the building is collapsing around her. One gasp of breath, then she starts to sob.

This night

'We both know what happened, Rob. Let's not attempt to rewrite history.'

'Excuse me? You gave me the brush-off.'

'Only because you'd planned your globe-trotting bit with your girlfriend and you didn't even have the decency to tell me. What was I supposed to do – hang around waiting for you for a year?'

'What?'

'I overheard you calling her and talking about tickets and stuff – you'd already decided to go, so don't start giving me a load of crap about how you only went nursing a broken heart because I'd rejected you.'

Rob paused, frowning, remembering.

'But that's not right.'

'I *heard* you. It *is* right.'

He shook his head.

'Uh-uh. Yes, Chrissy jumped the gun and bought the tickets, but I'd only planned to go for three months and it was only a casual thing with her anyway. She and I split up before we'd even boarded the outgoing flight.

The only reason I stayed away so long was because I was so cut up about you, if you want to know. I thought we – you know exactly what I thought, Miranda.'

Their eyes met. Miranda's lips parted, but she could not find the words,

'Hi, we're back!' A footstep on the path. 'What are you two up to out here, skulking in the bushes?' Joe smiled, keeping it light.

'We're not *up to* anything. I'm just having an illicit cigarette away from Herr Kommandant,' Miranda said. 'How was your dinner?'

'It was fine. Look, I know it's none of my business, but you should know that Simon's getting a bit twitchy about all this.'

'About all what?' Rob dug his hands deep into his pockets.

'*This.*' Joe gestured. 'You two.'

'There is no *us two*,' Miranda and Rob said exactly together. 'Jinx!' At the same time. A shared glance.

'For Pete's sake! Have a bit of sense, will you both? If you can't get through life without shagging each other in secret, then fine, get it out of your systems. But there are other people to consider here. You can't start locking yourselves in the bathroom or sneaking out to the garden. It's just not on. Think about Simon. Tamsin. And I'm sure I don't need to tell you to consider Anna, Miranda. Not to mention the effect it's having on Kath. Even Giles is tense as anything. Come on, folks – keep your hands off each other for two minutes and sort it out when you're back in London, then I won't have to spend my anniversary dinner listening to my wife drive herself crazy with worry over you two idiots.'

'She's *not*.' Miranda pulled her stole closer around her shoulders. 'Is she?'

Joe nodded.

'I'd better come in with you.' She looked back at Rob as she turned to go. He raised his hand in silence.

Thursday

Down in the depths

And she is sitting . . . on a rock on the seabed. Down
here, so deep, it is cool and dim, with little light from
the surface. She pushes off from the rock, trying to give
a good kick, but her glide is slow and heavy, as if she
is dragging a dead weight. Her tail feels like a strange
thing, awkward, unwieldy, as if it no longer belongs to
her. It tows sluggishly along, lumbering behind like a
clunking caravan. She sinks even lower, scoops up a
handful of sand from the bottom, lets it fall through her
splayed fingers, then swims slowly on.

Ahead, now, she sees a weak shaft of sunlight slicing
through her grey-green world. Pushes towards it, pulling
hard with her slender arms. Her tail skims the bottom,
gritty sand catching in her scales, swaying thickly from
side to side like some slow-prowling shark.

Towards the light, towards the light. As she nears,
she suddenly sees that it is not one shaft, but two.
She swims straight for the nearer one, curling round

to watch her scales shimmer in the welcome, wet sun. Reaches out her hand to the farther beam. Too far, too far. Stretches her whole body, pushing, lengthening as the light seems to hold itself in, receding from her grasp. Almost, almost. Closes her eyes, concentrating, feeling her scales fanning apart, the muscles pulling, aching. She can do this, must do this. Knows she must. Fingertips push, push hard, harder – now just catching the light, her nails pearly and gleaming, her fingers like some strange sea creature basking in the warmth. She tips her head to check, to see her fin-feet spotlit in the other beam beyond, her toes now no more than shadows in the veined V of her tail fin. She hangs there for what seems an age, bridging the sunbeams with her body, longing to rest. At last, she pikes sharply and arcs her arms round and back to relieve them.

A small shoal of fish swims by, moving as one, their pewter patina dabbed with bright blue just below the eye as if by a childish paintbrush. She waits for them to pass. Now there, beyond, an octopus hangs in the brackish water. Dark, dark blue, almost black, its rubbery, wetsuit skin flecked with specks of white, eyes downcast and yellow, glinting like fading torches. Anna raises a hand in greeting. The octopus coils its legs, loose springs in the water. So many legs. Too many. She moves a little closer. Suddenly, the octopus divides before her eyes, the two halves tearing slowly, painfully, pieces of skin flaking off, floating towards her. The water bubbles violently around her, boiling, as the flesh wrenches and tugs, screeching as those legs skid and shove against the slipping sands. *Can't see – bubbles – in her eyes – her hair – can't breathe – water boiling – churning – legs coiling – reaching for her – slimy skin sticking to her – pulling – sand sucking –hissing – pushing now – pushing as hard as she can – air – light – up.*

Gasping for breath. Crying out. Crying.

'Anna! Anna! Wake up!' Miranda held her daughter firmly, made her look into her eyes, know that she was awake. Then she rocked her gently to and fro, shushing in her ear, stroking her hair. Anna sobbed, gulping and gasping, her face red and wretched. 'You're OK now, little bean, Mummy's here, you're safe now.'

'It's all right, Anna-Banana.' Simon carefully stepped across Luke's mattress and perched on the edge of the bottom bunk by Miranda, stroking Anna's back. 'It was just a bad dream.'

Anna shook her head.

Polly and Luke were sitting up sleepily, dazed and blinking in the light, looking around, disorientated.

'I'm sorry, folks,' Miranda said. 'Anna had a bad dream.'

Kath appeared in the doorway.

'Sorry, Kath – I'm afraid they're all awake now.'

'It's OK. Don't worry.' Kath knelt down on Luke's mattress to comfort him.

Miranda started to stand up.

'Don't go!' Anna looped her arms around her mother's neck, and locked her fingers tight.

'Sssh, sssh – I'm not leaving you.' Miranda scooped her close and picked her up. 'Come on – let the others get some sleep, OK? Let's go downstairs and have some nice warm milk.'

Anna nodded sleepily. She reached out her hand for Simon.

'You come, Daddy.'

He kissed her cheek and nuzzled her, nose to nose.

'Course I'm coming.'

In the kitchen, Miranda passed Anna over to Simon so she could heat the milk. She clung to him like a monkey, her head pressed against his shoulder, her tears wet on his bare skin.

'Tell me your dream, hmm?' He lowered himself into a chair. 'Was it very horrid?'

She nodded.

'Not a dream. It was a thinking.'

'OK, a thinking then. What happened?'

She shook her head.

'Hmm?' He looked over at Miranda, frowning.

Miranda blew on the surface of the milk to cool it slightly, held it out.

'Careful – it's hot. Don't you want to tell? You know, once you say it out loud – even if it's really scary and horrible – then it's not so bad any more, it's just like a silly story.'

Anna shook her head again and took the cup of milk, slurped noisily at it like a toddler. Over her head, Miranda's eyes met Simon's, two foreheads furrowed in concern. Simon squeezed Anna a little tighter; Miranda softly stroked her damp hair back from her face.

'Back to bed now, my little banana, hmm?' he said into her hair. 'We're all pooped.'

Another shake. Simon turned to Miranda, silently questioning. An answering nod.

'OK. Come into our bed for a little while then. Just till you drop off.'

A sleepy nod.

Together, they slowly climbed the stairs.

Crispy bits

Kath was woken by a soft kiss on her nose.

'Happy anniversary, wife. Sit up.'

'Can't. Too sleepy.' She burrowed further beneath the duvet, then peeped open one eye. 'Hello, husb. Happy anniversary.' Opened her other eye, intrigued. 'Ooh, what's that?'

'Breakfast.'

She scrambled to sit upright, yawning widely.

''m so tired.' She looked down at the tray as Joe settled it in place across her lap. 'This is nice. Why are you being so nice?'

'Hush up, I'm always nice.' He flicked out a paper napkin and tenderly tucked it into the top of her baggy T-shirt. 'Anniversary treat – have it while it's hot.'

Tea. Toast. Two soft-boiled eggs with two rashers of well-done bacon on the side for dunking, just how she liked it. The eggs were decorated: one had a smiley face, shakily drawn in felt tip, the other was covered in pink daisy-like flowers and said 'HAPPY ANNIVErsary', the last few letters somewhat shrunken due to lack of space.

Polly and Luke stood beaming by the bedside.

'We did the eggs, Mummy!'

'I did this one.' Luke pointed. 'All by myself.'

Kath leaned forward to kiss them both, trying not to dislodge the tray.

'Lucky me to have such lovely and talented children.'

'OK, kids. Off you trot. Go down and get Auntie Miranda to give you some Coco Pops.'

Kath smiled down at her breakfast, then up at her husband.

'Oh, look at you,' he said, brushing just beneath her eye with his thumb. 'You old soppy.'

'Not soppy.' She sniffed. 'Just happy.'

'Two boiled eggs and a cup of tea – is that all it takes?'

She nodded.

'Pretty much.'

'I knew I shouldn't have splashed out on that vulgar diamond bracelet . . . ' He whipped aside another paper napkin to reveal a small box.

'Oh, Joe, please tell me you haven't gone mad? The kitchen—'

'Don't fret, K, it's extremely modest. Go on, open it.'

She carefully prised open the lid. Inside was a thin gold chain, with a tiny diamond set into a small gold flower.

'Oh, Joe! It's beautiful!' She looked up at him, beaming. 'Is it really real?'

He nodded and poured her tea.

'It's really real. And also really small, you'll notice. Honestly, it didn't cost much. Suspiciously cheap really. Probably fell off the back of a lorry.'

'In that case, if I don't have to worry, I love it even more.'

'Have a look underneath.'

She lifted out the small cushion of wadding to reveal a tightly folded piece of paper with a torn edge. Spread it out, puzzled, looking at him. A page from a magazine. Started to read out loud:

' . . . Please help – I have recurring athlete's foot and—'

'Not that side. The other side.'

It was an advert for a fitted kitchen company. Kath flushed a light shade of pink.

'This is that one we both loved, but decided we couldn't have—'

'Yes, but someone kept the ad hidden away at the bottom of the breadbin.'

'Did they . . . ?' She took a sip of her tea. 'Well, I'd practically forgotten it was there. Sort of.'

'It's OK. If you want to drool over a picture of an integrated dishwasher, I reckon I can live with that. It's not like it's a photo of another man.'

'No. I keep that tucked into my knickers.' She chopped off the top of a boiled egg and dipped in the end of a piece of bacon, closed her eyes in reverence. 'Heaven. Complete heaven.' Scooped out the firm white from the lid. 'But why did you bring the ad down here?'

'Because . . .' He raised his eyebrows up and down.

'What? No! You can't have done. We can't afford it.'

'Too late! It's ordered. No protests.'

'But—'

'Eat up your egg, woman. Rob's come up trumps – he suggested we fit it ourselves, so it's miles cheaper and he'll stop me making a hash of it like I would if I tried to do it on my own. I ordered it online yesterday on his swish laptop. We're both taking ten days off once it's ready and he knows a good plumber who won't rip us off.'

'But – Joe, you didn't—'

'No, I didn't rob a bank and, more to the point, I didn't ask your dad for a loan. You know me better than that, K.' He picked up a piece of her toast and nibbled one corner. 'I bit the bullet and rang my parents.'

'And they're really lending us the money? I can't believe we're actually going to have a proper kitchen . . . like real grown-ups. Thank you, thank you!' Kath kicked her feet excitedly under the covers, then she laid a piece of bacon onto the toast and offered it to him. 'It's the crispiest bit. This is how much I love you. You're my most favouritest husband.'

He bent to kiss her.

'You have it – and that's how much I love you, not nicking your last crispy bit. I'll leave you in peace.'

Miranda found Joe in the kitchen, where he was crouching in front of the dishwasher, peering at the dial.

'Am I doing something wrong? I'm not used to this sort of cutting-edge appliance. Ours is an antique, wind-up model.'

Miranda laughed.

'This one's got to be at least ten years old.' She took over, turning the dial to the correct setting and pressing it in. 'Happy anniversary, by the way. Kath having a lie-in?'

'Yeah, she needs it.'

'I'm sorry about last night – well, this morning – waking everyone up, I mean.' She opened the fridge and started

337

checking their supplies, noting what she would need to cook the grand anniversary dinner that evening.

'Don't be daft. It happens. Anna's OK now, is she? Poor little mite. That was a bad one, wasn't it?'

Miranda nodded.

'Mmm. And she wouldn't tell us what it was afterwards.'

'Wonder why not?' He frowned. 'Maybe she didn't want to say it out loud in case it made it even more real?'

'Maybe. I said I'd take her into town later for a cream tea and to see the boats in the harbour. Do you think Polly and Luke would like to come, too?'

'God, you wouldn't really take them, would you?' He looked like a man who'd just come in from a hailstorm to sit by a blazing fire.

'Sure, why not? I really meant to give you both a proper break before, but the week's sort of zipped by, hasn't it? I presume you'd like at least some couple time on your anniversary? We'll be a minimum of two hours, I reckon – maybe nearer three if we happen to stumble into the toyshop at some point.'

'Miranda, you're a star.' He grabbed her by the arms and kissed her on the cheek. 'But, hang on, you can't manage all three, can you? Luke has a way of wandering off if you take your eyes off him for even a second. It's like he has an antenna tuned into danger. If there's a hazard within half a mile, Luke will head straight for it. Is Simon going, too?'

'Who knows, Joe? Who knows? Communicating with Simon at the moment is like trying to send semaphore in patchy fog – occasionally, I get lucky and there's a sudden glimmer of sun and the message gets through. The rest of the time, I'm waving flags and there might as well be a thick brick wall between us for all the good it does.'

'Ach, we all have phases where things are a bit rough. When you're in it for the long haul, you have to expect a few bumps along the way.' He smiled. 'Well, ask him if you catch a moment when there's a spot of sunshine, eh? If not, maybe one of the others could lend a hand?'

Miranda looked doubtful.

'Rob's babysat before. He can manage.'

She wrinkled her nose.

'Possibly . . . '

'Ah. OK. Maybe not Rob then. I can't keep track.'

'Well. We'll see.' She checked her shopping list once more. 'Joe – in return . . . '

'Aha! All is clear to me now.'

'No – it's just, could you keep an eye on Anna for half an hour or so? I'm not sure where Simon is and I want a fast walk, not a doodle along stopping to look at every single seagull and blade of grass. I'm desperate for a breath of fresh air.'

'A breath of fresh gale, more like. I think Simon took her for a walk already.'

She sighed.

'It's a bit windy for Anna.'

'*You're* going,' he pointed out.

'That's completely different. I'm indestructible. Did she have her warm jacket on at least?'

'No idea. I think so. Probably. Don't fret.' He squeezed her arm. 'No-one's indestructible, not even you. You wrap up warm, too.'

'Yes, dear. And Joe – do me a favour? If anyone asks, you don't know where I am.'

Choices

Out of the garden gate. At the top of the steps, she looked down to the beach. Anna and Simon were at the far end, crouched down by a rock pool, intently gazing into it. Their heads were huddled close, Anna's dark curls next to Simon's close-cut, dead straight hair. Now Simon reached forward, and plucked something from the pool. He held out whatever it was to Anna and the pair studied it for a little while before returning it to the water. Anna stood up suddenly and said something to him, then raced off towards the far end of the beach. He leapt to his feet and ran after her. From here, Miranda could see how he was reining himself in, running so that he and Anna were almost neck and neck before finally pretending to run out of energy so that she could pip him at the post. Slowly, they walked back along the beach, eyes down, scanning the sands for good shells or stones, as always. Oh Simon, she thought, *Simon.* How easy it was to love him – from a distance.

Miranda turned then and headed up, away from the beach, towards the cliff. At the top, she tugged off her scarf and let herself be buffeted by the wind for a minute, breathed in the briny air. She walked briskly along the path, hunching her shoulders against the cold, tucking her head into her upturned collar like a tortoise. Out on the water, a speedboat bounced over the waves, scooting across the surface like a skimmed stone. Now, what was it to be: worrying about Simon? Worrying about Rob? Worrying about the letters? What fun to have so much choice. Her mind jumped between them, thoughts racing from one to the other, zigzagging back and forth fruitlessly. Maybe she should just keep on walking and never go back? Solve all the problems by pretending they were nothing to do with her, start a new life with a clean slate.

Over the sea, the gulls swooped and dived. She moved closer to the edge, watching one particular bird, her gaze following it as it sharply dropped to the water. Far below her, the waves frothed and crashed against the rocks. Instinctively, she drew back from the edge. If you were a really brave person, she thought, you'd simply take one bold step forward and then – *voilà* – end of all problems! End of dilemma, end of fear, end of Miranda. They'd have to fight it out amongst themselves and you'd be out of the equation. She shuddered slightly and forced herself to walk on. If she could drink herself to death on decent claret, then maybe . . . but smashing her head open on sharp rocks? Uh-uh. Besides, even if she were the worst mother on the planet, taking a dive and leaving Anna with a lifelong legacy of grief and pain and guilt was hardly likely to improve the situation.

If Rob really were Anna's biological father, then wouldn't that all just work out peachy? Yes, but what if he weren't? What if . . . ? Maybe she should run off just with Anna? Forget the men altogether? Not such a bad plan. But what about Simon? No matter how much he got up Miranda's nose, he still meant the world to Anna; she could not, would not, take her away from him. But if he gave her no choice? If he walked out because he simply couldn't stand to share a house with Miranda for one more minute, even if it meant becoming a Sunday father to Anna? OK. Well, that she – they – would have to live with.

Her mind wandered again. Dear God, the letters. At least they're not really your problem, are they? You could leave it, you don't have to do anything. Yes, yes you do, you know you do. But she didn't even have them any more. There was no choice. She would have to find a way of getting them back. She stood up and wrapped her scarf more tightly around her neck. In all this horrible mess, this was one thing she maybe couldn't make any worse, and she was the one person, the only person, who might possibly make it better. She tugged her belt tighter and set off back towards the house.

It was windier than she'd realized and she shivered as she walked along, quickened her pace. She hoped Simon would have taken Anna back inside. Miranda stopped at the top of the beach steps and cautiously craned her head over to see if they were still down on the shore. They were at the far end, partially hidden by a large rock, crouched on the sand. They seemed to be making shapes or writing perhaps with sticks, Simon's head bent low near Anna's, leaning in close to her, pointing now, telling her something. Anna's face tilted towards his as she listened.

There was a sudden shout as Anna looked up and caught sight of her mother and waved wildly. Miranda waved back and Simon poked his head up from behind the shelter of the rock and raised his hand. He beckoned her down and Anna called out to her, though her words were lost in the wind.

Miranda descended the steps.

'You should go in – it's getting chilly,' she called as she came closer.

'I'm not cold,' Anna insisted. She had Simon's scarf wrapped round her. 'Look at our picture – we're doing art in the sand.'

'Ephemeral art – it'll be all the rage.' Simon nodded further along the sands.

'What's emeph – ephem—?'

'Ephemeral? It means something that doesn't last long, like a cut flower—'

'Or a box of chocolates when I'm in the room,' Miranda added.

'True. It's because the waves will come in and wash it all away, you see.'

'Can we take a picture of it?' Anna asked.

'Good idea. Wait here. I'll go and fetch my camera.' Simon ran off towards the steps.

Miranda stood with her back to the sea, looking down at the sand sketches.

'These are wonderful!' She walked carefully around them. 'Did you do all of them?'

'Me and Daddy did them together. But I did this bit – and those over there – all on my own.'

'Oh, this is the Mermaid, isn't it?' Miranda paused by a figure with billowing hair, as if blown by the wind; the ends of the tail were edged by tiny shells. 'It's beautiful.'

'It's before she got turned into the rock.'

'And that's Daddy, isn't it?' Miranda pointed to another figure. 'And that one's you . . .'

'Yes.'

'Aren't you going to draw me, too?'

'I *did*. You're over there. See?' Anna pointed higher up the sand.

'Oh.' Miranda moved closer. 'Yes. I see me now. It's a really good drawing – I like the way you've done my shoes.'

She could see Simon coming back down the steps with his camera.

'Um, why didn't you draw me with you and Daddy?'

'There wasn't enough room. The rock was in the way. It's too big to move.'

'Yes, of course.' Miranda waved at Simon. 'I'm going in now to get lunch ready, OK?' she told him. 'Don't be long, will you?'

'Sure. Ten minutes tops.'

'Fine.' She dug her hands deep into her pockets, then picked her way over the stones towards the steps.

Below par

Polly and Luke were playing in the garden when Miranda came back through the gate. Kath and Joe were huddled at the table, clutching cups of coffee.

'Hiya. Joe says you've offered to take the horrors into town for tea.'

'Yeah. No biggie.'

'It is to us, you know it is. But can Simon help you? Rob and Tamsin have gone off to look round some castle.'

'Oh, have they? That doesn't sound quite their cup of tea?'

'Perhaps they wanted some time on their own,' Kath said, looking into her coffee. 'I don't think they'll be back for hours. I'm just about to make some lunch. Are Simon and Anna coming back?'

'Yes, they won't be long. I'll give you a hand.' Miranda sidled casually towards the house. 'Give me five minutes.'

Inside now, running up the stairs. The door to Kath and Joe's room was open, the chair and bed strewn with various pieces of clothing. Hang on, she couldn't start searching through other people's belongings. Even if it were all in a good cause. Maybe the letters would be left out somewhere, that wouldn't be so bad, would it? Wait. Think a second. This is Kath. Where would she put them? Miranda crossed to the chest of drawers, pulled open the top one. Yup – Kath's underwear and the letters tucked in at one side, almost exactly as Miranda had placed them in her own room. She put them inside her coat and quickly locked herself in the bathroom to read that final letter once more, to make sure.

Afterwards, she slipped them beneath her own mattress, and went downstairs. Kath was in the kitchen.

'I'm doing fish fingers for the kids, OK? Are you happy with just odds and ends for us? Cheese and ham and salady bits?'

'Perfect. I'll get that together as you're doing the kids. Don't forget – we're having a big meal tonight, so save plenty of room.'

'You're the one going off for the cream tea!'

'You're right. I should stay here. Perhaps go for a jog.'

'No, no, you can't. You've promised now. Joe is counting the minutes.' Kath waved the fish slice around. 'Give my dad a shout, will you? Tell him lunch is nearly ready. I think he's outside on the phone.'

'No,' Giles was saying. 'Absolutely not. It's out of the question.'

Miranda raised a hand in greeting, keeping her distance. Then she jerked her thumb towards the house and mouthed 'lunch', held up five outstretched fingers. He nodded and gestured for her to stay. Awkwardly, he tried to leaf through a stack of papers on the garden table in front of him, which threatened to blow away. Miranda quickly leaned on them and Giles smiled his thanks.

'. . . to paragraph twenty-six in Part Four. No, the following clause . . . that's correct . . . indeed . . . I hope to be back on Monday, possibly Tuesday . . . Speak to Clive if you need to before then. Or call me on my mobile. Good. Yes. Goodbye.'

Giles shook his head slowly.

'Dear God, preserve us from Bright Young Things.' He struggled to gather up his papers and Miranda straightened them for him.

'Lunch will be ready soon.'

'So I gathered. I know it's a cliché that country air sharpens the appetite, but I'm certainly finding it true this week.'

'If my appetite were any sharper, I'd start eating the furniture.'

'Ah, Miranda . . .' He shook his head, smiling. 'You've no idea how refreshing it is to watch a woman actually *eating* a meal instead of rearranging it with her fork. All my female colleagues seem to have declared themselves Nil by Mouth – except for alcohol, of course.'

'Diets always make me even more obsessed with food.' She looked down at her midriff. 'Still I am such a chub at the moment. I did join a gym, and I went diligently for, ooh, about a fortnight. I kid myself that having the membership counts as being virtuous.'

'Gyms are a preposterous waste of time and money, aren't they? What's the point of driving somewhere to be cooped up in some sweaty basement cycling on a machine that takes you precisely nowhere?'

'You're right. I should give the membership money to charity and walk everywhere instead.'

'Take up golf.'

Miranda made a face.

'You may mock, Miranda, but I bet you'd grow to love it. I could coach you a little perhaps if you'd like?' He smiled warily. 'Or am I being patronizing again?'

'Not at all – but can you really see me in a cardigan and tweed skirt, striding along the fairway?'

He paused then looked into her eyes.

'I can see you in many things. True, a tweed skirt wouldn't be my garment of choice . . . and, for the record, I don't see you as a – a *chub*, was it? I don't see you that way at all. I consider your curves one of life's great pleasures.'

'Giles . . . '

'Forgive me. I know, I know – you're about to tell me that I've overstepped the mark. It was inappropriate.'

'No, it's fine. Really. I've been feeling particularly worn out and unattractive recently. Thank you for reminding me that I'm at least capable of being sexy on a good day.'

'It wasn't so very . . . disappointing, was it?' He cast a cautious glance towards the house. 'Back then?'

'No.' She squeezed his hand. 'Quite the contrary. It was lovely. I'm sorry if it seemed that way even for a moment – I was in a bit of a state, what with my dad . . . and . . . and everything.'

Giles stroked the edge of her hand softly with the tip of his thumb.

'I'd better go in and set out lunch,' she said. 'But Giles? Would you be able to spare me a few minutes afterwards?'

He looked at her, his eyes bright and hopeful.

'I mean, not about that – but – I – it's just I need to – to discuss something with you.'

'Of course.' He looked down then and released her hand.

That Sunday morning

Miranda has amended last night's breakfast order to coffee and toast for one. Thank God Kath and Joe have been whisked away to some secret hideaway hotel last night so her absence from breakfast will barely be missed. Certainly Rob won't notice, that's for sure; he's probably left by now in any case, hot-footing it back to his real girlfriend, thankful he managed to get away from clingy Miranda, all right for a quick fuck, but that's that, thank you, a silly flirtation brought to its final, natural conclusion. Now they could both return to their normal lives and if they saw each other at Kath's, they would smile and say how are you and peck each other on the cheek, the brother and the best friend, cordial, pleasant, no more than that.

She starts to cry again, tears falling down her face. 'You're being pathetic!' she tells herself out loud. 'Stop it immediately!' Gulping back tears and clenching her fists tightly. Now she is not even sure why she is crying. 'What did you expect?' she demands. 'That you'd flit off into the sunset together? How could you be so ridiculous? So romantic? You, of all people!' Miranda, passionate yet pragmatic, who's never had any time for sentimental notions of Mr Right. Unthinking, she stretches out for the phone. As her hand closes around the receiver, she realizes. Nearly thirty years of turning to her father in times of trouble – ever since she fell over when she took her first few steps – is a hard habit to break. How long will this go on? How long will she think, 'I must tell Dad that, he'll get a real kick out of that,' how many times will she imagine she catches sight of him in the street ahead of her?

It isn't right. Even if someone has died, you should still be able to phone them at least. OK, fair enough that she can't sit in the kitchen with him anymore, talking their way through a pot of tea together, can't scold him for trotting off to give a lecture wearing an egg-stained jumper or one of his awful old knitted ties, but not being able to chat on the phone, that was truly appalling. Sorry, God, you cocked up there, this whole death thing is long overdue for a bit of a rethink. She pictures her father taking up the matter with God, absent-mindedly chewing one leg of his spectacles while he listens to God's point of view, then putting a contrary position with his usual consummate clarity and unshowy intelligence – challenging but not pushy. Her eyes fill with tears again, this time for her father, the deep, deep ache of missing him. Dead less than a month and she knows this pain is not about to evaporate overnight. Time heals all wounds? Miranda cannot imagine that this feeling will ever lessen.

Kath is out of the question, needless to say. Which leaves – who? No-one. She can just imagine what her mother would say if she were to ring up in tears, saying she'd just slept with her best friend's brother. 'Of course, people often go off the rails after a major bereavement.'

She would be reasonable and non- judgemental, tremendously understanding yet completely clueless. Then she would pronounce, 'I do hope you used protection, Miranda. It has been known for women to try to get pregnant when they're grieving. Subconsciously, I mean. It's utterly natural, of course, the need for continuity, new life and so on. But not a good idea, needless to say.' Her mother, who talks to under-age schoolgirls about contraception, never off duty. And then Miranda would have to lie, say, 'Of course I did. Honestly, Mum – how stupid do you think I am? I'm not fifteen, I'm a responsible adult.' Ha!

A knock at the door. Coffee. Thank God. She wipes her face on the sleeve of her dressing gown and opens the door.

'Oh, Miranda, good morning, my dear.' Giles smiles and averts his eyes slightly. 'I hope I haven't wakened you?'

'Not at all, I've been up for ages. Do excuse me . . .' she gestures at her state of undress. 'I thought you were my morning coffee.'

'Alas, no.' He pats his pockets and laughs lightly. 'I've come empty-handed, how rude of me.'

She smiles and wishes she'd had a chance to wash her face.

'Sorry, I must look an absolute sight . . .'

'. . . only of radiance. Forgive me for disturbing you—'

Behind him, the waiter appears.

'Coffee and a breakfast basket of pastries, was it?'

'Oh – I ordered toast actually.'

The waiter hovers, balancing the tray on one hand.

'Never mind, that'll be fine, thank you. Ah, it was just for one . . .'

'They said two.'

'No, it's one – oh, it doesn't matter.' She starts hunting for her purse, chasing round the room saying, 'Hang on, hang on . . .'

Giles discreetly tips him and the waiter leaves.

'Well . . .' He stands just inside the door. 'I'll get out of your hair. I was just off. I couldn't leave without saying a proper farewell etcetera.'

'Please – join me for coffee now you're here.'

'I'm sure you have to get on . . . ?'

'No. Really. It's fine. Won't you stay? If seeing me in my bathrobe won't put you off your croissant?'

It is a throwaway remark, simply to break the slight awkwardness she feels standing there with the door open and her bare legs on view, even though she is more covered than she had been in her dress last night.

'Hardly.' Giles lets his gaze linger on her for a moment. 'Many a woman would long to look so ravishing first thing in the morning.'

Miranda feels herself flush. Is he really meaning to flirt with her so blatantly or is he merely flattering her out of habit? Giles has always been extremely complimentary towards her, referring to her as the Fair Miranda, yes, but that's just the way he speaks, isn't it? It's a strange, over-the-top style he has, a sort of over-formal, flattering mode of address that comes across as slightly self-conscious and outdated, almost as if he's trying to seem older than he actually is. She's always regarded his compliments as little more than exaggerated politeness. It was just Giles being Giles. Wasn't it? She recalls his watching her during the wedding reception, his gaze openly lingering, his warm hand firmly on the small of her back as he danced with her, the way her skin unexpectedly tingled beneath his fingers.

'I'm sure Simon would beg to differ.'

'Ah. Not everyone recognizes the pearl in his palm. Until it's gone, of course.' He takes the coffee she passes him and waves away the offer of milk and sugar, the basket of pastries. 'I gather he . . . was unable to make it?'

'Yes, he got called away – there was an unexpected—' Miranda catches his expression, that beady glance; she sighs, thinking what's the point, you're fooling no-one. 'We had a huge, horrible row yesterday morning and he called me a selfish, spoilt brat – which I am, of course, and I said some pretty foul things too and, well . . .' She shrugs and leans forward to pick out a Danish pastry, glances up to catch Giles looking down the front of her robe. Instinctively, she lifts her hand to tug it closer around her, then hesitates a moment. Raises her hand further and instead tucks a strand of hair behind her ear. She stays in the same position, poised over the basket, frowning as if she can't quite decide what to choose, knowing that he is looking, longing, drinking her in. She senses his gaze travel over her, grazing over the soft, downy hairs on her extended forearm, delving, diving into the tempting shadow between her breasts.

'Please—' She holds out the basket towards him, her eyes meeting his now, her lips curving softly. 'Are you sure you won't have a little something?'

His smile. Eyes gleaming, openly interested now. His guarded look, the look that she now realizes she regards as his habitual expression, is gone. He looks younger suddenly, his face softer, hopeful, decidedly attractive.

'Well . . .' He leans forward, further than necessary, his hand brushing hers as he extracts a croissant. 'Perhaps I will.'

The last letter

Miranda knocked on the door.

'Come!' His voice was commanding and peremptory, reminiscent of the head teacher at Miranda's old school. She stuffed the bundle of letters into her handbag so that she could wipe her clammy palms on her trousers, then squared her shoulders and entered his room.

'Giles.'

He stood up at her entrance.

'Well, well . . . the fair Miranda said she would brave the lion in his den and here she is. This is a pleasure. I thought perhaps you had changed your mind.' He removed his reading glasses and laid them to one side.

Miranda attempted a smile.

'I do need to talk to you – but maybe now's not such a good time? If you're busy?' Felt herself wanting to chicken out. She couldn't imagine he ever saw anyone without an appointment. Bit her lip to stop herself asking, 'Should I check with your secretary?' Miranda looked down at her feet, pressed her toes down into the floor. These are not just my shoes, they are really *my* shoes, she reminded herself – they once existed only inside my head and now here they are, real and tangible, on my feet, protecting me from cold and wet and sharp stones. The protection from cold and wet was a moot point with these particular shoes – open-toed mules in soft camel suede – she knew, but then it was the principle that counted. I am a person who has made things *happen*, she told herself. I have my own business. *I am a grown-up.* She looked him in the eye once more. *Of sorts*, she amended in her head.

'I can easily come back later if that would be better?'

Giles folded his newspaper one-handed and drew his thumb and finger along the crease.

'I'm all yours.' He offered her the room's sole chair, where he had been sitting, and waited for her to sit before he lowered himself onto the nearer of the twin beds.

'You remember what you once told me? I mean – after we – after – at Kath's wedding – you said—' She ground to a halt. Why was this so difficult?

'You want to know if my offer still stands, is that it?' He laughed suddenly. This was the kind of laugh he directed at some of his colleagues, she imagined, a laugh that said 'you poor, stupid fool'. She flushed and pulled her handbag onto her lap like a shield. 'Has Simon finally driven you away? Frankly, I'm astounded that it's taken this long.'

'Strangely, no – actually.' Her voice was louder, angrier than she expected and she saw him blink, taken aback.

'Well, it does stand.' His voice was softer now, deep in his throat and slightly husky, as if he had a cold. 'Of course it does.' Looking at her now, really looking at her.

'Oh, *Giles* . . .' A button of his shirt had come undone and through the gap she glimpsed a flash of grey, curling chest hair. She stood up and came across to him, buttoned up his shirt without a word, as if he were no more than a child. His hand covered hers, held it against his chest, his beating heart. He looked up at her then – with such deep longing that it almost made her gasp; she could only meet his gaze for the briefest moment. She shook her head almost imperceptibly.

'I'm sorry,' she said. 'I can't even think about this now, I really can't.' She closed her eyes for a moment. 'It's been one hell of a week.'

Giles cleared his throat and patted her hand awk wardly, laid his own hand on the newspaper once more.

'Of course. An old man like me – what would you want with me when you could have anyone you choose? *Anyone.*'

'No. Don't be silly. It's not that. And you're not old. You know I—' She stopped herself. 'It's a bit compli-cated. I'm with Simon.' She shrugged, as if she had no say in the matter. 'That's all.'

'Well, I hope the fellow knows what he's got.'

'Mmm.' Remembering various recent endearments: *You can be such a fucking shrew, Miranda.* 'Well, we have our share of problems . . . but we're – we're working things out.'

Giles drummed his fingers on the newspaper.

'So, what did you want to see me about then? Some legal matter? I'm glad I still have my uses.'

'No – I mean – yes, of course you do – not just like that – oh, Giles – you remember, you told me that time – about Kath. You said she wasn't your daughter – you *swore* she wasn't. You said there was absolutely no doubt in your mind.'

'That's quite correct.' He nodded decisively. 'You know Connie was canoodling with that piano teacher fellow, that much was crystal clear. Sneaky lunches, disappearing for the whole afternoon, hastily terminated phone calls. Besides – look at Kathryn! You only have to look at her to see she's not a real Yorke! Runty little thing. And no backbone – she can't even control her own children. They're practically wild.'

'Giles, you're being ridiculous! No-one expects children to only speak when they're spoken to nowadays. And you're wrong. Completely wrong. I know Kath doesn't look much like you, she takes after Connie, but she *is* your daughter, I know she is.' Miranda dug into her handbag for the letters. 'You were right about the piano teacher, but only up to a point: he did love her. Kath found some letters he wrote to Connie.'

He looked taken aback for a moment, then quickly restored his expression of impassive calm.

'Well, well. Love letters. How very intriguing.' Giles held out his hand for them.

'They're private.'

'Then why bring them to me? They're evidence – surely I am the best judge?'

'They're not *evidence* – Giles, no-one's on trial here.' She sighed. 'But they are proof. You misjudged your wife.' She pulled out the letter she had placed on top of the pile. 'Just read this one.'

He fumbled for his reading glasses once more, extracted the letter from its envelope. Miranda watched him read it right through twice, his eyes flicking back as he returned to certain passages.

I've waited so long for you, then yesterday I waited and waited for hours . . . Why didn't you call at least? . . . I know you only want to do what's right . . . but can't you see he'll never make you happy? I've waited so long, dreaming of making love to you, of holding you in my arms, my bed at last. Please don't say all our dreams have come to nothing. Please, call me. Just call me. That's all I ask . . . If it's all over, at least have the courage to tell me . . .

She saw his shoulders slump, his mouth twitch with reined-in emotion.

'Giles . . . I'm sorry . . . it must be upsetting—'

He rallied at once and shook his head.

'It's a long time ago.'

'Of course, but still—'

'This is inconclusive.' He refolded the letter and replaced it in the envelope. 'Even if she didn't turn up to that particular assignation, she could have gone to bed with him later. This proves nothing.'

'But she didn't, Giles. That's the last letter. She must have broken off all contact.'

'But she kept his letters.'

'I don't know how she *felt*. I'm only talking about what she *did*. You can't find someone guilty just for *thinking* something, can you, Giles?'

A dry laugh.

'Yet you expect me to judge without knowing all the facts?' He reached out for the letters once more.

'But won't you find them . . . distressing?'

'I'm not some snivelling victim, Miranda. I daresay I can cope.'

This time, Miranda handed them to him.

'Please – I must have them back as soon as you can. I have to return them before Kath sees they've gone.'

She paused at the door, then came back and bent to kiss the top of his head. Giles closed his eyes and she heard him inhale, breathing in her scent. She laid a hand on his shoulder.

'It's not too late, you know,' she said. 'Don't let it be too late.'

Past times

They are lying in bed, side by side, in Miranda's hotel room.

'We'd better get up,' she says, propping herself up against the pillows behind her. 'Aren't we supposed to have checked out by now?'

'They can wait.' He turns towards her and kisses her lips lightly.

She smiles and pats his arm through the quilt.

'Really – I ought to be heading off. I have to get back to London.'

She raises her eyes to meet his gaze, but for once his usually impassive, assessing demeanour is gone. His eyes are bright and shining, his expression soft, open, playful.

'Miranda?'

'Yup.'

'Was it . . . nice . . . for you?' Doubt clouds his clear blue eyes for a moment. She looks at him again.

'Yes – I'm sorry – it was lovely.' She smiles warmly. 'It really was – it's just . . . well, you know, this is pretty weird, isn't it? I'm feeling a bit freaked out. And it's been a rather emotional weekend one way and another for – for various reasons. Sorry. It's not you – it's just–' She shrugs. 'This. *Us.*'

He nods.

She smiles again, more briefly.

'I really must get up.'

Giles politely turns his back and reaches for his clothes while she pulls on a bathrobe.

'Yesterday really was an amazing day – the food, the flowers, the music – it must have cost you an absolute fortune, Giles.'

'Well, it's important to do these things properly. I could hardly have people saying I would only stump up the cash for half a pint of beer and a couple of rounds of stale sandwiches, could I?'

Miranda opens the wardrobe and grabs her trousers and top for today, flings them on the bed.

'And Kath looked so beautiful – just glowing with happiness. You must have been bursting with pride.'

'I can't seem to find my socks.'

She starts to hunt for them, kneeling on the floor to look under the bed.

'Here they are. With her hair up, Kath really looks very like Connie, doesn't she?'

'Hmm? Yes. Yes, she does.'

'She's like you around the eyes though.'

Giles snorts and sits on the bed to put on his shoes and socks.

'What?'

'I don't think Kathryn takes after me in any way whatsoever.'

'How can you say that! I know her eyes are a different colour – and she hasn't got your height – but the way she looks when she's concentrating hard and she does this funny little frown – exactly the same way you do—'

'Miranda, you're mistaken.' Giles stands up and puts on his shirt.

'No, I—'

'Miranda.' He does up the buttons and squares his shoulders. 'Trust me on this. Kathryn does not take after me. I'm a hundred per cent certain of it. Do you understand me?'

Miranda frowns, completely puzzled for a moment, then laughs.

'Oh, Giles! You're not implying that Connie slept with the milkman, are you? That's the silliest suggestion I've ever heard.'

'We can all be deceived by appearances. My wife evidently wasn't quite the angel so many people seem to have taken her for.'

'But Giles – you must be mistaken. I don't believe it.'

'Still . . . it's true.'

'What – you're saying you walked in and found her at it with someone else? Come on.'

'No. I didn't catch her *in flagrante delicto* – but she was undoubtedly having an affair. With her piano teacher. I found a note he wrote to her, which she'd hidden, and she was spotted having a surreptitious lunch with him by a colleague.'

'And did you confront her? What did she say?'

'I asked her – extremely civilly – if she had enjoyed her lunch and she flushed a tell-tale deep red and started muttering some preposterous excuse about having run into him by accident, and then I said that if she was planning to repeat the experience, she might do better to pick a rendezvous where she was less likely to be spotted by all and sundry and that, when having piano lessons, it was usual to meet somewhere that actually had a piano – for the sake of appearances at the very least. Her response was that she was giving up the piano altogether, as she wasn't progressing as fast as she would like, so she wouldn't be seeing her tutor again in any case. And I said I was extremely glad to hear it and the next day I rang up our nearest school and offered them the piano.'

'But that doesn't necessarily mean—'

'Miranda. I'm not a fool. Kathryn is a very bright and pleasant young woman in many ways – but it's clear to me that she's not my daughter and there's an end of it.' Giles puts on his jacket and comes towards Miranda. 'Needless to say, I would prefer you not to speak to Kathryn about this. I don't regard the unfortunate fact of her origins as being in any way her fault and I see no reason for her to suffer for it.'

'No. No, of course not. I wouldn't dream of it.'

'Let's not spoil this morning by fretting over – unhappy memories. Please.' He lays his hand on her arm and she darts forward and kisses him briefly. 'Shall I . . .' He clears his throat. 'Would it be – might I call you in London perhaps?'

'Ah, it's a little awkward right now.' She smiles tightly. 'Best leave it for a bit, do you mind? It's just that things with Simon are a bit . . . you know . . .' She shrugs.

'Of course. You know where I am. Give me a call some time. Whenever you like.'

Peace at last

The house was quiet at last. Beautifully, but almost eerily, quiet. Giles was sitting reading in the garden, enjoying the balmy afternoon. Miranda and Simon had gone to town with the children. Rob and Tamsin were out sightseeing.

'Hear that?' Joe cocked his head, as if listening.

'What?' Kath frowned.

'Nothing. Lovely, lovely nothing. No shouting, no crying, no falling down the stairs, no arguing, no snarling, no squabbling, no banging, no crashing, no hurling of heavy objects—'

'And that's just the grown-ups.'

He smiled and beckoned her towards the stairs.

'Follow me, wife. I have something important I need to show you in the bedroom.' He took her hand and led the way.

'What about Dad . . . ?'

'No, he's not invited. It's a private show.'

'What if he gets bored or something and comes looking for us?'

'He's not Luke's age, he's sixty-two. He'll work it out.'

'But it could be embarrassing . . .'

'I never met anyone as easily embarrassed as you. OK, tell you what, why don't I bellow out the window "Don't bother us for an hour or two, Giles, I'm about to give my wife a good hard seeing-to." Then he won't need to wonder where we are, will he?'

'God, I think you would, too.'

Joe crossed to the bedroom window and started to open it.

'No, no!'

'So easy to wind up . . .' He came closer and kissed her, then they quickly began to undress, yanking off their crumpled T-shirts and worn jeans, Kath's greying bra and knickers with the failing elastic. Joe pulled back the covers and they leapt into bed. 'I want to point out that just because we're having sex on our anniversary doesn't mean it's going to be reduced to an annual event. It's rare enough as it is.'

'Sssh,' she said, lightly nibbling his neck. 'Stop moaning. There are plenty of more important things for you to concentrate on . . .'

After a minute, he reached for her and pulled her on top of him.

'Come and squash me, wife.'

She smiled down at him, dipped her head to kiss him.

'Hello, you.'

'Hello back.'

'Ah . . .' they said, moving together now, unhurried, at peace. '*Ah . . .*'

Staying up late

'Bedtime, darling.' Miranda shooed Anna up the stairs. 'Do your teeth and face and I'll be up in a few minutes.'

'Maybe I could have a little bit of supper with the grown-ups?' Anna clung to the banister halfway up and stood on one leg, the other held out in front with pointed toe.

'Or maybe not.'

'It's not very late.'

'Teeth! Hurry up.'

'But we're on *holiday*.'

'Go on, chop chop.'

'Just half an hour.' Anna took one step downstairs again.

'No.'

'Quarter of an hour.' Another step down.

'It's not up for negotiation, Anna. Don't waste your energies trying to haggle – it won't make the slightest bit of difference, I can assure you.'

'What does haggle mean?'

'Trying to get something cheaper or arguing for a better deal.'

'Is it like when—'

'Stop spinning it out, missy. Bed. B-E-D. Right now.'

'I want to haggle.'

'I'm sure you do. Not tonight. We can haggle tomorrow.'

'But I want to have a go now.'

'I don't care. It's not a democracy, I'm in charge. Bed. This minute!'

Anna backed up a step.

'You're really mean. Daddy lets me stay up some times. When it's a special occasion.'

Thank you, Simon, she thought. *Why is it always me who gets stuck with being the Nasty Cop?*

'Yes, I'm a mean mummy, poor you. It's not a special occasion.' Miranda started up the stairs, ushering Anna in front of her.

'It is. It's Auntie Kath and Uncle Joe's wedding anniversary – you're all having champagne and nice treats. It's not fair.'

'Nothing's fair. Yes, it's special – *for them*. It's not a Bank Holiday for the whole country. Or – ' catching Anna's look, 'or a late night for you.' She leaned forward to kiss her daughter on the forehead, tucked a curl of hair back behind her ear. 'I promise to save you a posh choccie, OK?'

'Can I have two?'

'Two then – to eat tomorrow, not now. If you hurry up and brush your teeth without any more fuss.'

'Can I choose?'

'Hmm?' Miranda could hear the clattering of plates downstairs.

'What chocolates I want?'

'No. Tell me and I'll save them for you.'

'I need to see the little pictures.'

Miranda sighed.

'Tell you what, you hurry up and get into bed and I'll bring it up and you can pick, OK?'

Anna slowly retreated to the bathroom, climbing up the stairs backwards.

Miranda ran back to the kitchen to rescue the salmon. She transferred it to a platter and began to peel off the skin. Simon came in, cheeks flushed from a bout of chopping wood for the fire.

Miranda smiled.

'You look healthy. Having fun?'

'Yes, actually. I'd almost forgotten what proper physical exercise feels like. My arms hurt. In a good way.' He came closer. 'That looks delicious.'

'I hope so. It's a bit overdone, I think.' She poked at the flesh with a knife.

'Looks wonderful to me. I'm *so* hungry. What are the rest of you having?' Simon put his arms around her from behind and she turned her head towards him, slightly surprised. He rested his chin lightly on her shoulder for a moment, then printed a kiss on her cheek.

'Just going to wash my hands.'

'Oh – can you pop up and check Anna's doing her teeth properly?'

'Course.'

Miranda craned her head round the door of the sitting room.

'Supper's in about five minutes, everyone. Can I have a volunteer to open the wine?'

Giles started to get up, then sank back into his chair.

'I'm not sure I'll be much use to you, I'm afraid.'

Rob sprang to his feet and followed her into the kitchen.

'What are we having? Red or white? Both?'

'Bubbly to start – if you could open that while I finish up?'

'Sure thing.' He took out two bottles from the fridge. 'Glasses?'

'Up there.' She waved at a cupboard, then began rapidly chopping parsley to stir into the mayonnaise. 'Did you have a good day out with Tamsin?'

'It was fine.' He dropped his voice to a harsh whisper. 'What else was I supposed to do, hang around like a sick dog, seeing if you wanted to spare me five minutes?'

'Don't be like that. Please.' She put down her knife. 'I just need some time to think.'

'Don't we all.' He sighed loudly. 'OK, OK. Sorry.'

There was a discreet, controlled pop as he expertly opened the first bottle.

'A drop for the chef?' He stood beside her, looking at the skinned salmon surrounded by waves of curly lettuce. His voice was low and smooth: 'Nice smell.'

'Rosemary roast potatoes – in the oven.'

'Uh-uh. More like Chanel, I'd say.' He handed her a half-filled glass, waited for the foam to fall. Miranda steadily focused on the bubbles in the liquid.

'Perhaps you'd better give some to the others? They must be dying for a drink by now.'

He nodded and took the bottle through to the other room.

Alone in the kitchen, Miranda closed her eyes for a second, then took a swig of her drink. Right, concentrate,

concentrate – what was next? She transferred the mayonnaise to a pretty bowl and checked on the potatoes once more. OK. Starter.

They were sitting eating their salad of grilled goat's cheese with warm roast peppers and toasted pine nuts when a small figure suddenly appeared beside Simon.

'Oh, hello, little lady!' Giles, sitting opposite, raised his glass to her.

'Anna! What are you doing up? You're supposed to be in bed,' Miranda said.

'Oh, leave her. It is a special occasion after all. Five minutes won't do her any harm.' Simon smiled and leaned back in his chair. Miranda glared at him: *not helpful.*

'You said you were going to bring me up the picture thing. For the chocolates. You promised.'

'We haven't even opened them yet. Go on back to bed.'

'What are you eating?'

'Goat's cheese salad,' Rob said through a mouthful of the same. 'It's gorgeous. Want to try a bit?' He held out a forkful and she stepped closer towards him.

'She won't like it, it's too strong.'

'I want to try.' Anna nibbled a piece from Rob's fork, then scrunched up her face and turned to her mother. Miranda duly held out her napkin for Anna to spit it out.

'Here, have a sip of water to take away the taste.' She handed her a glass. 'Not too much or you'll be up and down all night like a yo-yo.'

'Is that champagne?'

'Yes, it is and no, you can't.'

'Ohh – give her a sip!' Rob called out. 'Just for the toast – aren't we doing a toast?'

'I thought we'd do it in a minute.' Miranda frowned at him.

'Well, we're all here now. Shall I?' Rob raised his glass. 'Um – right. Joe, what can I say? Little did I think when I first offered you a few grand to take Kathy off our hands that you would stand it this long . . . Nine years. Well done, mate, we reckon it was a bargain. If you make it through to next year, we'll see about a bonus. Keep up the good work.'

Everyone duly laughed.

'To Kathy and Joe – happy wedding anniversary!'

'Happy anniversary!'

Miranda gave Anna a sip of her champagne.

'And now it's time for bed. No arguments.' Miranda kissed Anna.

Anna went to kiss Simon.

'I'll come and tuck you up in a minute.'

Anna kissed Kath.

'Happy anniversary, Auntie Kath!'

'Thank you. Nighty-night!'

'Happy anniversary, Uncle Joe!'

'Night-night, petal.'

'Stop spinning it out!' Miranda got to her feet. 'Excuse me while I shepherd my errant offspring back to her pen.'

'What about a goodnight kiss for your Uncle Rob then?'

Anna ran to him.

'You're not her uncle,' Miranda and Simon said at the same time.

'No.' He looked directly at Miranda. 'I'm not, am I? Still . . . if Kathy counts as her auntie . . .' Rob pulled Anna onto his lap and held her tight for a moment, his eyes fixed on Miranda's as he rubbed his cheek against Anna's, their dark curls an undivided mass. Miranda sent him a warning look, then focused on topping up everyone's glass. Rob blew a raspberry on Anna's neck and started tickling her under the arms until she was giggling hysterically.

'No! Stop!' Anna caught her breath, then slid off Rob's lap and leaned against him proprietorially, looking up at her mother. 'He can be my uncle if I say so.'

Then she went to kiss Tamsin.

'So can I be your Auntie Tamsin?'

Anna stood still for a moment, considering.

'. . . Um, I'm not sure actually. Mummy – how many aunties am I allowed to have?'

'We'll discuss it in the morning – off to bed now. It's far, far too late for you to be up as it is.' She propelled Anna towards the door.

'Night-night, everyone! Off we go!' Miranda called.

'No, Mummy! I didn't kiss everybody night-night!' Anna broke away and ran to Giles, then stopped abruptly in front of him.

Giles looked up at Miranda for a second and she managed a half-smile. He stayed where he was, waiting, apparently unsure what to do next. Extended his uninjured arm. Anna looked round for her mother, confused, then Giles leaned forward and kissed her awkwardly on the top of her head.

'Goodnight, young lady.'

'Night-night, Auntie Kath's daddy!'

He smiled at her. 'You could call me Uncle Giles if you like.'

'Um.' Anna shook her head and looked at him as if he were being silly. 'I think you might be a bit too old to be an uncle actually.'

'Anna! Don't be rude! Go to bed now!'

Anna seemed on the verge of tears. Simon stood up and laid his hands on her shoulders.

'She didn't mean to be rude. There was no need to shout at her. Look, you've upset her now.' He swivelled Anna around. 'C'mon, sweetie, off we trot.'

Miranda bit her lip, then started clearing away the hors d'oeuvres plates.

'I'm terribly sorry, Giles. Kids say these things all the time – she didn't mean it.'

'Of course.' Giles patted his lips with his napkin. 'It's fine.'

'She could call you Gramps or something.' Rob laughed and reached across Kath for more bread.

Kath and Miranda both frowned at him.

'Good to see you haven't lost all sense of filial respect, Robert.'

'Hey!' Rob glanced at his father's face. 'Take it easy. I was only kidding, Pops.' He topped up Giles's wineglass, as if to console him. 'You're not really fussed about ageing anyway.' Emptied the bottle. 'Are you?'

A pause. Giles shrugged.

'No more than anyone else, I imagine.'

'I thought you liked being a respected pillar of society? You're not hankering after your lost youth, are you?'

Miranda tried to catch Rob's eye. God, he could be so stupid sometimes.

'Of course not. I have no wish to return to being a *spoilt* and *callow* youth.' Giles pointedly avoided looking at his son. 'I think being young is decidedly over-rated, if you want to know. Young people seem to think they know it all, when in fact the vast majority of them–' he took a gulp of wine and eyed Rob over the rim of his glass, 'are astonishingly ignorant. Even those who have had the benefit of an expensive education.'

'Well, you paid for it, so maybe I'm not the stupid one? If you really think I'm an ignorant lout, maybe you should ask for a refund.' Rob drained his glass, tilting his head right back, then started drumming his fingers on the table.

'That goat's cheese was delicious, Manda!' Kath got up and started clearing the dishes.

'Yes. Very tasty. Thanks, Miranda.' Joe tried to balance the plates awkwardly on top of each other without removing the cutlery.

'Hey – you two sit down – you're the guests of honour. Rob? Give me a hand?'

'I'll help, too!' Tamsin leapt to her feet as Rob took the stack of plates from Joe.

In the kitchen, Miranda clunked down the dirty dishes.

'Honestly, Rob! What on earth did you say that for? You know how sensitive your dad is about his age.'

'Well, he should have grown out of it by now. And look how rude he was to me! How come he's allowed to be sensitive but I'm not? You ought to be having a go at him, not me. Why are you defending him? You ought to be on my side.'

They stood close together by the worktop, arguing head to head as Miranda opened drawers and cupboards, grabbing serving spoons and dishes.

'It's not a question of sides. He lashed out because he was upset – his pride was wounded. All I'm saying is—'

'Um. Sorry, where do I put this?' Tamsin was standing in the middle of the room, holding the basket of bread.

'Anywhere!' Rob and Miranda said together, barely turning to look at her.

Tamsin plonked down the basket on top of the dirty plates and walked out.

'God, could we have any more prima donnas here?' Miranda picked up the salmon on its platter.

'Ha! You can talk!'

'Oh, shut up.' She suddenly squealed as Rob playfully pinched her. 'Careful!' She nodded in the direction of the bowl of parsley-flecked mayonnaise, gesturing for him to bring it. 'Well, isn't this fun? Ding, ding! Ready for Round Two?'

The importance of being married

'So how long have you two been married?' Tamsin asked Simon.

'We're not married actually,' Miranda answered, leaning across Rob to serve up the potatoes.

'But we've been together over ten years.' Simon helped himself to French beans.

'Don't you believe in marriage then?'

Simon shrugged.

'Never seen the need. I think we're fine as we are really.'

'I don't see how a piece of paper makes any difference.' Miranda passed Tamsin a plate. 'After all, when you have a child together, you can't have more of a commitment than that, can you?'

'Who wants more water?' Simon got to his feet, preparing to squeeze round the side of the table.

'It's all right, Simon.' Miranda leapt up. 'I'll get it.'

'I don't know though . . .' Joe said through a mouthful of salmon. 'I can't speak for anyone else, but I think it *is* different.'

'Of course it's different.' Giles nodded and leaned back in his chair. 'Legally, morally, socially. There's no comparison. Marriage validates and recognizes a relationship in the eyes of society – which certain people like to wave aside, but it's all-important.'

'I don't give a toss what society thinks of my relationship,' Simon said, not looking at Giles.

'Actually, that's *not* what I meant.' Joe's voice was quiet but they all turned to look at him. 'I think it's different *emotionally*. Well, it is for me at any rate. When I married Kath, I didn't think it was possible to feel any more for her than I already did, but,' he took her hand and squeezed it, 'once we were married, our love felt more . . . solid—'

'Just like her home-made sponge-cake!' Rob laughed. 'How romantic!'

'OK, so that's not the right word maybe. But you're wrong, Rob. It *is* romantic. I'm not talking about that heady feeling when you're first in love or have the hots for somebody, it's different. *Better*. Yes, it is – a, a *solid* love, like it's the bedrock of your whole life, underpinning everything else and giving you a sort of core of strength and security. Like when I have to deal with crap at work: yet another government directive or more bureaucratic shite or my boss being a total prat, when it all gets too much, I always think, "Well, I've got Kath and the kids and that's all that matters – so bollocks to the lot of you."' Joe looked down at his plate.

Miranda came back in and thunked down another bottle of mineral water.

'That's *such* a nice thing to say.' Kath cosied close to him and kissed his cheek.

'Well, it's true.'

'You're *so* lucky, you two – you have no idea.' Rob leaned forward to grab the mayonnaise. 'Though do you think it's necessarily marriage that makes the difference? Surely it's to do with finding the right person – someone who makes you feel like that? God, if *I* – uh, pass the – the uh beans there, will you, Simon?'

Tamsin flushed deeply and clutched her empty glass as though it were a lifebelt. Kath and Miranda both glared at Rob. Two or three seconds of silence stretched across the table, then everyone started talking at the same time. Miranda launched into a self-deprecating story about a series of minor crises at her shop, portraying herself as a clumsy oaf in a perpetual panic, tripping over shoeboxes and arguing with manufacturers in Milan in her lousy Italian. The others laughed loudly, appreciatively, eager to erase the awkward tension. Simon leaned close to Tamsin and offered her some wine, but she dumbly shook her head and murmured no, thank you.

In the kitchen, Miranda was scraping the plates when Rob came in with the serving dishes. She turned towards him.

'I know, I know – don't give me a hard time. I didn't mean to say it – it just came out. I'm an idiot.'

'Yes, you are an idiot. Oh, Rob – how could you? It was hideous. Poor Tamsin – did you see her face?'

He lowered his voice.

'Why the concern for Tamsin all of a sudden? You didn't seem all that fussed about her feelings yesterday, did you? Can't remember your saying then, "Oh, no, Rob – we mustn't – poor Tamsin!"' Rob clunked the dishes down on the worktop. 'Don't start getting all self-righteous on me now – who are you to start moralizing? Jeez, you're getting as bad as Simon—'

'Sssh!'

'As bad as Simon in what way?' Simon swept into the kitchen, holding the platter with its skeleton of salmon.

Miranda tugged open the dishwasher door and started loading it, crashing the cutlery into its holder from a height.

Rob and Simon stood face to face, only two or three paces apart.

'In what way?' Simon repeated.

'Well, since you ask – in the way of being a smug git trying to claim the moral high ground while making the rest of us feel we should be grovelling in the dust at your feet. The only difference being that you at least really *are* a virtuous prig whereas God knows Miranda wouldn't know a moral if it came up and smacked her in the face – Jeez, if you—'

A plate smashed to the floor.

'Shut up!' Miranda shouted. 'Just shut up!' Kath and Joe came hurrying through.

'What's going on?' Joe said.

'Calm down—' Rob took a step towards Miranda.

'Don't tell me to calm down. I can't stand this any more. All this arguing and back-biting and shouting—'

'Manda—' Kath's voice was barely audible amid the fray.

'Actually, you're the only person who's shouting,' Rob pointed out.

'Why are you being like this? You're spoiling everything. Just *stop* it – *stop it* – I can't do this – I can't—'

'You know why I'm being like this—' Rob grabbed her wrist suddenly and she cried out in surprise.

Joe and Simon moved forward as one.

'Oi! Come on, mate. That's enough.' Joe laid a hand on Rob's shoulder, stayed there, solid in the centre of them, protecting them from themselves. 'Come on,' he said again, drawing Rob away. 'Let's have a coffee and chill out for a minute, eh? Come outside and have a fag.' Rob didn't speak but let Joe lead him out to the garden.

Kath scurried across to the sink and started filling the kettle.

'There, we'll have a nice pot of coffee, hmm? And where are those choccies? Manda?'

Miranda stretched up to a high cupboard and brought them down. Stood there holding them, looking down at them as if they might contain some magic solution. Kath came closer. There was a drop of water on the lid and Kath wiped it off with her thumb. Another drop landed by her thumb. Another.

'Oh, Manda . . .' Kath put her arms round her friend and Miranda crumpled against her.

Simon came forward.

'Miranda, we really need—'

She shook her head, mouth gaping open, a black hole of wretched despair.

'Maybe not now, Simon, hmm?' Kath turned and smiled up at him. 'Can you just give us a minute.'

He stayed a moment or two, moving awkwardly from foot to foot, then he nodded and left the room. After a little while, they heard the front door open quietly and close again.

Miranda was stretched out on the sofa in the sitting room, sipping a hot whisky, while Kath massaged her feet. Giles tapped lightly on the door and poked his head into the room.

'Anything I can do?'

'No, thanks.' Miranda tried to smile. 'I'll be fine in a bit. It's just . . . things. Too much excitement, as they say – there'll be tears before bedtime.'

'Ah. Well. Let me know if I can – perhaps – help in some way.' He paused by the door, then looked at Miranda. 'In *any* way.' He nodded then left, quietly closing the door behind him.

'Kath?'

'What?'

'I'm sorry.'

'What for?'

Miranda shook her head, staring into her whisky.

'For everything. For spoiling your anniversary and being a vile old drama queen and making everything such a bloody mess—'

'Oh, you haven't.' Kath waggled one of Miranda's feet to and fro, as if teasing a child out of a sulk.

'I *have*, Kath. I've messed everything up, I really have. And I've made everyone else unhappy too.'

'Come on, it's not that bad. Just a silly row.'

'It *is* that bad. You don't know. It's awful. And I – I – ' She started to cry again, roughly wiped her tears away with her sleeve. 'I don't know how to fix it. Today I kept thinking how much better everything would be i I were just to disappear completely – vanish off the fac of the earth.'

Kath squeezed her foot.

'Don't ever say that!' Kath's voice was suddenly loud and certain. 'Never, ever say that. Why is it your job to fix it anyway? I know you always want to be in charge and be the person who makes everything happen. But give yourself a break. Do what the rest of us do ninety per cent of the time: slump back on the sofa and just leave it. Stop rushing round trying to make everything work all the time. No-one's dying or anything after all, are they? Let it wash over you and just *be*.'

Outside, a car engine revved into life, crunch of tyres on the gravel parking space, a brief screech as the car swung onto the road.

Miranda and Kath had changed into their dressing gowns and were in the kitchen, enjoying the calm predictability of clearing up, when Rob came back in.

'Has anyone seen Tamsin?'

'She went up to bed ages ago, I think,' Kath said. 'Didn't she?'

He shook his head.

'I think she's gone.'

'What – you mean *gone,* gone?' Miranda asked.

'Yup. Her clothes have gone and you know Tam – never separated from her wardrobe for long.' He rubbed his hand through his hair. 'Shit.'

'What about her car?' Kath suggested.

He went outside, then quickly returned.

'Nope. It's not there. She's definitely left. Oh, for fuck's sake – some fucking holiday this is.' He took a step towards Miranda. 'Happy now?' Then he turned sharply away from her and thumped upstairs to his room.

A quick word

Miranda was in the hallway, about to go up to bed, when Giles opened his bedroom door.

'Miranda? Might I have a quick word?'

'Really?' Her shoulders sagged. 'I'm pretty wiped, to be honest. Is it important?'

He nodded, thoughtful.

'Yes, I would say so. I'll try to keep it brief.'

'Fine.' She pulled her robe more tightly around her waist, tugged at the satin lapel. Followed Giles into his room. He gestured for her to sit down.

'I'm happy standing – as this won't take long.'

'Miranda. Sit down.' His voice was strong and commanding. '*Please.*' She sank onto the bed.

'Well.' Giles sat back and crossed his legs. 'Where does one begin?'

'Giles . . . I'm quite tired.'

'Of course. Forgive me. Well, straight to the point then.' He cleared his throat, then looked up at her. 'She *is* mine, isn't she?'

This would almost be funny, thought Miranda, if it weren't such a complete bloody nightmare. Still, at least she'd had some sort of rehearsal now.

'I'm sorry?'

'Don't feign obtuseness, Miranda, it isn't your style. I'm talking about Anna. As you know.'

'Don't be silly, Giles. Of course she isn't *yours.*'

'Did you or did you not get pregnant during the weekend of Kathryn's wedding?'

'It was a month or two later, I believe, M'lud.'

Giles shot her a look and drummed his fingers on the arm of the chair.

'I believe Anna described herself as being eight and a quarter? Children tend to be rather precise about these things.'

'Have you been taking notes?' Miranda folded her arms. 'She was conceived some time *after* that weekend.'

'One hates to be picky about minor details, of course, but . . . how do you know *exactly* when conception took place?'

'God, Giles – women do know these things. As far as I remember, it wasn't even until my next cycle. Anyway, you can tell from the scan. They're amazingly accurate now.'

'Are they really?'

'Mmm. Plus I know when I started having morning sickness and bloody sore nipples if you want all the tedious details. I just *know.*'

'I see. Now would you say that Anna takes after Simon or . . .'

'I'd say she looks more like my side of the family really. Obviously.'

'And those eyes. Where would you say those appeared from? Simply a gift from the Almighty?'

'You never met my father, did you? If you had, perhaps you wouldn't feel the need to ask these preposterous questions.'

He shook his head.

'Miranda. I've been watching the child. This evening, when she was sitting on Robert's lap – really, the resemblance couldn't have been more striking. They are obviously related. Clearly, she must be his half-sister.'

Miranda met his eye and sighed.

'If you've finished with this interrogation, I think I'll slope off, OK?'

'I believe a test is in order, don't you?'

'I'm sorry?'

'A test, a DNA test. Extremely simple matter nowadays: a non-invasive cheek swab or a sample of hair.'

I know, she thought. You think I haven't investigated all this? How many times had she imagined finding some way to sneak a few hairs from Giles, from Rob, from Anna. Rummaging in their bins for used dental floss like that crazy celeb case in the papers? Once testing had started to become widely available, she'd tenta-

tively made enquiries. The first company explained
that they wouldn't carry out tests without the knowledge and signed consent of the donors. Government
guidelines, they said. Further investigations unearthed
another company who seemed not remotely bothered
about government guidelines. They'd be more than
happy to do it, they said, but when she hesitantly
outlined the unusual nature of her predicament, they
explained that, in that case, cut hairs wouldn't do. The
possible fathers were *related*? Hmm. She would need
buccal cells from the lining of the cheek or hair that
had been pulled out at the roots, including cells from
the follicle. And how the hell was she supposed to get
those ever so casually? Have Rob and Giles round to
dinner and drug them? That was her problem. But the
company's lab could do the tests, they promised. As
long as they had samples from the possible fathers and
from the child, it could be done. They wouldn't even
need a sample from Miranda. Great, she thought, I'm
no more than an irrelevance.

'That should resolve the matter easily enough.'
    'Would it?'
    'Yes. I should think so.'
    'In what way exactly?'
    Giles's eyebrows shot up.
    'Then we would know the facts of the situation and
could proceed accordingly.'

'I see. So let's say – theoretically – you have the test and it proves you're – that you are etcetera, etcetera – so then what? How would we proceed?'

'Well, clearly there would be more than one avenue open to us . . .'

'Hmm-mm.'

'Naturally, I take my responsibilities extremely seriously. At the very least, I would expect to make a financial contribution towards Anna's upkeep, education and so on. However, I see no reason why I shouldn't be rather more involved than that . . .'

'Involved?'

He nodded.

'Yes. I'm not an unreasonable man, Miranda. I can see that your position is really quite awkward with regard to Simon and it wouldn't be right to oust him completely from his paternal role, given that to all intents and purposes he has acted as her father in good faith, yes?'

'He loves her more than you could possibly imagine. So I guess that would be a yes.'

'I see. Well, perhaps, once you have notified Simon of the actual facts of the matter, then it would be in order for me to make regular visits to the house and then to take Anna out for tea and so on, as a kind of uncle figure initially, then we could move on from there, and reveal the truth to her when she is at an age to have some understanding of the complexities of these things.'

'Giles, I'm thirty-eight and I don't have a clue about the complexities of these things.'

'Ah, Miranda. Why do you belittle yourself? I have always considered you immensely bright. As well as beautiful.' He paused, fiddled with his sling, wincing. 'Of course, there is another alternative, which I presume has also occurred to you?'

'Enlighten me, in case it hasn't.'

'We could create a more stable environment for Anna. Together. I meant what I said before.' He stood up and moved towards the window, then half turned, speaking to her over his shoulder. 'I'm sure my feelings for you are no secret.'

Miranda opened her mouth to speak, then closed it again.

'Don't say anything right now. Give it some serious consideration though, won't you?'

She turned to leave.

'And we will want to sort out that test as soon as we're back in London.'

'Honestly, Giles – if you're so bloody keen on DNA testing, why the hell don't you organize one for yourself and Kath, for God's sake! I don't understand you at all. Why the fuck are you hankering after a child you barely know and who's probably not even related to you in any case, when you have a perfectly wonderful daughter already only you don't pay her the slightest attention and she thinks you don't even like her! I mean, have a bit of sense.'

He flinched, then bowed his head. His fingers fumbled with the corner of a newspaper.

'Giles—' She stepped cautiously towards him and lightly laid her hand on his shoulder. 'I don't know when to keep my bloody big mouth shut. I'm sorry. I'll go now.'

He held up his hand as if warding her off, and said nothing.

Friday

The last day

Miranda handed Rob a mug of coffee and waited.

'Thanks. Any milk?'

'Rob, do you know you haven't once offered to make so much as a cup of tea for anyone else?'

'I have. Course I have.' But she could see a half-smile creeping across his lips.

'When?' She stood facing him, then leaned casually back against the worktop. 'Name one time.'

'Er – yesterday! I came in from the garden and I said, "How about a coffee?"'

'Ha! And Kath leapt up as usual and said, "Of course – who else wants one while I'm making it?"'

'I can't help it if she misunderstood me.'

'It was fine, Manda. I didn't mind.' Miranda avoided meeting Kath's eyes; she knew she couldn't resist that beseeching look: *please don't argue.*

'I think she understood you perfectly well.'

Rob grinned back, unabashed.

'It's just strange how the Yorke men somehow always manage to avoid doing anything domestic.'

Giles lowered his newspaper.

'Are you accusing *me*, Miranda?'

'You'd make a better defendant than a lawyer, Giles – that is such a good wronged-innocent expression.'

'I'm not a barrister, Miranda, as you know. Perhaps you haven't noticed that I have sustained a serious injury to my right arm?'

'I do notice that you can manhandle a broadsheet paper well enough – which I can barely master with two hands – yet you can't even open the fridge to get milk.'

She felt someone nudging her leg. Usually, she would assume that it was Anna, or Polly or Luke. Now, she knew without looking that it was Kath, urging her to stop.

Giles dropped the paper onto the table.

'Well, I daresay few mere mortals can come up to your exacting standards, Miranda. Especially if they're men.'

'That's so unfair!' Everyone turned to look at Kath, unexpectedly loud for once. She flushed, but carried on. 'Miranda never expects anything from anyone that she doesn't demand of herself. She works incredibly hard and she's done practically all the cooking and she's always tidying up after everyone. And she was just – she was only trying . . . to be fair . . .' Her voice tailed off.

Miranda suddenly felt her eyes fill, touched by Kath's loyalty. She had never heard Kath raise her voice to Giles, yet she had done for Miranda what she would never do for herself.

Rob raised his eyebrows at Miranda, trying to make her an ally once more. There was a sudden thud from upstairs and Kath hurried out, grateful for an excuse to leave, as Simon came in. No-one said a word and he looked from one to the other.

'What's going on now? Or do I not want to know?'

Rob leaned back against the fridge and sipped slowly at his coffee.

'Miranda's telling us off for being lazy boys. We were so scared, weren't we, Pops?'

'Your *partner* gave us a rap across the knuckles. She expects me to whip up a three-course meal with my arm in a sling apparently.'

Simon stood straight and looked directly at Giles.

'Why did you say it in that way? *Partner*. Like it's a dirty word.'

'Did I? I was not aware that my intonation was especially offensive.' Giles returned Simon's gaze with an expression perfectly hovering between utter boredom and amused condescension.

'Si. It's OK.' Miranda, her voice soft.

He didn't turn from Giles.

'Yes. You know it was. Your *partner*, you said, as if it were something weird or laughable.'

Giles smiled.

'Your assumption rather than mine, I surmise. What would you prefer then: cohabitee? Common-law spouse, I suppose, technically. Live-in *lover*? Or is that not quite . . . *accurate*?'

'Dad! Hey – that's enough!'

Rob and Simon both took a step towards Giles, but Rob laid his hand on Simon's arm. For a few moments, they stayed like that. Miranda couldn't move, felt as if her feet were made of lead, her voice stuck and solid in her throat.

Then Simon slowly shook his head and pulled away.

'You're nothing but a sad, envious old man.' He turned to go, then paused. 'I feel sorry for you,' he said.

Kath came back in and avoided looking at anyone directly.

'Um, now who's up for a quick stroll on the beach?' she asked the kitchen table. 'We could probably all do with some fresh air. We're only getting a little testy with each other because we've been cooped up inside all morning.'

Rob drained his coffee in one go and put his mug on the worktop, then made a show of carefully placing it in the dishwasher.

'Not me. Don't think I'm up for playing at happy family outings just this minute, Kathy.'

Miranda merely shook her head and left the room.

'Dad? How about you? Please come, hmm?'

Anna came skipping into the kitchen, wearing her warm jacket and blue wellington boots.

'I'm ready first!'

'Good for you, Anna.'

'And Mum says I can have a choc ice from the icebox.'

'Before lunch?'

'Yes, 'cause it's our last day. She said I could.'

'OK. Dad – are you coming?'

Giles smiled.

'All right. Yes, perhaps that is a good idea.'

'*Kath*?' Joe's voice, calling from upstairs. 'Have you seen Luke's jacket?'

'You two go on ahead. We'll be right behind you.' She dashed off and ran upstairs.

The incredible shrinking man

Anna carefully peeled the wrapper open on her choc ice, leading the way to the back gate. There, she turned towards Giles at the top of the steps to the beach.

'You have to be quite careful on these steps actually,' she said very seriously, looking at his injured arm. 'You can hold my hand if you like.'

'Well, I – ' Giles hesitated, then reached out his left hand to take Anna's. 'Perhaps I will. Thank you.'

'I promise not to go too fast.'

At the bottom, they picked their way across the rocks to the damp expanse of the sand.

'Do you want to know how to skim stones?' She looked up at him, slowly licking her choc ice. 'I can show you.'

'I'm not sure I can – with my arm. Shall I try with my left hand?'

She nodded and held out a stone towards him.

'This is a good one, see?' Small fingers stroking the surface. 'You've got to find one that's all smooth and flat or it won't bounce.'

He took it and stood facing the waves.

'Here,' she said, tugging his jacket to turn him side-ways on. 'This is how you do it.'

'Ah. Well, yes – you'd best show me how.'

She pulled at his left arm.

'You have to go down a bit lower. That's what my daddy says. He's ever so good at it.'

'Ah.' He swallowed and clutched his stone in his hot hand. Tried to crouch, his balance off because of his arm. 'Like this?'

She nodded. He swung his arm out and forward, sending the stone skittering across the surface.

'You did it!' Anna clapped her hands together.

Giles stood up straight again.

'You're very tall, aren't you? I'm tall for my age, too.'

'Are you? I'm six feet two. Used to be more, but I've shrunk a bit.'

Anna laughed.

'How did you shrink?'

'I don't know. You just do as you get older. Didn't you know that?'

She shook her head slightly, lips clamped shut. 'Well, it's all right,' he added. 'It doesn't matter really.'

'Will you shrink any more?'

'Probably. I shan't be able to help it.'

'How much? Will you just get smaller and smaller?'

He smiled and crouched to look around for another stone. Suddenly lost his balance and sat back on the sand.

'Oops. Who knows – maybe I will?'

'Will you be the same size as me?'

He laughed.

'If you keep growing, perhaps we'll meet in the middle?'

'Yes. And then I'll be bigger than you. And you'll get smaller and smaller and then you'll be the same size as Luke—'

'And then no bigger than a – a – cat, say?'

'Then a little tiny kitten . . .'

'Then a mouse . . .'

'Then a beetle!'

'Then an ant.'

'And then you'd disappear – and we'd all come looking for you but we wouldn't be able to find you not even with a magnifying glass or a binoculars or anything.'

'Yes!' They laughed.

'You should probably get up now,' Anna pointed out. 'When I sat on the sand, I got a wet bum.'

'Wise words.' He struggled awkwardly to his feet. 'I suspect you may be right.' Giles craned his head over his shoulder, trying to see.

Anna stepped behind him and brushed at the sand on his trousers.

'Hmm.' She looked serious. 'It's not too bad actually. Mum put mine in the washing machine.'

'Good idea.' He looked down at the shore. 'Shall we find some more stones?'

She nodded and passed him her empty choc ice wrapper without comment. He held it in his hand, looking at it for a minute as if it were a rare artefact, then he folded it sticky-side in and tucked it into his pocket and resumed the search for the perfect stone.

Anna picked up a dark stone, nearly black, banded with white.

'Look.' She held it nestled in her palm as if it were as fragile as a bird's egg. Giles took it between his finger and thumb.

'I'm not sure it's flat enough.'

'Not for throwing!' She frowned at him, her eyebrows angling into a V. 'For *keeping*.'

'Oh. I see. I'm sorry. I didn't realize.'

'These white bits are quartz, you know. That's what makes it a special stone.'

'It's very . . . ah . . . pretty.'

She nodded seriously and he handed it back to her.

'I'm sure it'll make a fine addition to your collection.'

Anna turned it over and over in her hand, then enclosed it in both hands, cupped to form a cave. Held her hands to her mouth and blew into them.

'It's lucky now, 'cause I blew on it,' she informed him. Then she pressed the stone into his hand. 'You can have it if you like. I've got lots like this one already.'

The stone was still warm from her hands, her breath. Giles stared down at it in his large palm for a moment, then his fingers curled round it and he clutched it tight.

There was a sudden shout from above their heads as Kath called to them from the top of the steps, coming to join them.

The tide turns

Giles and Kath stood on the beach, watching the children playing at the shoreline. There were shouts, squeals as they jumped back at the last moment, the waves reaching for their shoes.

'They're looking well,' Giles said.

'Yes.' Kath dug her gloveless hands deep into the pockets of her coat. 'Yes, they're great just now.'

'Polly's getting a touch of your mother around the eyes, I'd say.'

'Really? I always thought she took after you more.'

Giles's mouth twitched into something that might have been a smile.

'Kathryn?'

Joe called to them, then came over.

'Think I'd better take the kids back up in a minute, Kath. They're all getting a bit peckish.'

'I can come.'

'No, you stay here. I can manage.' He called out to the children.

'Anyway . . .' Giles resumed.

'Hmm?'

'I would like to speak to you about something.' He paused, weighing his words.

'Oh. OK.' She waited, still keeping an eye on the children. After a minute, when he still hadn't spoken, she turned towards him. 'What is it? What's the matter? Have I done something wrong?'

'It's – you see, the thing is . . .' He cleared his throat loudly then began again. 'The possibility has occurred to me . . .'

'Oh! Hang on!' She rushed off and scooped up Luke, who had fallen over in the shallows and was crying. She cuddled him close, then passed him to Joe, who led the children back towards the house.

Having handed Luke over, Kath returned to Giles.

And now they were alone on the beach, with only the calls of the gulls and the hushing of the waves.

'The little man all right, is he?'

'He's fine. Just soggy that's all.'

'It doesn't do to cosset children too much, Kathryn. Boys especially have to learn to toughen up if they're to survive out there in the big bad world.'

'Dad, can we not have this conversation again? I think you'll just have to accept that we don't agree about this stuff. I don't regard cuddling my children or picking them up when they've fallen over as "cosseting", OK? The "spare the rod and spoil the child" approach has been pretty much discredited.'

Giles looked down and reached into his jacket pocket for one of his cigars.

'I make no pretence of keeping up to date with the latest vogue in childcare. I was never a devotee of Dr Spock and I doubt whoever it is nowadays is much of an improvement.'

'I don't think cuddling one's children is down to a mere whim of fashion, is it?'

'Times have changed, Kathryn, whether you choose to acknowledge it or not.' He passed her the matches. 'Would you mind?' Hunching close to her for a moment to shelter the flame from the wind.

'Well, your parents were affectionate towards you at least some of the time, weren't they? I mean, they didn't keep you locked up in the attic or anything?'

'As you know, I have no taste for this repellent obsession that people seem to have in endlessly going over their pasts. I find it self-indulgent and tedious and I have no intention of peddling my childhood as some woe-is-me sob story.' His eyes were almost closed, screwed up against the cigar smoke and the salt gusts of wind. 'Quite the contrary. In many ways people might regard my upbringing as immensely privileged. We were relatively well off, I had a decent schooling and so on. But things were different then. As you know, my father was an RAF officer – I barely saw him at all until after the war and then, from the age of seven, I was away at school, of course.'

'But your mother?'

'She was a fine woman. Highly capable and not unintelligent.'

'I didn't mean that. Did she cuddle you?'

'If I want a psychiatrist, Kathryn, I'll seek out a reputable one with a proper training. I hardly think that a couple of weekend counselling workshops qualify you to analyse me.' He tapped his cigar ash onto the sand, then he sighed and carried on. 'She kissed us goodnight, certainly. But there wasn't all this . . .' He waved his hand round and round as if to indicate a whirling carousel of excessive displays of affection. 'And then I was away most of the time. One wouldn't have dared attempt to cosy up to Matron, I can tell you. Fearsome woman – I'm not sure woman's even the correct term. She was more like a battleship, steaming along the corridors, crushing small boys against the walls as she passed. Still, I don't recall many of the boys being all that bothered about –' he waved his hand once more '– all that sort of thing. Mostly, we concerned ourselves with endless devious plots to get more food. We'd have made rather good spies, I sometimes think – we became quite clever at it. Cuddles?' He snorted. 'I shouldn't think there was a boy there who'd choose a kiss from his mother over a slab of fruitcake.'

'Poor you.'

Giles recoiled slightly.

'I wasn't asking for pity. I have no complaints. I reaped the benefits of a first-rate education.'

'Yes, but . . . '

'And it certainly didn't do me any harm, did it? Have I turned out so very badly?' He gave a dry laugh.

Kath squeezed his arm.

'Course not, Daddy.' She put her hands back in her pockets to warm them. 'What did you want to say to me before?'

'Oh. That. Nothing major.' He exhaled a puff of smoke and tapped the ash off his cigar. 'Well, perhaps that's not quite accurate. Recently . . . very recently, in fact, I have been thinking about various . . . matters . . . however . . . to do with the past and so on. And it struck me that there was a possibility that I might not have . . . treated you and your brother . . . one hundred per cent . . . equally.

I believe I should acknowledge that I might have, you know, not been quite . . .' He stood facing rigidly out to sea. '. . . As . . . as I could have been. Perhaps I should have been – could have been – more . . . more – ' he swallowed and his voice faltered and grew faint, '*fatherly* . . . '

Kath tried to breathe. Standing at his side, unable to look at him. Before her, sea and sky swam together in a blur. She tried to frame an answer, something, anything, even if she could just manage to mumble 'mmm'. But she could not speak. At the edge of her vision, she saw him turn to face her now.

'Kathryn?'

Still she could not look at him, dared not open her mouth in case all that was held there should burst out of her in a torrent. But it was too late. The wall was already breached.

'Kathryn?' Concerned now, his hand on her arm, twisting her round, seeing her face. 'Oh, my dear!'

She crumpled to the sand as if she had been felled and held herself, wrapping her arms around her head as if to ward off heavy blows. An unearthly sound tore out of her, a wild, strange keening like the gulls.

Giles dropped awkwardly to his knees, losing his balance. He scrabbled close to her across the sand patting her shoulder clumsily, touching her hair with his one good hand, saying her name over and over. At last he gathered her to him, rocking her, his little girl holding her close.

'I'm so sorry – I'm so sorry – please forgive me. Kathryn, Kathryn, my little Kathy. *Forgive me.*'

The answer

Rob looked out of the car window, tapping his fingers on the door handle, as Miranda drove to the local shop for provisions.

'Well, call me impatient, but I'm pretty much done with sitting on the reserve bench now, if that's all right with you. So . . . what's it to be, Miranda? Are you in or out?'

'Are we planning a bank robbery?' She stared resolutely ahead, trying to focus on the road. 'What do you mean, in or out?'

'You know exactly what I mean. I'm not spending another nine years wondering what the fuck happened between us. Do you want to be with me – or not? Yes or no? How hard can it be? Shall I rephrase the question?'

'Rob, you make it sound as if we're at a restaurant – now then, what's it to be, the beef or the chicken? Don't you think it's just a teensy bit more complicated than that?'

He sighed and wound down the window. Lit up his last remaining cigarette.

She glanced across at him for the first time. He ostentatiously craned his head out of the window, blowing the smoke outside.

'Complicated? Actually, no I don't. Not really.'

'Oh, for God's sake – bring your stupid head back in before it gets chopped off by a bloody branch!'

'Hear that, world? She cares!' he bellowed out of the window. 'She cares!' He started fiddling with his empty cigarette packet, tugging out the silver paper and folding it over and over again. 'OK, so there are a few complications – possibly – arrangements-wise – but the basic question couldn't be simpler.' Rob cast a glance at her. 'You think I'm just being simplistic and thick? Nice to know that you share my esteemed parent's opinion of me.'

'No-one thinks you're thick.'

'No? What was all that ignorant youth stuff then last night? I notice you stayed conspicuously silent in my defence. Cheers.'

'Really, Rob. Have a bit of sense.' She came to an abrupt halt, nose to nose with a white van coming straight at them. 'I know, I know. I'm giving way.' Miranda twisted her head round and reversed at some speed into the nearest passing place. Waited there a minute, hands gripping the wheel. 'Giles is so envious of you, can't you see that? You've got *everything* to look forward to. What does he have? A fat pension. Big deal. It's not much consolation if you have to spend it all by yourself, is it?'

'Ah yes – every morning I wake up, whistling a merry tune as I think about my rosy future. What do I have to look forward to? At least he enjoys his work.'

'Come on. Have a heart.'

He snorted.

'Had one of those. It got trodden on by a desirable dame in chi-chi shoes.' He half smiled at her, let his hand rest by her side. She covered it for a moment with her own, then moved it back to the gearstick.

Miranda pulled into the next lay-by.

'Rob. I'm not ready to have this conversation right now.'

'Aren't you? Oh, right then. Let's defer it for a couple of years until you are, shall we? I've got nothing to do but hang around waiting to have a real life.'

She sighed and put on the handbrake, switched off the engine. He sat watching her for a moment, but she said nothing.

'So I guess I can take that as a no. Final answer?'

'This is so hard.'

'Yeah, yeah. Well, that says it all. I don't need a diagram. Spare me the lengthy explanations. Let's crack on, shall we?' He checked his watch, started tapping his foot. 'I need more fags.'

'If it were just me, it would be different.'

'Don't blame it on the kid. So you come as a Buy One, Get One Free? So what. I'm cool with it. Jeez – she is *my* kid.'

'We don't *know* that,' Miranda reminded him. 'We don't know that at all. What if – if we have a – the DNA tests done – and – and she *is* Simon's after all? Or

– or – whoever's. Would you still be up for this cheap package deal if it included *someone else's* eight-year-old child? Would you be so keen to help her with her maths homework or to – to hold her hair back when she's being sick or to check beneath her bed for trolls at night?'

He laughed.

'*Trolls*? That's a new one.' A shrug of the shoulders. 'Or *whoever's*? Don't tell me there are another six suspects in this identity parade?' He shook his head, without waiting for an answer. 'Well, OK, it wouldn't be the same. Of course it wouldn't – you couldn't expect that – no-one could. But, hey, I'm pretty easy-going, aren't I? She's a cute kid. We'd get along fine.' Rob turned to face her. 'Anyway, what's the problem? We'll get back, have the test done, and – bing-bong – there you are. We'll know. End of suspense.'

Miranda slumped back in her seat.

'You want me to uproot Anna from the man she knows as Daddy, from her home, then you find out she's not yours and you decide on that basis whether you'll be able to love her or not?'

'No. I'm sure I'll love her. Give me a sodding chance, Miranda – I practically only just met the girl.'

'So why do *I* have to decide now? Why not wait for the test, then we can . . . see . . .'

'Oh no.' He gently turned her face to make her look at him. 'No, no, no. I'm prepared to take the risk – so

412

why aren't you? Either you . . . have strong feelings for me and you think we can make a go of it – or you don't. Come on, logically it's much more of a big deal for me – at least she's *your* child whoever the dad is. It's *you* I want to be with, Manda – and if it turns out that Simon *is* the father – well, OK, we'll be a stepfamily. Not the end of the world, is it? Anna will survive. Kids are tough these days. They're streetwise, they adjust. And if she has a crappy time, hey, she can turn it into a bestselling memoir, OK?'

Miranda looked appalled.

'Hello? *Joke?*' Rob rolled his eyes. 'God, you have been living with Simon too long, you've had a sense of humour bypass. Come on, you can't tell me you're really happy with him?'

'I admit we're having a bit of a bad patch at the moment.'

'A bad patch? Jesus, the guy's barely said a nice word to you the whole week. Is that what you want for the rest of your life?'

She shook her head dumbly, tears pooling in her eyes.

'Hey, I'm sorry. Hey. Don't cry. Have you got a tissue?'

She pointed to the glove compartment. He pulled out a tissue and dabbed at her face.

'You can't make Simon the reason for not giving me a chance. That's crazy.'

'I'm not. I don't know why he's being – the way he is. Maybe we haven't got a hope in hell of ever getting back to normal, to the way we used to be.' She took the tissue from him and wiped her face roughly. 'But I have to try. Even if it doesn't work, it can't be just because *I* baled out for my own selfish reasons. I'm sorry.' She started the engine again and pulled out. 'Anyway, you know the two of us couldn't hack it in a real relationship. Not long-term.'

'Not if you won't even give us a chance. You're just being a coward.'

'Maybe I am . . . but I'm not taking chances with my daughter. It doesn't work like that. If it were just you and me, we could swan off tomorrow and if we drove each other crazy and had to call it a day, then so what? We'd rub our bruises and move on. But I'm not gambling on Anna's behalf. I can't do it.'

'You don't consider me a safe bet then?'

Miranda pulled sharply into the hardstanding in front of the small village shop.

She turned to face Rob.

'I think you're *amazing*. Wonderful in a thousand ways. I would love to sail off into the sunset with you . . . but it's too late for us to embark on a fairy-tale romance, isn't it? We're too old – OK, *I'm* too old, don't say it. I'm too tired, too jaded and, frankly, just too bloody scared. If it had happened for us nine years ago, it would have been different. *Maybe.* Or maybe not.

But it's too late for us.' She looked into his eyes. 'I'm sorry,' she said.

He reached out and stroked her cheek with his thumb.

'Oh, Miranda,' he said. 'So am I, so am I.'

An important question

It was late afternoon. Simon pulled on his fleece and stuck his head round the kitchen door, looking for Miranda.

'Fancy a walk?'

She looked up from her book, then out of the window.

'Is it cold out?'

'Not too bad.' He shrugged.

Miranda checked her watch.

'I ought to be making a start on supper soon.'

'Not for a while yet surely? We won't be long – only half an hour. I promise not to drag you all the way to Land's End, OK?' He jerked his head towards the door. 'Come on.'

Miranda grabbed her coat and scarf and they walked down the garden in silence.

'Up or down?' she asked.

He nodded towards the cliff path, striding ahead of her, pulling on his gloves. Turned round briefly.

'Keeping up? Isn't this fun?'

'Call me stupid,' Simon came to a halt at the clifftop and turned to face Miranda. 'But what I can't work out is which one it is.'

'Don't be deliberately cryptic, Simon. Which one is what? Who? What are you on about?' Miranda, clutching at the last few seconds of normality before her whole life unravelled beneath her feet. She found she was hoping – actively hoping – that perhaps Simon just thought she was having an affair. That she could handle, after all. She had comebacks aplenty if he went down that route. She reminded herself that she didn't actually have sex with Rob, so she could deny that without lying. OK, it wasn't for want of trying, she hadn't exactly been fighting him off on the bathroom floor, but – looking at the matter from a purely technical point of view – no penetration took place, which was surely what mattered. There was a time for absolute truth and a time for a more Clintonesque approach to veracity, she felt. She just had to hope that Simon's questions wouldn't be too precise. Or she'd have to lie outright. She planted her feet squarely and prepared to defend herself.

Simon tucked his gloved hands into the pockets of his fleece and stood there, looking at her.

'I think the time for the outraged-innocent stance has come and gone, don't you?'

Miranda sighed and faced him full on.

'Fine, Simon, whatever you say. As you're the one

who clearly has an agenda, while I don't have a clue what's going on, why don't you just crack on and accuse me of whatever it is? My hands are getting cold.'

'Where are your gloves?'

She nodded in the direction of the house.

'Here. Wear mine.'

'I'm OK.'

'Take them.' He passed them to her and she put them on. If anyone were watching us from a little way off, she thought, they would mistake us for a happy couple perhaps – see, ah, he cares, he's giving her his gloves. They were his thick Gore-tex gloves, navy blue with ribbed cuffs. Not what Miranda would have chosen to wear, but very warm. She sniffed in the cold air and dug clumsily into her pocket for a tissue.

'Warmer?'

She nodded.

'Mmm. Thank you.' Looked down at her feet and stamped them. Forced herself to look up again and meet his gaze. 'Well?'

'Well . . . so, the question is then . . . is it Rob . . . or . . . is it, and I can't believe I'm having to ask this . . . Giles?'

'You're accusing me of having an affair?'

'Are you?'

'No.' She thought for a moment. 'Of course not.'

He waited.

'So is that it?' Knowing it wasn't, couldn't possibly be.

'Miranda, I'm not sure if you take me for some kind

417

of pea-brained halfwit, but it's obvious that *something* has been going on. I presume – *hope* – that it's not some weird ménage à trois involving both of them because, frankly, that's a bit off the graph even by your decidedly elastic moral standards, but clearly . . .' He shrugged and looked out to sea.

'Clearly *what*? When would I have had a chance to sleep with either of them since we've been here? And Giles has his arm in a sling, for God's sake. Even if I'd had the slightest interest in doing so,' she thought to add. 'When would I be indulging in these wild orgies? I've barely been out of your sight all week.'

He turned back to face her, waiting once more.

'I haven't been keeping a twenty-four-hour watch on you, Miranda, because – well, what's the point? If you're determined to sleep with other men, then no doubt you'd find a way and if the only way to stop you is to guard you day and night, then that's not really the kind of relationship I've always dreamed of, you know? As for this week, I have no idea what you've been up to but, frankly, I'm not even terribly interested. What I'm talking about, Miranda – as I'm sure you are well aware – is the past.'

'I've never had an affair with anyone else since we've been together.'

'Not an affair necessarily. The question I'm asking, as clearly you're determined to make me spell it out so you can pretend you don't already know full well what I'm talking about, is this: which of them is Anna's biological father? Is it Rob? Or is it Giles?'

Miranda's jaw dropped and she felt as if her legs would give way beneath her. Simon started, his outrage momentarily forgotten. Then she steadied herself and his mask of cold anger returned.

'Clear enough for you?'

'I – I—' She shook her head. 'How can – what makes you – why? Why? Why are you saying this?'

He shrugged.

'Because it's true. God knows I wish it weren't. But it is . . . isn't it? Or is there some entirely other third person in the picture that I should be worrying about? Clearly, Kath and Joe's wedding was a lot, lot wilder than I'd realized.'

Miranda looked away, out to sea, to the steely grey water shifting far below, and the jutting headland beyond.

'What makes you think she's not yours? You shouldn't get yourself into a paranoid state just because I'm a dreadful old flirt, you know.'

'Miranda. Please. Give me some credit. How can you know me so little? Do I go around accusing people on the basis of my own irrational hunches? Hardly. I suspect, I research, I check my facts, and then, only then . . .' He faced her. 'I had a DNA test.'

Her head jerked up and her eyes met his.

'Anna, too, of course. She's not my child. No question.

I can show you the results and I can quote from their letter: "The alleged father is excluded as the biological father of the child . . . Based on testing results obtained from DNA analysis, the probability of paternity is 0%." *Nought per cent,* Miranda. Nought.'-

'When? How? Maybe there was a mix-up at the lab? A mistake? It happens. No-one's infallible, you know. Remember, there was that case where—' He met her eyes and she had to look away.

'No, Miranda. No mix-up, no mistake. Believe me, if there were the slightest possibility . . . You're always saying I love to be right? Well, not this time. You know, I'd always had this niggling feeling at the back of my mind, but I'd suppressed it, told myself I was being ridiculous, paranoid. Then, you know what finally tipped the balance? Two things really. I was in at the paper, just sitting at Michael's desk, waiting for him to come out of a meeting and my eye fell on this feature about how many children in the UK aren't in fact fathered by the man who believes he's the father. The kind of piece I wouldn't usually give much credit to, frankly. Statistics drawn from too small a sample, so-called experts trotted out to make dramatic-sounding pronouncements, etcetera. But still . . . one in seven, it said, maybe even as high as one in five. I was sitting there, looking around the room at the other men – editors, staff writers, stray freelances like me. I could see nine men without even moving from the chair. So, statistically, I thought, one of us . . . at least one of us . . . and what if it's me?'

'But that's silly. That's like saying one in ten men are gay, and if none of the others is gay, then therefore you must be.'

He looked at her, waiting, and she let him continue.

'And then I came home and told you I'd had a blood test which showed I have a very high cholesterol level and that the doctor suggested we might want to get Anna checked out, and what did you say? Oh, no, Simon, let's not worry her – I'm sure she's absolutely fine.'

'But that's true! I meant that. I didn't want—'

'As I was *saying* . . . I suspected, so I checked it out while you were away. But, you know what? I was *so* desperate to be wrong I nearly didn't open the results. Maybe I should have thrown them away. What I didn't know is who the father might be. Well, that's not entirely true. I had my suspicions. Obviously, Rob was at Kath's wedding and you always flirt embarrassingly with him so the thought did cross my mind. And then when you tried to get us to cancel the holiday – well. That kind of clinched it. And since we've been here, I've spent a lot of time watching them both. She does look like Rob, you know, it wouldn't take an expert geneticist to notice the resemblance. But does she look like him because she's his daughter – or because she's his half-sister, that's what I need to know. *Giles?* Is it possible?' He shook his head, his face desperately pale. 'I presume you've noticed that he can't take his eyes off you?'

'Oh.' She bowed her head for a moment, then looked into his eyes once more. 'I'm sorry. I really am.'

'So am I.' He shoved his hands into his pockets. 'Shall we walk? It's too cold to stand still.'

She nodded and they continued along the path.

'So – what do you want to do?' she asked him.

'I was going to ask you the same question.'

Miranda turned towards him, puzzled.

'Well, it's not really up to me any more, is it? I mean, you will be leaving, right? I haven't missed anything, have I?'

'So you are definitely planning to be with him?' He frowned. 'It *is* Giles then? You've avoided answering me, so it must be.'

They walked on a few paces in silence. 'Miranda? I need to know.'

'Why do you? You've found out the big secret, congratulations. I've ruined everything. OK, you want the whole truth, I'll tell you – I slept with both of them! Father and son – not at the same time, if that's what you're thinking – but within the same weekend so I don't have a bloody clue myself! You think I haven't regretted it almost every single waking fucking moment? Great, so now you know – call me whatever you like, say I'm a slag, a bitch, a disgusting no-good whore – you think there's anything you could possibly say to me that I haven't told myself a million times?' Tears streamed down her face and her voice was hoarse and desperate. 'Oh – Simon

– I know I've been a bloody disaster of a human being, I'm not making excuses for myself.' She ground to a halt, exhausted. 'But, really, what difference does it make who it was if it wasn't you? It should have been you – God, I wish it was – but it wasn't. I've spent the last nine years hoping – telling myself – that it might be you, probably was you, and wishing I could undo it all but—'

'You wouldn't want to undo Anna!'

'No.' She smiled at him for the first time. 'Of course not. She's the best thing that's ever happened to me.'

He nodded.

'Yeah. Me, too. Well . . .' A flash of pain darkened his eyes. 'Guess I can't even say that any more.'

'Don't say that. Don't ever say that.'

They walked on, hunched against the wind.

'I understand that you don't want to be with me any more, Simon. I can't blame you for that – who would? If you feel you have to leave, then of course that's your choice, but I must ask you please, please would you carry on seeing Anna? Even if she's not yours *biologically,* she is *your* child in every other way. You can't just drop out of her life – please, for her sake – no matter how much you may despise me, don't punish her – none of this is her fault—'

He stopped suddenly and turned towards her, clutched at her arm.

'You think I don't know that? For God's sake, Miranda! You think I'd – I'd take it out on her?' His hand dropped to his side. "You really see me as some kind of monster, don't you?'

'No. I *don't*. I absolutely don't. I just . . . I'm trying to think of Anna. Oh, Simon, this is such a bloody mess. I'm sorry.' She sniffed and dug into her coat pocket for a tissue to wipe her nose. 'Anyway. How long have you known?'

'Since your last trip to Milan. I took the samples while you were away, sent them off and that was it. I couldn't believe how easy it all was. As easy as brushing your teeth really.'

Her brow furrowed.

'But that was almost three months ago. You *can't* have known that long.'

''Fraid so.'

'But that doesn't make sense. Except . . .' She thought of the trumped-up rows, the irritable manner, the undercurrent of anger bubbling beneath so many conversations. 'Why didn't you say anything? Why didn't you confront me the moment I came back?' She stared at him. 'I know things haven't been . . . at all good between us recently. We seem to grate on each other's nerves – and – and – I thought you seemed – somehow – you've been – well, so angry with me, but why didn't you say? I don't understand.'

'Don't you? Really? Think about it.'

'Jesus, Simon – I think about little else.'

'So why didn't you organize the tests yourself? Or did you?'

Miranda shook her head.

'I found out about them, of course I did. God, every time there was another high-profile case in the papers, I thought about it. You can't escape from it. But there was the small matter of obtaining a sample without your knowledge for one thing . . .'

'You didn't need to do that. You could have asked . . . the other man – men – in question to agree to the test. Then you'd have known.'

'It wasn't that simple. For a start, he – *they* don't know.' She let out a breath. '*Didn't* know. That it was even a possibility. But that wasn't it. I didn't do it because – it sounds stupid but I told myself that as long as I didn't *know*, if I wasn't sure, then – maybe it was all right and she was almost certainly your child after all. But, if we had the tests, well . . . then I *would* know, wouldn't I, and – and – if she weren't yours – then – then I'd have to do something about it and live with the consequences. And – and – well . . . and nothing. I'm sure that sounds crazy and pathetic and illogical to you, but that's the way it was. That's it.' She looked into his eyes. 'But why didn't *you* say?'

'Isn't it obvious?'

She watched his face, his mouth tightening into a thin line. Waited for him to carry on. He half turned away from her, fixing his gaze in the distance, far out to sea. A minute passed.

'Because,' he said.

Still she said nothing.

'Feel free to interrupt,' he added. 'You do normally.'

He blinked repeatedly in the chill wind, staring at the seagulls as they dipped and soared by the cliff.

'*Because,*' he said again. Simon shook his head then and his lips clamped shut. She saw his shoulders hunch, small jerks of his head.

'Simon?' Miranda came forward so that she was level with him, but he turned his face away. She laid a hand on his arm, but he shook it off and took a step towards the edge, '*Simon! No!*' Miranda shouted above the wind. Clutched his arm tight. He turned and stumbled towards her, tried to push past her but she grabbed both his arms. 'Tell me!'

'We're not married – if she's not even mine – then I – I—' His features crumpled then and sobs lurched from him in spasms. 'Can't you see? Why don't you see! I thought I'd lose her!'

'Dear God.' Miranda pulled him close against her, cradling his head on her shoulder. 'I'd never do that. Never, Simon. Never, never.' Stroking his hair now, kissing his face, his wet cheeks, saying the words clearly into his ear. '*Never, never.*'

Nine years ago: Going home

Miranda takes her time packing, carefully folding her clothes and neatly tucking her toilet bag and hairbrush

426

into her case instead of hurling her things in at speed the way she usually does. Simon has not phoned to speak to her the whole weekend and she, equally stubborn, hasn't called him. Now, the thought of the empty flat makes her feel physically sick. She is not ready for this, not grown-up enough for this. If only she could delegate the next few hours to someone else. She imagines setting down her case in the hallway, coming into the kitchen. There will be a brief note on a single sheet of paper – no, too wasteful, on the back of a used envelope – propped up on the table, the place where they always leave each other notes. Only this time it won't say 'Chicken casserole in oven – back in an hour' or 'We're out of loo paper and coffee. Have you hidden the pliers? Sx'. The casual ordinariness of everyday life when you belong to a couple. The glorious, wonderful ordinariness that she'd never appreciated while she had it. No, there will be no more than a few brief lines explaining that it's all over. Will it say 'Dear Miranda' at the top? Perhaps just 'Miranda—' or, as casual as if he'd popped out for a pint of milk, a truncated 'M'?

The traffic on the way home is dreadful, the roads slicked with rain; sitting in yet another jam, she looks around her at the occupants of the other cars: couples, returning from romantic weekends away, families with bored children misbehaving in the back seat, squabbling and picking their noses and sticking out their tongues at other drivers. She makes a goofy face at a child with its nose pressed flat against the rear window and tries not to think about her own weekend. Now, sitting here in her car, she thinks she must look like a normal person. A man in the next lane fiddles with his radio, then casually glances across at her and yawns widely, frowns and looks away. Perhaps he's turning away in disgust, thinking, 'That woman's clearly a harlot.' Harlot. A strange word. Archaic. Biblical. Jezebel – that sounded much better, exotic and intriguing. Either that or she has some kind of personality disorder. But tomorrow she will get up, shower, dress, and pretend to be a normal person. Who would suspect what she had been up to? Who could possibly suspect it? She doesn't even believe it herself and she was there the whole time. Maybe she could just forget the whole thing, edit her own memory, tell herself it was no more than a preposterous, crazy dream, unpick it like an old jumper, unravelling every strand until it simply ceased to exist.

For once, she manages to park in the same street as her flat. When she tries to unlock the Chubb, she realizes that Simon hasn't double-locked it. Thanks a bloody bunch. Normally, he was the one who was obsessional about locking up, berating Miranda if she dared to run down the road for a newspaper without deadlocking the front door. She sighs audibly, theatrically – better to feel angry than abandoned. Enters and dumps her case on the hall

428

floor. The place is silent. She is in no rush to read Simon's note, so she avoids the kitchen for the moment. Instead, she enters the sitting room; she'll put some music on loud, have a glass of wine – or three – fill the space with noise.

It is dark in here and she quickly crosses to the windows to open the blinds. A sudden noise behind her makes her gasp.

Simon is stretched out on the sofa, sound asleep and occasionally emitting a sudden pig-like snort. Miranda leaves the blinds down and kneels on the floor beside him in the dimness, looking at his face. His glasses are set on the side table and, without them, he looks younger, softer, less intense. The characteristic crease between his brows has smoothed out in sleep, the crease that deepens when he reads the newspaper or when he thinks that Miranda is somehow, as so often, missing the point. Watching him now, sleeping like a child, Miranda feels a dark well of shame and guilt and grief and love swell inside her. Tears pool in her eyes and spill silently onto her cheeks, running down inside her collar.

His eyes flutter open, then the crease forms once more.

'Hi,' he says.

'Hi.' She attempts a smile. 'I didn't think you'd be here.'

Simon pauses, frowning at her.

'What's up?' He reaches up his arm to wipe away her tears with the cuff of his shirt.

She shakes her head.

'Did you want me not to be here then?'

Miranda laughs, still crying. It is such a Simon-ish thing to say, expressing something back to front.

'What?'

'No, no, I didn't. I don't. I mean I don't want you not to be here – I do want you to be here – I—'

He pulls her close, burying his face in her neck, hugging her tight.

'I nearly left. I meant to. I went and tramped all over Epping Forest for most of yesterday, crashing through the undergrowth like an angry bear and telling myself how horrible you were. Then I bought a newspaper and sat in a café and it was weird – I kept expecting you to grab a bit of the paper without asking, I kept looking up, expecting to see your face in front of me, hear your voice saying, "Oh! Listen to this!" or "God, this man's a moron – get this." But you weren't there. It was like you'd died or something. And I knew that if I missed you that much when you were away for just one weekend, then I wouldn't last very long without you. I miss being annoyed by you.'

He cups her face in his hands, then kisses her, holding her, enfolding her. Pulls back for a moment the better to see her face, kisses her lips, her nose, her damp eyelashes. Tentatively licks away her tears.

'Why didn't you phone me then?' she asks.

'Why didn't *you* phone *me*?'

'Because I'm a stupid, stubborn fool who'd rather be right than happy.'

'Oi, that's my line.'

He stands up then and takes her by the hand.

'I'm sorry,' she says. 'You were right before. I am a horrible person, I know I am.'

'Hush-hush,' he says, putting his finger against her lips and leading her into the bedroom. 'That's no way to talk about the woman I love. Hush-hush.'

Minor worrying

Anna quickly clambered up the ladder into the top bunk and got under the duvet.

'Mummy?'

'Yes, darling?' Miranda leaned against the bunk and rested her chin on her crossed arms.

'You know Zoë in my class?'

'Yes?'

'Well, her parents are getting divorced. Her dad's moved out and now if she wants to talk to him, she has to phone him.'

'Oh, poor Zoë. That's very sad. Do you think she's very upset?'

Anna turned on her side to face her mother.

'She's not crying or anything . . .'

'But? Is there something else?'

'It's only . . . well, when it's lunchtime she keeps giving away all the food in her lunchbox. She says she isn't hungry. She gave me her raisins the day we broke up. I don't think they were organic, but they were much more chubbier than the ones we have.'

'That's not good, Anna – she must eat properly. Does your teacher know?'

Anna shook her head.

'Zoë said we weren't to tell.'

'Well, we'll see.' Miranda sighed. 'Poor Zoë. Thank you for telling me, darling – you did the right thing.'

'And you're not cross that I had her raisins?'

'No, course not.'

'And Mummy?'

'Settle down now. Time to go to sleep.'

'It's not fair – Polly's not in bed yet and she's much, much younger than me.'

'She *is* in bed – you know she's in her parents' bed.'

'You promise she isn't downstairs with the grown-ups?'

'I promise. Cross my heart. She's in bed – I saw her myself.'

'Mummy.'

'I have to go down now – we're having our supper soon, I can't leave Auntie Kath to do it all. It wouldn't be fair.'

'Oh please – just one more minute. Please?'

'One more minute then.'

'Mummy? It's only married people who get divorced, isn't it?'

'Yes, of course. You know that.' Miranda stroked her daughter's hair, then suddenly stopped. 'Hey – have you been fretting, little bean? You haven't, have you?'

Anna shook her head vigorously, but her forehead puckered into a frown.

'No. But . . . well, you know how you and Daddy don't like each other any more—' she blurted out.

'Oh, darling, that's not true! Is that what's worrying you?'

'No. I'm *not* worrying.' Her brow remained furrowed. I'm only *asking*. You said I must always ask any questions I want to. You said it's good to ask lots of questions.'

Miranda smiled, then carried on stroking Anna's hair back from her face.

'Well, that's right – it *is* good. But, listen – you're not to worry about Mummy and Daddy, OK? Grown-ups are very silly a lot of the time, and sometimes they get a bit cross with each other, but they usually sort themselves out in the end, and there's absolutely no need for little children to worry, OK?'

'I'm *not* little.'

'Well, big children then.'

'*Why* are you and Daddy so cross the whole time?'

Miranda bent to kiss Anna's forehead, then stroked her cheek.

'Are we really? We don't mean to be. And you know we're not cross with you, don't you? I'm sorry. I hate to think of you worrying. There's no need to, little bean – sorry, *big* bean – honestly there isn't.'

'What's it called when it's like a divorce only you're not married?'

'Anna – no-one's getting a divorce. Or a separation. It's called a separation, I suppose, if you're not actually married.'

'Will you have one of those?' Anna chewed her lip.

'I don't want you to worry about this.'

'Do you promise not to?'

Miranda looked into those enormous blue eyes.

'We're not planning to separate, Anna – we wouldn't do that without telling you, would we?'

'But do you *promise*?' Anna started to sit up. 'You have to promise!' Louder now. '*Promise!* Say you'll never have one – never do a separation. Cross your heart and hope to die!'

'Sssh, sshh!' Miranda laid her back down. 'Hush now – you'll wake Luke. Calm down – you're getting yourself all revved up for no reason.'

Anna was still trying to sit up.

'Lie down.' Miranda kept her voice calm and level. 'Come on, don't be silly – you're working yourself into a big old tizz, you know you are.' She tucked the duvet in tightly around Anna's shoulders. 'There we go. Grown-up lives can be very complicated, OK? And you are right

Daddy and I have been a bit cross with each other recently – but no-one's divorcing or separating right this minute and whatever happens you must know that Daddy and I both love you very, very much. And even when we're being cross and silly, it doesn't ever mean that we're cross with *you*, OK?'

Anna said nothing.

'Hmm?'

Anna nodded silently.

'And you're not to worry any more, OK? Promise me?'

Another nod.

'Good. We can talk about it a bit more tomorrow if you want to.' Miranda planted a kiss on her daughter's brow. 'Snug as a bug in a rug?'

'Mmm.'

'Settle down now and go to sleep. Early start tomorrow remember – you said you wanted to help me with the packing. Nightie-night then, little bean.'

'Mummy?'

'Go to sleep now.'

'When's Polly coming in?'

'In a bit. They'll bring her later. *After* you're asleep. They'll be quiet as mice, I promise. You just go to sleep. Night-night now.'

'Nigh-night.'

Miranda carefully stepped over Luke's mattress and out onto the landing.

Last chance

It was funny getting dressed without the lamp on, but there was enough light from the landing to see. Anna quickly pulled on her trousers and jumper over her pyjamas and carefully tiptoed barefoot over Luke's mattress. She could hear them downstairs. Uncle Rob was the loudest and she liked the way he laughed – it was a big noise, the kind of laugh a lion would do if lions laughed. You think of lions going hunting and eating other animals, zebras and gazelles and buffaloes and things like on that nature programme, they eat them raw, but Miss Strauss said that mostly what lions do is sleeping and resting, so they are more boring than you expect really. Mummy was talking now. Anna could not hear what she was saying, but she could tell it was her mother. Daddy's voice was more quiet. Auntie Kath's was the most quietest of all. Sometimes she looked like the hamsters they have at school, she had quite big cheeks and she looked a little bit scared like a hamster, like when it was frightened that you weren't going to pick it up properly like the time that Marcie dropped it on the floor and it ran behind the paint cupboard.

Anna knew she was not really going to become a mermaid, that was a silly wish, she knew now what she should have wished for, but they were going back first thing in the morning tomorrow so she had to go right now. One night, Mummy went for a walk on the beach just before the grown-ups had their supper and she said it was beautiful with the sun sinking into the water and she said the tide was out, so now was the time to go. If she was not going to be a mermaid, she could definitely be a secret agent or a spy. Or a cat burglar. She could be quiet as a mouse when she wanted to and the grown-ups forgot she was even there and she could hear everything they said.

Downstairs now, tiptoe, tiptoe. The wellies were lined up in the hall. She grabbed her own bright blue boots and paused by the front door. No. This door was too noisy. But there was a torch there, lying on the shelf next to a jumble of fleeces and jackets. It was still light now, but nearly sunset, she thought, so she would take it for the way back. Pleased with herself for being so well prepared, just like a proper spy. Tugged out her turquoise fleece. Quickly scampered along the hall and peered into the kitchen. Empty. They were all in the dining room. She could hear the chink-chink of plates and knives and forks. Pad, pad across the kitchen floor.

'Is there any more wine?' she heard her mother say. The scrape of a chair against the floor as someone got up.

Quick, quick now. Hurry, hurry. Into the pantry, then she opened the back door and quietly closed it behind her. Squatted down next to the wall outside to put on her boots. Pulled her fleece over her head. Heard Uncle Rob calling through, 'Red or white? There's both.'

'Then for God's sake let's have both!' Mummy shouted back. 'It's our last night after all!'

She stopped in the garden for a moment and crept close to the dining-room window, which was all lit up with candles. Stood on tiptoe, just able to see in. Rob came back with a bottle in each hand. He offered some to Daddy, but Daddy put his hand over his glass and shook his head.

Anna stepped back again and turned, running down the garden to the gate, then slowing down for the wooden steps, being careful now. Jumped the last two onto the rocks. The beach was empty, completely empty. She had never, ever, ever been on a beach all by herself before. She turned in circles, arms out like a bird, exulting in the space. Wanted to stop and draw in the sand again with a stick or the sharp point of a stone or the knobby bit on the end of her torch, but no, hurry now. Running across the pale, dried-out sand, running, now sloshing through the shallows, not even ankle-deep, snug and dry in her bright blue Wellington boots.

The last supper

'That was delicious. Another fine meal – thank you to the chefs!' Joe pushed his plate away and raised his wine glass to Miranda and Kath.

'To the chefs!' the others echoed.

'Oh, Joseph . . .' Kath said.

'Yes, I will clear away and load the dishwasher, petal. I know I have my uses. Let me digest for a minute.'

'Noooooo, not that. You wouldn't go and shift Polly to her bunk, would you? Before you get too knackered. I've gone all floppy. Please, oh please?' She turned to Rob. 'Last night, we left it until we went to bed and one of us was rather tired and one of us was rather drunk, and we were so tempted just to roll her off straight onto the floor instead.'

'I'll do it later. I promise.' Joe leaned back in his chair. 'I'm so stuffed.'

Miranda looked at his stomach.

'When's it due?'

'Hmm. What do you think? I'd say I'm about six months gone.'

Rob smiled.

'Do you know what it is yet?'

Joe looked coy.

'Well . . . we'd sort of rather it was a surprise, but secretly I'm betting it'll be a big, bonny lasagne. It's just a hunch, mind you.'

'Anyone for a port?' Giles got up and went through to the kitchen.

Miranda did an ostentatious double take.

'Was that really Giles, fetching something from the kitchen?'

'Thank you, Miranda!' he called back. 'I heard that!'

'You were meant to!'

Kath shucked off one shoe and gently poked Joe's leg.

'Husband?'

'Mmm?'

Simon stood up.

'Orders for coffee? Tea?'

'Peppermint tea for me, please,' Kath said. 'Joe? Please go and move Poll. Go on.'

'In my condition? Really?' He made a show of levering himself upright, then slowly left the room, puffing loudly and clasping his hands beneath his stomach.

They were sitting in a mellow daze, the air rich with wine and coffee and candle smoke, when Joe came back in again.

'Um, Miranda? You didn't move Anna into your bed, did you?'

'No, course not. Why?' She looked up at him, saw his expression. 'What is it?'

'Maybe she's down here? Did she come down for a glass of water?'

Miranda stood up at once, ran through to the kitchen, calling Simon.

The daze dissolved. Quickly, they searched the house, looking under the beds, in the wardrobes, checking behind the curtains, calling now, louder, more urgent.

'*Anna!* Come on – that's enough now! We know

you're hiding! It's not funny any more!'

Back upstairs to the children's room, where Polly and Luke were sitting up in bed.

The adults converged in the doorway of their room.

'Why is everyone *shouting*?' Polly said. 'You're all very naughty to be so noisy.'

Joe came and sat on the edge of her bed.

'We can't find Anna, Poll. Do you know where she's gone?'

Polly shook her head in silence.

'Did she say anything to you?'

Another shake of the head.

'You didn't see her?'

The smallest of pauses.

Kath came and squatted next to the bed.

'What did you see, Polly? You must tell us.'

'I might've been dreamin', I don't know.'

'Poll?'

'Did you see her? When?'

Polly rubbed her eyes and yawned.

'Poll?'

'When I was in your bed . . .'

'Yes?'

'The door was open a little bit . . . and I think she went down the stairs. But I might've dreamt it.'

'When was that?'

'Don't know.'

'Oh, please think, Polly – think!'

'I *don't* know. Don't be cross with me, it's not my fault.'

'Well, was it still light? Was there light coming through the curtains?'

She thought for a moment, then nodded.

'I think so. She was wearing her pink jumper and her trousers with the little hearts down the side. Will you get me some like that?'

'Not just pyjamas? Are you sure?'

A small nod.

'Oh, *God.*' Miranda turned, clutching for Simon's hand.

'OK, everyone. One person – Kath? – stay here – everyone else, help us look outside.'

'Did anyone see the torch that was right here by the door?' Rob called out. Shaking of heads.

'There's one in our car.' Simon rushed outside to get it.

In the garden now, looking under the bushes, a twilight game of hide-and-seek, calling, shouting. Miranda ran to Simon.

'The beach, Simon. Quick – bring the torch!'

Down the rickety steps, two, three at a time, clattering down them at breakneck speed.

Into the darkness

Across the narrowing strip of dry sand, the beam of the torch bounced as Simon ran over the rocks, slipping and stumbling, shining it into every corner. Again and again, they called Anna's name.

'What if she went out to the Mermaid?' Miranda's face was as white as the full moon above.

Simon held her tight.

'Why would she do that? Surely she wouldn't?'

'To *wish*!' Her whole body was shaking uncontrollably. 'Because of *us*. Oh, God, oh God . . .' She ran along the water's edge, looking out to sea, calling. 'I can't see! I can't *see* anything. Simon – can you see?'

'My binoculars,' Giles said.

'Where are they? I'll get them,' Rob volunteered. 'I'll be faster.' He ran for the steps, seemed to leap up them almost in a single bound.

'I think we should ring the coastguard.' Giles took out his mobile phone. 'And perhaps the police, too.'

And then, tearing through the night like a bolt of lightning, a single, terrible scream.

They all turned to see Miranda, dropped to her knees in the water, bathed in moonlight. She was clutching something in her hands, something now drained of its usual brilliant colour, no longer bright and blue but silver-grey in the moon: a single, small wellington boot.

Miranda staggered to her feet and tried to run into the water, heading blindly into the waves, stumbling on the unsteady sands. Simon waded in after her, lifting her bodily, pulling her back to shore.

Rob streamed down the steps, waving the binoculars and a larger, more powerful torch. The beam shone out, a ray of light panning back and forth over the surface of the water.

'The Mermaid!' Miranda shouted.

Rob pointed the torch, while Simon angled his from further along the beach, catching the Mermaid in the twin shafts of light. The water covered the craggy base, the unmoving tail of stone, fused as one with the rock, up above her hips, lapping at her waist.

There, there now – a flash of turquoise in the crossed torchbeams. They shouted again: *Anna, Anna, Anna.*

Giles aimed his binoculars at the rock.

'There she is! Look!' He passed the binoculars to Miranda.

An oval of frightened white. Then, faint across the water, half-snatched by the wind and the shushing waves:

'D-a-a-a-ddy!'

'Simon! Quickly!'

Simon was by Miranda's side in an instant. He grabbed the binoculars.

'I see her! Wait here.' He turned to Rob. 'Keep that light on her.' Kicked off his shoes and yanked off his heavy jacket.

444

'Let *me* go.' Rob offered the torch to Simon. 'I'm a strong swimmer.'

Simon shook his head and ran straight into the ocean, waded a few dragging paces until he was thigh-deep then plunged headlong. Miranda handed Giles the second torch.

'Please – guide him. Watch him. For me.'

He nodded and she lifted the binoculars once more.

'Where's the coastguard? Where are they? You said they were coming! Oh, Giles – where *are* they?'

He faced her.

'They *are* coming.' His voice was level and steady. 'It's all right, Miranda. They're on the way. They'll be as fast as they can.' Giles beckoned Rob and handed him the second torch. 'Keep this steady on Simon.'

Giles took the binoculars from her and looked out to the rock again, then passed them back.

'Look there – ' He directed the binoculars for her. 'Can you see? Anna's caught by her hood on the rock – she can't fall.'

'He's reached the rock!' Rob called.

Miranda watched, seeing Simon scrabble at the wet sides of the stone.

'Oh, no – it's too wet – he can't climb up it.'

Rob tugged off his trainers. 'I can help him.'

'Yes – no – there – he's found a handhold,' Miranda reported. 'He's – yes – I think – yes – he's on it.' At last, she breathed out and the tears streamed down her face.

'He's there. He's with her.'

'Stay there!' Rob bellowed across the water, holding his hand up flat.

A weak beam shone back at them. The torch that Anna had taken with her. Simon waved it back and forth.

At last, another light appeared, arcing from the left beyond the headland. The light slowly swept the water then held steady, homing in on the Mermaid and the answering gleam of Simon's fading torch. And now, heaving into view, ploughing through the waves, the speeding form of the lifeboat.

Miranda stood, flanked by Rob and Giles. Together, they huddled close to her, sheltering her from the wind, steady and strong, like pillars of rock on the wild shore.

Saturday

Afterwards

It had been a long, long night. After the rescue, Anna
had been taken to the nearest hospital to be checked out.
Aside from the grazes on her hands and legs, she was
physically unharmed, but clearly in shock. She clung
to Simon like a limpet, while a doctor assessed her
condition and asked her questions. There was no real
need to keep her in hospital, they said. Keep her warm
and wrapped up, give her a hot, milky drink to help her
sleep, stay with her so she knows she's safe. Get her own
doctor to see her once you're back home.

They emerged into the corridor, and Giles and
Rob leapt to their feet, their faces pale and drawn.
Simon carried Anna, her sleepy head resting against
his shoulder, her thumb in her mouth, though she
had long since given up sucking her thumb. Miranda
walked close alongside, her hand on her daughter's
arm. Together, they walked through the brightly lit

corridors of the hospital towards the exit and the promise of sleep.

A new journey

Two cars: three children, six adults. God, it's like the beds all over again, Miranda thought. Who goes in which car? She didn't have the energy even to think about it. Maybe Kath was right – she should just leave it and let it be someone else's worry? As long as she was in the same car as Anna, everyone else could do whatever they liked. She went back into the house to check that they hadn't left anything behind.

Kath was in the kitchen, wiping down the worktop.

'I think they bring in a cleaner, babe – don't go mad.'

'Force of habit.' Kath turned round to face her. 'I've been thinking,' she said. 'About the journey home. Now that we've only got the two cars.'

'Good. I can't think any more. I'll go with whatever you decide.'

Kath fiddled with the cloth in her hands.

'Um . . . Rob's coming in our car . . .'

'Fine. I told you, I really don't mind.'

'But I'd like to be with my dad.'

Miranda raised her eyebrows.

'Sure. Whatever you like. But you can't fit both o'

them in, can you? Not with Luke's child seat? It'll be much too squashed.'

'No.' Kath shook her head. 'We can't. Do you mind if I come with you?'

'Of course not, silly. No need to ask even.'

'So Dad can come in your car, too? That's not . . . awkward?'

Miranda came and stood by her friend, removed the cloth from her hands and dropped it into the sink. She put her arms round Kath and gently clasped her.

'No, it's fine. Of course he can.' She paused. 'Hang on. Maybe I'd better check with Simon first . . .'

Miranda went outside to where Simon was loading up the boot.

'Hi.'

'Hi. Nearly done. Have you had a final recce?'

'I'm just doing it now. Si?'

'Hmm?'

'Kath wants to come with us. Rob's going in the other car. Is it OK if we take Giles, too?'

Simon sighed, then shrugged.

'Why not? Guess I'd better get used to it. We're all family now.'

'Si?' She moved closer to him.

'What?' His face softened and he granted her a half-smile.

'I'm sorry,' she said, looking into his eyes. 'I'm really

451

and truly very sorry. For everything. For making such a God-awful old muckheap of it all.'

He put his arms around her and hugged her briefly.

'What's done is done, Miranda. I can spend my life wishing it were different, fill every second of every day with blaming you and hating you – God knows that would be easy—'

'And possibly fun?'

'And possibly fun, too.' He smiled. 'Or I can find a way – some way – of trying to deal with this – what we have here – whatever it is. There's no one perfect way to be a family—'

'I don't think we're going to be up there on the podium when they're handing out the Perfect Family medals.'

'No. I guess not. What I do know is that I love Anna. More than ever – is that odd? Doesn't feel odd to me. I still think of her as mine.'

'She *is* yours, Simon. In every way that really matters. I do believe that.'

'Well. Thank you. Thank you for that at least. You know what?' He looked down, then perched on the edge of the boot. 'I'm going to hang on in there, Miranda. We'll have to find some way of making this family work – no matter that it's not like other families, so what? So we'll have to chuck away the rule book and muddle through somehow. I'm not going to be the one who jumps ship just because it's too tough or weird or because I can't deal with it. I *will* deal with it. It's not

Happy Families, but it's what we've got and maybe we can find some good in it. There *is* good in it . . . and you know . . .' He stood up again, took a step towards her. 'It's not that I don't love you anymore. God knows, all this would be so much easier if I could just forget you, forget it all and walk away, but I can't. I still *care*.'

She nodded.

'Me too.' She lifted one hand to touch his cheek for a moment, then turned towards the house. 'I'll go and recce.'

Joe and Rob loaded the other car. Miranda kissed Polly and Luke goodbye, then stood still, not sure whether to turn away or to take her leave of Rob. Joe came up and gave her a hug.

'Drive safely, eh? Maybe we can all meet up for lunch on the way back?'

'Good idea. Call us on my mobile.'

She nodded tentatively at Rob. He slung his bag in the boot, and came towards her.

'Hey,' he said.

'Hey.'

'No crazy driving, all right? Precious cargo. Promise?'

'I promise. Cross my heart.' She criss-crossed over her chest. 'Take care, OK?'

'Mmm, you too.' He bent and kissed her tenderly on the forehead.

She folded her arms tightly, holding herself together. A tiny nod.

Simon put Giles's case into the rear, waiting for him to say goodbye to Joe and the children.

'Perhaps you'd better sit this side, Giles? To protect your arm.'

'That's thoughtful, thank you.'

At last, the luggage was loaded. Joe drove off, tooting his horn, while the others waved.

'I think I'll drive for a change, if you don't mind?' Simon said.

'Sure. Go ahead. Good idea, I'm too sleepy.' Miranda got into the front passenger seat.

Kath quickly climbed into the middle, followed by Anna, then Giles carefully lowered himself onto the back seat on the other side of Kath.

Miranda flipped down the sunshield and looked at them in the make-up mirror.

'All right there in the back row, everyone?'

Simon turned round in his seat.

'All buckled up?' He put the car into gear. 'Right then – off we go!'

Giles patted Kath's hand next to him, tilted his head to smile at Anna.

'Now then . . .' he said, turning towards his two daughters, 'who wants to play I-Spy . . . ?'

THE END

Acknowledgements

Grateful thanks to the following:

For information on the legalities and possibilities of DNA testing, The Paternity Company, especially Bill Thomas; website: www.thepaternitycompany.com

Additional help and advice from:

DNA Solutions; website: www.dnanow.com

and Cellmark Diagnostics in Abingdon, Oxon.

Denise Schwarz, my lovely neighbour, who also handily happens to be a geneticist.

Nessa O'Neill's name is included in this book as the result of an auction in aid of the charity WarChild; website: www.warchild.org.uk

And thanks also to the following:

Alan Finch, Julian Hague, Patrick Janson-Smith and Presley Warner

Larry, who is a wonderful husband but a tough taskmaster: 'So, how many words did you write today, darling?'

Jenny Finlay, née Strauss, for telling me helpful stuff about being a mother

My sister Stephanie, for her unflagging cheer-leading over the years

Linda Evans, my enthusiastic and, in this case, extremely patient editor at Transworld/Black Swan

My fantastic former agent Jo Frank, who has strangely decided to retire from the business. I knew it was a mistake to make her read the forty-fifth draft . . .

My new agent Stephanie Cabot, who is something of a Superwoman and amazingly nice to boot.